Lessons in French

Lessons in French

LAURA KINSALE

sourcebooks
casablanca

Published by Sourcebooks Casablanca, an imprint of Sourcebooks, Inc.
P.O. Box 4410, Naperville, Illinois 60567-4410

ISBN 978-1-61523-866-8

Printed and bound in the United States of America

To Ventoux, the Peter Pan of Great Pyrenees dogs,
Who reminds me that
Life is scary and fun, and if you don't know what to do,
do something odd,
Play even if you don't have someone to play with,
And be sure to dance for joy.

Lessons in French

One

LADY CALLISTA TAILLEFAIRE WAS A GIFTED WALLFLOWER.
By the age of seven and twenty, she had perfected the
art of blending into the wallpaper and woodwork so
well that she never had to dance and only her most
intimate friends greeted her. She could sit against the
pink damask in the ballroom or sit against the green
silk in the refreshment chamber. She didn't even have
to match to be overlooked.

"Did you hear that a carriage came to Madame
de Monceaux's!" The scarlet plume on Mrs. Adam's
headband swayed alarmingly as she leaned near Callie's
ear. "I believe it is——" But she suddenly broke off
her confidence and took Callie's hand. "Oh, do look
down! He is starting this way again."

Callie obeyed, instantly developing a profound
interest in the catch on her bracelet. She had not quite
succeeded in becoming completely invisible at these
affairs. There were always the gentlemen of a certain
category who solicited her hand, just in case she might
be clutching her eighty thousand pounds in it, Callie
supposed, which would save them the trouble of a
stop at the bank as they carried her off.

"There, you are safe!" Mrs. Adam said gustily, as if Callie had barely scraped through with her life. "Let him pour the butter-boat over Miss Harper, if she is so foolish a girl as to listen to it."

Callie let go of her bracelet. She had found that looking down and discovering a flounce had come loose from her hem, or a stone had worked its way into her slipper, was evasion enough to discourage the hopeful abductors. Even for eighty thousand pounds they were not very persistent. She was, after all, Lady Callista Taillefaire, who had been jilted three times. Even a gentleman with dishonest designs would have to ask himself what, precisely, could be wrong with her.

She had wrestled with this question herself. Indeed, she and her father and her sister and their acquaintance and all the local gossips and probably two or three of the wiser village goats had spent a good deal of time dissecting the matter. No satisfactory answer had been agreed upon. Her father had attributed it to the general decline of British manhood into riot and villainy. Her sister, Hermione, felt that Callie showed a deplorable lack of respect for the fashion in caps. The gossips largely blamed it upon Napoleon. During the French wars, they had blamed everything on Napoleon, and even five years after Waterloo he had not outlived his usefulness in that regard. The goats, being commoners, very properly kept their opinions to themselves.

It was Callie's own conclusion that she was quite plain and had red hair, and she was very stiff and shy with gentlemen, even after she became engaged to them. Perhaps more so after she became engaged to them. Her eyes were neither brown nor blue, but some grayish green middling color, her nose could politely be described as Grecian, having barely escaped the threat of Roman, and her fair skin flamed with unbecoming splotches of pink in the slightest touch of wind.

It was also true that she had a habit of lugging newborn calves into the kitchen from time to time, which might be considered eccentric in the daughter of an earl. But since her family had taken care that no rumors of this peculiarity should escape beyond Shelford, Callie felt that she was not held to be actually dangerous.

Mrs. Adam eased her ample figure from her chair, giving Callie's hand a squeeze and a pat. "Bless me, there is Mr. Hartman going in to tea. I must speak to him about the altar-cloth, but I will be back directly. You'll be quite all right now that the sets are forming."

Callie nodded. Having escaped the looming threat of being dragged off by her hair and ravished, or at least required to dance, she dared a glance at Miss Harper as the young lady took her place. The girl seemed to be enjoying her swim in the butter. Callie gazed at the couple, imagining herself—suitably embellished with golden hair and flower blue eyes and eyelashes that were the toast of England—dancing gracefully through the figures. She made light and witty conversation. Her smile pierced the fortune-hunting gentleman to his heart. He was so taken with her that he forgot all about her fortune and fell desperately in love for the first time in his cynical and dissolute life. He vowed to give up gambling and drink on her behalf, and fought several duels with men of vague but wicked demeanor in defense of her honor.

Finally, when she refused him, having selected from among her large following a gentleman of steadier nature, he threw himself from a sea cliff, leaving a poem of unrequited love in which Callie was thinly disguised as a mythological heroine with a name at least eight syllables long, which she would look up later. The poem was published in all the papers and made the ladies weep over it in their boudoirs.

She blinked, realizing the music had paused. The gentleman who had thrown himself from the cliff in despair was conversing with Miss Harper on the topic of how many sunny days the town of Shelford had enjoyed so far in the autumn.

Callie could never think of what to say to gentlemen. She could feel her cheeks turning splotchy if she tried. There had been one, once, who had been so easy to talk to that she had quite lost her head over him, but that had not turned out well. It was quite settled by now. She was born to be a spinster. The gentlemen would have to declare their undying devotion to other ladies. Callie would be too much occupied with developing a delicate constitution and a dependable recipe for tapioca jelly.

Her father, of course, had understood none of this, because he loved her. He had thought her pretty and stubbornly refused to be convinced otherwise by the abundance of evidence. As long as he lived he had persevered in escorting Callie to each London season, arranging betrothals, signing settlement papers, and raging almost to tears each time the gentlemen broke it off. By the third time, Callie had really been more distressed on her father's behalf than on her own. She was not by nature a violent person, but she had given serious consideration to sewing a teasel-burr into her former fiancé's unmentionables, or even perhaps recruiting a live black beetle for this mission, but decided in the end that it would be a disservice to the bug.

In any case, she had found no occasion to tamper with his personal linen, although the lawyers had been pleased to make his bank account smart by the removal of ten thousand pounds to avoid a breach-of-promise suit. He had departed on a ship for Italy with his beautiful, penniless new wife, while Callie sat with her crestfallen father in the study and held his hand.

The thought of it made her wrinkle her nose, blinking back the sting. She missed her father painfully, but it would not do to let her eyes fill with tears in the midst of a country dance. She turned her face down, brushing her nose with the feathers of her fan, concentrating on the swish and thud of the dancers' feet on the wooden floor and the off-key note on the pianoforte, waiting for the moment to pass.

It was only a local assembly, nothing so glittering as a London affair, but still Callie would not care to make a scene. For a year after the Earl of Shelford's death, she had at least been spared the agony of any social occasions, but now that they were out of mourning it was her duty to accompany Hermione.

Callie kept a careful eye on her sister's partners. It was up to her to make certain no fortune hunter stole Hermey. Their cousin Jasper wasn't precisely the sharpest needle in the pincushion, and since his elevation to the earldom, his lady wife was most anxious to see Callista and Hermione packed up and departed from Shelford Hall. An early wedding for Hermey would be just what Lady Shelford liked, and she would not be particular as to the groom. Any person would do as long as he wore trousers and promised to take Callie along with her sister.

So Callie put on her gray gloves, hid her red hair as well as she could under a lavender turban, and sat herself at her guard post on the row of satin chairs along the wall, watching her sister dance with a most suitable baronet. He had taken leave from his promising position as an undersecretary in the Home Office and traveled up from London particularly to pay his compliments to Lady Hermione. Along with his addresses, it was to be hoped, though that had not yet transpired.

Her favored position in the Shelford assembly rooms overlooked the dance floor and the entry. She had only to lift her lashes to see each newcomer, without any noticeable turn of her head. It was late now. The crush of people in the arched doorway had long since cleared, and so she merely glanced when a single figure appeared there.

For an instant she looked away again calmly, seeing only another smartly dressed gentleman who paused to watch the dancers. It was as if recognition struck her heart a moment late—a sudden rush of heat to her face, a squeezing of her throat. She found she could not catch her breath.

It was him.

She threw a panicked look toward him, knew it certainly, and then had nowhere at all to look or to run. She was alone on the wall of chairs. Mrs. Adam was vanished to the refreshment room, and everyone else danced. She stared down at her toes with desperate concentration, hoping and hoping and hoping that he would not recognize her.

He might not know her. She had not instantly recognized him. He was older. Of course he was older—one could hardly suppose that she herself had reached the advanced age of twenty-seven without him doing the same. In the first blink of a look, she had seen a dark-haired, handsome gentleman; it was only with her second panicked glance that she knew his face: sun-darkened and harder, all the smiling promise of youth matured to a striking man.

He stood with a quiet confidence, as if it did not concern him to arrive late and alone, or to receive no welcome. Any number of people here knew him, but no one had seen him yet, save Callie—none who acknowledged him, at least. He had been gone from the vicinity for nine years.

Callie fanned herself, staring at her lap. This was Mrs. Adam's news, of course. The carriage arrived for Madame de Monceaux. Her prodigal son had come home.

It was glad tidings. Callie was pleased for his mother. The poor duchesse had so longed for this, failing as she had been over the past year. She had clung to those infrequent letters from France, read them aloud over and over to Callie, and made them both laugh until Madame's cough overcame her and Callie took her leave.

For herself, Callie was terrified. Laugh she might over his written words—but she could hardly even breathe for the strange and sick feeling that she felt at the sight of him.

He might not even remember her. He had never mentioned her in his letters to his mother. Never asked after her, though he demanded to know how everyone else in Shelford fared in a long list of names and reminiscences, which showed that he had not forgot their small country lives while he consorted with kings and great people in Paris.

A pair of black evening shoes appeared in the limited range of her vision. She kept her face hidden down in her feathery fan and worked frantically with the catch on her bracelet, but the black shoes did not take the hint and move on. Closely fitted white trousers, the tail of a fine blue coat—she was so dizzy that she feared she might faint.

"Lady Callista?" he asked in a voice of low surprise.

She thought desperately of pretending she had not heard him over the music. But she remembered his voice. It was the same timbre, full of warmth. Evidently it still had the same dire effect on her senses.

"Come, I know it's you," he said gently. He sat down beside her. "I can see a stray lock peeking out from under that prodigious lovely turban."

She drew a deep breath. "No, can you? And I was so hoping to be taken for a Saracen." She tucked at the nape of her neck without looking at him.

"You've mislaid your camel, it would appear. How do you do, Callie? I must say, I didn't expect to find you here in Shelford, of anyone."

She found enough courage to lift her head. "You've come to see your mother," she said. "I am so glad."

He returned a sober man's look, a stranger, no longer the wild boy who had been careless of any burden. His dark eyes did not smile at her. She saw in a short look that he had a scar on his left cheekbone, and a little crooked bump to his nose that she did not remember. The marks only served to make him appear more an untamed gypsy than ever, even severe and stiff in his formal clothes.

"I've come to her, yes," he said. He paused, tilting his head a fraction. "But you—I thought you must have left Shelford long ago."

"Oh no, I have clung here like a limpet." She opened her fan and closed it again.

There was a little silence between them, filled with the violins and the dancers' noise and prattle.

"You have not married?" he asked quietly.

Somehow, Callie had supposed the news that she had been jilted three times must have reached the farthest corners of the earth. It was certainly common knowledge everywhere she had ever set foot. But it seemed that France had been spared the intelligence.

"Indeed no," she said, looking up at him fully for the first time. "I don't propose to marry."

He would find out the truth soon enough. She could not bring herself to mention it. But at the way his eyebrows lifted, she suddenly feared he might think it was because she still bore some strong feeling for him—and that was worse.

"I've become quite celebrated, you see," she said, fluttering her fan. "I have driven no less than three terrified gentlemen from the altar, not counting yourself. I don't tally you in my record keeping, but if you would like to do me the honor and then break it off, it would add immeasurably to my eminence. Four would be a nice round number."

He seemed slow to comprehend her. "Four?" he asked blankly.

"That is the sum of one and three," Callie said, beating her fan with a nervous velocity. "Unless there has been some recent alteration in events."

"Are you saying that you've been betrothed three times since I left?"

"It is a wonderful accomplishment, is it not?"

"And they all—"

"Yes." She snapped her fan closed. "That is what I've been doing, you see—becoming engaged and being jilted. And how do you account for your time these past years, my lord duc? Have you indeed recovered your ancestral properties and fortune? I sincerely hope for it; it would give your mother so much happiness."

He stared at her a moment, as if he did not quite understand the language that she spoke. Then he recovered himself. "I've had success, yes," he said. He did not elaborate on it. "I think it has given her strength."

"And will you return with her to France?" Callie asked.

"That would be impossible. She's not well enough."

"I hope you won't leave her again soon."

"No. I don't plan to leave until—" He hesitated. "I've no intentions to leave."

"She will be delighted to know it. Please reassure her directly. She will be anxious."

"I will. I have. I'll speak of it again, so that she is sure."

She dared another glance at him. He was turned toward her, looking directly at her. He gave her a quirk of a smile, so familiar that she could hardly recall to breathe.

"Have you ripped me up enough yet?" he asked. "I was not one of your jilts, Callie."

She knew the splotches were burning on her cheeks. "I beg your pardon! I've no notion what made me speak so!" He was the only gentleman outside her own family she had ever been able to talk to at all.

"The tip of your nose is turning pink."

She hid it quickly in her fan.

"A charming portrayal of an ostrich," he said, "but I'm afraid you'll suffocate in those feathers. We'd better dance, so that you can thrash me about the head with them instead."

Callie realized with alarm that the music had paused and the sets were reforming into couples. "Oh no, it is a waltz—"

But he was standing, holding out his gloved hand to her. Callie found herself lifted by the strong clasp of his fingers, in spite of her intentions, drawn irresistibly as always into whatever adventure that Trevelyan Davis d'Augustin, duc de Monceaux, comte de Montjoie, and seigneur of any number of exotic-sounding *villes* somewhere in France, might propose.

He led her to the floor and bowed. Callie curtsied and turned her face aside, terrified to look at him as he rested his hand on her waist. She had only waltzed in public three times, once for each of her betrothals. People were already staring at them. Mrs. Adam had just come from the refreshments—she stood stock-still in the doorway with a look of horror on her face. Callie saw her start forward in determination, as if she would tear Callie bodily from his indecent embrace, but the music began and his firm guidance swung her into motion.

Callie held herself as far from him as she could, barely allowing her fingertips to rest on his shoulder, trying with little success to make her fan lie down instead of fly in his face. She could scarcely recall where to put her feet, but he directed her with simple assurance, looking down at her as they spun around, smiling that intimate half smile.

"I never hoped I'd be so fortunate as to discover you here," he said warmly. The room seemed to whirl past with the music, everything a blur but him.

Callie could hardly comprehend that she was dancing with him. She glanced up and then away again, feeling oddly weightless, as if he carried her on air just by the light touch of his gloved palm.

"I must beg of you a favor," he added, squeezing her hand a little.

Callie nodded, gazing at his shoulder. It was handsomely clad in a tailored coat, a broader and taller shoulder than she recalled. He was familiar and yet unknown—far more intimidating than the grinning and unruly youth of her memory. Her heart and breath felt as if they had deserted her, declaring they were off to join the navy and might come back to visit in a few years if she were lucky.

"Can you recommend to me a decent cook?" he asked.

The prosaic question pulled her from a momentary dream of… of something. She missed a step and caught herself, flushing deeply as he lifted his chin to prevent the feathers of her fan from obscuring his face entirely. "Oh," she said, gaining control of the wayward fan. "Don't say that Mrs. Easley has taken to drinking again?"

"I fear so. I came in hopes of stealing a seedcake or two to save us from starvation."

"That woman!" Callie exclaimed, dropping her hand. She almost stood still on the dance floor, but he lifted her glove and kept her moving. "She's beyond saving," she said severely. "But has your mother not had nourishment? I sent a whole haunch of beef to her two days ago!"

"Thank you." He smiled. "But I don't know what's become of it, bumbling fellow that I am in these domestic matters. There was some broth, which is all that it seems she'll take, in any case."

"She must have more than broth!" Callie did stop then, causing a brief flurry as the other dancers found a path around them. "I'll go to her directly."

"No, do not trouble—"

"It's no trouble," Callie said, drawing away from him. "Only let me speak to Mrs. Adam. She'll see my sister home in the carriage. It's too late for the cook-shop, but I'm sure I can find something of substance in your kitchen if Mrs. Easley hasn't sold it all to that wicked butcher's boy."

He shook his head. "You need not. I beg your pardon, I didn't mean to interrupt your entertainment."

Callie waved her fan in dismissal. "That's hardly an affliction to me. I'm happy to go to your mother."

He hesitated, frowning down at her. For a moment she thought he would refuse again, but then a wry look came into his dark eyes. "In truth, it would be a blessing. I found the place in disarray, and I hardly know how to set things right."

"I do," Callie said. "Pray go and tell your mother I'll be with her directly."

Something brushed Trev's face in the darkness as he fumbled at the door. He cursed under his breath and pushed a trailing ivy out of the way, finding the latch with some difficulty. He didn't bother with the bell—there was no maid to answer it. The place was overgrown, the garden gate falling to pieces. He let himself inside and pulled off his gloves, stuffing them into his pocket instead of laying them on a table he already knew to be grimy with dust.

If it had been a roulette wheel to balance, or a boxer's bloodied head to stanch, Trev could have managed well enough, but the mysteries of a hearth and home were baffling to him. His sisters and mother had always seen to all of that: supervising the linen and directing the servants. They would have been aghast if he or his majestic grandfather had interfered or inquired about the smooth running of the household. Not that Trev had ever been inclined to do so. But even he could see that the rambling old house at the edge of Shelford was falling deep into disorder, and his mother's deteriorated condition appalled him.

She had hidden it well. Not once in her letters had she begged or even hinted for him to come, even after Hélène had died. He saw now that he should have come then; he had wanted to, but he had hidden certain things himself, and it had not seemed possible at the time.

The considerable amount of money he'd been sending to Shelford for the past few years had obviously gone astray. Surprising, but not inconceivable, considering the circuitous route he had arranged

for the funds to take. Trev narrowed his eyes. He
hoped that somewhere in France, a certain banking
correspondent was enjoying his remaining interlude
of good health.

He felt his way to the stairs. There were no candles
or spills, not even a rushlight. But he remembered the
low ceiling and heavy railing well enough. He made
his way up to his mother's chamber. The lamp he had
left with her still burned low.

She was sleeping. He stood for a moment, watching
her labored breath. His mischievous, sweet-faced
maman—he had hardly known her for herself when he
saw her. She was drawn, her cheeks sunken, her lips
parted, thinned by the effort to take in air. But she had
a trace of a smile, as if she dreamed a pleasant dream.

Trev scowled. He hardly cared to admit the vast
feeling of relief that he had felt when Lady Callie
offered to come. It was not something he would have
asked of her. They were all but strangers now. But
still, the moment he had recognized her, it was as if
no time had passed; he had wanted to sit down and
confide everything in her, his shock and fear at his
mother's illness, his consternation at the state of the
house, his amazement to find Lady Callista Taillefaire
here in Shelford yet.

Unmarried.

He put that thought away, not yet ready for the
surge of anger, the wound that lay behind it. Even
that surprised him—he had supposed himself long
ago over that juvenile affair. But they could still be
friends, it seemed, for which he was glad. He liked
Callie. Admired her. What other lady of her position
would stop dead in the midst of a waltz and insist upon

coming instantly to the aid of a Frenchwoman who had no earthly claims upon her?

He smiled a little. A lavender turban, with that hair. Only Callie: oblivious to every fashion, as sweet and shy as a wild doe. He shook his head and sat down on the edge of the bed, lightly touching his mother's hand.

"May I have the honor of this dance, Mademoiselle?" he murmured in French.

Her long lashes fluttered, dark against her pallor. She lifted them. "Trevelyan," she whispered, curling her hand about his. "*Mon amour.*"

He raised her hand and kissed her cool fingers. "I cannot permit these indolent airs," he said. "You wish to encourage my rivals, I know it. I will have to shoot them all."

She smiled and spoke to him in English. "You enjoyed the assembly?"

"Of course! I engaged myself to two beautiful young ladies and had to leave by the back window. I've fled to you for aid. Will you conceal me in your wardrobe?"

She gave a faint husky laugh. "Let the girls meet… on the field of honor," she said in a weak voice. "Nothing to trouble about."

"But their mothers might pursue me!"

"*Alors*, I'll dispatch their mothers myself, by poison."

He squeezed her hand. "I see now where I come by my unsteady nature."

She returned the pressure, gripping his fingers. "Trevelyan," she said suddenly and hoarsely. "I am so proud of you."

He maintained his smile down at her, finding nothing to say.

"You have succeeded where even… your grandfather failed. I wish only that he and your father were alive to see it."

Trev gave a slight shrug. "I was fortunate."

"To regain the whole! Even Monceaux!" She struggled to sit up and began to cough.

"Do not be carried away by raptures, I beg you," he said. He stood and propped pillows about her. "Save that for when I take you back to Monceaux in a gilded coach, with half a dozen outriders and three footmen up behind."

She closed her eyes and leaned her head back. She smiled, breathing with difficulty. Her fingers trembled as she put her hand on his arm. "You know that's not to be."

"Only two outriders, then. Elegant economy!"

"Trevelyan—"

"Come, do not quarrel with me. I cross the sea to your side, and you refuse to accompany me to dance, you will not eat—I've been forced to apply for reinforcements. Lady Callista desired me to say that she will be here presently."

"Ah, she is too good."

"Indeed, she is an angel. If she can produce a supper, I shall marry her out of hand."

"I'm certain that she can." His mother breathed deeply. "But… three engagements in one evening, my love?"

"No, do you think it excessive?" he asked in surprise.

"Trevelyan." She smiled up at him. "I am so happy." She held tight to his hand as her chuckle turned into a gasping cough.

Two

M RS. A DAM HAD NOT HESITATED A MOMENT WHEN SHE heard. Disapprove she might of Callie waltzing in the arms of a suspiciously French émigré, but the news that Mrs. Easley had succumbed to the bottle again was sufficient to excuse all. "That woman!" she hissed, uttering everyone's favored description of Mrs. Easley. "Take Lilly with you. Tell her to fetch the arrowroot custard that I meant for midday dinner. That will do well for Madame's lungs, the poor lamb!"

Armed with the custard and a mission, Callie did not feel so shy as she made her way into the back door of Dove House. She was always better when she had a task at hand.

While Lilly swung the lantern so that shadows flew all over the scullery, Callie wrinkled her nose at the odor of sour milk issuing from a pail on the floor. The air was cold and damp, the hearth a dark pile of abandoned ashes.

It appeared that nothing had been done in the kitchen for a week or more. On the slate floor lay a square case-bottle marked *Hollands.* Dove House had always had a faintly shabby air, being a sublet property for as long as Callie could remember, but Madame de Monceaux and her daughter Mademoiselle Hélène had kept a pretty garden and fitted up their spotless, neat parlor in a charming continental fashion. Callie feared that Madame must have taken a serious turn for the worse, to allow things to come to this pass.

She pulled off her gloves and folded back the calash hood from over her turban, set Lilly to washing bowls and cutlery, and located a candlestick from amid the disorder of the pantry. As she made her way up the short staircase, she wished strongly that she had not been absent for nigh a month with her sister and the new Lady Shelford, drinking the vile waters at Leamington and knitting enough length of Shetland wool to tie up a haystack in garters. Between helping her cousin Jasper to correct the muddle he had made of the estate books in that short time, and attending to the various small disasters that had arisen on the home farm, she had not paid a call at Dove House since her return, only sent the beef over Lady Shelford's objection that a hare would have been quite sufficient.

She could hear Madame coughing, and so she only knocked once before letting herself in. Somehow she had expected that Madame would be alone—Callie froze when she saw Trevelyan turn and look toward the door.

All her shyness swept over her again. "Oh!" she said. "I beg your pardon for intruding. I'll send up the maid."

As she began to close the door, he strode toward her. "Come in, my lady," he said, catching the door by the edge. Then he took her hand and made a bow as he relieved her of the candle.

Callie looked at his bare hand holding hers and then toward his mother. Madame de Monceaux held a handkerchief to her mouth, but she put it down and smiled such a warm welcome that Callie felt a little more at ease.

"I'm afraid I've neglected you, ma'am," Callie said. "I am so sorry. I didn't hear of Mrs. Easley until tonight. Will you take some arrowroot pudding?"

"My dear," Madame whispered. "Do not be concerned with me, but I would be grateful for anything you might discover"—she struggled for breath—"for my son to eat. You find this house in a sad state, I fear!"

Trev gave Callie a meaningful glance. He still held her hand in a firm clasp, as if to keep her. "She'll take arrowroot, I assure you," he said. He glanced toward his mother. "I had a great deal to eat at the assembly, Maman; I couldn't consume another bite."

Callie knew he had not eaten anything at the assembly. In the flickering shadows from the candle, his face seemed grim. As Lilly came into the chamber with a tray, he let go of Callie's hand and went to prop pillows at his mother's head. Then he stood back uncertainly, looking like a man in a sickroom—helpless.

"The fire has gone out in the kitchen," Callie said, offering him a task elsewhere. "Is there someone who might see to it?"

"Jacques," he said immediately. "I'll speak to him." He made a courtesy toward his mother, bowed again to Callie, and left the room.

Relieved at his departure, she took the tray from Lilly's hands and arranged it for Madame. It was a natural thing; she had often done so for her father. The

Frenchwoman lifted her lashes and gave a faint thanks. "I must apologize—" she murmured.

"Don't worry yourself, ma'am," Callie said briskly. "When the fire is rekindled, Lilly will bring up some tea." She sent the young maid downstairs and busied herself with an inventory of the medicine glasses and spoons on the bedside table, watching from the corner of her eye as Madame lifted an unsteady morsel of the pudding to her mouth. "How pleased I am that your son has come home!"

Even in her weak state, Madame's face seemed to come alight. She laid down the silver. "It is such bliss to me, Lady Callista. You cannot conceive!"

"But you must eat, you know, so that you have the strength to entertain him in fine style."

Madame de Monceaux picked up the spoon dutifully. But she laid it down again. "My dear—" She turned and gave Callie a wistful look. "You have been such a friend to us these years."

Callie lowered her face. "It's my pleasure to do what I can."

"The whole town has felt your kindness. But my family—you have been good to us beyond any hope that we... can repay you."

"Indeed, no, ma'am. Don't speak of repayment. Please do eat a little more!"

"I know your father did not approve of—any intimacy, may God bless him," Madame said. "I didn't blame him."

Callie had been fifteen when the émigré family moved into Dove House. Her father had been willing enough for her to take lessons to improve her French with Madame and her daughter, but in his curt summation, whatever wealth and rank the Monceaux had held before the Revolution, by the time they reached Shelford they were living upon little but pride and thin air, however refined it might be. And when her papa had discovered, somewhat belatedly, that a handsome son of Callie's own age had returned from school to live with his grandfather and mother and sisters, the earl's coolness congealed to ice. The French lessons at Dove House had ceased.

At least to her father's knowledge. Callie had taken some further lessons at Dove House—if not entirely in French.

"That was long ago," she said. She sat down on the chair beside the bed and locked her fingers together nervously.

Madame took several slow bites, pausing for breath between each one. "I thought once—" She gazed down at her tray. "I thought—perhaps—I detected an attachment between you and Trevelyan."

"Oh no!" Callie said instinctively. She held herself rigid. Madame had never mentioned such a thing before.

"Ah—I am full of nonsense in my head tonight." She smiled a little. "It was long ago, as you say."

Callie sat mute, unable to steer between the treacherous shoals of conversation she perceived threatening on each side. She wondered if taking recourse to the sal volatile and burned feathers on the nightstand would help.

"I do think he has matured well, do you not?" Madame said faintly. "Though he took a fall from a horse, he told me—such a shame, that it has marked his face. He was always a perfect Adonis." She drew a hoarse breath. "So says his doting maman!"

"Is the pudding sweetened to your taste, ma'am?" Callie said in a stifled voice. "It's from Mrs. Adam. Tomorrow we'll see into procuring a woman to cook."

"So good she is, Mrs. Adam! She has warned me again and again against Mrs. Easley, but—you know—she is not such a bad woman, after all." Her voice trailed off into a small cough.

Callie did not need to be told that Mrs. Easley had been all the cook that Dove House could afford. "I'm sure that we can find someone more suitable, now that your son has returned." She was a little vexed that every subject seemed to lead back to Trev, but it was hard not to be glad at the look of relief on Madame's pale countenance.

"Oh yes—everything is so much better now!" the duchesse said.

"I'll make inquiries directly. And until we locate someone, we can very well spare the undercook and a maid from the Hall." Callie paused. "If Lady Shelford approves," she added belatedly, recalling that she no longer had charge of the housekeeping staff at Shelford Hall.

"Do not trouble yourselves at Shelford! Trevelyan will—" Madame lost her sentence in a fit of coughing. It grew worse, lasting so long that the tray shook and the Frenchwoman struggled for air.

Callie finally took the tray and helped Madame to lie down, keeping her own countenance calm with an effort. Hardly a spoonful of the pudding had been eaten, and every gasp seemed weaker. Madame lifted her lashes when the spell at last diminished, clutching the coverlet.

"Oh, Callie," she whispered with a faint sound of despair. "I don't want to leave him all alone."

"Rest now," Callie said, stroking her forehead gently.

The duchesse closed her eyes. She breathed shallowly, her lips working as if she would say more. But she sighed instead, holding on to Callie's hand. A single tear slid down the side of her face.

Callie stopped in the kitchen door, still startled at the sight of him, even though she should have been perfectly prepared. He sat at the kitchen table, watching Lilly measure tea into the pot, but he sprang up as Callie entered.

"Jacques! The tray." He glanced at a mountainous man who stood wedged between the table and a sideboard. "She didn't eat well?"

"Not very well," Callie admitted quietly, surrendering the tray to the scarred and gnarled hands of his hulking servant. "Lilly, you needn't carry up the tea after all. She's lain down to sleep now."

"Bring it to the parlor," Trevelyan said. "There's a fire started there."

Callie had been about to see if she might discover some supper for him, but he was already at her elbow with a light touch that had resolve in it. She glanced about quickly for Lilly as she found herself propelled up the short stairs and across the dark hall to the parlor. She did not really think he was going to despoil and plunder her person, or anything nearly so interesting, but the town of Shelford would be honor-bound to assume so, having exhausted the latest volumes of *The Lady's Magazine* and *La Belle Assemblée,* and being in grave want of a fresh topic of conversation.

In the firelit room, he set the chairs back from the hearth. "I beg your pardon. I hope you may draw a breath in here," he said. "I don't remember that the chimney used to smoke this way." He placed a chair for her. "I won't keep you long, I promise. Miss Lilly, you'll remain with us after you pour out the tea."

"Yes, sir." Lilly curtsied willingly. Mrs. Adam's pert maidservant was not always so eager to oblige, but she was clearly enthralled by a handsome gentleman who called her "Miss."

Callie was fully conscious of the master stroke he delivered in complimenting the maid and openly ordering her to remain as chaperone. Lilly was sure to portray it in a positive light to Mrs. Adam. From there it would be passed to all the society of Shelford who might be supposed to have any business to comment upon Lady Callista's concerns. This comprised a large circle, even discounting the goats.

His manners could be faultless when he cared to exercise them—a strict grandfather of the ancien régime and a gracious mother had seen to that. He perfectly comprehended the most arcane demands of courtesy, even if he had always been equally pleased to disregard them at his whim.

"Lady Callista—tell me—what do you think?" he asked bluntly as he sat down.

Callie bit her lip. "She's very happy that you're here."

He made a sound in his throat, a half-angry laugh. "Overdue as I am, you mean. God forgive me." He closed his hands on the arms of the chair for an instant and then said, "I'll summon a medical man from London tomorrow. What can some country surgeon know?"

Callie only nodded, watching Lilly pour the tea. She feared that another physician could do no more than ease the way a little, but she did not wish to say so.

"Please, if you can aid me in finding some staff— the expense is no object," he said. "A housekeeper and cook and some maids. And someone who can coax this abominable chimney to draw. Whatever is required. I wish the best that can be had, but I have no notion how to discover them."

"Of course. I'll commence to look directly in the morning. We can find a temporary cook and a maid in a few days, I think," Callie said. "But the neighborhood is thin of help, I fear. A good housekeeper may take some weeks to procure."

"Weeks!" he said.

"In the meantime, I'll make certain that things are managed better here."

He looked up at her. Callie met his eyes for just an instant. She saw the same flash of knowledge and despair that she had seen in his mother's face. "I would be grateful," he said. "What an insufficient word."

"I'm truly glad if I can be of use," she said. "I haven't many duties to engage me at home now."

"No? But surely you're busy at Shelford Hall."

She gave a small shrug. "Lady Shelford wishes me to have more leisure since my father died, and not fatigue myself with concerns about the staff."

"I see." His mouth flattened. "She's jealous of you there."

As ever, he said outright what Callie kept concealed and shrouded in her heart. It was like a lifting of a burden she had not realized she carried, to have someone who understood. She could not agree with him openly, not in front of Lilly, but she gave him an appreciative glance.

"I can't conceive of anyone who could manage Shelford better than you, my lady," he said. "But doubtless that's what vexes her."

Callie felt the splotches coming to her cheeks. "I don't fault her. Truly, it's confusing for the servants, to have two mistresses."

"I suppose. Still, if she feels that she can spare you, then her foolishness is our gain, if you'll turn your excellent talents to us."

"I'll be glad to do all I can," she said. She lifted her eyes long enough for a quick smile and lowered them before he could perceive the rush of gratification that she felt at his words.

They sat for a moment without looking at one another. Callie sipped her tea. She was vividly aware of Lilly in the chair behind her. She suddenly found a hundred things she wished to say to him, questions to ask, where he had been and what he done. She struggled for a commonplace to fill the silence, but commonplaces always eluded her.

"You remain at Shelford, then?" he asked at last.

"Only until my sister marries. Then I'll go with her, to keep her company."

He stood up suddenly. "Forgive me, but that is a precious waste."

She shook her head. "It's what I wish."

"To leave Shelford Hall? But, Callie—"

"It is what I wish," she said firmly. "And Hermione has promised she will not marry any gentleman who won't allow me to bring my bulls." She paused, realizing how unseemly that had no doubt sounded, and felt the red splotches bloom brighter on her cheeks. "Pardon me," she said. "But—you know what I mean." She blinked and averted her gaze in embarrassment, seizing the opportunity to stare into the dregs of her teacup and wonder what the scenery would be like in the outer reaches of Mongolia, if God would only answer her prayer and transport her there at once.

"Yes, I know what you mean," he said. His voice held a hint of a smile. "Tell me, how does the magnificent Monsieur Rupert go on these days?"

"Rupert has passed away," she said, on firmer conversational ground there.

"God rest him." He clasped his hands behind his back. "I'm sincerely sorry to hear it. I was hoping to see him again."

She lifted her eyes, surprised at the note of genuine regret in his voice. "Thank you. But he was upward of eighteen years, you know, and had a good and fruitful life. I've kept two of his sons, and a particularly promising grandson. In fact Hubert has developed so well that I didn't even enter him at the Bromyard fair this year, because he's taken first premium there once already. We're going directly to the county exhibition at Hereford next week."

"Directly to Hereford. Indeed!"

"Yes, and I feel certain he'll win one of the silver goblets." Her voice gained confidence. "His sire took first place last year among the Bulls of Any Breed, and Hubert is a finer animal on several counts.

Only—I'm hoping that Hermione's husband will like them all."

"The man would be a fool not to adore them, I'm sure."

"Well, he need not write poetry to them," she admitted. "Some good pasturage will be sufficient."

"No love poems, of course," he said gravely. "He wouldn't wish to make Lady Hermione jealous. But surely an ode would be appropriate?"

She felt a smile lurking at the corners of her mouth. She pressed her lips together to conquer the quiver and put down her cup. If only he would not look at her quite so, with that gleam in his dark eyes. It had always made her think foolish, outrageous things. "I should see if there are any eggs to be had for your supper. I believe Madame said there was a hen nesting under the rosebush when I called last month."

"No, I'm already a devil to keep you so long. It's far too late for you to be tangling among thorns and sulky chickens," he said. "Jacques will drive you home, and I'll lie awake and pine until you return. So do not tarry long, my lady."

Callie stood up. "You've had no supper."

"Not for the first time. I promise you won't find me expired of hunger, as long as you return promptly at sunrise. Or a little earlier, if you can manage it." He gave her a hopeful look. "Say, five or ten minutes from now?"

She shook her head slightly, trying to remind him of Lilly. It was impossible that he meant anything by such absurd things as he always said—she should know that well enough—but still she could feel her thought-less heart flame with long-silent memories.

His carriage held the scent of him. Even after he had closed the door and stood away, after the driver had clucked to the horses and the carriage began to roll, in the dark interior of the vehicle she breathed a faint perception of his presence, a hint of sandalwood and polished leather.

Lilly sat up on the roof with Jacques, to direct the way to the gates of Shelford Hall. Inside, Callie ran her hand over the velvet seat of what was certainly an elegantly appointed traveling chaise. She could not see it well by moonlight, but she had discerned the coat of arms painted on the door. She would have thought Trev would drive a curricle, or even a cabriolet, something light and fast, but instead it was a great ponderous closed vehicle like her father's carriage.

A bit too much like her father's carriage. That ceremonial vehicle stood yet in the coach house, only used on Sundays and for funerals. Enclosed and dark and set a little away from the stables, as it had always been, left to quiet and seclusion each week after the wheels had been cleaned of mud and the seats brushed down.

She stared out at the slowly passing shapes of trees and hedges, all blue-white and black under the rising moon. Not for a long time had she thought about her father's carriage as anything more than the conveyance that she and Hermione, and now Lord and Lady Shelford, mounted inside to drive to church. But tonight, in a different carriage, with the thought and scent and touch of Trevelyan d'Augustin all about her, that other memory rose vivid and inescapable.

It was Trev who had first perceived the commodious possibilities of the coach. It was not something Callie would have considered. But then, she had not been considering anything very rationally at the time. She had been so in love, and so besieged by the sensations he could evoke just by glancing down at her with that faint perceptive smile at the corner of his mouth—one of the peahens in the yard would have been more likely to hold a sensible exchange on the matter of where they might safely meet.

His kisses she had already experienced. She was an authority on the topic. Trev said so. He said her kisses made him feel as if he were dying, which she had taken as a compliment, because his made her feel exactly the same way, and it was indeed a great deal like dying, or disintegrating, or falling down some infinite well that had no name but led somewhere that she was sure she had to go.

It had led, in fact, into her father's carriage. Even now, years later, she moistened her lips and closed her eyes and put her gloved fingers to her mouth at the thought of the dim coach interior, lit only by a thin line of daylight that fell down from some high window and through the curtains, a streak of brightness across the red velvet seats. And silence, but for his breath at her ear and throat, and the little noises she made as he touched her. Protest and pleasure and fear almost to panic that someone would discover them, but when he had kissed her there and even *there*, his tongue and teeth on her breast, tugging through her gown, she had gasped and clung to his shoulders and begged with tiny whimpers.

He'd sat up a little, his hair all mussed in the dusky light, looking as if he could not remember who he was. Then he had freed the buttons on his trousers and guided her hand, kissing the side of her neck. When she touched him, he shuddered and bruised her skin as he closed his teeth. A low sound in his throat seemed to make sparks shower down through her whole body.

She arched up against him, pressed and tangled as they were on the seat, his leg over hers and her skirt all askew. She felt his hard man's part slide against her thigh, their fingers twisted together over it, as if both of them searched and prevented at once. She wanted him closer and pushed him away, frightened and seeking for more.

As she pressed her legs together, he worked his fingers inside her, finding a place that made her sob with smothered pleasure. She'd tried to suppress the sounds that came from her throat, but he kissed her breasts again and thrust his fingers deeper, growling in his chest as he drew a half cry from her, delight and confusion and desperation, wanting and wanting and pushing herself up to meet his hand. She could hear herself panting, and him, their breath coming harder, mingling and rising until she felt a wave of such intense pleasure burst through her that she did cry out, forgetting everything but him. He rose over her, pressing himself hard into that intimate place, not his hand now but the thick head of his erection pushing for entry.

"Callista!"

The sound of her father's voice seemed to echo even now, as if he stood there yet, the door to the carriage flung open and Trev moving suddenly to sit up. Remembering, Callie bit down on her fingers so hard that it hurt through the glove.

Trev had tried to conceal her, but there was no hope of it. Only an instant of bewilderment, and then her heart had seemed to burst in horror. Sickness rose in her throat. She had barely been aware of Trev's quick move to arrange her skirts; she had seen only her father's face, a nightmare against the shadowed brick of the coach house wall.

"Get down," her father said in a whisper.

Callie had scrambled past Trev, stumbling down the stairs, her gown and hair in disarray. Her father had not touched her. He stood back, his hand working on the riding whip he carried, as Trev swung down after her in one swift move.

"Callista," he said. "Go back to the house."

Trev started to speak, and her father struck him across the face with the whip.

Callie made a choked cry. She took an instinctive step toward Trev as she saw the line of blood well across his cheekbone. His face was white, utterly still. He stared at her father without speaking.

"Go to the house now, Callista," her father said. "Or do not expect ever to enter it again."

She had run. She had turned away and run from the stable yard, up the front stairs, run blindly through the hall and up to her room. She had not seen Trev again. He had vanished from Shelford, from his family, from her life. Not even his mother had known where he had gone until years later, when he began to write from France.

Late in the evening of that dreadful day, after she had sent back a tray from her room, having no appetite to swallow anything, her father had come to her. Callie was too mortified to do more than sit at her dressing table with her fingers gripped around her comb until the teeth bent. She had glanced at him once, but the expression on his face was unbearable. If it had not been her father, her own staunch and self-possessed papa, she would have thought from his red-rimmed eyes that he had been weeping.

"Callista," he said, "I will not chastise you. You lost your mother when you were very young, and perhaps I haven't—perhaps your governesses—" He paused, rubbing his hand over his eyes. "I'm convinced that you did not comprehend."

She sat silent, allowing him to excuse her. She well knew she had been wicked. Anything and everything to do with Trev was a transgression. She had kept it secret because she had known that with perfect clarity. All she had to say for herself was that he made her lose all shame and reason, and that was no defense.

"I must—" He turned his back on her. "I must ask this. Did he—ah—"

He seemed to lose the tail of his sentence. She felt the ivory teeth of her comb break with a tiny snap. She stared down at the red marks on her fingers.

"He claimed that he did not utterly soil and ruin you," her father said in a rush. "I cannot—I will not—take the word of a blackguarding French scoundrel, but if you tell me that is so—" His voice changed. He seemed almost to plead. "Callie, I will believe you."

"He didn't, Papa," she said quickly, flushing so hot that she felt feverish. Callie perfectly understood what he meant. She was as well acquainted with certain facts of life as any farmer's daughter would be. But

she should not have touched that place where Trev
had guided her hand, or let him do what he had to
her—what girl of any slightest modesty would not
have comprehended that!

Her papa let go of a deep breath. "I see."

She picked at the tiny broken teeth of her comb.
He turned back to face her. Callie stared at her toes.

"My very dear," he said. "Oh, my dear. I'd have
given my life to spare you this. He's a villain of the
lowest sort. I know that he made you believe he loved
you, or you would never have been so rash, but,
Callie, Callie…" He gazed at her, his eyes damp. "It is
all lies. You're a substantial heiress. You're underage.
These wretches with their polished address, they're full
of any pretense in order to get you into their power."
His lip curled with scorn. "But he'd never have
touched a penny of your fortune. It's well protected
for you, I've made certain of that. He knows it now,
if he did not before."

She had nodded. She had not wholly believed him.
Trev's sweet falsehoods had been still too close then,
the way he made her feel too vivid to disbelieve.

Trev had said they would fly to the border to be
married, because neither of them was of age. In the
years after, she was amazed to look back and think
that she had ever had the nerve to fall in with such
plans. But then she had always done so, whether it
was a secret jaunt to see the finish of a horse race,
amid a very mixed crowd of rowdies and questionable
gentlemen, or a visit to the graveyard by a full moon.
She had known he was wild, but she had trusted him.
It had not seemed so bad or frightening to slip out
of the house at midnight, as long as Trev would be

waiting for her under the ancient yew that guarded her window.

No doubt those escapades had hardened and habituated her, rather like the criminal classes, to accept without serious question his idea that it would be a grand adventure to elope. Of course she had known it was an iniquitous thing to do, and that her father deeply disapproved of Trev and would never countenance a marriage between them, clandestine or otherwise, but all that she somehow had put aside in her euphoria that someone as splendid and handsome and enthralling as Trevelyan loved her.

She had barely been seventeen. She was not so naïve anymore. The point had been borne in upon her by three subsequent gentlemen just how unlikely it was that Lady Callista Taillefaire would inspire any true romantic passions in the male heart.

"Well," her father had said gruffly. "I wish for you to go to your cousins in Chester for a time. But we'll take a visit up to Hereford first. You and I. There are some cattle sales I wish to see, and you will advise me on what I should buy. You'll like that, eh? We'll depart tomorrow, as soon as your maid can make ready."

So she had gone away for a few months and then come home. Her father had made her excuses well. No word of her indiscretion had ever been disclosed, no hint or insinuation of it whispered over the years. Shelford was a small place, and she was notorious for her triple jilting, but not even the most scandalous gossip had ever connected her name with Trevelyan's.

Not even his family had known. Madame de

Monceaux had spoken often of her bewilderment and grief, and his grandfather cursed the boy to damnation for his capricious desertion of his family. Callie felt heavily to blame. After she was allowed to return, she had quietly done everything she could for their welfare, but the occasional pheasant or basket of fruit from Shelford Hall was a poor recompense for the loss of a son.

Callie gathered her shawl about her, sitting up as the carriage turned in at the gates of her home. She looked out the window at the fields along the drive, their dim, silvered expanse dotted with the dark humps of sleeping cattle. The Hall was a high black shape, a few windows glowing softly here and there along the length of its regular facade.

The coach rolled to a stop. Lanterns glinted on the broad stairs as Shelford's footman opened the door for her. Callie unclasped her fingers, aware of a secret lift of her spirits as she stepped down from the carriage. Trev had come home. She was needed at Dove House early in the morning. But she made no request for a mount to be ready or a maid to be prepared to accompany her. She would rise before dawn and walk by the back way to his den of iniquity, so that she would not be seen in the village.

In truth, Trev might be a practiced villain, but she feared that he had not required much practice to lead her astray.

Three

IT WAS IMPOSSIBLE TO HAND CALLIE INTO A CARRIAGE without skeletons rising up to point accusing fingers at him. Trev had been exquisitely polite as he bid her good night. Fortunately there was little moonlight, so both of them could direct their full attention to the mundane matter of safely negotiating her way onto the steps. He watched the carriage lumber into the darkness of the narrow, tree-choked lane.

He was beset by skeletons in Shelford. His mother, whom he had neglected beyond shame. His sisters, lost to scarlet fever, lying in graves he had not visited. His grandfather, unmourned and full of condemnation, rising up like some vengeful character from a play by Shakespeare. And Callie—shy, passionate, a very much living reminder of one of the more reprehensible moments in a notably careless career.

He still found it difficult to comprehend that she had not married. When he had left, he'd been sure that she would be wed within the year, if not sooner—as soon as her father could arrange for it.

He had not cared to stay and watch the ceremony. He was a contemptible French scoundrel, so he went to France. To his bloodthirsty delight, he'd found that Bonaparte had good use for young men with bruised hearts and even more deeply lacerated pride. For a few years Trev had labored under the name of Thibaut LeBlanc and shot at Englishmen, starved hideously, looted Spanish peasants, and learned how far down he could plunge into brute existence. What final vestige of pride or humanity he retained was burned out of him at Salamanca. He had not rejoined the crushed remnants of his company as they retreated; he'd surrendered instead to a British aide-de-camp who recognized him from their school days, and spent the rest of the wars in the reasonable comfort of various officers' prisons, interrogating French captives for Wellington's staff.

He might have gone back to Shelford after Waterloo. Instead he had remained in France. He'd begun to write to his mother, but somehow he had not told her of the battles or the ruin he had found at Monceaux, or the burned-out shell of her childhood home in Montjoie. Somehow he had written instead of how he would win it back for her, the fabled château and the titles and everything she had lost.

He knew all the stories. His grandfather had made certain of that. Instead of nursery rhymes, Trev had been weaned on tales of the Terror, of his father's heroism and his mother's sacrifice. His father had not surrendered, like Trev, but gone as a true nobleman to his fate. His mother had barely escaped the mob. Trev owed his life and his baptismal name to one Captain Trevelyan Davis, an enterprising Welshman who had smuggled her and her five young children across the channel just two days before she gave birth to him.

In spite of the bloody backdrop, his childhood had been golden. He didn't miss a father or a country he'd never known, but he remembered his pretty mother laughing while she taught his elder brother to dance. Trev had worshipped Etienne as only a seven-year-old could worship a dashing brother of thirteen. Those had been the sweet, carefree times, the years of perfect boyhood bliss. Then one day Etienne had tried to raced his hot-blooded horse past a carriage, and amid a crush of wheels and his mother's frenzied grief, Trev's brother had died, and the sunny world of childhood ended.

From that time, it was Trev's duty to regain all that had been stolen. Like a personal guillotine, that expectation had hung over him, repeated with every blessing his grandfather said at meals, in each letter sent to him at the English school, repeated whether he fell ill or whether he recovered, when he was thrashed and when he was praised, repeated until Trev had been sure he would throttle his grandfather, or shoot himself, if he heard it one more time.

He had done no such thing, of course. Instead he had seethed like the silly, mutinous boy he'd been, at least before all the gold and silver plate was sold and he had to leave school and move with his family to the modest house at Shelford. After that he talked to Callie and made her laugh. An agreeable alternative to murder, making Callie laugh. She always tried not to and always did. It changed her face, made her eyes tilt upward and sparkle in the hopeless attempt to stifle her giggle, just as it had tonight.

A bird called in the dark garden, a trilling whistle that made Trev turn his head. He stared into the shadows.

Then he put his hand in his pocket and felt for the pistol he carried, realizing with some annoyance that another of his skeletons had dropped round for a chat.

"Come away from the house," he said softly.

With a rustle, a figure moved out of the tangled gloom, shoving the overgrown bushes aside. A chicken squawked and fluttered. The visitor uttered a heavy-handed curse and came through the gate.

"Quiet, you codpiece." Trev walked across the open yard with his hand still in his pocket. When he reached the back of the small stable, he stopped and turned. "What do you want?"

"Bill Hayter is beggin' a new match, sir."

Trev gave an exasperated sound. "I told you I've done with all that. He's been paid off. Let him go to another operator if he wants to publish a challenge."

"But the stakes—"

"I will not act as stakeholder, damn it. Do I have to place an advertisement in the papers?"

"The gentlemen of the Fancy don't trust no one but you, sir." His visitor was only a black silhouette.

"Then they may go hang," Trev said cordially.

"Sir," the man said in a plaintive tone.

"Barton—my mother is dying. A low, unfeeling fellow I may be, in the usual course of things, but I find this concerns me just a little. If you suppose I'm going to saunter off to make book at some fight that would like as not be broke up by the sheriff and land me in the dock, you may reorder your ideas."

"I'm sorry, sir. I'm sorry to hear that." Barton was silent for a moment. Then he said tentatively, "Do you think, after she passes on, God bless 'er, that you might…"

"I might have you strung up and disemboweled. I might do that."

Barton gave a gloomy sigh. "Very well, sir." His feet shuffled on the gravel. "But I don't know what's to become of us."

"For the love of God, you had two percent of sixty thousand guineas not a fortnight ago. How'd you manage to spend twenty years' wages in two weeks? Or need I ask?"

"We ain't got your head for a numbers game, sir," Barton said humbly. "You're the lucky one. Charlie botched the calculations, and we come up short to pay out on St. Patrick when he won at Doncaster."

"That short? You'd better marry an heiress and be done with it."

"Ain't no heiress would have me, sir," Barton said.

"Then follow my example. Become an honest man."

Barton gave a snort. Then he began to chuckle.

"Go on," Trev snapped. "Get out of here before you wake the dead."

Callie was sitting at her dressing table, dreaming of escaping from pirates, wielding a sword like a musketeer while Trev kicked a scalawag overboard at her side. As her maid unwound the length of purple silk from Callie's head, Hermione peeked inside the door, interrupting Trev's desperate lunge to pull Callie from the path of a cannonball.

Her sister slipped into the room, holding her wrapper close about her. "You're home," she said. "I was hoping you wouldn't be too late. Mrs. Adam said they hadn't a thing to eat at Dove House."

"Nothing," Callie said. "And I'm afraid Madame has not long to live."

"Poor woman." Hermione walked restlessly to the window, plucking at the latch as if it were not closed properly. "But her son has come home? High time for that, they say. I didn't see him; is he a tolerable gentleman?"

"Oh yes. Elegant manners." Callie watched her sister in the mirror. Hermey took after their mother, everyone said, with skin of smooth perfection and soft golden brown hair falling loose now down her back. The maid plucked at the ends of Callie's own red braids and began to unravel and spread them over her shoulders.

"Elegant," Hermey said. "Well, that's to be expected, I'm sure. He's Madame's son, after all. And a duke, or whatever sort of title they have over there now." She stopped her agitated pacing and made a sweeping flourish with her thumb and pinkie finger, as if she were taking a pinch of snuff. "So very continental!" There was a flush to her cheeks, a high color that was unlike her.

"Crushingly modish, I assure you," Callie said lightly.

"I'm sure you took him in dislike, then. It was good of you to offer to help."

Callie did not correct her. "I intend to do what I can for them," she said merely. "I mean to find some servants and see that the house is put to rights."

"Of course." Hermey made a distracted wave of her hand. She turned away and turned back again. "I was surprised to find you gone, though. I was looking for you after the waltz."

"Yes, I told Mrs. Adam—"

"I know. It's no matter. Only——" She hugged herself. A half smile of excitement curved her lips. "Your hair is so pretty when it's down! It looks like copper waves."

"Hermey." Callie tilted her head quizzically. "What mystery are you keeping from me?"

"Sir Thomas is coming to call on Cousin Jasper tomorrow!" she said breathlessly. "He told me so!"

Callie smiled at her. "Already!"

"Oh, Callie!" Hermey clasped her hands together, chewing her knuckles. "I'm so afraid!"

"Afraid? Of what, pray?"

Hermione took the hairbrush from the maid's hands. "Be so good as to go upstairs, Anne," she said primly. "I'll do that."

The maid curtsied and left the room. Hermey watched the door close behind her and then began to brush out Callie's hair. Callie could feel her sister's fingers trembling. "Hermey!" she exclaimed. "What are you afraid of?"

"It's just that——he said... he said he would do himself the honor of calling on the earl tomorrow. That means he's going to ask, doesn't it, Callie?"

"I should think so," Callie said. "He had no business saying such a thing to you if he didn't mean it."

"I'm twenty," Hermey said. "Twenty! And it's my first offer."

"Well, you needn't make anything of that. You couldn't come out while Papa was so ill, and then you had to wait out the last year in mourning. You haven't even had a season."

"I know. But I'm almost——" She stopped, looking conscious.

"On the shelf?" Callie drew her hair over her shoulder, working at a tiny tangle. "Goose! I'm on the shelf, not you. You'll have your choice of suitors if you wish to wait until spring and go up to London. I hope you won't leap at this one if you don't like him."

"I like him," Hermey said. "Very much!"

Callie parted her hair and caught it, winding it about her head. Sir Thomas Vickery seemed a kind and quiet gentleman, the perfect sort of person to be perpetually an undersecretary. He rather reminded Callie of herself, which did not impress her greatly, but she could find nothing to object to in him. Indeed, she could only be glad that Hermey, who was a little flighty, seemed to prefer a steady man. And he was drawn to her sister's vivaciousness no doubt—which would be just as well if the three of them were to form a household. At least there would be one person to make conversation at the dinner table.

"Well, then," she said. "If you like him that much, I advise you to wear that blue straw bonnet tomorrow and be in your best looks. I don't know how he can help himself but propose if he sees you in it."

"I think he will," Hermey said. "I know he will." She went and sat against the bed, still holding her wrap about her and shivering as if she were cold. "No, anything but blue, Callie. I think I will wear the apple green. Or the spotted lilac with the cream ribbon. Oh, I can't think. I don't care what I wear!"

"Calm yourself, my dear," Callie said at this astonishing statement. Hermey always cared what she wore. "It's really not so frightening. I've had three offers myself and survived them all."

"I know. I *know*!"

She looked so distressed that Callie rose and turned to her. "What is it? Now, do not cry, love! I never thought you would be full of nerves over such a thing. He's the one who should be anxious, and I've no doubt he's quaking in his shoes this minute at the thought of making an application to you."

Hermey gave a choked sob. "Oh, Callie! I'm going to tell him that I want you with me or I must refuse him, and I'm s-so afraid he will say no to it."

Callie paused. She met her sister's unhappy eyes. Then she turned and reached for her nightcap, bending to the mirror and tucking up her hair. "You will tell him no such thing, of course!" she said briskly. "You mustn't make a cake of yourself just when he's proposed, you silly girl. Do you want to frighten him out of the house before you have him fairly caught?"

"But I will tell him!" Hermey took a deep breath. "I don't care if he won't agree. I won't leave you here alone with that… that—oh, I don't know what horrid name to call her!"

"Hush," Callie said, as her sister's voice rose. "He would think you addle-brained, my dear, just when he's declared his deep love and abiding respect for you, to be told that his bargain is two for one."

Hermey bit her lip. "Is that what he will say? That he loves me?"

"Certainly. That's what they all say."

"Well, if he truly does love me, then he'll let me have you with me. And your cattle too!"

Callie laid her robe across the chair. She crossed to the bed and gave Hermey a hug. "Perhaps he will. But pray do not tax him with it at the very moment that the poor man makes his offer. There will be ample time to talk of such things later."

Hermione caught her hand as she pulled away. "Callie. I will not leave you here with her. I couldn't bear the thought. I won't speak of it to him tomorrow, then—but I promise you that I will." She lifted her chin defiantly. "And if he doesn't agree, then I will jilt him."

"Excellent!" Callie said. "It's high time we started to even up the score."

An hour before sunrise, Callie was already making her way along the lane to Dove House. The autumn air lay heavy with fog. They were still far from any snap of frost, but the coolness of nighttime had begun to promise a chill. She pulled her hood closer and assured herself that this early start was merely because she wished to avoid awkward questions from Lady Shelford, not for any reasons having to do with pining or being missed or anything of that nature.

She meant to prepare a breakfast, leave it set out on the parlor table under covers, and return to Shelford Hall before anyone would suppose she had done more than make an early visit to the farmyard. No one belowstairs at the Hall had questioned her need for bread and bacon and butter. They were accustomed to any odd request from Callie for her animals. But Dolly, Lady Shelford, was another matter. It would require some marvelous persuasion, Callie feared, for her cousin-in-law to approve of lending out the undercook. Callie wasn't hopeful about her prospects of success.

In the shadowy silence before dawn, she let herself into the scullery at Dove House and laid out her burden. The kitchen was empty, but the fire had been banked properly and took no great effort to revive. She envisioned a frigid wind blowing across the side of a mountain. Casting herself as the pretty daughter of an old shepherd, she built up the fire to a hot blaze in order to warm the rich and handsome traveler she and her faithful dog had just rescued from the Alpine snows.

After she had renounced his fervent offer of matrimony in favor of the handsome-but-poor blond mountain guide who had loved her since she was a child in the flower-strewn meadows, she slipped upstairs to look in on Madame de Monceaux. As she ascended, she could hear a ponderous snoring all the way from the attic and supposed that the massive Jacques had found himself a bed. When Callie peeked into Madame's chamber, the duchesse seemed to be resting quietly, her breathing shallow but regular. Barely visible in the shadows, Trev slept in the bedside chair, propped against the wall at an uncomfortable angle.

Callie paused. His mother must have passed a difficult night, if he had sat up with her for all of it. As she closed the door, trying to keep it from squeaking, she resolved to find at least a maidservant and a cook by dinnertime, even if she had to gird herself to beg Dolly for the loan. The situation for hiring in Shelford was dire, with the opening of a large new pottery not four miles from the town. Even Shelford Hall had felt the pinch in trying to replace the increasing number of staff who had left since the new mistress had taken management of the house. But Dolly had only looked coldly uninterested when Callie suggested that wages might be increased to compete with the manufactory's lure. Callie was entreated to calm her anxiety about a pack of disloyal servants and concern herself with more refined topics.

It was still dark outside when she set the teakettle on the hob and arranged rashers of bacon in the skillet. She stared down at the sizzling meat, deep in thought as she considered where best to begin inquiries. The innkeeper, Mr. Rankin, might have news of a prospective cook, since he was on the post road and received all the intelligence first. And Miss Poole always had her finger on the pulse of the young girls available in the district, looking out for help in her mantua-shop. A girl too clumsy to do good needlework would be perfectly useful at Dove House.

"Good morning."

A husky voice made her look round quickly. She dropped the big fork and turned as Trev stepped down into the kitchen, his black hair tousled and his neck cloth hanging rumpled and loose.

"That smells delicious," he said. "And the cook is a charming sight too." He leaned against the wall wearily. "If there is coffee to be had, I believe I may be able to carry on to the next hill."

"Coffee," Callie said, flustered to find him down so soon. "Oh yes. Let me look out some berries from the pantry. Good morning!"

He smiled. "What can I do to help you? I'll carry out a violent raid on the rosebush, if I can unearth it in that jungle of a garden."

"No, do sit down, if you don't mind to eat in the kitchen." She waved at the scarred old table.

"There's bread and butter. I fear your mother passed an uneasy night?"

His brief smile evaporated. He stood straight and came to the table to sit. "She was better after midnight, I think. I don't know. Perhaps it's only a bad spell, and she'll be recovered presently." He looked up hopefully.

Callie kept her gaze averted, setting the skillet off the grate. "I pray so. When I saw her a month ago, we sat up in the parlor, so perhaps with better nourishment she'll find her strength." It was too difficult to admit that she feared the duchesse was failing badly.

He ran his hand through his hair. "I'll send Jacques to London today. I want a man of reputation to attend her."

Callie laid bacon on a plate. "Let me fetch the coffee-berries."

When she came back to the kitchen, he was gone. But by the time she had roasted the berries on a fire-shovel and ground them, he returned. His great, tall manservant ducked a shaved head through the door after him. Jacques didn't linger to eat but only made a very creditable and gentlemanly bow to Callie before he went out the back door. She glanced after him. He was dressed neatly but oddly for a servant, in billowing yellow trousers and top boots, a colorful scarf tied about his throat. She had not noticed the night before that both of his ears were thickened and distorted in shape. If he had not been so well mannered and gentle in his moves, she would have thought he had been one of those horrid pugilists, the ones who came into the country for their illegal matches and caused all her farm lads to lose their wits and talk of taking up fighting as a trade.

A faint light of dawn showed against the sky as the manservant went out. When he was gone, Callie became conscious that she was left alone with Trev in the kitchen. He had not yet shaved, but he had straightened his neck cloth and brushed the wilder curls from his hair. It didn't seem awkward or improper; indeed it seemed comfortable when he sat down again at the table and began to slice the bread. Callie set out plates and cups, the chipped and elegant remains of a set that had once borne garlands of flowers and gilt rims.

She strained off the coffee when it boiled. Trev had speared pieces of bread on a long-handled fork, toasting them at the fire with surprising expertise for a French duke of royal bloodlines. He dropped the golden brown pieces off the fork onto a plate.

Callie was indulging herself in gentle daydreams, now the mother of a promising young family in a Normandy farmhouse, preparing breakfast for her dashing husband while he was home on leave from his naval command. He looked so drowsy because they had spent the entire night making passionate love that would no doubt result in another fine son. After breakfast they would take a stroll through the seaside village and cause the other wives to sigh over his gallantry and prizes. She served out the bacon on two plates and sat down across from him. "I hope the coffee is what you like."

"Everything is exactly what I like," he said. "You most of all."

She shook her head, feeling herself grow pink. She put down her knife and fork. "I must go and find the eggs."

"Don't go," he said quickly. "I won't be outrageous, I promise you."

Callie hesitated. Then she picked up her fork, trying to keep her eyes down on her plate and not gaze at him like a moonling. They ate in silence for some moments, while she lectured herself with unspoken vehemence on the folly of a plain woman of twenty-seven years, thrice rejected, having any thought at all about a silver-tongued rogue's careless compliments. If she had been more skeptical of him nine years ago, she would not perhaps have suffered quite so painfully.

"It must be quite interesting to grow the grapes for wine." She made a plunge at casual conversation.

He shrugged slightly. "They're grapes," he said, as if that entirely covered the subject.

"Did you find the vineyards at Monceaux badly damaged?" she asked.

"Oh no." He drank a deep swallow of coffee. "Even raging revolutionaries like a good claret."

"I hope your absence won't cause too much disruption in the work. It's harvest time there, is it not?"

He lifted his hand carelessly. "There's a vigneron to take care of all that."

"Oh yes," she said, remembering. "The evil Buzot!"

He glanced up with a sharp look, as if her mention of the name startled him.

"Madame asked me to read her letters aloud," she said hastily. "I hope you don't mind."

"Ah, then you know of Buzot." He sat back in his chair. "The fellow howls at the moon and drinks the blood of innocent babes, I assure you. I haven't caught him at it, but that's only because I'm afraid to go out after dark."

"How vexing. But he makes such excellent wine from your grapes."

"Oh, magnificent wine!" he said affably. "It's my belief that he's sold his soul to the devil."

"No wonder that you keep him on." She nodded, buttering bread. "It can't be easy to find someone with such impressive credentials."

"I don't suppose any midnight covens are scheduled to convene in Shelford?" he inquired. "We might discover an exceptional cook."

"I'm afraid that would be quite ineligible. There's no saying what she might put into the pot and pass off as a chicken."

He put down his cup, his eyebrows lifted in alarm. "I hadn't thought of that. Scratch the coven."

"I think we should start with Mr. Rankin."

"Ah. And what has Mr. Rankin to say to it?"

"He still keeps the inn—the Antlers, you know—and will be our prime informant. You mentioned that funds were not greatly restricted?"

"Hire the chef out of Buckingham Palace if he can appear promptly."

Callie peeked up at him. The only overt signs that he was now a very wealthy lord were his excellent carriage and elegant dress. He seemed to be traveling without pomp, or any retinue beyond Jacques. She rather liked him for it, that he had not changed his ways on regaining his family's riches and titles. Dolly had insisted on every point of ceremony since her elevation to the Countess of Shelford. Cousin Jasper's vague indifference to the dignity of his new title only seemed to goad his wife into greater concern for his position. She made certain that the smallest mark of respect toward the earl should not be overlooked.

It was a relief to escape, even for an hour, from the stifling atmosphere that had been established at Shelford Hall. High form and etiquette always made Callie feel as if she should consult Burke's Peerage to make certain her name was actually in it, and discover how she ought to address herself in letters.

"I'll pass by the Antlers on my way back," she said, on a more comfortable subject, "and have them send over a hot dinner by noon. That must suffice for now, but their victuals are very plain, and I think it best to have a cook in the kitchen, so that Madame's appetite can be tempted with more delicate fare."

"Thank you. I hadn't even thought of sending to the inn."

"If you'll excuse me, I'll go up and attend your mother and make her comfortable before I go."

"Thank you, Callie." He pushed himself to his feet as she rose. "Thank you. I can't believe—" He shook his head with a baffled sound. "Who are these chuckleheads who let you slip out of their grasp?"

Callie was conscious of a sudden rush of blood to her cheeks. "Hardly that. They were made to pay handsomely for the privilege of relinquishing my hand, I assure you."

"So I should hope," he said. "Blackguards. Are you a great heiress, then?"

"Well, yes," she admitted. "At least, I suppose I am. After the last settlement—it does tote up to a rather large sum."

"How much?" he asked bluntly.

She bent her head. "Eighty thousand," she said in a smothered voice.

"Good God."

"So you see," she said, lifting her face, "I'm hardly an object for compassion."

"May I make you the object of my violent and unrestrained ardor?" He made a motion as if to loosen his neck cloth. "I'm a bit tired, but perfectly willing."

"My calling hours are from twelve to three, if you wish to importune me violently," Callie said, dropping a quick curtsy. "But now I must see to your mother."

"Thank you." He gave a weary snort. "How many times have I said that? I'll try if I can to achieve some originality when I've had more sleep."

She paused on her way to the door. She had meant only to say that he had no need to thank her, but something in his tired smile made her touch his arm. "I'm so glad you've come home," she said softly.

He stood still for a moment. Then abruptly he gripped her hand. "Oh God, I can't even think how to tell you—" He seemed to hear the desperation in his own voice, and let go of her with a rueful laugh. "Well. You'd better make your escape immediately, before you find me pressing kisses to your feet. Or somewhere equally improper."

Callie ducked her head. She lifted her skirts and hurried up the steps out of the kitchen.

The fog still lay heavy when she reached the pasture, softening and obscuring the trees and hedges. Hubert stood waiting at the gate, a dark shape in the mist. As she came to the fence, he broke off his placid chewing and lifted his huge pink nose, snuffling loudly in expectation.

Callie pulled a loaf of stale bread from her basket. She stepped up on the rail. The bull nosed gently, tickling her fingers, and took the bread on his long tongue. He curled it into his mouth. Callie scratched his broad forehead while he chewed with an air of satisfied contemplation.

He had good reason to feel satisfied with himself. Hubert was an excellent specimen. He measured five feet six inches at the shoulder and eleven feet ten inches from nose to tail. He boasted a superbly mottled coat, red and black on a white ground. In addition to his size and beauty, he possessed all the highest perfections of a shorthorn bull: a clean throat, level back, impeccable big shoulders, ribs full and round, leading smoothly to long quarters. He had grown only one ring yet on his handsome horns, being just three years old, and his first crop of calves were on the ground this past spring, perfectly healthy and lively as larks.

She looked on him fondly as he blinked his generous lashes and turned his head to allow her better access to scratch behind his ear. She had been present at Hubert's birth, led him about at his mother's side when he was a baby calf, comforted him with treats when he was weaned, nursed the inevitable cuts and scrapes a young bullock inflicted upon himself by trying to reach that farthest blade of grass through the hedgerow, and brought him up to his impressive prime. Hubert was the pride of the county, a fit successor to his celebrated grandsire, Rupert.

Even though he was a mottled shorthorn, rather than one of the cherished local white-faced breed, she felt perfectly certain that he would take first premium at Hereford. In a few days she would have him begin his leisurely walk to the city with her most trusted drover, moving at just the right speed to maintain his weight and muscle, but still arrive in good time for him to recover from any loss or scratch he might suffer on the journey.

As Callie leaned across the fence to rub his ear, a sudden growling bark made her startle and grab the rail. Hubert turned his big head as a brindled dog charged from out of the foggy lane, roaring and snarling. It stopped, teeth bared, a yard's length from her skirt.

Hubert stamped a hoof, lowering his nose to look through the rail. The dog rushed toward him, snapping. In the flash of the moment, Callie threw her basket, sending a shower of bread on the dog's head. It shied off for an instant, then paused, its heavy muzzle turned toward Hubert, its pink lip still lifted in a growl, quivering in every muscle.

"Silly creature!" Callie said in a jolly voice. She stayed on the rail but forced her muscles to relax. "Now what do you suppose you're doing?"

The dog never took its eyes from Hubert. The bull had turned to face the threat, lowering his nostrils almost to the turf, blowing strong gusts of air against the grass. He began to paw the ground.

"What a funny dog!" Callie crooned in a quiet voice. "What a foolish boy. You don't think we mean to hurt you?"

A man's voice called out from the road. The dog pricked its shorn ears and turned. But it did not retreat.

Through the light fog, she saw a stranger hurrying toward them. He called the dog again. This time it obeyed him reluctantly, swinging away and trotting to his side.

"Beg pardon, Miss!" He reached down and grabbed the dog by the collar. "I'll put a rope on him."

Neither man nor dog were from the neighborhood of Shelford, where Callie knew every domestic creature and a good number of the wild ones too. The stranger wore a heavy overcoat and gaiters with an elegant top hat, a rather odd combination of country and city fashion. As he straightened up from tying the dog, he gave her a nervous smile, his mouth creasing too widely under high cheekbones.

"We'll go along now, Miss!" he said, touching his hat and dragging the dog as it snarled and lunged back toward Hubert.

She watched from the gate as his outline faded in the fog. He disappeared around the curve in the lane. The sound of the dog's barking diminished. One of those card sharpers and badger-baiters, she did not doubt, who would put his dog to fighting chained animals while he stood back and shouted and made his cowardly bets. Callie despised the breed. She hoped that he was merely passing through. The Bromyard fair had just ended, and fairs always attracted such men. She thought she would make note of it to Colonel Davenport. Just a word in the magistrate's ear, that whatever might be tolerated in Bromyard, such activities were not to be countenanced in Shelford's village.

Four

BY NOONTIME, THE INHABITANTS OF DOVE HOUSE HAD full reason to be grateful to Lady Callista. Not only had a hot meal arrived from the Antlers, but the innkeeper's wife came with it. Mrs. Rankin insisted that she would stay to attend Madame while his lordship's grace stepped down to the inn, where the barber was awaiting him with water on the boil. A pair of men and a boy from Shelford Hall were already at work clearing the chimney, and a basket of green apples sat on the front table, compliments of Lady Shelford.

"You must call on her this afternoon, Trevelyan," his mother whispered, lifting her hand weakly from the coverlet. "I shall undertake to survive alone for an hour, I pledge you!"

He hesitated. But Mrs. Rankin shooed him toward the door, saying that it was no such thing—Madame would not be alone. The innkeeper's wife was a tiny woman, but she had the self-assurance of a scrappy terrier, admonishing Trev to have his coat brushed before he presented himself at the Hall. He left her chiding his mother to take more beef stew or find herself sorry for it, for if Lady Callista learned that

Madame had not eaten well, it would be a great shame and a black stain on the honor of the Antlers.

She did not use those words, precisely, but she managed to convey the importance of the affair. Trev smiled as he closed the door. He was under no illusions. His family had always been treated with friendly condescension in Shelford, tolerated but hardly esteemed. It was Lady Callista's opinion that mattered to Mrs. Rankin.

It was Callie's opinion that mattered to him too. He submitted himself to the barber, had his boots polished, made use of one of the inn's bedchambers to tie a fresh neck cloth, compensated Mr. Rankin generously, and—having made himself plausibly presentable in a lady's drawing room—hired the Antlers' postboy and groom to put a pair to his carriage and drive him to Shelford Hall.

He arrived at half past two, which would give him the proper quarter hour to pay his respects and convey his gratitude if she had not been in jest about her calling hours. He hoped she had not. He carried a posy of soft white roses and russet-colored dahlias, cut ruthlessly from his mother's tangled garden and tied with a ribbon. Small thanks, but the best he could do.

The cream-colored limestone edifice of Shelford glowed like a Greek temple in the autumn afternoon, a symmetrical facade of pilasters and porticoes set in a gem green park. Chestnut trees dotted the rolling pastures, their leaves flaming with orange under the sun. Trev was perfectly acquainted with the outside of the great house, in particular the dark old yew under Callie's window, but he had never been invited to set foot inside.

A carriage was stopped before the stairs, disembarking a trio of well-dressed ladies. He recognized none of them, but he judged their gowns to be expensive. The chaise had a liveried footman, who sprang up behind as it moved away, grinding over the gravel down the drive. Trev touched his card case in his pocket. He reminded himself that he was a duke and a cousin of kings, even if they had been beheaded. He had a perfect right to the title of useless aristocratic fribble.

The front door had already closed behind the ladies by the time Trev walked lightly up the steps under the blank gaze of two footmen. He informed the porter that he requested the honor of calling upon Lady Callista Taillefaire on behalf of Madame de Monceaux, handed in his cards, and waited. He waited a very long time, cooling his heels on the stoop, trying not to feel seventeen years old again, with the cut of a whip across his face and shame burning in his throat.

At last the door swung open under another footman's white-gloved hand. The butler bowed. It was all a great deal more ceremony than he remembered from the old earl's days. The butler then had been an ally of his, an immensely tall fellow with a craggy, forlorn face. This new man was shorter and thicker, with a high reddish complexion in his cheeks. He looked as if he might have a temper. As Trev handed over his hat and gloves, he judged that the new fellow would peel to thirteen stone—not a bad physique for a middleweight boxer.

Their footsteps echoed in the domed vestibule, whispers of sound against the fluted stone columns and the marble floor. The butler showed him into an empty anteroom with a few stiff chairs and some paintings of cattle on the walls. Trev wished now that he'd merely left a note of thanks with the flowers, instead of sending up the cards. He felt as unwelcome at Shelford Hall as he ever had.

There was already sufficient indication that his family was not held in large regard here. The basket of apples from Lady Shelford might just as well have been a chilly announcement that no more was owed to Dove House than token civility. So it had hardly been a shocking blow when Mrs. Rankin conveyed the news that, due to some impending social event, Lady Shelford could not see her way to lending out the undercook even for a few days. The innkeeper's wife had delivered this intelligence with an eloquent shrug, as if it were exactly what one might expect.

"This way, sir." The stolid butler returned after some delay. The servant nodded briefly as he held the door open.

Trev followed him up the wide curve of the staircase, carrying his posy. From the drawing room came a loud murmur of voices. Quite a large afternoon gathering it seemed. Pausing in the doorway, he saw that the pleasant, sun-filled chamber held a number of visitors, mostly congregated about a young couple at the head of the room.

A quick glance round as he was announced did not reveal Callie among the group. He disguised his vexation, being utterly at sea without knowing which of these females might be Lady Shelford. No one moved forward to greet him, so he stepped into the room and stood a moment, listening.

It didn't take long to deduce that the pair of young people standing shyly by the fireplace were newly betrothed. Amid talk of a ball and a formal announcement, someone said gaily that Lady Hermione would be wise to order her bride-clothes early from Paris. Trev realized with a slight surprise that this was Callie's sister.

She did not resemble Callie at all. She was somewhat prettier, to be sure, but it was an ordinary prettiness, neither objectionable nor memorable. Now that he guessed who she was, he could vaguely recall a prattling and sociable child from his earlier days in Shelford, but little sisters had not interested him very deeply at the time. She seemed tolerable enough now, if perhaps a little too forced and gay in her gestures. Doubtless she was nervous at being the center of attention. A forgivable offense. But no hint of stifled mirth in her expression made him wish to tease a smile from her, as Callie's did.

Callie had mentioned going away with her sister when she married, but he had not understood that it was already a settled thing. He realized that he was frowning, and smoothed his face into a public smile as one of the women finally took notice of him.

She did not immediately move to greet him. He saw her give him the sort of cursory examination that any lady of the bon ton could perform in the flick of a raised brow. Trev waited with composure while she made certain that he was in all points comme il faut.

Her gaze lingered. He gave a small bow, finely calculated to avoid any presumption that she should notice him if she did not care to do so. She was quite beautiful in an unyielding way, her hair such a pale gold it was almost white, her features as strong and expressionless as some classical statue of Minerva. Her skin seemed so fine and thin that the bones showed too near the surface, as if she might crack like a marble stone if struck.

Trev made a deeper formal bow as she committed to walk across the room to him.

"Monsieur le duc," she said, holding out her gloved hand. "*Bienvenue.* I am Lady Shelford. Ah—flowers! Thank you. You must have heard of our happy news. But you shouldn't have left your poor mama. How does she do?"

He found himself giving up Callie's posy, having little choice as she took it from his hand and passed it to the footman. Keeping any hint of irony from his voice, Trev conveyed his mother's heartfelt thanks for the magnificent basket of green apples. He was surprised to find that Lady Shelford condescended to lead him to the tea table and see that he was served. He had not thought he would rate so high in her social calculations. She even lingered with him. He took advantage of it to extend his felicitations on the betrothal and casually hope that Lady Hermione would not go too far away from Shelford when she was wed.

"Oh, they will live in town," the countess said in an uninterested voice. "He has some sort of situation in the Home Office. His duties keep him tied to Whitehall."

"Ah. London." Trev would have liked to pursue this topic, but he could not find a nonchalant way to ask where Callie would pasture her bulls in London. "That will be a gay life for Lady Hermione," he said politely.

"Indeed." She did not appear gratified by the thought. "You're recently come from Paris?"

"No, I went direct to Calais from my home," he lied, avoiding any possible acquaintances of hers who he might have been supposed to encounter in Paris.

"Of course. You did not wish to delay." She touched his arm, allowing her gloved fingers to trail across the back of his hand. "You must tell me anything that can be done for your poor mother. I might send someone to help in the kitchen, perhaps?"

Trev lifted his lashes. He met her eyes and found an unmistakable look there, a flagrant physical aware-ness of him under her impassive smile. He was a great appreciator of women, and he knew well enough that his admiration was generally returned, but he avoided liaisons with females of easy principles. His grandfather and mother had been neither romantic nor reserved in their counsels to a hot-headed and well-favored young boy. Trev had been brought up with no illusions about ladies of society or ladies of the streets.

"You are too kind," he said. "I beg you won't put yourself to the trouble." He kept his voice neutral and his bow respectfully stiff. He felt vaguely insulted that she would make even a delicate advance at the same time she offered assistance. "I only wished to convey my thanks to Lady Callista for her help. She's not at home?"

"It would seem that she is not." The countess looked around as if she had no notion whether Callie was present.

"Perhaps I might write her a note," Trev said, when she did not make the offer.

"Oh. Yes, if you like." She gestured toward a carved secretary and turned away.

He wrote standing up, dipping a pen and helping himself to the paper. Only a sentence, conveying little but his mother's thanks, since he could discover no wafer to seal it. He had a notion that Lady Shelford was just the sort to take a glance at other people's correspondence. When he straightened, he found that she was watching him from the far side of the room. He folded the note. With a little less than courtesy, he gave her a nod and handed his letter to the footman as he departed.

As the porter held the door for him, Trev glanced over the curving drive toward the stable range. A thought occurred to him. He signaled to the postboy to hold his chaise and walked across the gravel toward the outbuildings.

He knew the way. Under the carriage arch, past the dim stall rows smelling of sweet hay and horses, then a goodly distance out along the walled lane with glimpses of a big kitchen garden through portholes in the brick. He was dressed for a drawing room, not a visit to the home farm, but he sidestepped the mud hole at the gate and evaded the importunities of a donkey. A pig watched him hopefully through the slats of its pen. Trev stooped to retrieve the remains of an apple that had rolled out and tossed it over the fence, receiving a grateful grunt in return.

A farm lad was shoveling at the manure pile, sending animal pungency into the air. He tipped his cap to Trev. "Afternoon, sir."

"Would I find Lady Callista here?" Trev asked.

"Aye, sir." The boy nodded toward the bigger cow barn. "M'lady's feedin' the orphan."

Trev had guessed something of the sort. He took off his hat as he ducked under a dangling rope and walked into the shadows of the barn.

He saw her bonnet over a stall partition, the brim bobbing energetically. He paused, looking round the wooden barrier. Callie stood bracing herself against the enthusiastic assault of a large calf on the bottle she held. Under a copious canvas apron, she was dressed in a pink silk gown with a pair of muck boots poking out from beneath the ruffled hem.

"Have you deserted the drawing room, my lady?" he asked.

"Oh!" She started but only glanced aside without showing her face from under the wide brim of the bonnet.

"You had a caller," he said. "I even had my boots polished."

"I'm sorry," she said in a voice he could barely discern. "I didn't expect—I shouldn't have gone away from the party, but—"

Her muffled words trailed off. She kept her face hidden. As he watched, she turned up the bottle to let the calf suck down the last of the milk. Trev took a step nearer. He tilted his head, bending a little, and saw that her chin was wet with tears.

"Callie," he said in dismay. "What is it?"

She set the milk bottle in the straw. The calf nosed it and licked at the nipple. There was a long silence, and then she wiped her cheek.

"My cousin has lost Hubert," she said in a small voice.

"Hubert?" For a moment he was bewildered, and then recollection struck him. "Hubert the bull? The one you're taking to the Hereford show?"

"Yes. Rupert's finest grandson."

"What do you mean, lost him? He's got loose?"

She shook her head. "No. Cousin Jasper lost him in a game of whist at the assembly last night. Colonel Davenport is coming tomorrow to lead him away."

"A game of—but Hubert doesn't belong to him! He's yours, is he not?"

"My father didn't specify it," she said. She gave a wan shrug. "I don't suppose it was something he thought of, to change his will over a bull calf."

"And your cousin put him up for stakes?" Trev said incredulously. "A bullock?"

She lifted her face. He saw for the first time that her eyes were red and swollen. "Colonel Davenport has tried to buy him for a year now. He's offered a great deal of money, but we never accepted. Cousin Jasper feels very badly about it. I think he was not himself."

"Was he drunk, the stupid devil?"

"I don't know. I shouldn't think so. He said was trying to be affable with the other gentlemen. Lady Shelford won't allow him to gamble for coin."

Trev scowled. "He sounds a very fool."

"He is not quite—" She pulled her apron from the calf's searching mouth. "He finds it difficult to be comfortable with people. I can understand it."

"I don't!" Trev said with exasperation. "What sort of man is this, to gamble away an animal when he knows he has no right?"

"He's the earl," she said simply.

"He should buy him back for you."

She drew a deep breath. "Yes, he did try. And Colonel Davenport said he wouldn't part with Hubert for any price now. He's going to show him at Hereford for the cup and then take him about the country to all the exhibitions."

Trev made a skeptical sound. "There's a price that would change his mind, I vow."

"Yes," Callie said. "No doubt." She pulled a wrinkled handkerchief from her apron and blew her nose. "But he turned down two thousand pounds."

Trev whistled through his teeth.

"In a year I might save that out of my pin money," she said thickly from behind the handkerchief. "But I don't know what he would accept. And Hermey is going to live in London. Where would I keep a shorthorn bull anyway?" Callie stared at the calf as it nuzzled her skirt. "It's only that—" She turned away, blowing her nose. "I shall miss him a little. I had not thought to say good-bye so soon."

He stood a moment, holding his hat, flicking his thumb against the brim. "This Colonel Davenport is coming tomorrow?"

"Yes." She took a deep, shaky breath and turned back. "I beg your pardon, I don't mean to burden you with my vapors. Did your mother take some stew?"

"I'm certain that she did. I left her under the command of the formidable Mrs. Rankin."

She smiled faintly. "I'm afraid we still have no cook. Lady Shelford doesn't wish to lend out anyone from the kitchen."

"So I heard."

"I'll speak to her again this evening. Perhaps I can persuade her," she said.

"No, Callie. No."

She glanced up. Weeping did not complement her; the puffiness about her eyes obscured any hidden spark of humor. He had a sudden desire to reach over and gather her close and promise that she would not lose Hubert or Shelford Hall or any of the things he knew she loved. With some effort, he resisted it. He had a bad habit of pledging things that were out of his power.

Instead, he said, "I don't wish for you to plead anything more from Lady Shelford. We'll muddle through without the undercook."

"There's a woman in Bromyard who might be in search of a new position. Mr. Rankin was going to inquire. I'll see him again tomorrow, after—" She paused. "After Colonel Davenport has taken Hubert."

She said it very bravely, which only made him want to beat this Colonel Davenport senseless and then run her cousin through the heart with a saber.

"Perhaps he'll change his mind," he said.

She gave him a tremulous smile and shook her head.

"He might," Trev insisted.

For a moment she looked up at him. "Please don't make me hope for it."

"No—I suppose—forgive me. I wasn't thinking. May I walk you back to the house?"

"Thank you. I would rather not go back quite yet." She caught the rope on the calf's halter and curled it around her hand, looking down.

"Don't cry, Callie," he said stupidly.

"No, no. I won't. I'm not."

He curbed himself fiercely from saying more. He could hardly bear to stand and watch her hide her face under the bonnet. "Good afternoon, then," he said. "When you go in, tell the footman that I brought the roses for you, not for your sister."

He arrived back at Dove House in a dark disposition. The ponderous carriage, purchased for the sole purpose of providing a suitably glossy background for the Monceaux crest, was no more than a nuisance now. The modest stable at Dove House was too small to house it. His mother could not even rise from her bed, so there was little hope that she would see it. As he stepped down at the gate, he told the groom to take up Mrs. Rankin and drive the vehicle back to be lodged at the inn.

The innkeeper's wife was descending the stairs as he entered, clearly in some haste to depart. "Beg pardon, your grace, she's sleeping, and I must be back to put a turkey on the boil, or there'll be no supper in the parlor. Shall I send your manservant over to you?"

"My manservant?" Trev asked. "No, he's gone up to London since early this morning."

She gave him a shrewd look. "I hope you don't take it in bad part that I say so, but I fear he hasn't gone nowhere. He's made himself more than at home in the taproom all the living night and day."

"The taproom?" Trev repeated in astonishment. "You're mistaken. He slept here last night and left at dawn."

She cocked her head. "Did he, your grace? But he told us that you'd put him up at the Antlers for your convenience."

"I did no such—" He checked himself and then swore under his breath. "Tell me, how tall is this manservant? Is he a big man?"

"Big? No, sir, not at all. He's less than a middling sort, I'd say." She looked at him with a growing alarm. "He is yours, ain't he not? He hasn't choused me with some Banbury tale of you putting him up with us?"

Trev's mouth flattened into a thin line. "Does he have a brindle dog with him?"

"Aye, that he does, one of them fightin' curs. We had to put it in the shed, and it barked all night until he took the thing out to walk at dawn. He said it was your grace's animal."

"Deuce take the fellow! It is not."

"Then he's not your servant, your grace?"

"My God, I suppose I must claim him." Trev tossed his hat down on the hall table. "Turf him out, Mrs. Rankin, and tell him to hie himself here at once if he cares to live another day. You may bill his board to me."

The landlady looked relieved. "I'll send him to you straightaway, your grace. And forbid him the taproom?"

"Oh, with my blessing. He won't be lingering in Shelford, in any event."

Trev cut short Barton's excuses and apologies, keeping him standing in the kitchen. "Spare me the sad tale! Doubtless I should have known to scout the local taproom for any pestilent acquaintance of mine engaged in a swindle."

"I didn't think you'd begrudge me and poor old Toby a bed, sir," Barton said reproachfully. "You never did a'fore."

"Try, Barton—try to recall that I've turned you off. You are seeking other employment."

"Sir." He shifted his feet, plunging his hands into his pockets. "Sir, I don't want no other employment."

"What is it you expect of me?" Trev lowered his voice to an exasperated hiss. "I'm done with blacklegs and sharpers. I have no work for you now."

"You kept on Jock, sir," Barton said, his head bent. "You found work for him."

"As a valet! And I suppose you'd like to be my gardener?"

Barton looked up. "I'll do anything, sir! Only don't cast me off. Charlie washed his hands of me, and now me an' old Tobe ain't got nobody."

"Barton—" Trev leaned his shoulders on the wall, crossing his arms.

"Please, sir! Don't say no. After all the years I've been with you." He swallowed. "Please."

Trev gave a heavy sigh. He rested his head back and closed his eyes.

"Has I ever failed you, sir?" Barton asked. "Has I ever botched what you asked of me?"

"A hundred times," Trev muttered. He would have felt kinder kicking the dog away.

"I'll do better! There must be something I can do for ye," Barton said, his voice cracking. "Please."

"All right!" Trev stood upright. "All right, then. Don't snivel, for God's sake. I have a commission for you."

Barton's wide-mouthed grin spread across his face. "Sir? You mean it?"

"A single commission. One."

"Thank you, sir!" The man held himself up to his best height. "Whatever you wish!"

"I want you to purchase a bull for me," Trev said, "from a Colonel Davenport."

Barton nodded eagerly. "I'm a dab at a haggle, sir, and you know it. What's your limit?"

"No limit. The animal goes by the name of Hubert. The cost is no object."

"No object, sir?" Barton said, looking doubtful. "For a bull?"

"Shelford's prize bull. Davenport's to come and take him off tomorrow. Wait until that's done before you make your approach. Keep it quiet."

"Oh, aye, sir. Mum as a post. Don't want to drive the price up, eh?"

Trev could hear his mother begin to cough upstairs. He turned. "The price be damned," he said over his shoulder as he headed for the door. "Just make certain you get the bloody beast for me, will you?"

Five

WITH PAINFUL EFFORT, CALLIE KEPT HER COMPOSURE as Hubert ambled down the lane. She could have no complaint about the provisions made for his comfort: the drover offered water and tied him behind a cart full of hay. An exultant Colonel Davenport leaned down to shake hands with Cousin Jasper and turned his horse, trotting ahead of the cart as the little procession moved off. Hubert walked away, swishing his tail happily each time he snatched at a mouthful of hay.

Callie disengaged herself from her sister's sympathetic hug and gave Cousin Jasper a bright smile as he tried again to stammer his regrets and apologies. The new earl wrung his gloves in his hands and looked miserable, blinking his wide brown eyes with a soft plea that she forgive him.

She had shed all her tears before dawn, brushing Hubert from his nose to his handsome rump, teasing out his tail pompom, buffing and polishing his hooves as if he were already going to a fair. It had given her something to do. Now, facing Cousin Jasper's wretchedness, she needed some further activity quite desperately.

"There, he's on his way. No more to be said." She interrupted the earl with ruthless cheerfulness. "Now I must walk to the village. Pray excuse me, Cousin!"

Hermey made no attempt to accompany her, for which Callie was grateful. She kept up such a brisk pace that by the time she reached Dove Lane, she was not quite so close to breaking down in tears, though she had to maintain a stern frown to prevent it. She had not intended to stop at Dove House, meaning to call first on Mr. Rankin at the inn and discover the news. But Trevelyan was just coming out, making his way through the overgrown garden.

He plucked at a long rose cane that attempted to grab his sleeve as he passed through the gate. "Good morning, my lady. May I give you my arm up the street? I'm engaged to escort this rosebush to the shops, but I'll fob it off."

Callie drew a deep breath. She felt her facade of forced cheerfulness slipping. "Good morning."

He tilted his head, smiling a little, looking at her with such unspoken understanding that she had a very strong urge to walk straight up to him, lay her head upon his elegantly tied neck cloth, and weep her heart out.

"You forget your mother, my lord," she said, taking refuge in a frosty tone. "Surely you don't intend to leave her alone? I can't think it wise."

He nodded in agreement. "Yes, it's always useful to pick a quarrel when one is feeling low. Come with me into the high street, and I'll undertake to start a brawl for your further diversion."

She felt a small smile welling up, overcoming the immediate threat of tears in her throat. "How civil of you."

"I know. Particularly as I'll be bound to wrinkle my only coat." He let the gate fall closed and took her arm. "My mother is much improved this morning, with some excellent nourishment and a good night's rest. Mrs. Adam has arrived with Lilly to undertake nursing duties, and I am expelled as a dangerous man."

She glanced at the house. "Mrs. Adam is here? I should go in and lend her help."

"No, you should not. She's certain that I intend to lure Lilly into the debauched harem that I maintain in the opium dens of Paris." He turned her toward the lane. "Be so good as to thwart me from this evil scheme. You can begin by distracting me with a walk to the post office."

She smiled, though it was slightly watery. "I see that it's my Christian duty, when you put it so. I only hope I may not succumb to your wicked plot myself."

"Oh, I have far more sinister plans for you. I mean to entice you to a dish of tea in the public parlor at the Antlers. I will certainly set a chair for you, and possibly I may even speak French."

Merely walking at his side, with her gloved hand resting on his arm, was rather alarming. She remembered that he had brought roses, though she had not told anyone they were meant for her. "Thank you for your call yesterday," she said shyly. "And for the beautiful posy."

"Hardly enough to convey my gratitude," he said.

She had not, of course, supposed the flowers were meant as anything more than an expression of thanks. "We'll inquire about the Bromyard woman at the Antlers," she said, grasping at a practical topic. "I have high hopes of her."

"The dahlias reminded me of your hair," he said pensively. "That deep copper color. Only a little darker."

"Oh," Callie said. She lifted her skirt and stepped over a tuft of grass. "I do hope she knows how to cook. Truly cook, you know. Something that your mother would like."

"And the roses—pretty and pale, with a flush of pink. Very like your cheeks when you blush."

"A blancmange, perhaps," Callie said brightly. "Or a custard."

"Your cheeks are nothing like a blancmange, I assure you, my lady. And certainly not a custard."

"A blancmange would be the true test of her skill," Callie said with difficulty. "I think we should ask her to make a blancmange."

"They're the classic strawberries and cream. Very English."

"Any sort of fruit trifle would make a good test, I agree," she said hastily. "But strawberries are out of season."

"Indeed, but they aren't," he said. He slanted one of those looks down at her that left her covered in confusion. It was very vexing. She ought to tell him to stop. But she didn't precisely wish him to stop. She rather wished to fall right back in love with him, like a veritable ninnyhammer, and believe against all fact and reason that he meant what he said.

"So you have met my sister and Lady Shelford?" she asked, her voice rather too loud. She could see some pedestrians in the sun-dappled lane, far down where it widened into something that could reasonably be called a street.

"Lady Shelford," Trev said. "I met her, yes. An awe-inspiring woman, to be sure. I'm afraid I didn't remain long enough to have the honor of an introduction to Lady Hermione. She was engulfed in well-wishers. Has a date been set?"

"Next month," Callie said.

"They're impatient lovers," he commented.

"But poor Hermey has had to postpone so much because of—" She hesitated, then said, "She's hardly been away from Shelford at all, or met any eligible gentlemen, until we went to Leamington to the spa. Our father was ill for a long time, you see, and then he passed away last year, so we have been in mourning."

"My condolences."

Callie did not look up at him. "Thank you," she replied in a small voice.

Trev guided her round the bowing white heads of Queen Anne's lace that encroached on the lane. He was aware that he should make a better show of sympathy. Callie had adored her father. He knew it well. But he would never forget that whip across his face. He remembered it every time he shaved himself, each time he saw the faded scar in the mirror. For months afterward he had dreamed of revenge with a hopeless violence that only fed on knowing his fantasies were absurd. He'd shot more than one unfortunate British infantryman with the Earl of Shelford in his sights.

She walked with her face hidden from him. He looked down at the tendrils of reddish copper hair that had escaped her braids and bonnet, tiny curls that lay against the nape of her neck. Callous bastard that he was, the glimpse of white skin, tender and soft, made his throat fill with some unnamed clash of emotion, with resentment and protectiveness and a potent spike of simple lust. She smelled faintly of fresh hay and mown grass, as she always had.

They could be friends. He truly wished for that. A friend would enter into her obvious distress with real sympathy, the way she had instantly come to his aid with his mother. He tried to summon words of kindness for her father's death, but they were not there. The only sort of words that came to him were sarcastic comments on just how pleased the old man would doubtless be to see her walking with him now.

Finally he said, "I'm sure you miss your father." It came out more stiffly than he wished, but he had said it.

"Yes," she said. "Very much."

"He cared a great deal about your welfare."

"Oh yes," she said.

Trev hoped that was sufficient. He bewildered himself with the fresh rage that overcame him. He had no right to it, as he had no real right to tease and flirt with Callie when he could go no further. Her father had rejected him as a penniless nobody of unsteady character, and that was in Trev's respectable days. Now he was one step ahead of the hangman's noose.

"He was very disappointed when I didn't marry," she said, so softly that he could barely hear. "He wished very much for that."

"Ah," Trev said. His rage found a new object: these three silly sods who had jilted her. He walked along for a few moments, all tame in his gentleman guise, gazing at wildflowers and trying to think of a kindly and understanding response. With sudden ferocity, he uttered, "I'd like to kill them all for you."

She gave him a startled glance. Then she laughed, causing the trace of a tear to tumble down her cheek. The sound made his heart rise amazingly.

"Thank you!" she exclaimed. "I've been so vexed that I can't do it myself!"

He took deep pleasure in the happy crinkle that appeared at the corner of her eyes. "Only tell me who they are," he said, giving her a little bow. "I'm wholly at your service."

She sniffed and smiled. "Perhaps it wouldn't be quite the thing," she said. "It would cause a vast increase in the number of widows and orphans in the country."

"Reproducing themselves rapidly, are they? Just what the world needs, more bloody fools. I'd best set about eliminating them without delay."

She giggled, with a little hiccup of a sob. "Trev," she said, holding his arm with her gloved hand.

No more than that. Just his name. She looked up sideways at him under her hat, that shy, half-laughing look that had always made him want to pull her down in a rick of new hay and tumble her under him and do lustful and luxurious things amid that sweep of loosened coppery hair.

"We'll start with Number One," he said. "He should be skewered first, for setting a bad example to the rest."

"Major Sturgeon," she said readily.

"Sturgeon," he repeated. "Sturgeon, as in the fish?"

She nodded.

"So you might have been—dear God—the Lady Callista Sturgeon?"

"Well," she admitted, "I did consider that."

"A mortifying thought. I'm not sure that we shouldn't let him live, for sparing you from this fate."

"No, he should be skewered," she said firmly.

"As you wish, ma'am. Will it be swords or a knife in the back? Or I could shoot him at dawn, if you like."

She considered this, pulling at the dried blossoms of a wildflower as they passed. She shook her head and scattered the seeds, dusting her glove on her skirt. "No—no duels, if you please. I wouldn't wish to see you put yourself in danger on my behalf."

"It would be an honor to put myself in danger on your behalf," he said gallantly. "But I'm a fair shot, I promise you. In the—" He paused. He'd been about to say that he'd been promoted to *tirailleur* and assigned to a battalion of sharpshooters in the Grande Armée because of his accuracy. "In the vineyards at Monceaux," he revised, "I can shoot a cluster of grapes from their stem at a hundred paces."

"Indeed! I'm sure that endears you to Monsieur Buzot."

"Oh, he only dislikes it when I make him stand with a basket and catch them."

She laughed aloud, her smile crinkling at the edge of her lashes. "You and the evil Buzot are well suited, Monsieur," she said reprovingly.

They ought to be, Trev supposed, since he had made up the man's existence out of whole cloth. "But please don't mention it in public, Mademoiselle," he murmured. "I haven't sold my soul. Only mortgaged it, you understand, at a very reasonable rate of interest."

"I quite comprehend the fine distinction."

"It's my belief," he said, putting his hand over hers and walking on, "that you are in grave want of excitement. Have you had one single adventure lately?"

"Hundreds, of course." She waved airily. "We are awash in adventures in Shelford. Only last week a goat climbed too high in Mr. Turner's chestnut tree, and I was called to talk it down."

"But I doubt you've climbed down from your window even once."

She hid again, looking down at the hem of her skirt. "I'm afraid I've left the acrobatics to the goats."

He kept his gaze on what he could see of her face, enjoying the play of emotion and denial at the corner of her lips. Callie showed everything in her mobile expression, which was why she kept it concealed so often, he suspected.

"Do you suppose you could still manage it?" he asked softly. "Perhaps I'll put you to the test one night."

"Trev," she said under her breath. "We are coming into town."

"Should I cover my face with a scarf?" he asked. "Or would you prefer a bag over your head?"

He could see her bite her lower lip. It wasn't fair to her, this provocation. He hardly knew why he was doing it. He could have discussed her sister's betrothal or his mother's health or the weather.

"So it's to be cold-blooded murder for Sturgeon," he said, ignoring his own better impulse. "And who else would you like me to slay before I flee the country? I'll require the names and directions of Numbers Two and Three, and their preferred methods of demise."

"Mr. Cyril Allen is Number Two," she said, lifting her chin. Her cheeks were quite pink.

"And what is to be his fate?"

"Oh, he should be strangled," she said strongly. "He told everyone in London that I wasn't quite right in my head and that's why he jilted me. And then he married his cook!"

"May I chop him into very small pieces first? I'll strangle him when there's not enough left to do else."

"Yes, you may," she said obligingly. "And I should like to have a slice of him put into her stew."

He gave a wicked chuckle. "I'm sure I can arrange it."

"Number Three has gone abroad with his exceedingly beautiful wife," she said, pursing her lips. "To Italy, I believe."

"That will be convenient. I can boil and render Mr. Allen and then, while I abscond to the continent, drop round to Pisa and push Number Three off the Leaning Tower."

"I suppose it would be described in all the newspapers," she said with relish.

"Quite likely. But your name need not be made public. 'He did it for the honor of a lady,' they'll say."

"Oh, that will cause a deal of frenzied speculation," she said in satisfaction. "Everyone will wonder who is this mysterious lady."

"No, of course it will be obvious I did it for you. Any constable could discover that. What else have these three fellows in common?"

She made a puff of dismissal. "No one would believe you did it for me."

"Why not?"

"Because." She stuck out her tongue at him. "Gentlemen don't do that sort of thing for me."

"They don't kill their rivals?" he asked in bewilderment. "These Englishmen are such dull dogs."

"Well," she said with that little glint of mischief. "Yes, they are, rather."

He grinned at her. They had somehow stopped walking. She was looking up at him shyly, a clear invitation on her lips. The fact that she had no idea of it only made the latent enticement more tempting. Humble Callie with her kissable mouth and laughing eyes; she'd be astonished if he gave her a lesson, right here in the public lane, in what a red-blooded Frenchman would do.

"Good morning to you, my lady!"

Trev looked up, startled by the loud voice. Callie's fingers left his arm as if it burned her. A portly gentleman paused before them, the fan of his white beard rounding out his face, spreading like an old-fashioned ruff over his clerical collar. He bowed toward Callie and nodded at Trev.

"Mr. Hartman," Callie said, sounding as if she could not catch her breath. "Mr. Hartman, oh yes." She became tangled in an introduction in which she could not seem to decide who to introduce to whom, or what anyone's name was. "That is—um, Monsieur—you'll remember our rector. Ah, of Monceaux. Monsieur... our parson!" She made a gesture of her hands as if she were shooing them toward one another.

"Of course." Mr. Hartman took off his hat with a practiced expression of concern. "I'm just on my way to pay a call at Dove House, monsieur le duc. I fear Madame is in a grave crisis?"

As he spoke, he assumed an odd affectation of an accent, so that Trev was *moo-shur l'duck*. The citizens of Shelford always took to French when they wished to put him in his place. Clearly Mr. Hartman did not approve of Callie's escort.

Her cheeks were the color of crushed strawberries. Trev was embarrassed too, caught enjoying himself while his mother was in a grave crisis. He was instantly annoyed with Hartman.

"She's a good deal better this morning, thank you," he said with easy English and a cool demeanor.

"Ah, she's improved." The news did not seem to please the parson. In fact his face drew downward into a more severe frown. "I felt deep apprehension from what I was told. I did not wish to leave her spiritually unattended at such a time."

"It's kind of you to come," Trev said dryly. As adherents of the Roman Catholic rite, his family had seen very little of Mr. Hartman over their years in Shelford. "But I have some hope she'll survive for a few more hours."

"Well, certainly. I didn't mean, of course—" Mr. Hartman sputtered a little. "I should be glad to provide any comfort that I may in her extremity."

"Lady Callista has seen that my mother has every comfort," Trev said. "I suppose it's not too late to alter her popish tendencies, but I advise you to hasten."

"Really, sir!" Mr. Hartman gasped. "I had no intention, I assure you!"

"But pray don't let us detain you while she's in her extremity." Trev could see by the look Callie gave him that he was being outrageous. He took her arm again. "We're on our way to the Antlers for tea, leaving her to her fate. Good day!"

With a little application of force, he walked on, carrying Callie along with him. She threw a quick good morning over her shoulder and then allowed him to direct her forward. They walked at a brisk pace as far as the crossroad.

He stopped so suddenly that her skirts swirled around his boots. With a harsh exhalation, he said, "I beg your pardon. But by God—what a meddling old crow. What does that fellow mean by calling on my mother now, when I daresay he's never set his foot in her house before?"

"He's a meddling old crow," Callie said wryly. "But you were perhaps a little disrespectful."

"Impudent, you mean. I suppose that will be all over town by noon."

"Oh no." Her mouth made a tiny quirk. "By the next quarter hour, I should think."

"Well then," he said. "Do you prefer the scarf or the bag?"

"Perhaps I should cover myself with a rug." They were nearly abreast of the first thatch-and-timber houses that lined Shelford's only street. No one else had passed them yet, but there were a few people walking and one horseman ahead. "Good morning," she said hastily, in response to a greeting from the gentleman who trotted past. Her steps were growing more unwilling as they approached the populated part of the street.

"This is a Mrs. Farr about to accost us, as I recall," Trev said under his breath. "Widely known for her kind soul and foul-mouthed cockatoo." He took off his hat and bowed, reckoning he'd best make an attempt to rehabilitate himself. "Good morning, ma'am," he said cheerfully.

"I declare!" exclaimed the apple-cheeked widow, dropping a quick curtsy toward Callie amid an abundance of petticoats spared from sometime in the last century. "Good morning, milady. It couldn't be our young Frenchman who has you on his arm, now?"

"Good morning, Mrs. Farr," Callie said softly. "Yes, indeed, here is Madame's son come to her."

"An excellent thing," Mrs. Farr said in her quavery voice. "There's nothing to top it. What a fine gentleman!"

"I trust you're as well as you look, ma'am," Trev said. It was easy to smile affectionately at Mrs. Farr. "And how does Miss Polly do these days?"

"Oh, she's as cross as ever she was. Just fancy you remembering Miss Polly!"

"How could I forget? That bird taught me how to have my mouth washed out with soap."

"Pshaw, you aren't supposed to hear what she says!" Mrs. Farr said, lowering her voice with a quaking chuckle.

"No? You should have warned me before I repeated it to my mother."

"Evil boy!" Mrs. Farr simpered. "You never did!"

Trev winked at her. "Come into the Antlers and sit down to a cup of tea with us, Mrs. Farr. Lady Callista has undertaken to help me find a new cook for Dove House. I've no doubt your advice would be invaluable."

"I should be glad to do what I can to help." Mrs. Farr picked up her skirts and stepped toward the inn with a briskness that belied her gray hair and ancient voice. "And to guard milady's virtue," she added with smug smile.

Trev bowed gravely. "Everything I know of vice, I learned from your parrot, Mrs. Farr."

"Pshaw, you never did!" the widow said, sweeping ahead of them into the door of the inn.

Six

THE ANTLERS BOASTED ONLY ONE SMALL PARLOR beyond the taproom, with just space enough for two tea tables and a small sofa set before the fire. The whiff of baking gingerbread gave the atmosphere a pleasant aroma. Mr. Rankin stood with his hands behind his back, leaning a little toward Mrs. Farr with a good innkeeper's solicitous attention while that lady wavered between the choice of the bohea or the souchong.

Trev excused himself to negotiate the cost of sending his letter postpaid. He had just come to an amicable agreement on mileage and postal notations with Mrs. Rankin when the blare of a tin horn made her hurry back into her kitchen. An open landau came rolling to a smart halt in the street outside. Trev glanced toward the door, his eye drawn by the sweep of a large cocked hat and a glimpse of uniform. He paused, watching the officer descend.

A dragoon guardsman, though he couldn't make out the badge. Since the war had ended, British uniforms had changed, aspiring to such stylish splendor now, that this fellow fairly glowed with heavy gold and scarlet, draped in braids and plastered with massive gilt facings across his chest. A tempting target for a marksman, Trev thought. He turned back to pick up his coins from the bar and toss his letter into the postbox.

The innkeeper did not quite abandon his other guests, but he came out of the parlor with a rapid step. Trev looked round again as the officer entered the door. The newcomer had a distinct familiarity about him. Trev caught the man's moment of hesitation as they glanced at one another briefly, and saw that he also was recognized. But he couldn't place the face. A square-jawed, handsome English face; light blue eyes and a high forehead... it could be from any of a thousand past encounters. Trev had dealt with innumerable English gentlemen and officers, named and nameless, in smoky, dim-lit quarters and thronging crowds.

He gave a faint nod, received the barest acknowledgment, and they went their own ways, having agreed to ignore whatever passing acquaintance they might have had. Trev doubted it was the sort of thing a regimental officer would care to recognize in public. He was not eager to be forthcoming himself. It was bound to happen, of course—he would encounter gentlemen who had known him under other names and circumstances, but he hoped that they would match his discretion with their own. It was to no one's advantage to make a case of it.

He rejoined the ladies, sitting down to a conversation about the price of tea carried on largely by Mrs. Farr, with the occasional nod and "yes, ma'am," from Callie. She did not seem to be paying strict attention, for which Trev could hardly blame her.

"I don't care for your green teas," Mrs. Farr said decisively. "The half of them have been doctored with such abominable tricks that there's no saying what's in them. I won't have green tea in my house, I tell you."

"No, ma'am," Callie said. "Certainly not."

Mr. Rankin appeared at the parlor door with the officer behind him. "If you'll just take a seat beside the fire, sir." He ushered the new arrival into the room, accepting the man's hat and cloak. "The boy will see to your baggage. Will you be taking a refreshment? There's gingerbread just coming out of the oven."

"Cider will do," the officer said briefly.

Callie suddenly sat up and threw a look toward the newcomer. Such a horrified expression came into her face that Trev almost reached out to support her as she blanched, but then she put down her teacup and bent her head toward her lap, hiding any glimpse of her face under the brim of her bonnet.

Mrs. Farr entered into a discourse on Congo, with a pekoe additive, versus a good Imperial. The officer glanced toward their table with the brief disinterest of a stranger obliged to share a public space—and then looked again. It was a penetrating look directed at Callie, at the nape of her neck, where those singular red curls were as recognizable in Shelford as any sign hanging outside a shop. Trev watched a play of emotion in the man's face—the instant of detection, followed by a tightening of his thin lips, a straightening of his shoulders. The officer turned away abruptly and sat down on the sofa.

Callie was hidden, but her breasts rose and fell with a rapid rhythm. Trev moved his leg, pressing it against her knee in silent support and question. She turned her face entirely away from the fire, staring toward the window as if she could escape by flying through it. Her eyes were wide with alarm.

"But if you care for a black tea, duke," Mrs. Farr said, "you cannot go wrong with the Congo mix. Green gunpowder will kill you in a month."

"I'm sure it would kill you with one lucky shot, Mrs. Farr," Trev said. He looked at Callie. "Are you feeling quite well, Lady Callista? Would you like to go out into the air?"

She nodded, standing up, clutching at Trev's arm as he offered it. Behind her, the officer stood up at the same time.

"My lady," he said clearly.

Callie stood still, frozen like a deer at the sound of his voice.

"If you don't desire to acknowledge me, Lady Callista, I'll submit to your wish," the man said. His nostrils flared. "I will not inflict myself upon you." He glanced an instant at Trev, his aristocratic brows drawn together. Then he stared at Callie again. "But I would call upon you, if you would... if you would kindly give me consent to do so."

She wet her lips. "Oh, I—no, I—" She took a deep breath, staring down at the floor. "It would be very uncomfortable for me."

The officer's pale eyes snapped to Trev again. There was something... Trev held the look. It was as if the other man grew taut with a personal challenge, directly marking him. He might have thought it was jealousy, the way the two of them stood with their lips buttoned and their faces rigid, like a pair of thwarted lovers, but Trev had a strong suspicion otherwise. Unless Callie had participated in more romantic encounters than anyone who knew her could believe, this would be one of the infamous jilts. A major of cavalry, at that; Trev could read the insignia of rank now.

A fine coincidence. He didn't see how the fellow had any claim to resentment of another man at Callie's side.

The officer looked again at her, his jaw set hard. "My lady, if you might consider—"

"I believe Lady Callista has made her answer known to you," Trev interrupted.

The man ignored him. "If you would see fit, my lady—"

"How curious." Trev gave an audible sniff. "I could swear I smell a day-old fish."

Callie's fingers nearly cut off the blood in his arm. She made a sound somewhere between a choke and a whimper. The other man grew as scarlet as his uniform coat. White lines played at the corner of his mouth. "I'm speaking to Lady Callista, not to you, sir."

"I don't wish to speak to you," Callie said in a rush.

The officer stood very still for a moment. "As you wish, then, ma'am." He bowed stiffly and walked out of the room, casting Trev one more venomous glance as he left.

"Oh." Callie's voice trembled. She sat down with a plop.

Mrs. Farr leaned over, patting Callie's hand and peering into her face. "Poor dear, you're ashen as a sheet. But the nasty gentleman is gone now. There, you see, he's calling for his carriage."

Callie put her fingertips to her cheek, drawing a deep breath. "Pardon me, I didn't mean to cause a scene. Thank you, Mrs. Farr." She lifted the cup that the widow poured for her and took a convulsive gulp of tea.

"Number One?" Trev asked matter-of-factly.

She swallowed again and made a face, wrinkling her nose over the cup. "Major Sturgeon." The saucer rattled as she put down the tea and looked at Trev. "What a peculiar shock," she said weakly. "So odd, as we were just…" Her voice trailed off. "Forgive me. I'm very startled." She gave an unsteady smile. "I must thank you for skewering him so neatly."

"Oh, you skewered him quite well yourself," Trev said.

"I hope so," she mumbled.

"What a very rude fellow," Mrs. Farr said. She peered at Callie with new interest. "I'm sure you ought not to know such a person, milady."

"No!" Callie said instantly. "I don't. That is—" She bit her lip. "I really don't know him at all, or wish to. I hope that you don't suppose—that anyone should think—oh, please don't mention—"

"I wouldn't breathe a word!" Mrs. Farr said, which Trev took to mean she would wait at least until Callie was out of sight before she began to spread the tale. He didn't care for the speculations that were likely to result from a story of some stranger accosting Lady Callista in a public inn. But as Callie floundered through a disjointed sentence, he could see that she was unable to summon any coherent explanation in the face of Mrs. Farr's growing curiosity.

"Major Sturgeon is beneath Lady Callista's notice," he said abruptly, judging that the truth was better in this case than the rampant conjectures that were bound to occur in a place like Shelford. "As a man who broke his word to her, he deserves no recognition from her, or from anyone who stands her friend."

"No, is *that* who he is?" Mrs. Farr gasped. "One of those villains who cried off on our Lady Callista? I declare, that he would dare to show his face in Shelford! That he would dare to *speak* to milady! Does he suppose he can worm his way back into your graces and propose again?"

"He is married now, Mrs. Farr," Callie said gently. "Doubtless he would simply like to express his deep regret or some such thing."

"His deep regret that his wife is an ill-tempered shrew, one hopes, and marrying anyone but you was the greatest mistake of his sorry life," Trev remarked.

Callie rewarded him with a tiny smirk. She seemed to be recovering her composure. "Oh, I should like that. I might have let him call, if he were going to say that."

Mr. Rankin paused in the door, peering in with a puzzled look. "Did the gentleman say he was leaving?"

"Driven off with his tail between his legs," Trev said.

"But he left his bags."

"Throw them into the street," Trev advised and enjoyed Callie's sudden giggle.

"He said he was staying the week," Mr. Rankin protested.

"Oh dear." Callie bit her lip. "What can he want in Shelford for a week?"

"Did he annoy you, milady?" the innkeeper asked anxiously. "He seemed a perfect gentleman, and so I was sure I ought to offer him a seat in here, instead of the tap."

"No, no, it was nothing," Callie said.

"I believe he recalled an urgent appointment," Trev said. "With a halibut."

"Indeed, I hope he found nothing to offend him about the Antlers."

"It was nothing of the sort, I assure you, Mr. Rankin." Callie sat up in her chair. "The gingerbread smells delicious; I hope we might taste it soon. And have you had a reply from the cook in Bromyard?"

"I have, milady. I was about to tell you when the officer gentleman arrived. She is at liberty to start on Saturday, and sent a recommendation from her employer. But two other families wish to take her on, and she advises that she cannot accept a post for less than thirteen shillings the week."

"Thirteen shillings!" quavered Mrs. Farr. "For a cook-woman?"

"Oh—she is in great demand, then?" Callie asked.

"I fear so, milady. I understand that the only reason she was willing to entertain my inquiry is because she would prefer to live within a day's drive of her family in Gloucester, and the other offers are farther afield."

"But why is she leaving her employer?"

"She's been these past ten years with a lady who now intends to make her home with a married daughter, due to her declining health."

Callie looked at Trev. "Thirteen shillings is a shocking swindle."

"No doubt she scents my desperation," he said. "My want of a convincing blancmange has carried all the way to Bromyard."

"I suppose if she's been with a lady in declining health, she must be accustomed to producing meals to tempt a delicate appetite," Callie said.

"The letter describes her just so, milady," said Mr. Rankin. "I'll fetch it for you." He bowed and went out.

"I think we might be wise to leap at this," Callie murmured. "Thirteen shillings or not."

"I'm wholly in your hands," Trev said. "She may gouge me to her heart's content if you think she can provide what my mother requires."

She gave a decisive nod. "Very true. There's no use in trying to haggle her down. We haven't the luxury for that. Mr. Rankin—" As the innkeeper returned, she took the letter and perused it briefly. "I believe we must request her to come as soon as she may. If you'll bring me a pen and paper, I'll write out an offer."

"Make it fifteen shillings," Trev said.

"Fifteen?" Mrs. Farr groaned. "I hope my old cook doesn't hear of this, or I shall have no peace."

"I understand you, Mrs. Farr, I do!" Callie peered into the inkpot that the innkeeper provided. "But truly, it's a crisis. You may tell Cook that the duke is French and has no sense, and it's only to be expected that he'd be choused."

"Make it eighteen shillings," Trev said grandly. "Make it a guinea!"

"A guinea!" Mrs. Farr emitted a scandalized cry and took a deep draught of her smelling salts.

"You see?" Callie said, dipping her pen. "A complete flat. Fourteen is our firm offer."

He winked at her. She gave him a bright glance and then bent to her task.

Callie parted from Trevelyan and Mrs. Farr outside the door of the Antlers. Trev had offered to escort her on any further errands she might have, but she declined, cravenly unable to endure more inquisitive looks and interested greetings. She walked down the street, hardly knowing where she was going. She was by no means accustomed to so much disorder in her feelings. For some years now—for nine of them, to be exact—she had found her pleasures in the quiet rhythm of seasons and animals. They had their certain habits and small adventures. They did not propose to come and see if she would climb down from her window at midnight, or jilt her and then request to call on her with a burning look. They might make her laugh with delight or weep with loss, but they never made a compliment to her complexion.

She had, of course, imagined a thousand times how she would accept the groveling change of heart from each of her suitors, starting with Trev. He was to have written her passionate, brooding letters and declared that his life was forfeit if she would not have him. That was after he had become unthinkably wealthy and recovered Monceaux, and declared on his knees that her fortune meant nothing to him and never had. He would take her penniless from the side of the road and threaten to shoot himself, or sail to Madagascar and become a pirate—which was just the sort of thing Trev would do—if she refused his love. After suitably ardent persuasion, she would reluctantly give up her plan to dedicate her life to good works and tapioca jelly, and accept his suit. Afterward they would become pirates together, and she would wear a great many pearls and rubies and skewer British officers.

Major Sturgeon, on the other hand, was to have behaved with considerably more circumspection, no doubt because her imagination had matured a few degrees by the time she grew out of her teens. He would have seen her across the room at a London ball, having pined in silence for many years. But now, at the sight of her, he could no longer contain his feelings. He would write her a sonnet and send it anonymously. It would be full of remorse and regret, and he would stand in the rain outside her house and stare for hours at the door. She thought perhaps he would finally find a way to come into her path and beg to call on her, only in a rather more tender and miserable tone of voice than he had used in the Antlers' parlor, rather than sounding as if he would like to call her out.

In perfect honesty, she would have been quite content to leave these reveries safely in her head and omit any actual experience of them. Instead of Trev, it was Major Sturgeon who seemed to be assuming the role of brooding corsair, which was disconcerting in the extreme. She had no inkling of why he could possibly wish to call upon her. Their betrothal had been broken off through the medium of a letter, with no specific reason given but that he felt himself unworthy of her hand. Since he had shortly thereafter felt himself worthy to become engaged to another woman, she drew the obvious conclusion that she had not satisfied his requirements in a wife. Her father had been of a mind to forcibly alter Major Sturgeon's decision on the matter but submitted when Callie begged him not to do so. She had no desire, she told her papa, to marry any gentleman who did not wish to marry her.

It had all been very unpleasant and mortifying from start to finish. She recalled very little about Major Sturgeon himself, as she had only met him when he was on brief leave from Paris, and once again after Waterloo, and hardly spoken to him during the few times they were in company. He was quite a handsome man, very firm of jaw and military in his bearing, always in uniform when she had seen him. That was why she had recognized him after so long. Very few active officers in full dress crossed her path—none, to be precise—and she quite clearly remembered the imposing stiffness of his braids and shoulder epaulets. But there was a certain swashbuckling air about him now, in all his scarlet and gold, a resolute sweep in the way he removed his cloak. The intense manner in which he looked at her was unnerving.

To make things yet more unsettling, the instant antagonism between the two gentlemen had been palpable, and magnified by Trev's careless insolence. She had heard of duels being fought for less insult than he had offered to Major Sturgeon. It was one thing to tease about skewering and pistols, but the idea appalled her in reality.

However, she could not deny that it had been gratifying to have Trev stand by her. Very gratifying. In truth, the whole encounter had made her daydreams seem quite pale in comparison.

She found herself at the only corner in Shelford, gazing blindly at a new poster plastered over the old ones on the greengrocer's wall. It displayed the image of a bullbaiting, showing a colossal spotted animal in combat with two huge dogs. The advertisement was for a butcher shop in Bromyard and made great news of that old wives' tale that meat from a baited bull was the more tender.

Callie scowled. Colonel Davenport would be using Hubert for breeding, not baiting, but his resemblance to the imaginary bull made her shiver. This type of ancient nonsense caused poor creatures to be tortured for hours, when they ought to be dispatched with a single well-placed blow. Her father had taught her to patronize men who knew their trade. They did not allow the animals to suffer through lack of skill or carelessness. But this sort of cruelty was maddeningly common, made worse because it pleased the fairgoers and sporting crowd.

She reached up and ripped the bill down, tearing it into pieces. Shelford's grocer owned the butcher shop too and would no doubt thank her for obliterating an advertisement for one of his competitors from the wall of his own property. She thought of buying some stale bread for Hubert, remembered that he wasn't there, and blew her nose into her handkerchief, trying not to burst into tears in the center of Shelford's village green.

"Married at Blackburn, Henry Osbaldeson, aged 95, to Rachel Pemberton, spinster, aged 71." Trev read by candlelight from an ancient copy of *La Belle Assemblée*. "Do you suppose she's given him an heir yet?"

"And twins by this time," his mother said faintly. She sat propped up on pillows, cradling a tisane without drinking from the cup. "I'm sure that journal may have ten years."

Trev flipped to the front page. "Eight." He raised his wineglass. "To the health of Mrs. O! Let us hope she's still spending his money to this day."

She smiled and plucked at the coverlet with her long fingers. "Myself, *mon trésor*—I hope you will not delay so long as Mr. O to take a wife."

Trev realized he had wandered onto dangerous ground. "I vow I won't wait a day past eighty."

She gave a sigh. It turned to a cough, and he reached for her medicine glass, but she shook her head. "No, I don't wish to… sleep." The color was very high in her cheeks, so that she looked younger, almost a girl in the candlelight. "Trevelyan," she said. "Tell me, have you ever considered to… propose to Lady Callista Taillefaire?"

"Certainly. I've offered myself to her several times," he said casually. "But alas!"

"Alas?" His mother tilted her chin. "Do not tell me she refused you."

"Not everyone appreciates my virtues as you do."

She pursed her lips. "I dare say that Lady Callie… I believe she… has some appreciation."

"Do you? I'm flattered. Her father was of another opinion, however."

She frowned a little, a pretty sulk, like a thwarted child.

He turned a page. "Mr. Thomas Haynes, of Oundle, will soon publish a treatise on the improved culture of the strawberry, raspberry, and gooseberry," he announced. "This can't possibly animate us so much, however, as the news that the Rev. James Piumptre has made considerable progress in printing his *English Drama Purified*, and it will appear in the early spring."

She put on a smile, only half attending. Trev feigned a concentrated attention to the journal, watching her fold the edge of the coverlet over and over with her fingers.

"It was before, then?" She looked up searchingly at him. "You asked her before you went away?"

He turned the magazine in his hands and rolled it into a cylinder. "Don't let us speak of this, Maman. Lady Callista has no desire to wed me, I assure you."

"But with Monceaux, the circumstances have so much... changed."

"Exactly. She would not wish to move to France, and leave her sister, and go away from all she knows."

"I think she might be willing."

"Maman—" he said.

"She can't wish to be a... spinster all her days."

"Please," he said, tapping the rolled journal against his fist. "Please."

She drew a deep, unhappy breath. "You love her."

"Damn," he said, staring into the dark corner of the room.

They sat without speaking. Trev felt all his lies and failures hovering on his tongue—only the knowledge that he would disappoint her yet more kept him silent.

"Is it money, Trevelyan?" she asked at length. "I know you have not told me... the whole. Do you have no money?"

"I have a great deal of money, Maman. A very great deal of it."

That he could say with full truth. She looked at him, her eyes large and brilliant in the unsteady light.

He drained his wine and set the empty glass on her table. "Come, madame le duchesse, don't you want me to find a girl of the old blood, to dignify Monceaux with her prestige?"

"No," his mother said. "I want you to be happy. Lady Callie would... make you happy."

He smiled wryly. "I'm not so sure I would make her happy."

"Why not?"

"You know what I am, Maman. Unsteady character."

"You were only a wild boy. Your grandfather—he could not help himself to drive you mad. I tried to say to him..." She trailed off and shrugged. "He could not help himself. He wanted everything to turn back... as it was."

"Yes, I did try single-handedly to restore the monarchy, but Bonaparte would have none of it. And then Wellington stole a march on me and did the thing himself."

She reached toward him across the coverlet, smiling. "You have accomplished what mattered most to us. Your father and your... grandfather would be so proud, to know we were in possession of Monceaux again."

It was almost worth it when she gave him such a look of gladness. He wondered briefly what it would be like to deserve it. He took her cool hand for a moment, then released her.

"Well, I will not weasel you about Lady Callie," she said contritely. "But perhaps you will... consider what I say."

"Weasel me?"

"Yes, as they bait and persecute those... poor creatures in their burrows, you know."

"'Badger' me," he corrected. "You will not *badger* me."

"Oh. But I may weasel you, then?"

"I feel quite certain that you will, Maman," he said.

Seven

THE NATURE OF HIS CONNECTION TO MAJOR STURGEON occurred to Trev over his morning coffee. It struck him full blown, apropos of nothing but a chipped white cup that reminded him of one he'd used in the Peninsula.

"*Putain,*" he muttered slowly, looking up, his eyebrows lifted.

Jock turned round, his big head bent down to clear the low beam over the hearth. "You know yer mama won't like you to be saying them filthy words in French."

Trev took a sip and grimaced. "I'm sorry to sully your pretty cauliflower ears with my language lessons, '*Jacques,*' old son, but your coffee deserves it." He always gave his manservant's name that little Gallic moue of accent, partly to encourage the unlikely impression that he was actually French, and partly just to torment him.

Jock snorted and returned to clattering with black pots and skillets. Sleet pattered against the small square window, promising an ugly day, but Jock had not stinted on the coal fire. The huge hearth gave out a steady heat. Trev stared at his valet's massive back, drinking the foul brew and frowning pensively.

Salamanca. It was easy to recall everything because it had been at Salamanca. The scalding sun of July, the dust and smoke—it seemed dreamlike now in the wet chill of an English autumn. Trev had been a new prisoner, brought in under Geordie Hixson's guard, both of them still panting from exertion and heat in the British cavalry officer's tent. Geordie had started to say something about sending Trev to the rear, but the words were interrupted by a new barrage of shelling from the dead ground to the west, exploding so close that a handful of spent shot pelted against the canvas. A pair of aides and a sentinel ran out to discover the range, leaving the tent empty but for Geordie and his commanding officer, both of them bent over the map in grim discussion of the reconnaissance.

Trev hadn't known the field officer's name or given a damn. He'd just been relieved and ashamed and sick of starving; sick of the sound of artillery and what he had become. He wasn't even concerned about the guns so close; it had seemed no more than a pretty irony to be killed by French cannon a bare half hour after his surrender. When Wellington's wounded courier had staggered in, covered in blood and black soot, with orders to attack immediately into the teeth of the unseen battery, Trev had barely taken note of the dying man's words. The courier had expired almost at his feet, but all he'd felt was that numb wonder at how the poor bastard had managed to make it so far after being shot in the chest.

He remembered a brief silence from the guns, and the blood from the courier's mouth. Then Geordie's officer had ordered the body carried back outside and laid by the man's horse.

The strangeness of that order had not penetrated Trev's mind. It was only Geordie's protest and expression of shock that had even caused him to look up at the field officer. Into that same challenging, pale-eyed stare he had met yesterday.

Trev remembered Sturgeon.

Trev and Geordie had carried the corpse, left it as if the courier had fallen from his saddle. As if the orders to attack the battery had never arrived.

When they returned, Geordie stood at attention, staring expectantly at his commanding officer. The guns thundered again, and Sturgeon ordered him to call for the tent to be repositioned behind the knoll. Geordie stood still and then requested permission to speak. Sturgeon snapped at him to shut up and strike the tent. The young aides galloped in a few minutes afterward from their reconnoiter, cursed at the courier's death wounds, and hauled the body into the shade of a tree while the tent was struck.

Nothing else happened. No attack on the French guns had been mounted. They moved down behind the safety of the hillside. Not long after, Trev had been taken in a set of light irons to join the other prisoners in the rear.

He had never heard any more of it or given the incident particular thought. There had been far more pressing concerns on his mind than some nameless British officer's decision in the heat of battle, as long as it didn't include shooting at him. He'd put the memory away along with all the other things he didn't care to dwell upon. Wellington had soundly crushed the French at Salamanca, so it made no difference to anyone, except perhaps a few French and British soldiers who would have died and hadn't.

But here and now—Trev suddenly appreciated that he had been a witness to a court-martial offense. Sturgeon had been ordered to attack, and he had acted as if he'd never received the order.

"Son of a…" Jock dropped the coffeepot with a hiss and clang, sending dark liquid over the floor. He added several more colorful words, holding his fingers in his other hand and blowing on them. Then he looked down at his stained trousers—the fashionable yellow ones—and let out a string of expletives that would have burned the ears off a bosun's mate. "My buttercup cossacks!" Jock's deep bass cracked. He grabbed a dish towel, daubing in a frenzy of vigor.

Trev squinted one eye at the stain on Jock's billowing trousers. "I fear they're past hope," he said, heartlessly honest.

"Thirty guineas!" The valet's voice reached a pitch that Trev had not supposed it could attain.

Trev put down his cup. "Damme, you spent thirty guineas on those things?"

"Worth every groat, sir," Jock snarled.

Trev would admit that they made the big man look quite the Cossack. All he required was a saber and some tassels hanging off his ears to be fit to ravage a town. But Trev made it a strict policy never to mock his valet's sense of style. He did not care to have one of those ham-sized fists in his teeth.

"You'd better take them down to the inn directly and find out a launderer," he advised. "Perhaps they can be boiled."

"And shrink to nothin', and bleach besides," Jock mourned.

"Then you can give them to me," Trev said soothingly. "I'll wear them to bed, like a sultan's pajamas."

Jock made a rumbling growl, stalking toward the kitchen door.

"You're certain this doctor has our right direction?" Trev asked after him.

"No, sir, I told 'im to go to Madrid," Jock snapped, holding the door in his giant paw so that a gust of freezing wind blew in Trev's face.

"You're so fetching when you're savage," Trev murmured.

The door closed with a solid thud, shutting out the sleet. Trev contemplated the dark splay of liquid trickling across the stone floor, oozing its way toward his polished boot. He heaved a sigh and got up to find a mop.

Callie had been out to feed the orphan calf and back to change long before her sister and Lady Shelford joined her in the breakfast room. She sat beside the window, gazing out at the drooping trees and sleeting rain, trying not to dwell upon the empty gate where one large and placid bull had not been awaiting his morning treat.

"It's my sister's *personal* correspondence, ma'am." Hermey paused by the door, allowing Lady Shelford to precede her into the room. "She is quite mature enough to dispense with anyone's approval of any letters she may receive."

The countess was carrying a sealed missive. She ignored Hermione and held it up, looking at Callie. "I do not think it suitable for Lady Callista Tallefaire to be in clandestine communication with a bachelor, however mature she may be. Not in this house!"

"Clandestine!" Hermey exclaimed. "Oh, that is not true! It was delivered quite openly!"

Callie stood up, a familiar tightness forming at the base of her throat. She could not bear a scene with Dolly, not just now. "What is it?" she asked dubiously.

"It's a letter addressed to *you*, Callie," Hermey said hotly, "and she has no right to keep it from you!"

"I'm sure it's only a note from Mr. Rankin about the cook for Dove House." Callie looked at her cousin's wife. "Please, read it if you like, ma'am."

Dolly held the note, looking down at it. Callie could see that there was an imprint of deer antlers upon the cover, the inn's insignia. She hoped that Lady Shelford would not decide to throw some obstacle in the way of hiring a cook.

"Most unseemly," Dolly said, lifting her pale and elegant chin. "I don't know why you wouldn't use an appropriate intermediary when dealing with a common innkeeper."

"I've known Mr. Rankin since I was a little girl, ma'am," Callie said.

"Indeed." She walked across the room and handed the note to Callie. "Pray leave any reply beside the table in the hall, and it will be forwarded for you. You need not concern yourself to convey it in person."

"Thank you, ma'am." Callie kept her voice gentle. She wished only to escape the room. Hermey could not wed her baronet and give them an opportunity to depart quickly enough for Callie. She took the note, laid it down beside her cup, and offered to pour some tea. She did not want to retreat too hastily, for fear of arousing new suspicion. There was a slight chance that the letter was from Trevelyan—it was thicker than a mere confirmation of the cook's acceptance needed to be, and he might have used the inn's stationery to write. She dreaded to open it here. His earlier note to her had been quite unexceptionable, but with Trev there was no predicting.

"I've already had my tea," Hermey said as Callie filled a cup for Lady Shelford. "Come up to my room, Callie, when you've done with yours. I want to tell you what Lady Williams said to me yesterday. You won't credit it, but she insists that striped redingote only needs to be edged with blue fur to make a winter coat. Pink and blue for winter! Can you just imagine what a sight I should make? Come and help me choose another lining."

Callie took advantage of this transparent scheme, since they both knew that Dolly found nothing so tedious as discussing anyone's wardrobe but her own. "Perhaps the coquelicot wool you purchased in Leamington?" she asked.

The countess made a sound of revulsion. "Please, you can't mean it, Callista. That garish poppy orange? It should be burned, to spare me having to look at it again. You ought to have bought a few more yards of the primrose I'm going to use for my pelisse, Hermione, as I advised you."

"I think the coquelicot would be lovely," Hermey said loyally. "Come with us, ma'am, and we'll spread it out on my bed with the pink. You'll see."

"I couldn't bear to look at it," Dolly said.

"I'll come." Callie took a perfunctory sip of tea and then walked to the door, carefully timing her excuses to coincide with the arrival of a footman with Lady Shelford's barley water. "I can bear to look at anything."

"Yes," Dolly murmured, "we've noticed."

Callie walked with Hermey to her sister's bedroom. Neither of them spoke. As soon as the door closed, Hermey turned. "She's jealous! I vow it. You should have seen her yesterday, pawing at Madame's son. It was revolting. She can't even tolerate that he brought you a posy from his mother, of all things!"

"Oh dear, I hoped no one knew of that."

"Why shouldn't anyone know it?" Hermey demanded. "He made sure to correct the footman about it, and rightly so. I hope he may elope with you and put her in her place!"

"I'll be certain to write to you from Madagascar if he does." Callie broke the seal on her letter.

"Perhaps that's from him," Hermey said, leaning over her shoulder.

"No doubt these are my instructions on how to make a ladder out of bedsheets." Callie stepped away. "You laid the coquelicot wool in your cedar trunk, if I recall."

"You noodle, you don't truthfully think I'd pair that with *pink*?" Hermey shook her head and put her hand over her eyes. "And I won't peek, I promise."

Callie looked down at the letter. It was directed to her, under cover of Shelford Hall, in a precise, broad hand that she did not recognize. She had not really expected it would be from Trev, but it was not from

Mr. Rankin, either. She frowned, allowing the damp outer wrap to fall away.

My dearest Lady Callista Taillefaire,

I humbly beg you will accept my heartfelt apologies for causing you distress at our recent encounter. Such was far from my intention. My only possible defense is that, in my wonder at seeing you, I allowed my feelings to overcome me.

Yet I cannot pretend that I came to Shelford without the express hope of calling upon you. I had intended to request your permission in writing before I imposed myself. However, I found myself taken utterly off guard to realize that I was in your presence. I think now that I should have picked up a newspaper and feigned that I did not exist. Indeed, how should I suppose you would even recognize me—instantly, as I did you?

You think me a scoundrel, of course. And so I am. By what audacity I make this request, I myself can hardly fathom. You have and you should refuse me. Nay, I think you would be even more disgusted if I should tell you that my wife, God rest her soul, passed away these two years ago, and it was not a happy marriage, to my shame.

What a botch I make of this. I am not a man to whom words come easily. I do not wish to impose myself on you, and yet I would do what lay within my poor power to stand your friend and amend the unforgivable.

I have removed from the Antlers so that you

*may be easy, and will remain a guest at Col. Wm
Davenport's house at Bromyard until Friday. I
believe you are acquainted with him, as he tells me
he has recently obtained a singular bullock from the
Shelford stock.*

*Do I have any hope that I have not sunk myself
beneath reproach? If Friday passes and I have no
sign of it, I shall know and leave you in peace.
God bless and keep you, Lady Callista.*

*Yr Servant,
John L. Sturgeon, Maj.
7th Royal Dragoon Guards*

"Oh, do tell me what it is!" Hermey made an impatient little hop. "You look as if you've seen a ghost!"

Callie drew a deep, shaky breath. "Indeed. I believe
I have." She handed the letter to her sister.

Hermey snatched it and read, bouncing on her heels.
Her mouth began to open wider and wider. She looked
up at Callie as she finished. "And who is this gentleman?
Is he a scoundrel in truth? Callie! Oh my, what have
you been up to while no one was attending?"

"I haven't been up to anything, I assure you. I was
once engaged to marry Major Sturgeon. You don't
recognize his name?"

"Oh," Hermey said. "Ohhh." She sank slowly
down onto the window seat and read the letter again.
Then she looked up. "You've seen him?"

Callie nodded. "He came into the Antlers
yesterday morning, when I was discussing the cook
with Mr. Rankin."

"What did he say?"

"Very little. He requested to call on me, and I refused, and he looked as if he'd like to run me through. And then he left. I can't imagine what he supposes to gain with this." She sat down on the dressing stool and pulled her shawl closer around her in the bedroom's chill. "Oh, I hope he will not persecute me all week."

"Persecute you! But it's so romantic!"

"Not in the least." Callie lifted her chin. "His wife has died, bless the poor woman, and now he wishes to take another look at my fortune. No doubt he needs a mother for his orphaned children too."

Hermey looked down, still holding the letter. "No, I suppose… you would not consider it."

"Certainly not. The man cried off, Hermey. Don't you even remember how angry Papa was? No reason given, but then Major Sturgeon up and married that Miss Ladd within the two-month. It was ghastly."

"Yes, but—it was all so long ago, wasn't it? He's had a change of heart."

"I doubt that very much. I suppose you were a bit young to know the particulars. You must have been no more than—oh, fourteen perhaps, at best."

Hermey bit her lip. "I do remember that it made you cry."

"Merely on Papa's behalf," Callie said staunchly.

"Men are horrid." Hermey stood up and flung the letter. It fluttered into the air and gently down onto the carpet.

"Well, I've not had much luck with them, but I'm sure that you'll find it a very different matter." Callie leaned down and retrieved the letter. "For one thing, you would never wear coquelicot with pink."

Hermey gave her a distracted smile and sat down again on the window seat. She toyed with the new ring on her hand, tracing her fingertip round and round the opal cabochon. Callie watched her sister's profile against the gray light. Quite suddenly, she remembered Hermey's fear that Sir Thomas Vickery might not wish to have a spinster sister intrude on his marriage. "Oh—" she said and stopped herself.

Hermey looked up.

Callie avoided her eyes and spread the paper on her lap. She felt a tightness in her throat, something threatening to fill her eyes. She cleared it with a cough.

"It's such an odd letter," she said, pretending to read it again. "My first impulse was to tear it up, but I must confess—this part where he admits he's making a botch of it..."

"Perhaps he's realized he made a botch of it years ago," Hermey said fiercely. "Which he most certainly did."

"He does say it was not a happy marriage. Perhaps he was..." Callie tapped her fingers on the sheet. "Well—things can happen, I suppose. Gentlemen find themselves... embarrassed."

Hermey looked at her aslant, her neat eyebrows raised. Callie did not know if she understood.

"I think perhaps he was in love with this other lady," Callie said.

"Oh poo. Then why did he ask you to marry him?" Hermey asked naïvely.

"Papa arranged it. But—" She broke off, at a loss to explain to her sister that it was quite likely Major Sturgeon had not been faithful to Callie during their engagement. "I'm not the one to cause a gentleman to forget his prior feelings, I don't think."

Hermey rose abruptly and crossed the room. She sat down on the bench and gave Callie a hard hug. "This dreadful major doesn't seem to have forgot you, though. I wish you may make him fall wildly in love, and then give him the cut and let him pine away until he dies of consumption."

"While writing poems in a garret."

"A freezing garret. With rats."

Callie turned the letter and squinted at it. "I'm not certain Major Sturgeon could bring himself to write a poem."

"For you, he would do anything!" Hermey opened her arm in an eloquent wave.

"Hmmm," Callie said. "Perhaps I will subjugate him and marry him after all, and keep him enslaved to my smallest wish for years."

"Yes! Exactly like Sir Thomas," Hermey agreed.

"I daresay it would annoy Dolly to have him call on me."

Hermey's eyes widened. "Oh *yes!*" She caught Callie's arm. "Oh, you must. For that alone."

Callie looked down at the letter. She blinked. "Yes," she said resolutely. "Yes, I think I must."

The London physician did nothing to allay Trev's worst apprehensions. He had ordered Jock to bring back the finest professional man he could locate, and the valet had gone right to the top, it seemed. Dr. Turner came with excellent credentials, chiefly that he was an esteemed friend of Sir Henry Halford, president of the Royal College and physician in ordinary to the sovereign. According to Sir Henry's letter, Trev could repose his full confidence in Dr. Turner, to whom Halford preferred to delegate his regular practice while he was in attendance on the king.

With that strong a recommendation, there seemed little hope that Turner's discouraging opinion could be dismissed as quackery. He didn't even try to replace the medicines with his own concoctions, as every other doctor Trev had ever known had done. After the examination, he sat with Trev in the parlor, writing instructions in a businesslike manner, before he finally looked up and said in an even voice that the duke would be wise to help his mother to put her affairs in order.

His meaning struck Trev like a blind-side blow in a sparring match. He had thought tentatively of future concerns, of course. He'd even sent his letter just yesterday to the French Chapel Royal in Little George Street, to request the attention of a priest to his mother's illness. Merely as a comfort, because he knew she must have been unable to attend any mass herself for some time. Certainly not for any idea of immediate danger. But to have it said so frankly, by a medical man... Trev found he could not seem to grasp the news. He only sat motionless, gazing at the physician's pen as it scratched across the page.

When he finally composed himself far enough to protest that she had been improving since he arrived, Dr. Turner merely nodded. That was characteristic of such cases, the doctor said; the patient underwent a sudden burst of energy and activity just before the final crisis, caused by migration of blood from the lungs to the heart. The winded speech and high color in his mother's cheeks were a sign of this phase. It might last a few days or a month, but she was much debilitated, and the doctor did not think she had a great deal of strength to spare.

Dr. Turner had brought with him a nurse, and a surgeon to assist with bloodletting. Trev was not fond of surgeons. He recalled too well the sensation of faintness and nausea that had accompanied the bleeding treatments his grandfather had insisted upon until Trev was old enough to bodily rebel. He had not let a knife or lancet touch him since the age of eight, and he didn't intend to allow it again, however imprudent and eccentric that might be. He didn't think his health had suffered a jot from keeping his ill humors shut up inside, though he was willing to admit it might have contributed to his dubious character.

He imagined trying to speak to his mother about putting her affairs in order and felt a familiar and potent urge come over him—the strong desire to be elsewhere. London. Or Paris. Or better yet, Peking. He hardly realized that Dr. Turner was rising to depart, or even felt the sleet on the back of his own neck as he escorted the physician under an umbrella to lodging at the Antlers. He woodenly expressed his gratitude for the doctor's forethought in making a professional nurse available for as long as his mother might require it, and promised to convey all instructions to the local surgeon. When he stood in the street again, he could think only that he needed fortification before he could face his maman. Not to put a fine point on it, he needed to be deeply, blessedly, besottedly drunk.

Not at the Antlers, of course. Nowhere in Shelford. Feral instinct pointed him toward a small alehouse that he recalled having passed on the Bromyard road. He was not a habitual tippler; he liked to keep his wits about him too much for that, but barring Peking, drink seemed the only recourse. He began to walk, holding the umbrella until the wind threatened to collapse it, and then put his face down and strode into the stinging drops.

At the pace he set, it was hardly more than a quarter hour before he saw the low thatched roof and cheerful smoke rising up through the sleet. As he pushed open the door, the scent of damp, sweaty wool and home brew engulfed him, carried outside on the rumble of laughter and talk.

He shoved his way in among the crowd of laborers and idle sportsmen. The Bluebell was clearly one of those places deplored by moralists in lecture and print, where all levels of society mingled on free terms. A convivial gathering to escape the weather, relentlessly masculine but for a barmaid who could give back as good as she got—it was just the situation Trev preferred at the moment. He used his smile to ruthless advantage, obtaining a tankard from the barmaid and a jeer from the table she ignored on his behalf, but he bought them all a round and dragged up a stool, downing his ale in one long draught. He knew well enough how to purchase a welcome here.

The crowd was in the middle stages of alcoholic mirth, singing bawdy songs and wagering on whether a carter could lift a table on his back with five men atop it, when a pair of gentlemen joined the company. They stood near the door, peeling out of wet overcoats and checking the oilskin covers on the locks of their rifles.

Trev left off watching the carter's losing struggle and glanced at the newcomers as they hiked their guns into a rack. It took him a moment to recognize Major Sturgeon, dressed as he was for shooting and wet to his skin. The two men seemed in excellent humor in spite of the weather, hanging a bulging game-bag beside their guns. Sturgeon's companion appeared to be some respected local squire. Men touched their forelocks and vacated the inglenook by the fireplace, leaving the best seats open for the new arrivals.

Trev set his stool back on two legs, his elbows propped behind him on a table. The others were laughing and yelling at the carter now, goading him for his defeat, while he shouted back, red-faced, demanding another try and making himself look a fool on top of a failure. He was clearly not the sort to take a ribbing.

Trev lifted his mug in the air and began to sing "The British Grenadiers." He raised his voice over the carter's hot complaints. "Whenever we're commanded to storm the palisades," he bellowed in good John Bull style, "our leaders march with firelocks, and we with hand grenades!" By the time he got to *"tow, row, row, row, for the British Grenadiers!"* he had his own table singing along at the top of their drunken lungs. He finished off his ale and saw Sturgeon looking at him with a cold gaze. The rest of the tavern had taken up the song in loud chorus, forgetting the carter in their new enthusiasm.

A familiar sense of waywardness possessed Trev, a moody antagonism riding on the lift of ale and latent violence that he could always find in a place such as this. He flipped an insolent salute to Sturgeon. The officer only stared back. His good humor seemed to have evaporated.

Trev wondered if the major had realized what basis they had for acquaintance beyond their meeting at the Antlers. From his scornful expression, Sturgeon appeared to bear Trev a marked dislike, considering only their brief contact the day before. So Trev followed up the grenadiers with more songs in a military mode, offering a few British camp tunes he'd learned from the wounded Light Bobs who'd hobbled alongside him in the baggage train. None of those tattered infantrymen had been in a patriotic mood, and the lyrics were all highly disrespectful, in addition to being lewd, taking cheerful and deadly aim at worthless officers and lack of pay. As he'd expected, there were enough worn-out soldiers in the Bluebell to approve this theme. They took it up with fervor.

Trev could see Sturgeon's face growing ever more rigid. As the major's lips curved in disgust, Trev sat back, gulping ale, abandoning the thin skin of gentility. He knew this wild temper in himself—he'd regret it later, but at the moment it was amusing. Sturgeon deserved an insult, by God, for crying off on Callie.

With a wink and a lift of his mug toward his prey, Trev plunged into a song about a deserter, singing merrily in celebration of cowardice. It was a lampoon of "The British Grenadiers," set to the same melody, but the words turned upside down. Instead of storming the palisades, this grenadier hero repaired to town a little too early in the verses, and found a girl who cried "Hurrah, boys," and fondled his grenades. The twist in the usual words had the men at Trev's table laughing so hard that they were spitting.

Trev could see the furious color rise in Sturgeon's face. Still he grinned and plowed into the next stanza, where the craven grenadier turned tail, stuck branches in his unmentionables to impersonate a bush, and ended up with a promotion. In the original ditty, he'd been made into a grenadier sergeant, but Trev slotted "major of *dragoons*" into the verse instead, which fit the cadence better anyway. His tablemates were almost prostrate with hilarity. The man next to Trev gripped his shoulder as they all leaned together and howled, *"Tow, row, row, row, row, row, row, for the British Grenadiers!"*

He was well into the third round when the voices round him died away to a sudden quiet. Trev recovered his balance as his neighbor let him go. His chair legs hit the floor, an audible thud in the new silence.

Sturgeon stood over him, white and stiff. "You puling French bastard."

Trev rose from his seat. "*Oui,* Monsieur?" he said politely and made an unsteady bow. He had not expected to draw blood so soon.

"Shut up, you fool."

Trev gave him a sweet smile. "But what have I said to offend you?"

Someone giggled drunkenly behind him. Sturgeon's lip curled. "It's enough to know what you are."

"Indeed." They were of a height, with Sturgeon at an advantage in weight. Trev drew a breath to clear the ale fumes from his brain. "But explain further, my friend. What am I?"

"*Blackmail,*" Sturgeon hissed through his teeth, almost a whisper, so low that Trev wasn't sure if he'd caught the word or if the major had called him a blackguard. He wondered if he was more inebriated than he had thought.

"I fear you must speak more plainly," he said, "if you wish for everyone to hear."

The major drew his lips back over clenched teeth. He reached out and gripped Trev's lapel, but said nothing.

Trev pried his fist loose, thrusting it away. "You may unhand me," he said coolly. "And be sure that I know what *you* are. We've just been singing about it, eh?"

The major seemed to swell, the blood beating in his temple. "*Shut up!* You nauseating bloodsucker, shut up."

"I'll tell you what's nauseating," Trev said in a conversational voice. "A man who insults a lady and then comes skulking back and bleating for her favor. Keep your distance, Sturgeon; she doesn't wish to see you."

"You dare! *You!*"

"Of course I dare. Do you suppose she has no friends to take her part?"

Sturgeon was dead white with rage. "By God, I ought to kill you, you slimy little French worm."

"You son of a whore," Trev said calmly. And then he repeated it in French, for good measure.

Sturgeon stood so still that Trev could see the faint tremor in his fingers as he yanked off his glove. In the slow instant, Trev felt his own blood rise with a mad pleasure. A decade of rage pressed in his chest, lost years, impotent shame that he had stood and taken that blow from Callie's father and left her to be slighted by a man like this. With a sense of fascinated doom, he watched Sturgeon fold his glove over his fingers and lift his arm.

A duel, it was to be. He was that much an English gentleman.

The major slapped him across the face, the glove a brisk snap against his skin. "Name your weapons."

Trev hauled back and struck with a right cross before Sturgeon's mouth was even closed. He put his full weight and five years of ringside training and all his hatred for arrogant English gentlemen behind it, smashing Sturgeon's jaw with an impact that he felt all the way to his heart, deep down in his chest.

He caught the officer utterly off guard. Sturgeon went down backwards, sprawling against a table. Men leaped up to stay clear. Someone grabbed Trev's arm, restraining him. He turned round and threw another punch, hard to the gut of the major's esteemed comrade. The man doubled over. Trev jerked free of some eager bystanders and saw his tablemate hurl a blow at Sturgeon before the major could launch himself at Trev.

People scrambled, yelling and shoving at one another. Chairs toppled and bottles smashed. The barmaid shrieked in frustration as the Bluebell descended into a drunken melee.

Eight

ACCORDING TO HOARY TRADITION, THE YEW TREE outside Callie's window had been planted at the behest of Edward I. She had never had reason to doubt this fact—its girth was a full twelve feet round, and the thick old branches were gnarled and scarred enough to have seen six hundred years. They had certainly witnessed a visit by Henry Tudor to the abbey that had once stood in place of Shelford Hall, and been singed by the flames of Cromwell's troops. Two elopements, a sermon preached by John Wesley, and a murky incident involving the tenth countess, which could have been an attempt at burglary, an abduction, or a practical joke—all were on the list of known escapades in which the old tree had played a role.

There were a few escapades in its more recent past that were not a matter of public record. Callie was already certain, without even trying to peer down through the moaning and whipping branches, exactly who was waiting at the foot of the ancient yew. The sharp double click of two pebbles, and then the raucous howl of a tomcat: she should not remember that signal at all, but she had recognized it from a dead sleep

it seemed, her eyes springing open at the first rattle
against the glass. She was out of bed and pulling on her
dressing gown before the hoarse yowl died away.

She paused before she pulled open the shutters,
putting her palms to her face. Woken so suddenly, she
could barely gather her wits. Her cheeks were hot, her
heart thumping. Surely he did not truly suppose she
would climb out of her window *now*. At the age of
seven and twenty. A spinster. In this weather!

The yowl came again, insistently. She drew a breath
and folded the inside shutters back, kneeling on the
window seat. Through the glass, she could see only
swaying black shapes of branches in the night outside.
The dark mass of the yew obscured everything else.
The tomcat called a third time, ending on a muffled
human note, almost a plea. Callie made a small moan
and pushed open the window.

Chilly air flowed in, sprinkled with icy drops. The
damp, musty scent of the yew enveloped her as she
leaned out. She could not see the ground. "Go away!"
she hissed. "For pity's sake, are you mad?"

"Callie." He pitched his voice low, just loud
enough to be heard over the rushing sound of the
branches and the wind. "I need help."

She squinted down, gripping the wet windowsill.
She had expected him to laugh and urge her to join
him on some ridiculous exploit.

"I'm sorry," he said. "I can't go…" The rest of his
reply was lost amid a gust of wind in the branches.
"Would you…" Only snatches of words reached her.
"…my mother. I need…"

She could not make out more. In the murk, she
could just barely discern a pale shape that might have

been his face. But there was distress in his voice, not taunt or coaxing. "What is it? What's happened?"

He made no reply to that, or if he did she couldn't hear it. She sat back on the window seat, pulling her dressing gown tight about her waist. Trev had never come asking for help, not this way. It was some crisis with his mother. And she could not blame him for coming to her window instead of sending a message. He wouldn't want to wake the staff, or involve Dolly, not at this time of night. Callie wasn't eager to do so herself.

She leaned out again. The branch nearest her window, the big one with the special crook where she had always taken the first step, was impossible to see. And really, she had no intention of climbing down from her window—it was simply beyond the pale.

She thought of telling him to meet her at the cow barn, but one of her farm lads would be sleeping there. The boxwood maze would be miserable on a night like this. The gamekeeper would be on alert for poachers in the wood, and a groom was always on night duty in the stables.

Truly, the range of possibilities had not altered much in the past nine years.

She cupped her hands around her mouth and called down as softly as she could. "The carriage house."

"Bless you!" he responded instantly. The vague shape below her vanished.

Callie wore her oilskin overcoat and work boots. She had made her way out the servants' entrance, locking the door behind her, prepared to say that she was going to tend the orphan calf if she'd encountered any of the staff. But no one stirred, not even the hall boy snoring on his cot by Dolly's bell.

It was all too easy, as it had always been. She should have been born a housebreaker.

The door to the carriage house was closed. She could see enough by the light of the lowering clouds to let herself in, but it was utterly black inside.

"Trev?" she whispered. "Are you here?"

She heard the carriage springs squeak with some sudden move.

"Callie?" His voice sounded muffled and shocked.

"Of course," she said. She had no idea why he had mounted into the carriage itself. "What's happened? Is it your mother?"

There were more sounds, and then the creak of the door opening. "Callie. You didn't have to come out."

She paused in consternation. "I thought you needed help."

She heard him moving on the steps, and then suddenly he bumped against her in the dark. He sucked in a swift, sharp breath and then touched her arm, resting his fingers there as if to steady himself.

"You're not hurt, are you?" she asked, uncertain of the sounds.

"Ah," he mumbled. "A little."

She could smell strong drink on his breath, something she had never noticed with Trev before, though it was common enough among the older gentlemen of her acquaintance.

"I only need a place to sleep," he said, enunciating his words carefully. "I can sleep in the carriage."

"What's happened?" She pulled off her gloves and fumbled in the deep pocket of her overcoat where she always kept a cache of useful items. "What have you done to hurt yourself?"

He blinked and squinted at the flare of her brimstone match. "I fell."

"Fell?" She peered at him. He was holding his hand up against his chest. Even in the flickering light she could see that it was badly swollen. He had a bloody cut on the side of his jaw.

"From my horse," he said, standing back from her. He leaned against the carriage wheel. "I'd... rather not go back to Dove House just now. Need a place to rest until morning."

She could see that his coat was torn at the collar, and his neck cloth hung down in complete disarray. She frowned, trying to discern if he had any other injury.

"I don't want Maman to see me like this," he said thickly.

"I suppose—yes." She looked at him in consternation. "It might frighten her."

He ran his good hand through his hair, disheveling it even further. "The doctor from London attended her this morning."

"What did he say?"

The light flickered, casting shadows on his face. "He said she has a week or two, perhaps." His voice was not quite even. "A month at most."

Callie tilted her head. "I'm sorry," she said softly.

The match went out. They stood in the dark. She could hear him breathing almost as if he were laughing. "God damn it," he said. "God damn me to hell. I ought to shoot myself."

"Nonsense," she said stoutly. "You've only had too much drink. No wonder you took a tumble. You'd no business going mounted, not in this state." She fished again in her pocket for a candle stub. "Let me look at

your hand. I'm sure once it's bound up, and you're set
to rights, your mother won't be upset to see you. Did
you take any other hurt?"

"No," he said. He paused. "I don't know. A little
bruising. I may have cracked a rib."

She touched the candle to another match. "I'd best
send a boy for the surgeon."

"No," he said strongly. "No surgeons."

"Only to bind you up. I won't let him bleed you."

"No surgeon," he said.

"But—"

"I haven't taken any serious hurt." He scowled,
turning from her candle. "If I can just rest a few hours,
I'll be off in the morning."

She held the light over a metal trunk. "Sit down.
Let me see your hand."

He blew out a breath of air and sat. Callie set the
candle stub in a rusty sconce and sat down beside
him. He allowed her to open his fingers and moved
each of them in turn for her. She was no surgeon, but
she had dealt with enough animal injuries to have a
good deal of experience in judging their extent. He
tensed a little, especially when she pressed gently at
the swollen joints along his fist, but made no sharp
move.

"I don't think you've broken anything," she said.
"But it would be best to bind your fingers. There will
be some bandages in the carriage boot."

She left him sitting on the trunk and felt about in
the dark boot for the horse supplies, returning with
scissors and cloth. As she bent over and wrapped his
hand, she could feel his breath move softly against her
temple and hair.

She tied off the bandage tightly and cut the ends. Then she straightened, standing between him and the carriage. It loomed behind her like a huge and awkward keepsake, a ponderous memento, as if a hidden package of love letters had suddenly mushroomed into an elephant, standing there swinging its trunk back and forth with gauche shyness.

"Well!" she said brightly. "Another adventure."

He remained sitting, his head turned a little aside as he looked up at her. "Another adventure," he said with a smile that held no humor. He closed his bound fist, holding it up against his shoulder.

"Does it hurt when you breathe? You think you might have cracked a rib?"

"I'm all right. Thank you, this helps a good deal."

"There's little enough I can do, if you won't see the surgeon."

"I'm all right, Callie. Sit down with me for a moment."

She felt her pulse beating faster. But he appeared more distracted than amorous, which made her ashamed that she was feeling quite animated by his company in the middle of the night in highly improper circumstances. She sat down, her oilskin rustling.

For a few moments, they were both silent. Callie watched the gleam and sway of light on the black carriage paint. Several layers of fabric and oilcloth separated them, but not enough to prevent her feeling the solid shape of his shoulder against her arm. She wriggled her toes inside her work boots. They were cold, but her cheeks felt flushed.

Unexpectedly he took her hand, locking it within his. He lifted it and bent his head and pressed his mouth to her fingers. She watched him in astonishment, feeling as if it were some other lady sitting in her place with his lips and cheek resting against her hand.

"I have to leave Shelford now, Callie," he said.

She blinked. "Leave?"

"I can't go back to Dove House. Would you—could I ask you to call on my mother? And tell her…"

He stopped, as if he could not think of what he wanted to say.

"You have to leave now?" Callie repeated stupidly. "What do you mean?"

He gave a short laugh and kissed her hand. "I'd rather not explain. I'm a brainless bastard, will that suffice?"

She was bewildered. "But… how long will you be gone?"

"For good," he said roughly.

"Oh." She stared at him.

"I've had one adventure too many, I'm afraid."

"But… I don't understand. You must leave Shelford now?"

"Perhaps you'll understand tomorrow, or the next day."

She remembered suddenly that she had written to Major Sturgeon, giving him permission to call on her tomorrow if he wished. She opened her fingers. Trev let her go.

She had thought, while she was penning her stiff invitation to the major, that Trev would be certain to hear of it eventually. Without precisely hoping that he would be angry or jealous, she had indulged in a lengthy reverie in which the news had brought him rushing to Shelford Hall to propose to her, perhaps after knocking Major Sturgeon down at the door.

Now Trev said he was leaving. And while it would have been rather pleasant to imagine this had something to do with her—that he had heard she was entertaining a flattering proposal, and was withdrawing his presence forever because of a broken heart, that was not only preposterous but clearly would be far more devastating in reality that she could have imagined. A sense of quiet panic rose in her.

"You can't leave your mother now," she said. "I can't believe you must leave now."

He made an unhappy sound. "Will you tell her that I was called suddenly to Monceaux? Or London. To my agent there. Tell her I'll be back soon."

"But you said you aren't coming back."

He did not answer. Callie stared at his profile in dawning comprehension.

"You want me to lie to her," she said.

"No." He sat back and gave a slight laugh. "No, I misspoke myself. I shouldn't have asked such a thing. A gentleman should tell his own lies."

Callie stood up. "Something terrible has happened." Her voice quivered. "What is it?"

He rose with her, so close that she could smell the damp scent of his skin. "Nothing terrible has happened yet."

She felt his arm slip about her waist. It seemed unreal, as if she stood in a dream where nothing made sense. "Yet?" She felt close to tears. "You're going back to France?"

"It doesn't matter." He leaned his forehead down, resting it against hers. "Would you let me steal a kiss before I go?"

"Why?" she whispered, her voice breaking.

"Because my mother says I love you." His lips grazed her temple lightly.

Callie made a small painful sound. "Oh, of course." She stood back, holding her chin up. "The way the chaperones say I have a very nice smile, and can't understand why I never took. Why do you have to go away?"

His arms tightened, drawing her back to him. He bent his head and kissed her lips, his skin warm and a little rough against hers. "Callie, do you remember this?"

She was breathing deeply, poised between anger and weeping and disbelief. But the brush of his mouth on hers made her close her eyes, all the daydreams of years past coming real. This was Trevelyan, the only man who had ever touched her this way, who had ever made her want to be touched this way. It had all long ago faded into reverie, deep and dangerous and hidden in a secret corner of her mind, as far away as if she had only imagined it.

He was very real now. Very masculine, scented of drink and wood smoke and sweet tobacco like the gentlemen when they returned from hunting or supper at a club. And more than that—the special, particular scent of Trev himself, different from anyone else, fixed in her mind with a certainty that she had not known she possessed until she recognized it again.

He kissed her. She began to feel that sensation he had always made her feel—as if she would lose herself in some sweet, aching fall toward oblivion as long as he held her this way. He made a sound low in his throat, an echo of intense pleasure. It seemed so implausible, so impossible to believe that he could feel it too. Yet he kissed her deeply, pressing her to him. She could feel the stiff binding round his fingers, just touching the back of her neck, a strange reality of starched cotton amid the dreamlike dimness.

He leaned his shoulders against the great wheel of the carriage, drawing her off balance to him, kissing her throat and her temple and her hair. Through the oilskin coat and thin protection of her night rail, her whole body touched his. She felt wildly outside all bounds of decency and civilization. All her forbidden daydreams were concentrated in Trev, in this shadow love and outlaw fancy, waiting just beyond the fence of her everyday life. She reached up and put her hands to each side of his face. It had been no more than memories, never something to depend upon or believe could come true. Only this was true—that she stood here in the dark with a man who was going away, as he had always been going away, always receding into remembrance and dreams.

"Wicked Callie," he said against the corner of her lips. "You shouldn't consort with drunken Frenchmen in the middle of the night."

She made a small whimper as he grazed her ear with his teeth. She gripped her fingers in his hair and pulled him closer.

His mouth hovered over hers. "I dream about you all the time," he murmured, his voice a little slurred. "Do you know that?"

"About me?" She slipped her hands down and held his coat, squeezing it in her fingers. "I don't believe you."

"I know," he said. "Damn it all."

"You say these things—"

"I know. I know I do. But some of them are true."

She forced herself to stand back a little, trying to be composed. "I don't even think you're real. I don't think this is real."

He let go of a sigh and stroked his bandaged finger-tips lightly across her hair. "If only it weren't. Maybe then my hand wouldn't feel as if a camel just stepped on it."

It was almost a relief to recall his accident. "You think the horse trod on you?"

"The horse should have kicked me in the head," he said. "I deserve it."

"Yes," she said, biting her lip. "I think you do if you leave Shelford now."

He slid his hands down to her waist, following the shape of her. "You'd better go back, wicked Callie in your boots and nightclothes, before I do something to deserve worse than that."

She knew what he meant. She thought of her room and her bed, warm and dry and safe. It was only a brief walk through the wind and rain, and a million miles away. Her whole body seemed to glow under his touch.

He drew her hard to him suddenly, opening his mouth over hers with a rough invasion. For an instant she was full of the delicious, smoky, sandalwood taste of him. She was seventeen again, and she was dying again, that infinite plunge into his kiss and his body pressed to hers, so familiar and so unknown.

He set her away as abruptly as he had kissed her. "Enough," he muttered. The flicker of the candle shadowed his eyes. "Give me a few hours' sleep now, and then I'll be on my way."

Callie gazed at him. As unlikely as it seemed to believe he was here, it was more impossible to believe that in a moment he would be gone from her life again. She hugged herself, shaking her head slowly, as if to clear her brain.

His lip curled. "You didn't suppose I'd be any less a cad than the rest of them, did you?" he said harshly. "Your father was right. You're well out of a connection with me, Lady Callista. I assure you it won't be long before you thank him for the second time."

She stood numbly, unable to summon any words amid the welter of feelings. She turned away and then turned back for a moment, as if to ask a question, but she could think of no question that he had not already answered with perfect clarity. In the dimness, all she could see was his rigid face, with that same expression of bitter disdain that he'd worn when her father hit him.

"Don't look at me as if I've swindled you," he snapped. "It's a dream. It was always a dream. Go back to the house." He took a step toward her. "Get out of here, you silly wretch, before we both regret it."

She turned and ran, her face and body hot with emotion, the way she had run before.

He was right, of course. It was a dream and always had been—another castle in the sky, dusted with just enough reality to make it more vivid and persistent than the rest of her foolish daydreams, her fanciful visions of being beautiful or adventurous or admirable in any number of highly unlikely ways.

Callie realized she had worn her muddy boots into her bedchamber and kicked them off. Being right about dreams did not buy Trev any gratitude from her. She tore off the wet oilskin and threw it on the floor. She hated gentlemen. She hated every single one of them, the ones who had jilted her and the ones who had not. They were useless, hopeless, impossible, and mean. He said he was a cad like all the rest, and she heartily agreed. Doubtless he had a wife already, or perhaps a dozen, and mistresses by the score back in France, all of them beautiful and charming and never at a loss for words. Women adored Trev, all sorts of women threw themselves at him, she had no doubt, and the least of them would be more appealing than Callie on a good day.

She lay facedown on her bed, not quite sobbing into her pillow, but huffing rather brokenly while she envisioned herself running them all through with a hay fork. She would have nothing more to do with gentlemen, or any other people for that matter. She would go and live with her animals, so that she wouldn't have to speak to anyone ever again. Residing under a hayrick in the fields, with only the cattle for company, would be a perfectly blissful existence in Callie's view. She could not imagine how she had ever considered any other arrangement.

She plumped up her pillow and beat at it. Indeed, she really didn't like people at all. She didn't like to make conversation or be looked at or have friends. It was all painful and hopeless, and it would be worse when she lived with Hermey and everyone pitied her the more because she was a useless spinster sister who had been jilted three times.

No—she loved Hermey—but she couldn't bear it. She refused to do it. She would become a hermit instead, or possibly a witch, and frighten little children by haunting some dark wood with her moans. She would adopt a large-brimmed black hat, the more out of fashion the better, and encourage a great number of cats to hang about her.

No one would wonder at this in Shelford. Everyone here would perfectly comprehend that she preferred animals to people. Particularly to gentlemen. Most particularly to French gentlemen. They could all join Bonaparte on that island of his at the ends of the earth, and very happily she hoped they would be there, drinking good claret and singing "La Marseillaise," while she lived out her life under a stump.

She fell asleep contemplating these joyful plans, her pillow soaked in tears.

Major Sturgeon stood very stiffly beside the mantel-piece in the lesser drawing room. Instead of his uniform, he had worn a dark green coat with exceptionally high collar points, so that his entire jaw was swathed in linen. Even so, his clothing could not obscure a great bruise and swelling that made his mouth and left eye appear oddly crooked.

Callie sat beside the garden window, as distant from him as was possible, which was not very distant in the modest chamber. She should have received him in the more formal atmosphere of the pink drawing room, but there was no fire laid there before Lady

Shelford's afternoon calling hours. Major Sturgeon had answered Callie's invitation with unnerving promptness, appearing at an hour of the morning that her father would have called encroaching. Taken by surprise, Callie had managed to clutch Hermey and pull her bodily to join them in spite of her sister's whispered protests.

They had entered in a rather clumsy stumble, but Callie managed to give the major a brief curtsy and introduce her sister. He bowed, with a narrowing of his eyes that could have been a wince of pain or an expression of delight. After the exchange of greetings, Callie and Hermey seated themselves. They all three fell into an awkward silence.

Callie found that it was difficult to ignore his swathed and swollen jaw. She racked her brain for some polite conversation, but all she could think of to say was, "Do you have the toothache?"

Hermey gave her an exasperated glance and broke the uncomfortable moment herself. "I'm very pleased to meet a longtime acquaintance of my sister's," she said.

"I'm grateful for the honor, Lady Hermione," he said, sounding as if his tongue were not quite working properly. "Your sister extends me more favor than I deserve." He bowed again toward Callie, with something that would probably have been a warm smile if it had not appeared to cause him considerable discomfort. "I apologize for my appearance. I took a fall from my horse."

"I'm so sorry to hear it," Hermey said. She looked at Callie expectantly.

Realizing that she could not avoid her turn, Callie said, "The horses seem rambunctious of late."

"Do they?" Hermey smoothed her skirt. "It must be the weather."

Another silence stretched to painful proportions. Hermey maintained a tranquil smile as she gazed into the distance, making it clear that she would offer no further aid.

"The gentlemen appear to have taken a considerable mauling too," Callie added, at a loss for any other subject.

"Merely a scratch," the major said, an understatement of substantial proportions. "I wished so anxiously to see you, Lady Callista, that I allowed myself to imagine my appearance was not so shocking as I fear it must appear."

Callie looked down at her hands clasped in her lap. He must be in great need of money. And since Trev, in spite of kissing her and informing her that his mother said he loved her, had shown more inclination to flee to France than to propose, the major seemed to be her only remaining hope to avoid either billeting herself upon Hermey and Sir Thomas for life, living out her days under the whip of Lady Shelford's sharp tongue, or residing permanently under a pile of hay.

She was quite certain that Major Sturgeon intended to sacrifice himself on the Altar of Mammon and offer for her hand again. There was no other discernible reason for him to call on her. Heiresses must be thin on the ground in London this year.

The new Earl of Shelford appeared at the open door. Callie jumped to her feet, startled to find her cousin abroad and fully dressed at this hour. She performed introductions again, vexed to discover a slight quiver of apprehension in her voice. She hoped he would not ring for his wife. If anyone could drive Major Sturgeon off, it would be her ladyship. Though in truth, Callie wouldn't have been ungrateful for that. Caught between wishing to be rid of him and the apparent necessity of marrying him, Callie subsided into confusion and sat down again.

Lord Shelford was eagerly cordial to the major, as he was to everyone. He rang for coffee, complaining that Callie had overlooked this obligatory aid to any gentleman's comfort. The officer apologized again for his appearance and informed Lord Shelford of his spill from the horse. While his lordship expressed dismay and sympathy, Callie mused on the coincidence of two gentlemen, out of the very small number of gentlemen of her acquaintance, falling from horses within the same few hours. Perhaps they had collided with one another.

"Ah, I'm charged with a message from Colonel Davenport to you, sir," the major said in a slurred voice to Lord Shelford. "That bull of yours has got loose from its paddock. He asks you to keep a lookout. He thinks it may have an idea of wandering home."

"Hubert, do you mean?" Callie looked up. "Hubert is loose?"

"I don't know how he's called," the major said. "The bullock that Davenport won from his lordship in a wager, as I understand."

"Oh yes," Lord Shelford said uncomfortably. "That bullock. He's wandered off? Dear me. I suppose he will come here, yes. Nothing more likely." He cast a nervous glance at Callie.

"How long has he been out?" she asked sharply, standing up.

"Only since last night." The major turned toward her, keeping his neck stiff. "The lad fed him in the evening and found the fence broke right through when he went out at dawn. Davenport's put out several of his men to search. He's a little apprehensive, since he had an inquiry from some low fellow the other day to purchase the animal. He turned it down flat, of course, but the man was offering an enormous sum."

"A low fellow?" Callie frowned. "What sort of fellow?"

Major Sturgeon cleared his throat. "I don't know if you are aware, Lady Callista, of the men they call sharpers. The colonel is slightly concerned, since he's had word that some celebrated fighting dog has come into the county in the past week. It's unlikely, of course, but with the sort of sum the fellow claimed to be offering, undoubtedly he had some idea of arranging a match for the betting crowd."

"A match?" Callie exclaimed. "Dear God, do you mean a baiting?"

"Nothing of the sort," the new earl cried. "Nonsense! Davenport's the magistrate; he won't allow any of that sort of thing hereabouts. Calm yourself, my dear. Oh please, don't look so frightened!"

"I am frightened!" Callie started for the door. "We must discover him. John, never mind that." She passed the footman carrying a tray of coffee. "Leave it here; my horse is to be readied instantly. I'll be down in five minutes."

"You're going to search, my lady?" Major Sturgeon was a step behind her. "May I have the honor of aiding you?"

"Yes, yes, of course," she said distractedly. "The more eyes the better. Are you mounted?"

"The groom is walking my horse."

"I hope it doesn't throw you again," she said. "If it does, I must leave you. We've lost hours already."

"You may abandon me bleeding on the road," he said. "I can see that this bull is of the foremost importance."

"He's my finest calf!" she said, leaving him in the corridor as she mounted the stairs. "And my best friend too. I should never have let him be taken off, never! Stupid wagers. Stupid gentlemen!" She hiked her skirt and pounded up the steps, wrinkling her nose. "I detest the whole lot of you!"

Nine

"A NEAT BANDAGE, SIR," JOCK SAID, GLANCING DOWN AT Trev's swollen fingertips. "Poleaxed him, I'll wager?"

"Went down like a dead tree." Trev leaned behind the door of the small stable at Dove House, brushing straw off his coat. "How is my mother?"

"Asking for you this morning," Jock said. "I said you was sleepin' late, havin' been out all hours conducting yourself ungentlemanly. Made her laugh. She wouldn't be bled, 'less you approved it."

Trev wiped his good hand over his face, trying to order his thoughts in the aftermath of too much ale and too little sleep. "Well, I don't approve it. Why put her through that, if there's no hope?"

Jock shrugged. "Doctors," he said, in comprehensive disgust.

Trev closed his eyes and opened them. "The constable hasn't been here yet, then?"

His manservant gave him a long, interested stare. "The constable. Should we be expecting the constable, sir?"

"I seem to have picked a fight with a local magistrate."

Jock drew his big body up straight. "Lordy," he said. "You knocked down a judge?"

"Most likely. It was a little… confusing. I know I punched his friend, the major of dragoons."

"That ain't a good thing, sir."

"No. In point of fact, it's a consummate disaster."

Jock nodded slowly. "Aye."

Trev leaned heavily against the rough wood. "I can't get snagged now. If I'm discovered in England, it'll be the gallows."

"You sure they'll send the constable? Was it self-defense? What can they take you up for?"

"Disturbing the peace, assault—we did some considerable damage to the Bluebell tavern."

"Nobody weren't killed, was they?"

"No." Trev scowled. "At least… not while I was there." He rolled his head back, resting it against the wall. "Mother of God, I hope not."

"You certain this magistrate'd recognize you, sir? It's a country place here. Maybe he don't know who you are."

"He may not. But his friend the major does. Called me a French blackguard. Or—" Trev hesitated. He turned his head, frowning, trying to recall their alcoholic brangling. "I'd swear he said blackmail."

"Damme," Jock said, squaring his enormous shoulders. "That's an insult!"

"I suppose I could blackmail him after all, if I cared to," Trev muttered. "But it was hellish more fun to hit him instead."

"You don't blackmail nobody, and you don't forge nothin'," Jock said fiercely. "When you was Monsieur LeBlanc, you always paid out fair and square. That's why I've stuck with you, sir, and that's why they still wants you back so bad to operate the fights. Ain't nobody we trust as much as you, and them judges can say what they like. We all know you didn't forge that bond note, and we know why you took the blame."

Trev gave his manservant a crooked smirk. "A touching encomium to my honesty. I could have used it when I was on trial."

"The Rooster knows why you did it." Jock gave a thrust of his chin toward heaven. "He knows. Mrs. Fowler's tucked up all safe and sound with her little boy, ain't she? Though she don't deserve a bit of it. You're too good a man for her, and so was Jem Fowler."

Trev shrugged. "It's the boy I cared for. And Jem. But the king won't pardon me a second time. Hell's bells, he can't. It would all come out if somebody recognized the duc de Monceaux as the same man as Thibaut LeBlanc while I'm standing in the dock. And even if they didn't, Christ, just think about it—I'm hauled before the bench while my mother's on her deathbed. What an edifying prospect for her last moments."

Jock grunted assent. He crossed his arms, his great muscles flexing. "This officer you decked knows you's LeBlanc, sir?"

Trev shook his head. "No, thank the Lord. We've a little history of another kind. But he'll be sure to lodge a charge against me and prosecute it all the way. Nothing more certain, with his friend being the justice of the peace. At best I'll be sitting in the gaol till Epiphany if I let them catch me, and fortunate if I don't rot there until the Easter assizes."

A hen clucked from somewhere in the shadows of the single stall. Jock turned his head, alert to any odd noise. But aside from a faint scratching in the straw, there was no more sound.

"Chicken pox!" Trev said, suddenly inspired. "You can tell the duchesse that I've broken out in spots, and the doctor said I must keep a distance until the contagion is past."

The manservant gave a skeptical grunt. "Chicken pox? You don't think she's such a greenhead as that, sir. Up to every rig, Madame is."

"Hmm," Trev said. He scratched his chin with the bandage. "No, you're right. Chicken pox—I think I've had it. I can't remember."

"Yer mama will. They all do."

"You'll think of something. I'd advise spots of some sort. Something that would keep me away for a fortnight or so."

"A fortnight?" Jock lifted his thick brows. "Didn't the doctor say—"

"I know what he said! It's burned between my ears. But I can't stay, Jock. For God's sake, how can I stay?"

They both stood silent. He didn't need to explain more of the consequences to Jock. If he wanted his mother to go to her final rest knowing her only living son was a criminal condemned to hang, all he had to do was get himself arrested. Thibaut LeBlanc had been given a rare royal pardon from his capital conviction for forgery, but it was provisional, based on his obligation to leave the country and not return. If LeBlanc broke his exile, the pardon was revoked.

"You'd surely better not get yourself snabbled," Jock said at length. "But it might blow over, eh? If they find out about yer mama being so ill, they might think twice about taking you up for a little disagreement between gentlemen."

"I can't chance it. I can't stay here openly."

"Aye. But if you was to go off for a few days, sir. Let tempers cool. If they come here, I can make 'em feel pretty ashamed for persecutin' of a poor lady who hadn't got long on this earth. You could come in at night to see her."

Trev squinted into the musty corner of the stable. He chewed his lip in thought. "It's risky." He nodded slowly. "But it might do. If I had a safe house."

"Lemme ask round for—"

A sharp, trilling whistle interrupted him. They both startled at the sound—familiar enough, but so close overhead that Trev had to crane his neck to see into the loft. "Barton!" he muttered in disgust. "What the deuce are you doing up there?"

His former accomplice showed his face between the rough-hewn beams, a straw of hay dangling from behind one ear. "I've got him, sir!" he hissed. "Tied up right out behind the shed."

Trev had a sudden nightmarish vision of Sturgeon—or worse, his friend the magistrate—bound and gagged behind the shed. "Who's tied up?" he exclaimed, taking a step. "Barton, I swear, if—"

"The bull, sir," Barton said. He scrambled round, causing hay and dust to drift down through the planks. He dangled from a beam by his hands, dropped, and recovered himself, dusting vigorously at his trousers.

"The bull?" Trev scowled at him a moment and then remembered. "Oh right—the bull," he said with a strong sense of relief. He watched Barton try to dig a straw from inside his neck cloth. His hand was dirty—completely black about the fingernails, and his clothes were marked with grimy dark streaks. "Well done, then. Well done, old fellow. At least something's gone right. Have you been sleeping in some bog? Clean yourself up at the pump and take the animal over to the Shelford home farm. Say it's to be presented to Lady Callista Taillefaire, with my compliments."

It was something he could do for her, anyway. He thought of how pleased she would be, and wished that he could see her face light up when she saw the creature, as he knew it would. "Try to get the manure out of your ears first," he added.

Barton fidgeted. He'd been grinning like a gargoyle at the praise, but his smile faded at this. "Present it to a lady?" he said. "I dunno if that's a good idea, sir."

"She'll be excessively pleased, I assure you. She's no common lady. How loud did you have to squeal for Davenport?"

Jock looked up sharply. Barton's glance slid sideways, an avoidance that caused a familiar drop in the pit of Trev's stomach.

"Davenport, did you say, sir?" Jock asked. "A Colonel Davenport?"

Trev glanced at his servant. "Aye, do you know of him?"

"Sir, he's the one give me the name of that London doctor. The Antlers sent me over to his place at Bromyard, thinkin' he'd know somebody in town. A very kind gentleman, took some of his time out to write me an introduction to the medical man." Jock's voice held an anxious note. "Sir... sir, he had law books in his study. And a lot of notebooks and proceedings. I think he might be a justice of the peace."

"A justice?" Trev gazed at him, slowly comprehending. "My justice?"

"Stocky gentleman, sir, with a red complexion and a mole beside his nose?"

Trev groaned. "Oh God. Let that be a lesson to me—first inquire if a fellow's done me any favors before I punch him in the bread-box. How much did you pay him for the bull, Barton?" he repeated. "I hope it was a fortune."

"Well, sir," Barton said brightly, "y'know how chancy my luck can be now and then! That fellow Davenport wouldn't take no price. He weren't kind to *me*, oh nossir. Had me flung out the door. He got all heated, he did, sayin' I couldn't pay nothin' he'd take." He giggled. "And I didn't have to pay nothin', as it happens."

"Barton! Damn you, tell me you didn't—"

"No, sir! Oh no, sir! I didn't steal him. I swear I didn't." He stuffed his hands in his pockets and leaned forward with a conspiratorial grin. "Ol' Tobe an' me just found him on the road."

Trev closed his eyes and dropped his head back against the wall. But he had only a moment to consider whether he would strangle Barton or drown the man. A brusque halloo came from the direction of the garden gate, a stranger's voice with an edge of resolve in it.

All three of them looked at one another. Barton lifted his thumb and forefinger in a familiar sign, pointing toward the hayloft. Trev glanced at Jock and jerked his chin toward the gate. The manservant gave

a curt nod. Without a word, they split company—
Jock striding toward the house and garden, Trev
and Barton scaling the ladder. Trev followed his
companion across the dusty boards to the open loft
door. Down in the walled yard, he saw an enormous
black bull lift its head from a pile of hay, chewing
calmly as it watched them.

"Barton!" Trev hissed, dropping from the bale hook
to land on both feet. He stared at the black animal
and then put his face into his hand in despair. "You
infernal imbecile. That's the wrong bloody bull."

Callie trotted along rapidly, only vaguely aware that
Major Sturgeon's horse kept pace behind her. She
had taken the shortcut into Shelford, jumping two
stiles and a hedge and trespassing on Farmer Dauncy's
orchard to reach the lane. She left word with everyone
she passed, calling Mr. Rankin out from the Antlers
and informing him of the emergency without even
dismounting.

Colonel Davenport lived at some distance from the
village, several miles along the Bromyard road. As she
rode she scanned the autumn landscape, searching for
a familiar flash of red and white hide among the laden
apple trees or across the fields. It shouldn't be difficult
to locate something as large as a bull, but they could be
amazingly easy to overlook. Hubert would be enticed by
the countless orchards or any fencerow that contained
sweet grass, still green under the holly and hawthorn
this late in the year. He could manage to obscure himself
quite nicely behind an overgrown hedge.

A brief pause at Colonel Davenport's house discovered only the empty paddock. The colonel himself was not at home. A stable lad showed her where Hubert had cracked the rails right through, tearing them out of the posts. Callie had dressed the boy down, quite unfairly, for the flimsiness of a fence that would not have held Hubert when he was a yearling, much less as a full-grown bull. It wasn't the lad's fault that Colonel Davenport didn't keep sturdy fences, but she was incensed. The boy seemed to think that Hubert must have smashed the rails with his horns, which would have alerted the whole neighborhood to his escape, but Callie knew better. All that would have been required was a long, slow, steady push by a bull that preferred to be outside the paddock rather than in it.

Whether he had been ready to go home or just stretching for that farthest blade of grass, she didn't know. From the colonel's house she took the route that the drover would have followed from Shelford. This led her back toward the village by a longer, more level way where a cart might ford the streams, in the direction of Dove House.

"Black henna, sir!" Barton whispered. "Not a bad job, eh? Started as soon as I had any light. For a while I didn't know if it would come up to cover the white, but he's turning pretty sleek now." He ran his hand down the bull's hind leg. "I see I missed a spot there on his left hock."

"Christ, where'd you get that much dye?" Trev demanded in a low voice. He saw now that there was blue-stained hay concealed under the fresh layer at the bull's hooves.

"Tanner, sir," Barton said solemnly. "Got thick with him over a pint of bitters."

"Naturally." Trev watched the dog, Toby, sniff at the bull's knee. "Now what the devil do you expect me to do with this animal?"

Barton looked anxious. "I dunno, sir. You didn't tell me I'd need to think o' what to do with 'im. I reckoned you knew your own mind on that, sir."

"I did," Trev said dryly.

"You was gonna give 'im to that lady, sir?"

"That was the plan. But she would be expecting a red pied bull, you see, with a bill of sale. This seems to be a black bull of uncertain origin."

"Hmm," Barton said, pursing his wide mouth. "So it does, sir."

"Quite."

"I didn't steal 'im, sir! I found him."

"We aren't going to argue the point with a constable, Barton. We're getting myself and my fellow fugitive here out of sight before anyone searches the premises."

"Yes, sir." Barton grabbed the lead attached to the bull's nose ring. "I know a way round the lane to the millpond. We can walk him down the stream and tie him up. Come along, old fellow." He clucked to the bull. "Toby, get him!"

At Barton's voice, the dog barked and nipped at the animal's heels. The bull turned its head and gave a half-hearted kick, but appeared to find the dog no more persuasive than a large fly. It blew a gust of air and lowered its nose, taking up another mouthful of hay.

"Quiet!" Trev snapped, as Toby began to bark and growl. "Do you want to advertise us to the whole county? Move along, you beast!" He picked up a pitchfork and waved the handle at the enormous bull. He'd seen drovers in the army hustling their animals along with staffs.

The bull blinked at him, all four feet planted solidly amid the hay, its jaw working in unhurried rhythm.

"Come along," Trev said in exasperation, brandishing the fork. "What's your name? Hubert. Hyah, Hubert!"

The animal turned fully at the sound of its name. With slow majesty, it lifted one hoof and then another, ignoring the pitchfork and ambling toward Trev. It lifted its massive nose to snuffle at his clothes, as if searching for something in his neck cloth. It was purported to be a shorthorn bull, but Trev could have sworn that the tips of its horns were as wide as his arm-span.

Trev backed away. The bull followed. "Hubert," he said, walking backward toward the gate. Hubert moved faster after him, deliberate now, his great hooves thumping in the dirt. He made a low sound, a sort of groaning, smothered bellow that made the hair rise on Trev's neck. He hoped to the devil that the thing didn't decide to charge.

"*Hubert!*" Callie pulled her horse to a halt in the middle of the lane. Major Sturgeon came up behind her. She waved at him to stop, straining her ears to hear over the sound of the horses and her own breath.

She could have sworn that she'd caught Hubert's distinctive bellow, a deep rumbling sound almost below hearing.

They had just passed Dove House. The garden gate was ajar, and the front door stood open. She had not forgot Trev, but the strange encounter in the night seemed so far from reality that today she was hardly certain it had even taken place.

A dog was barking furiously somewhere in the back of the property. She dismounted, throwing her reins to Major Sturgeon. It wasn't impossible that Hubert had wandered off the road and found his way inside the small stable yard, where she knew there had been some fresh hay put out for Trev's team. She was about to hurry round to the rear when a figure came skulking out the front door, pulling his hat down over his eyes. Trev's big manservant walked out behind him, pulling the door closed with a firm hand.

"Constable Hubble!" Callie said, relieved to see that Colonel Davenport must have set the parish officer on the hunt for Hubert. "Is he here? Have you found him?"

The constable looked up, recognized her, and pulled off his hat. "No, my lady." He glanced back at Jock uneasily and lowered his voice to a lugubrious whisper. "I ain't going to disturb nothin' further now, ma'am. I'm told there's mortal sickness in the house."

"Mortal?" Callie stopped short, feeling a wave of alarm for Madame. She looked toward Jock. "No... the duchesse is not worse?"

The manservant shook his gleaming head slowly and bowed it down. "She's real poorly, my lady." He spoke English with strong traces of a drayman's accent. "Mortal poor. She ain't got long, Doc says."

Callie had known this was coming, but not so soon. And Trev… where was Trev? She stared in dismay at Jock. "Is her son here?"

"On his way, my lady," Jock said gruffly.

"No one is with her?" Callie moved toward the door. She couldn't leave the duchesse alone if she was failing. She turned to the constable. "I must go in. But I think I may have heard him in the back, behind the stable," she said. Major Sturgeon came up and stood by her shoulder, but she only glanced at him. "Please do look, Constable, and send word up to me immediately if he's here. Then you can secure him and wait for Colonel Davenport."

"You're mistaken, beggin' your pardon, my lady!" Jock said strongly. "He's not in the stable, I assure you! I've had a message sent to him to come as soon as he can."

"A message?" Callie drew in her chin in confusion.

Constable Hubble twisted his hat in his hands. "Is my lady lodging a complaint too? Because I don't much like to make an arrest at such a moment."

Callie blinked. "Arrest?" Then she shook her head. "There's no one to arrest. You can't arrest a bull." She bit her lip, envisioning what damage Hubert might have done while he was on the loose. "Can you?"

The constable gave a hawking laugh. "Nay, my lady, I'm not here to arrest no bull. I reckon you mean the colonel's animal? I've kept a lookout for 'im this morning, certain enough, but I've a warrant here for—" He pulled a document from inside his coat. "For a duke of Mon-serks, says. Of French origin, residin' at Dove House, village of Shelford, hundred of Radlow, union of Bromyard, county of... etc., etc."

"That French fellow?" Major Sturgeon spoke at her elbow, a sharp note in his voice. "This is where he lives?"

Constable Hubble glanced up and nodded at Sturgeon. "Aye, sir. I'm after 'im, I can assures you. But his mama's in her last mortal coils, her man here tells me, and he's been called to come to her side. I'd as soon wait a little while sir, beggin' your pardon. There be no hurry to take the gentleman up. It can wait until his mama's left this world, god bless 'er."

"The duke?" Callie took a trembling breath. "I don't understand. You have a warrant for the duke?"

"Aye, my lady. Arrest warrant."

"Arrest!" She gasped. "For what?"

"Assault on an officer of the king's army, ma'am, and on a justice of the peace. That was Colonel Davenport himself, my lady, and this here military gentleman, if I'm not mistaken."

Callie turned to Major Sturgeon. She looked at his swollen jaw, and thought of Trev's swollen hand. With a speechless burst of insight, she apprehended that they had not, after all, fallen off their respective horses.

"Breakin' the king's peace, riot, and threatenin' behavior," Hubble added, reading from his warrant. "Attested to by John L. Sturgeon, Major, Mr. Daniel Smith, proprietor of the Bluebell tavern, list of other witnesses, statements taken on the spot, etc., etc."

She was still staring at Major Sturgeon. A warrant for Trev's arrest.

She closed her eyes for a moment and opened them. Trev had said she would understand today why he had to go away.

Her heart sank. It was a shock, but not entirely beyond comprehension. Ever since she had known him, Trev had played over the edge of safe and lawful conduct. He seemed to glory in discovering just how far he could go, how much he could get by with. She was probably fortunate to escape having a warrant for her own arrest, merely for having tea with him at the Antlers.

Major Sturgeon seemed vexed, as well he might if Trev had assaulted him. There had been an instant antagonism between the two of them at their brief meeting, a hostility that Trev had certainly done his best to encourage. She felt blood rising to her cheeks. Had it been over her? She could not imagine that two gentlemen had exchanged blows over Lady Callista Taillefaire. They would be more likely to consult one another on novel methods to escape her spinster clutches.

"I didn't wish to burden you with the details of a rather sordid encounter, Lady Callista," the major said, his voice still slurred by the swelling at his jaw. "I beg your pardon if I've bent the truth regarding my injury."

"Oh no," she said, turning away hurriedly. "I'm sure it's no business of mine how you came to be injured."

"Perhaps someday you'll allow me to tell you a bit about this 'duke,'" he said, speaking with considerable bitterness. "He claims to be your friend, but I don't think you should depend upon it, my lady."

"Indeed," Callie said. She was having a little trouble breathing. "Perhaps someday you will tell me. But now I really must go in to the duchesse." She turned and went quickly up the path to where Jock stood at the door.

"Let's just take a look in the stable yard, Constable," Major Sturgeon said behind her. "For this bull—and anyone else who may be there."

Ten

CALLIE HURRIED UP THE STAIRS OF DOVE HOUSE. SHE did not pause to knock at the bedroom door but went straight in, fearing to find the duchesse in very grave condition. Instead she found Madame sitting up in a chair, sipping at a cup of tea while a nurse changed the bedsheets with competent efficiency.

"Lady Callista!" Madame said in her soft, struggling voice. "Do come in. I am so... pleased to see you." She had to pause a moment in the midst of the sentence to catch her breath, but she was attired in a dressing gown, her hair arranged neatly and her color good.

Callie dropped her hand from the door knob. "Good morning, ma'am." She halted uncertainly. "I'm sorry to burst in upon you. But I thought—they told me below—I was most concerned, ma'am! I thought you were left alone."

Madame smiled and lifted her hand. "As you can see, my son has procured... an excellent woman to nurse me."

The nurse lifted her head for a moment and nodded curtly before she went back to work. She had a military air about her that made Callie feel as if she should salute in reply.

"But I'm impatient for a little company," Madame said. "I feel so much better that I must have a... caller to amuse me. I heard someone ring a little while ago, but still I am deserted, you see! My infamous son, he is sleeping very late."

Callie moved into the room. "You're feeling better, ma'am?"

"Much better." The duchesse smiled. "I do believe I could... dance."

Callie had never thought of herself as particularly shrewd, but she noted the contradiction between Jock's story to the constable and the evident truth that Madame was not on her deathbed quite yet. "I'm so glad," she said. "That's a great relief to me. But you haven't seen the duke today?"

The duchesse shook her head. "It is most vexing. I should like to send him down to see what is... all this clamor. Voices at the door, and I heard the strangest sound, my dear, you... would not credit. Nurse says I am dreaming, it's only a dog, but we have no dog, you know!" She shook her head. "And it did not sound like a dog at all. More as the very Horn of Salvation! But sinister. Very low. Almost I could not hear it."

"I heard a dog barkin', madam," the nurse said stubbornly. "Certain as I live."

"Yes, there was a dog too," Madame agreed. "But this was... different."

"Aye, and it may be that your mind is playin' tricks on you, madam, since you haven't yet been bled as the doctor directed." Nurse snapped the sheets taut across the bed. "Too much heat in the brain."

The duchesse made a little face, turning toward Callie so that the nurse could not see. She winked. "Yes, my brain is boiling," she said. "But I wish for my son… to approve my treatments."

"He'd best rouse himself out of bed, then, madam," the nurse said with the disapproval of the righteous for all those who did not rise at first light.

"Indeed," said Madame. "Before my head bursts! Perhaps, Lady Callista, would you be so good as to direct his… manservant to wake him?"

Callie opened her mouth, but nothing emerged. She was certain Trev was far away somewhere, fleeing the law, though she had no idea how to break this news to the duchesse. As she searched for some way to deflect the request, a low vibration rose beneath her very feet, a rumble that was just at the edge of hearing. The long and haunting note seemed to tremble in the walls themselves before it died away below hearing.

"*There!*" the duchesse exclaimed and was immediately overcome by a fit of coughing. She leaned over, struggling to breathe, while men shouted outside. Callie and the nurse hurried to assist Madame, but she waved, pointing to the door. The nurse was wide-eyed now, supporting the duchesse's thin shoulders as she coughed, looking up at Callie as if she had seen a ghost.

It was indeed a malevolent and unearthly sound, if one didn't know precisely what earthly beast had produced it. A surge of relief flowed through Callie, but Hubert's bellow had sounded so close that even she was startled. She looked out the front window, seeing nothing in the garden but the constable's coattails as he ran out of the stable gate toward the lane. He paused, looking up and down in both directions, and then ran across toward the opposite hedgerow. After a moment, a brindled dog raced after him, barking with all the offended frenzy of a shopkeeper chasing a thief.

She turned to the duchesse, who was barely recovering her breath. "Go!" Madame whispered. "I'm... fine! See what—" She lost her voice in another cough but waved so emphatically toward the door that Callie hurried to it.

"It's only my bull, ma'am; you needn't be alarmed," she said. She lifted her skirts and hastened down the stairs.

Jock stood in the open door with his back to her as she came down, looking out and pointing across the road. "That way!" he yelled to someone outside. Beyond his big shoulders, she caught a glimpse of Major Sturgeon dodging round the horses tied at the garden gate. "Follow the dog!" Jock shouted to him. "It broke through the hedge!"

She was about to dart past him to join the pursuit, when a brutal crash and a woman's scream from the direction of the kitchen stairs made her grab the newel post, turning. Lilly came squealing round the corner, colliding with Callie and springing back, her eyes wide. She stood still, put one hand over her mouth, and gestured wildly toward the kitchen.

Callie heard a familiar low rumble, a thump, and the sound of breaking dishware. "Oh dear," she said. She rounded the corner, already expecting disaster, but the sight that met her was rather more along the lines of a culinary apocalypse.

The kitchen at Dove House was not a large chamber. Four ancient stone steps led down to it from the main body of the house, and at the far end, it gave out on the rear yard. At the moment, the back door stood open, blocked by a brawny woman flapping her apron with both hands and breathing with such violent agitation that the sounds she made almost equaled the gusty snorts of the colossal bovine occupant who took up the largest part of the room.

For an instant Callie stood stock-still, completely confounded by the sight. She had already braced herself to find Hubert involved in this outlandish pickle, but it wasn't Hubert beside the overturned table. Amid the broken eggs, cooked carrots, and remnants of a perfectly browned apple pie, stood—not Hubert—but a black bull of equally gargantuan proportions, swishing its tail against the cupboard. He munched happily on a head of lettuce, showing no objection to the flour-sack blindfold across its face. As it swallowed the final head of lettuce leaf, Trevelyan—looking entirely the part of an unshaven and wrinkled fugitive from British justice—offered it a ripe tomato from the mess on the floor.

"Close the doors," he ordered with such a snap of command in his voice that Callie slammed the kitchen door behind her, nearly catching Lilly's nose in it. The new cook was a little less docile. She only dropped her ample apron to her lap and stood gaping in the open back entry. The bull snuffled, turning its blindfolded face up toward Callie, giving a happy moan as its nostrils flared.

The entire state of affairs came clear to her in a single burst of comprehension. She recognized Hubert—she should have done so instantly, only he looked so oddly different, like a familiar person wearing a peculiar wig. Trev would be hiding from the constable, of course, and for some absurd reason he meant to conceal Hubert too. They would have been in the stable yard and ducked into the kitchen as the first possible cover with the pursuit so near. She had been through just this sort of close call with Trev any number of times.

By instinct she hopped down the steps and edged past Hubert to reach the back door. "You must come inside." She took the cook-woman by the arm. "This is a perfectly harmless animal, I assure you, but there's a dangerous criminal and a vicious dog out there. Hurry now, shut the door!"

The cook from Bromyard gave a faint scream and banged the door closed behind herself as she stepped gingerly inside. Callie glanced at Trev. "What of Lilly?"

"And good morning to you too, Lady Callista." He grinned at her, that familiar slanted grin that made them instantly conspirators in crime. With a cordial bow, he added, "Jock can manage Lilly, but damn this great ox." He tried to offer Hubert the limp green top of a carrot, but the bull was attempting to turn blindly toward Callie, treading on a fallen bread loaf and shoving the table another foot toward the hearth. The cupboard tottered dangerously. "Can you keep him quiet?"

She lifted her skirt and climbed across the table leg to reach Hubert's head. The bull gave a deep sigh of contentment once she joined him, and ceased his attempt to destroy the kitchen furniture. He accepted the carrot top from Trev's bandaged hand with a gentlemanly swipe of his great tongue.

"What," Callie said fiercely, untying the blindfold so that she could scratch the bull's broad forehead, "are you doing?"

"Ah," Trev said with an airy wave of another carrot top, "we're just having a bite of breakfast, you see."

"I thought you meant to go—" She stopped, remembering the cook.

He gave her a glance, a compelling flash between them, awareness and a vivid memory of the night before. She looked down and shook away an apple peel that clung to her hem, clearing her throat.

"My lady! Pardon us!" The cook's voice quaked. "But—" She could not seem to gather any further speech as she pointed at Hubert with a muscular arm and shook her head.

"Yes, of course, you are quite right," Callie said in her most soothing-of-servants manner. "We must remove him. But not until we know it's safe."

"Safe!" the new cook said indignantly. "I didn't take this position to be attacked by cattle and criminals, I tell you, in my own kitchen, and on my very first day!"

"Certainly not," Trev agreed. "But I'm obliged to you for your courage. It's women of your iron moral fiber who saved England from Bonaparte."

The cook glanced at him. She took a deep breath, as if to reply sharply, and then straightened her shoulders a little. "I spe'ct so. And who might you be?"

"The duke," he said easily.

"The duke!" She made a puff of disdain. "Oh, come!"

Trev shrugged and smiled. The cook's lips pursed as she tried to maintain her indignation, but her frown eased. Ladies always melted when Trev smiled in that self-deprecating way. Callie had a strong tendency to soften into something resembling a deflated Yorkshire pudding herself, in spite of knowing better than anyone how dangerous it was to succumb.

"I'm one of those eccentric dukes," Trev said. "The French sort."

"Little does she know," Callie said under her breath, pulling Hubert's ear forward so that she could rub behind it. The bull tilted his head and moved it up and down with heavy pleasure. Trev took a step back as a horn waved perilously close to his face.

The door opened a crack. "They're on the way back, sir," came Jock's disembodied voice.

"Already?" Trev said. "Can't Barton even lead a respectable goose chase?"

"They don't look none too happy, sir. Sturgeon's got mud over half his breeches, and his sleeve's torn off."

"The work of the vulgar Toby, I perceive." Trev gingerly pushed Hubert's horn away from his face with his injured hand. "Doubtless this too will be added to my account. Keeping a vicious dog on the premises."

"Old Toby's all right," Jock muttered through the door. "Had all the sense knocked out of him in his line o' work, is all."

"Toby? That's *your* dog?" Callie asked, lifting her head. Before Trev could even answer, she had leaped forward in her thoughts. "That's a fighting dog!" She stared at him for an instant, her whole world tilting. "Why is Hubert dyed black?"

"A small misunderstanding," Trev said hastily.

"You stole him!" Callie exclaimed. "You were going to bait him!"

"Of course not. I—"

"Why is he disguised?" she demanded. "Why is he in your kitchen? And that dog." Her voice rose in pitch. "I'll never let Hubert be baited! He's—"

"Callie!" His voice cut strongly over hers. "Good God, do you think I'd do any such thing?"

She paused, biting her lip. Then she lifted the flour sack in bewilderment. "But I don't understand. Why is he here?"

"I was trying to get him back for you," he said roughly. He began to edge past Hubert's bulk as the door clicked abruptly closed. "Maudlin fool that I am. Keep him quiet, unless you prefer to hand him back to Davenport on a silver platter, and my head along with him."

Callie had to feed Hubert the entire overturned basket of tomatoes and raise the new cook's wages to two guineas a week in order to keep both of her charges in check while dogs and constables raged about outside. Trev and Jock seemed to be leading them a merry chase, with a few feints provided by Lilly from the upstairs window. In spite of her initial shock, the young maid had clearly thrown in with the criminal ranks. She showed some zest for it too. When Toby began scratching and barking at the kitchen door, she leaned out and rang such a peal about disturbing a house of illness that the constable tried to grab the dog himself, though all he seemed to get was a nip for his trouble.

Hubert paid no mind to the snarling threat from the yard, occupied with his tomatoes, but Cook finally grabbed a tub of dishwater in both of her beefy arms, braced it against the door, and opened the latch, dumping the whole over Toby as he tried to dash inside. He yelped and shied back. Cook slammed the door closed. The barking and growling ceased.

"Well done," Callie said in admiration. "Three guineas a week!"

Cook nodded shortly and crossed her arms. "Constables. Dogs. Can't have such 'uns in the kitchen, can us?"

"I should think not," Callie said, rubbing Hubert's ear.

"I warn 'er, my lady, I don't know how I'll serve a dinner on time," Cook said ominously.

"I think a light luncheon will be perfectly adequate. Perhaps you can…" Callie surveyed the wreck of the kitchen. "Perhaps a ham and mustard sandwich," she concluded faintly.

"Pr'haps," the cook said with displeasure. She nodded at the bull. "'Tis standin' on the bread, him is."

"Yes," Callie said helplessly. "I see."

Cook harrumphed in disgust. "Can't put food on the table with a bull in the kitchen, can us?" She rolled down her sleeves and turned resolutely to the door.

"Oh no, please don't go—" Callie's plea was cut off by the sound of the door thumping closed behind the cook with finality. She bit her lip in vexation, sure that was the last they would see of the new cook. She was astonished a few moments later to hear the constable and Major Sturgeon addressed in strong Gloucester accents. The cook's voice was soon joined by another, equally scolding. Callie recognized the nurse, who seemed to have abandoned her patient long enough to come down to the yard and rebuke the local officer of the law in no uncertain terms. Lilly's higher tones joined in, and the sounds, along with the major's clipped replies and Constable Hubble's pathetic attempts to mount a defense, receded.

Callie fed Hubert another tomato. After several minutes, the door to the hall opened cautiously. "Still here?" Trev looked around the corner.

She gave him a dry look. "Where did you expect us to be?"

"Can he turn about?"

Callie cast a glance round the room, measuring Hubert's length against the breadth of it. "In a word—no."

"Damn." Trev went away for a moment, then came back and opened the door fully, stepping down into the kitchen. "It's safe for now. They've retreated in disarray. Cook's gone for some bread at the shop. An excellent woman!" He grinned. "We'd fought it to a draw, but Sturgeon wasn't going to fall back until she rallied the forces."

"I've raised her wages to three guineas a week," Callie informed him.

"Capital." He offered another carrot to Hubert. "I could commit murder before her very eyes and keep her on at that rate. Now—what are we to do with you, my immense friend? Can you back him out?"

"I doubt it. I may have to lead him through the hallway," Callie said.

"I fear that you may. I pray for the survival of the floorboards. And after that, what are we to do with him?"

"What are we to do with him?" she echoed in surprise. "I should think that must be obvious."

"We must get him out of here, of course," Trev said. "But after that, I'll admit, I'm stymied for a plan."

"We'll return him to Colonel Davenport, of course."

"And what will we say to the colonel?" he inquired. "'Here's your bull, my good man. So sorry he fell in a tanner's vat!'"

Callie made an exasperated sound. "Why on earth did you dye him? It makes it appear as if you stole him."

"Ah. You perceive the crux of the problem."

She was silent for a moment, her gloved hand resting on Hubert's muscular shoulder. She lowered her eyes. "Did you steal him?" she asked softly.

"Well, no," he said. "At least, I didn't mean to."

She lifted her eyes, her head tilted a little aside, a hesitant upward curve on her lips.

Trev felt his heart make a certain sort of squeeze, the kind of pang that he direly wished to avoid, when she looked at him just so. He gave a flat smile and a shrug. "I'd intended to purchase him, if you will credit that."

"For me?" Her voice was barely above a whisper.

"Oh no," he said casually. "I meant to present him to some other lady. It's all the crack, you know. Flowers are so common."

She pressed her lips together and frowned. She wrinkled her nose, and then put her arm over Hubert's broad back and laid her cheek to his massive shoulder. "Thank you," she said quietly.

Trev examined the bandage on his hand, tugging at the knot. "An unsuccessful endeavor, as usual. What will I bungle next?"

Callie sighed. She lifted her head and stroked the bull's sleek hide. "We must give him back, you know. He's too valuable."

"I suppose," he said. "I prefer not to be too closely associated with the honorable deed, myself. Perhaps we could just turn him loose, to be found."

She considered this, shaking her head slowly. "I don't like to turn him loose. There are these sharpers lurking about. And there's no saying who might find him first, or that he might get tangled with some fence, or chased by dogs, or a fast carriage might come upon him suddenly in a narrow lane. Hunting gentlemen come into the country this season and drive as if they're mad. He might be hurt."

"True." Trev privately spared a moment's sympathy for any fast driver who happened to collide with Hubert.

"Besides, I think he would just come home again." A slight frown crossed her brow. "And if he were discovered at Shelford—dyed like this—" Her eyes widened. "Someone might think *I* stole him!"

He snorted. "You? No one would suppose that."

"With the Hereford show next week—" She stood straight. "Everyone knows we're going to it. Everyone knows I hoped to win. There's a great deal of rivalry within the county Agricultural Society."

"It's cutthroat, I've no doubt," he said. "But I hardly think anyone would accuse you—"

"They would," she said strongly. "Best Bull not over Four Years of Age—it's for the silver cup, you know! And there was a horrid scandal last year; I heard all about it from Colonel Davenport, though I couldn't attend myself. Mr. Painter was disqualified from ever showing at the exhibition again, because he had glued false hair over a sore on his bull's back."

"Shocking," Trev said with a grave look.

"It was! Very! No one would ever have suspected it of Mr. Painter. We supposed him to be a perfectly honorable gentleman. Now he doesn't dare show his face among honest graziers. No, I don't want to risk anything like that. I've seven heifers, four steers, a bull calf, and a pair of oxen entered, even without Hubert. And I'm not certain, now that I think of it, that it would look very well at all even if I took Hubert directly back to Colonel Davenport now. Not in this state, and so close to the exhibition. It might appear that I only pretended to find him and bring him back, while meaning to keep him out of the competition altogether. He can't be shown like this."

Trev pressed his fist inside the stiff curve of his bandaged hand. "So… we can't take him back, and we can't turn him loose, and we can't keep him at Shelford."

She shook her head. "I don't see how we can—at least until he grows out of this dye."

"How long will that take?"

"Oh my—his winter coat will be coming on, but—some months I should think, before there is no trace of it."

"Splendid," he said dryly. "We'll have to conceal him, then."

They both gazed at Hubert. He chewed rhythmically, with a faraway, dreamy look in his deep brown eyes. He swished his tail, thumping it against the cupboard with a sound like a hollow drum. Inside the cupboard, the dishes rattled.

"Perhaps some spectacles and a mustache," Trev suggested.

"Yes, and a bagwig," Callie said curtly. "He could sit on the bench and conduct the assizes."

Trev squinted at the bull. "He does resemble some of the judges."

She pursed her lips and gave him an arch look. "No doubt you're familiar with any number of them."

"Sadly I am, and I fear I'll come to know them even better if we don't discover some way to deal with this monster." He crossed his arms, leaning his hip against the overturned table. "If you believe we can't turn him loose, we must get him well away from Shelford, Callie, in truth. And rapidly at that. Is there anyone you trust to take him?"

She frowned and clutched her gloves together, holding them to her chin. In spite of his increasingly urgent anxiety for his own skin, Trev found himself hard put to suppress a smile at the look of earnest concentration on her face.

"I have an excellent drover," she said, "but he knows Hubert very well, and I wouldn't know how to explain it all. And where would we take him?"

"Somewhere among a great number of cattle would be best. A market or such."

"We can't sell him!" she exclaimed.

"I don't mean to sell him. Only somewhere that he would blend in among a lot of others of his kind for a while."

"I don't believe Hubert will blend very well. Particularly in this color. The only black cattle that are common are the Welsh type. They aren't so large, and you don't see many of them hereabouts. I heard there were a few at the last exhibition."

"The exhibition!" Trev stood upright. "We could take him there. Cattle by the score."

Callie gasped. "Are you mad? We can't let him be seen there!"

"It's perfect. It's an exhibition, yes? You don't have to enter for a prize. He's an alien bull, just come over from... from Belgium. Kept under wraps until he's revealed at the show. New blood, all that. We could even start up a rumor claiming he's larger than Hubert. And you would publish Hubert's dimensions—slightly reduced, of course—and express your displeasure with this upstart—"

Callie's mouth fell open wider and wider. She was shaking her head.

"It's hide in plain sight, you see," Trev said. "We'll offer a challenge! A hundred guineas. While everyone scours the countryside trying to find Hubert, so that the two can be compared, he's standing right in front of them. But they won't see it."

"You're mad! Of course they would see it. I recognized him instantly!"

"Did you?"

"Well, I—it did take me a moment to realize—but, I'm sure anyone who knew Hubert would see it quickly."

"How many in Hereford know him that well? He doesn't have any scars or nicks. It's not so easy to recognize an animal with no markings as one might suppose. I've seen enough dark horses to know, you may believe me."

She turned and gazed at Hubert, assessing his generous bulk and shaking her head. Trev could see that she was about to dispute him, when a faint cough from the door made them both look round quickly.

"Maman!" Trev exclaimed. "What are you doing down here?"

The duchesse leaned one white hand on the door-jamb, peering into the kitchen. "No, I ask you!" she whispered. "What does this animal do here?" Her eyes danced. "You and Lady Callista... have a scheme together, eh?"

"We're taking him out directly," Trev said. He moved toward the door, avoiding the smashed pie. "As soon as I help you back to bed."

"Oh no, do not suppose—" She coughed, clinging to the door. "You expect me to... be in bed... while all my house falls down!"

"Better that, than you fall down," he said, taking her arm.

"I will... sit up in the parlor," she said with dignity. Her voice strengthened. "I am much... better. We have a great deal to discuss, I think, Trevelyan."

"And where is that nurse?" Trev asked. He guided her away from the door, but she set herself against climbing the stairs.

"No. And no. I will... sit up," she said as firmly as her weak voice could manage. "And we will discuss, Trevelyan!"

"May I remove this bull from the premises first?" he asked courteously.

"You may," she said with a little smirk at him. "Only do not... destroy what Limoges ware I have left to me."

"I make no guarantee of that," Trev said, guiding her to a chair in the modest drawing room. "I can only hope he doesn't lodge at the turning and pull the whole place down around us."

❈

Hubert proved himself a splendid gentleman, worthy of his exalted lineage and genteel upbringing, in his transit from the kitchen to the front door. Following Callie and a trail of carrots, he moved one ponderous step at time, his big head swaying gently under the replaced blindfold. There were a few breathless moments at the turning, in which his hip caught on the doorjamb and the ancient floorboards squealed in protest at his weight, but a mighty shove against his rib cage by Trev, and Callie's encouraging voice, swayed him just enough. His hind foot found purchase on the top stone stair, and he pushed through.

Once he reached the garden, however, he summarily shed his well-bred manners and showed a loutish tendency to trample the dahlias and browse on the tender shoots of a sweet pea vine. Trev had tied the horses in the stable yard and made sure the lane was empty of passersby before they brought Hubert through the door, but he felt his alarm rising as the bull disregarded the carrots and planted himself amid the flower beds, cropping great swaths of blossoms and vegetation with each mouthful.

"Callie!" Trev hissed, pushing at Hubert's rump. "Move him along!"

"I'm trying!" she returned in a fierce whisper, as if they weren't standing in full view of the lane with a massive black bull taking up the twelve feet of garden between them. She clucked and tugged at the animal's nose ring. "Hubert! Walk on!"

Hubert flicked his ear, lifted his nose an inch, and then went back to tearing up daisies.

Trev had been praying that Jock and Barton's absence meant that the pursuit was still decoyed away.

Jock knew full well they needed time, and plenty of it, but Sturgeon had not left the premises willingly—not unless it was to go for a musket. So when Trev saw a flicker of motion through the leaves and overhanging branches far down the lane, a warning that someone was marching briskly toward them, he felt a surge of true panic.

"Someone's coming." He would have stampeded the bull in any way he could, but with Callie standing in front of the bull he didn't dare. She'd be crushed in an instant if the beast overran her. He threw a wild look round, saw a white expanse of bed linens hung out to sun over the side fence, and finished off Hubert's work by trampling down the delphiniums to reach them. He tore the sheets off the fence and waded back, dragging them in his arms, tossing the whole spread over Hubert's back. "Take the ends! We're airing linen."

Callie nodded, with a wide-eyed glance toward the lane. She grabbed a sheet corner, pulling it toward her. Hubert ignored the drape as Trev hurriedly arranged one edge over a rosebush, trying to cover him entirely under a tentlike affair of bed linens. Callie held out the ends, waving them up and down as if to shake out wrinkles while she made a pavilion over Hubert's lowered head.

To the nondiscerning eye, he might possibly resemble the lumps of covered garden bushes, assuming the bushes were small trees, but Trev feared he looked very much more like a bull with a pair of sheets and a counterpane laid over him. Trev was frantically trying to invent a reasonable tale to cover the situation when the advancing pedestrians appeared round the curve of the lane.

Trev looked toward them. Then he closed his eyes, let go of a harsh breath, and thanked every saint in heaven and a few well-known sinners in hell. It was only the new cook and his mother's nurse, with no other companions.

The cook paused a moment in her stride, gave the tableau in the garden an appraising look, and then walked stoutly forward, carrying her covered basket. The nurse stood stock-still, eyeing them suspiciously.

"Giving the linens an airing!" Trev said, trying for a lighthearted tone in the face of the nurse's glower. "We thought they could use more sun."

She did not appear to be amused. Indeed, she seemed to be making some effort to breathe, her chest rising and falling as she held herself ramrod-stiff.

"I told Nurse, him's a Frenchie duke," Cook said conversationally. "Eccentric."

Callie flapped one corner of her sheet a little, to free it from where it threatened to tear open on the tip of Hubert's horn as the bull lifted its head. He took a step forward. The sheets began to slip.

Trev speedily altered his tactic, injecting a note of curt haughtiness into his voice. "My mother is sitting up in the parlor, Nurse. She's been awaiting you for some time to help her back to bed. You may use the back entry. Cook, if you will delay a moment, I'd like to see what you've brought in that basket to tempt her."

"Ah, sir," the cook said, nodding. "As you likes. The kitchen door's back round that way." She pointed obligingly for the nurse.

With a little scandalized shake of her skirts, the nurse strode round the corner of the yard, avoiding a collapsed sunflower that lay across her path like a fallen soldier. She vanished just in time. Hubert was beginning to move, easing himself forward, his great nose lifted under the sheets in the direction of Cook's basket.

"What do you have there?" Trev asked.

"Bath buns," the cook said.

"Bath buns?" Callie exclaimed, taking a step back as Hubert pressed forward, moaning eagerly and trailing sheets. "Oh, thank the good Lord! Bath buns are his favorite. He'll do anything for them."

Eleven

"Seigneur," his mother said, her whispery voice drifting from the parlor as Trev attempted to pass the door unnoticed.

He halted. Most mothers rebuked their sons by their full names when they were in hot water, but Trev had simply been "Seigneur" since he was old enough to dread the word. He knew he should have left by the stable gate, but he'd hoped the nurse had escorted his mother upstairs and back to bed by now.

He considered feigning that he had not heard, but Callie was already stepping past him. She had lured Hubert to the rear of the property and established him comfortably in the closed stable, surrounded by ample hay spiked with scattered pieces of Bath buns to keep him occupied. Trev had feared that the bull would bellow again if she left him, but she claimed the hay and buns would be sufficient distraction for the moment. They'd left Callie's mount with him and tied Major Sturgeon's horse again at the garden gate. Now, as Trev paused, plotting how best to abscond before he was obliged to explain himself, she took his sleeve and called, "He's right here, Madame." She gave him a little tug toward the parlor door.

Trev made an accusing face at her. She knew perfectly well what that "Seigneur" portended for him. He could bear any number of whippings from his grandfather, but to have his gentle maman call him on the carpet was more excruciating by far. Callie gave him a pert glance and a mock curtsy. She turned back as if to join Cook in the wrecked kitchen, but the grim-faced nurse appeared at the parlor door.

"Madame wishes to speak to my lady also, if she would extend the honor," she said in a stern voice.

"Hah," Trev said softly. He smirked and gave a bow as he gestured for Callie to precede him.

She shook her head quickly, but he took her elbow and used his superior height and leverage to grossly unfair advantage, ushering her bodily through the parlor door ahead of him. Then he stood with her in front of him like a shield.

"You may go upstairs, thank you, Nurse," the duchesse said mildly. "And close the parlor door, if you please." She waited until the nurse had shut the door with an offended rattle. Then she broke into an impish smile. "I fear she is very much... shocked... at this household."

"I'd better speak to her directly," Trev said, seeing a chance of escape. "We can't afford to lose such an excellent woman." He turned toward the door, ignoring Callie's clinging hand and accusing look at his desertion.

"Seigneur!" His mother stopped him. "I believe that I can soothe her... pelt—or is it feathers?"

"Feathers, ma'am," Callie said in a small voice.

"Thank you, my dear. Please sit down. I can do that soothing of feathers well enough myself. I wish to speak to you, Trevelyan. Before I expire of curiosity, and have no need of any nurse."

Callie sank into in the nearest chair, gripping her fingers nervously. Trev determined to take some control of the interrogation, since it appeared to be inevitable. "Very well, Maman," he said briskly. "What would you like to know? It's about the bull, I suppose."

"Yes. The bull. And the constable. And the bandage of your hand. And the much shouting, and your coat... torn, and the dog... and... a scurrilous fellow running about... whom I never saw before... in my life!" She panted a bit at the end of this list, overcoming a cough.

"Scurrilous? That would be Major Sturgeon," Trev said blandly.

"I think she means that other fellow," Callie said, sitting up straight. "I saw him too, Madame." She gave Trev a sideways look. "And Major Sturgeon is not precisely scurrilous."

"I beg your pardon, my lady." Trev was not altogether pleased to hear her defend the major, even mildly. "I thought he was persecuting you. But I notice that you arrived in his company this morning. Do you like him better now?"

"He was helping me to find Hubert."

Trev would have liked to inquire further into just how that came to pass, but he deemed it wiser to steer the topic away from Sturgeon and any other reason the constable might be calling at Dove House. Hubert was one thing; a warrant for his arrest was another. "So kind of him," Trev said, dismissing the major with a sardonic glance at Callie. "I suppose I must explain why the bull was in the house, Maman. It was to protect Lady Callista's reputation."

"*My* reputation!" Callie gasped.

He bowed to her. "You'll recall that you said you didn't wish for anyone to suppose you had stolen him back from Colonel Davenport."

"Well, no, I don't wish for anyone to suppose that, but that isn't why he was in the kitchen!"

"Then why was he in the kitchen?" Trev asked.

"Because you led him in there, I must suppose."

"And why would I do that?"

"To keep the constable from finding him with *you*, I presume!" she responded indignantly.

"And why did I have him with me?"

"You said you had tried to purchase him from Colonel Davenport," she said. "But I don't know why you had him—"

"Yes!" Trev interrupted triumphantly. "Why did I attempt to purchase him?"

She blinked, shaking her head. "Well—you said you wished to—I thought—you implied that—" She bit her lip. "I thought you wished to give him back to me."

"There, you see?" Trev said.

She looked utterly bewildered. "See what?"

"I did it for you, my lady. I wished to please you."

"Well done, Seigneur," his mother said. "Our brains are quite cooked now."

He turned to his mother. "And you also, Maman," he said. "I thought you would like it if I did something to make Lady Callista happy."

The two women in his life both looked at him with their lips pursed, one with resentment and the other with dry amusement. "I see," his mother said.

"Well, I do not," Callie said. "Why is Hubert dyed black, if you were only trying to buy him back for me?"

"I must censure myself for that," Trev said, standing with his hands clasped behind his back, the better to look solemn and responsible. "I didn't call on Colonel Davenport myself, as I was preoccupied with my mother's situation." He glanced at Callie, to see if she would allow that as a defense. When she gave a little nod, acknowledging it, he continued. "So I delegated a… a gentleman of Jock's acquaintance, with full powers of negotiation to deal with the colonel. I told him to purchase the bull at any price. I may have said to bring him to me under any circumstances. I was perhaps unwise in my choice of words. Or my choice of an agent."

"Oh," Callie said. "Oh! Could this be the sharper who offered Colonel Davenport a huge sum for Hubert?"

"Quite probably. Almost certainly. You see, Lady Callie," he said, with an air of hurt dignity, "it was not to use him for baiting."

She cast her eyes down. "I never really thought you would do that."

"Thank you." Trev cleared his throat. "I'm obliged to you. But it seems that, after being—ah—dismissed from the colonel's presence, in a rather abrupt manner, with the word that the bull was not for sale at any price, my agent discovered the animal wandering free on the road. Being a brainless but determined fellow, he saw this as an opportunity to convey Hubert to me, taking care to disguise him first by dyeing him a false color. And so, Maman—" He nodded toward his mother. "We are now in a fix."

"But of course," she said, looking up at him appreciatively. "I am in awe of the… greatness of… this fix. What do you propose to do?"

"We must give Hubert back, ma'am," Callie said. "I can't keep him, I'm afraid, though I very much wish I could."

His mother seemed to ponder this, studying Callie. "My son told me of this ridiculous card game where he was gambled away."

Callie gave a small shrug. "It could not be helped. Hubert didn't really belong to me."

His mother reached out to touch Callie's hand. "I'm so sorry, my lady. I know you… love the good creature. And I commend you well, Trevelyan—that you try to buy him again for Lady Callista. But it is—yes—a fix." She sat back, giving Callie a sidelong glance. "So you will do… what Trevelyan says, then? My son is so clever to fix a fix, you know?"

"Do what?" Callie asked with a note of suspicion.

"The cattle show… up to Hereford," the duchesse said. "I heard a little. It sounds to me like an… excellent plan."

"Oh no, ma'am, that will never do. I promise you. I would not dare to take Hubert to a show while he's in this state!"

"Then what will you do with him?" his mother asked innocently.

Callie clutched her hands together. She opened her mouth and then closed it.

"I do believe that if he… remains here… he will be discovered from his… great bellow. It is a fine bellow, but… very loud."

"Yes," Callie said wretchedly. "I fear so. Perhaps—" She turned to Trev with a helpless look. "Perhaps I could stay here and try to keep him quiet."

"Until he sheds the dye?" Trev shook his head. "We'd never manage to hide him here that long. But I think I may have a likelier notion. It'll require a bit of nerve, but it ensures that Lady Callista wouldn't be accused of trickery and cuts short the whole imbroglio to a few days instead of weeks."

"Nerve?" Callie asked dubiously.

"Ah, but nerve is what Trevelyan has in abundance," his mother said, with an approving nod. "Prudence—now that is a house of another color."

"'Horse,' Maman," Trev said. "A horse of another color."

"A horse, then. What is this… scheme, *mon chère*?"

Trev paced to the window, looking out before he drew the curtains. Sturgeon's mount was still tied to the post. Jock and Barton seemed to have succeeded admirably in keeping the major and his minion at bay, but there was no saying when the reprieve would be over. Trev turned back to the darkened room. "We mean to get Hubert back to the colonel, yes? And I suggested that we pass him off as an imported animal and perhaps promote a contest as a diversionary course, which would do for a short time. Then—after it's been widely seen that she has no part in bringing him to the show, we'll have Lady Callista observe him there, 'recognize' him under the dye, and declare his true identity, with a suitable show of shock and dismay of course, at which time he can be handed over to his rightful owner, dye and all."

"Brilliant!" exclaimed his mother, overcoming a cough.

"Absurd!" Callie squeaked. "You mean for *me* to identify him? In front of everyone? I couldn't!"

"Why not? You'd only have to say the truth, that this is Hubert, and he's been dyed. You're in the clear. Let the others decide how he came to be that way. I'll make sure no one finds out."

"But—" She looked as if she might faint in her chair. "In front of everyone!"

"That would be best. It would make it convincing."

She gave a little moan, shaking her head. Trev couldn't help but smile as he watched her struggle with the idea. It appealed to him, this scheme, now that he had formed it in his mind—though he had the wit to keep some of the riskier details to himself until she was committed beyond recall. He resisted the urge to pull her up to him and kiss her into acquiescence, holding her cheeks between his hands and breathing his recklessness into her—a persuasion he'd used more than once in the past.

He would have kissed her now, but for his mother's presence. Not that it would shock his maman. Oh no—it was that she would be all too delighted.

"Come, you admitted to me that you've had no adventures lately," he said to Callie. "It'll be amusing."

She steepled her hands and pressed her fingertips to her chin, looking at him wide-eyed. In the dim light she was pretty and delicate, like a small white flower peeking out from under the shade of showier plants.

Trev felt such a rush of love that it was almost a pain in his chest and throat—he had to grip his bruised hand into a fist and drown the feeling in sharp physical hurt, mill it down like an opponent in a brutal match.

"A lark," he said with a smile and a shrug. "Like the old days."

"Oh, did you make larks with Lady Callista—in the old days?" his mother inquired, lifting her eyebrows.

"One or two," he said casually. "Long ago, Maman. Sometimes we took an outing. A—ah—a supplement to her lessons in French."

"That is alarming… news," she said, not appearing to be at all alarmed. "I must hope you did not lead my lady to… assist you in any of your regrettable… pranks."

"Regrettable! Come, do you call releasing a baboon amongst a crowd of spectators at a cockpit regrettable?"

"Trevelyan!" his mother said. "You didn't involve Lady Callista with… a cockpit, I pray!"

"I had no choice," he said gravely. "She was in charge of freeing the birds while everyone else was distracted."

Callie gave a stifled giggle behind her gloves. "Yes, I was, ma'am," she admitted, lowering her hands. "But no one noticed me, I assure you."

His mother looked at her with interest. "And what… became of the baboon?"

"Oh, Trevelyan made sure he was all right," Callie said. "They had been going to make the creature fight with a poor little monkey, but they both got away."

Trev chuckled. "A fine chase those two led us!"

"Oh yes. If not for that peculiar old gentleman you knew, no one would ever have caught them. But he was a marvelous handler of monkeys! It was quite astonishing, ma'am. He coaxed the baboon right down from a cottage roof!"

His mother nodded wisely. "How fortunate that my son... acquaints himself with marvelous... handlers of monkeys."

"Indeed it was, ma'am," Callie agreed. "But Trev was used to know all sorts of..." She trailed off suddenly, looking conscious.

"Riffraff?" his maman supplied in a helpful tone.

"The old fellow was perfectly respectable, I promise you." Trev gave Callie a wink. "For a gypsy, at any rate. I daresay they're dancing for coins to this day with him."

Callie smiled up at him warmly. He cleared his throat, having provided his maman with far more fodder for her impossible hopes than was prudent, and added regretfully, "But it's true, my lady—I suppose you could not consider such an unseemly trick now."

"Seigneur!" his mother chided. She leaned on the arm of her chair, looking less vigorous than she had a few moments earlier. But she said with staunch effort, "Lady Callista... is not... so poor-hearted... as that, I am sure."

Callie observed his mother with a worried expression. "But I *am* poor-hearted. Oh my. But I suppose..."

"It's in a humanitarian cause," Trev offered when she hesitated.

She glanced askance at him. "What humanitarian cause?"

"To save my skin."

"Ah," his mother said, breathing with difficulty. She was clearly losing strength. "I do hope you will...

rescue his... shameless skin, my lady. As a particular favor... to me."

Callie sat still, an array of emotions passing in fleet succession across her face. Then she stood up. "Yes, ma'am. I'll do what I can. But will you give me permission to ring for the nurse and lie down now?"

The duchesse smiled feebly. "Yes, I think that might be... wise."

"I don't see how this can possibly succeed," Callie said, tossing more hay into Hubert's pile. She put down the pitchfork and dusted her gloves. "How is a drover to walk him to Hereford, out and about on the public roads where everyone can see?"

"You say he'll do anything for Bath buns?" Trev's voice came to her hollowly through the spaces between the boards in the loft.

She looked up, squinting against a little fall of straw. "I believe he would," she admitted. "Particularly if they're stuffed with white currants."

"Then I'll get him there."

She wished to argue, but now that she had agreed to this outlandish scheme he seemed to be exceptionally reticent about the particulars, a circumstance which only heightened her anxiety. "And when he arrives?" she asked. "What then?"

"That puts me in mind of something," he said, his disembodied voice still muffled. "Do you have a chamber bespoke in Hereford?"

"Yes. We always stay at the Green Dragon."

"Where is it?"

"It's just in the middle of Broad Street, where the show is held."

"Good. How many nights do you stay?" he asked.

"I'd intended to stay all three."

"And who goes with you?"

Callie hesitated and shrugged. "No one."

"No one?" He sounded surprised.

"My father and I used to go together every year." She ran her gloved hand over Hubert's poll, stroking him. "But no one else has very much interest in a cattle show. Lady Shelford doesn't like it, but she didn't forbid me. So… this is the first year I'll go alone."

The boards creaked. He came to the edge of the loft and knelt down. "You won't be alone," he said with a slight smile.

She lifted her lashes. In the dusky light of the stable, his rumpled neck cloth and open shirt points made him appear carelessly dashing, like a dark poet or some hero from a novel. She always felt as if she were living inside a story when she was with Trev, swept along on the excitement of some plot outside her own making.

"You'll bring an abigail, won't you?" he asked.

"Oh yes, of course." She awoke from the brief reverie that he had meant she wouldn't be alone, because he would be there. "Though—" She remembered that she hadn't yet lit upon on a substitute for the lady's maid that she and Hermione shared. She stopped gazing up like a moonling into his face and busied herself with arranging the pitchfork on a hook. "Well, I must have someone, at any rate. Hermey needs Anne at home for the next fortnight, what with all the callers and visitations. Sir Thomas is taking her on a number of outings, and Lady Shelford has invited a great crowd of people for the hunting and a masquerade ball or some such." She sighed. "It's so difficult now to keep staff. I don't require anyone with experience. I might even borrow Lilly now that your mother has a nurse, if Mrs. Adam will spare her to me."

"Perfect," he said with a grin. He rose and vanished again, keeping watch from some hole in the loft in case Major Sturgeon should return.

Callie looked down at her toes. It really was quite all right. They would have one last lark and save his skin, and then... the rest of her life, she supposed.

She pulled her gloves on tightly. "I should go," she said, taking up a notch in her horse's girth. "He'll be quiet now until this hay is gone. But be sure to keep a full manger and a bucket of water in front of him."

"We will. The lane's empty if you make haste. Wait—do you still have that medicine box in your cattle barn?"

She paused, holding the reins in her hand as she looked up at the loft. They'd used to use the medicine box as their secret place to exchange messages. "Yes, it's there."

He made a satisfied sound. "Check it every morning."

"What of the key?"

For a long moment there was silence. Then he said quietly, "I still have it."

Callie stood looking up at the bits of straw and cobwebs that dangled from the boards. She swallowed a slight, strange ache in her throat, anticipation and pleasure and pain all mixed, and turned away.

"Can you use the mounting block?" he asked, his voice oddly gruff.

"Yes, of course." She didn't look back, though she heard his boots hit the dirt of the stable floor as she led her horse outside.

"You'll have a message from me," he murmured. The door closed behind her with a wooden growl and thump.

Being cordially disliked by Lady Shelford did not afford Callie any relief from attending the teas, dinners, and house parties that the countess—once released from the punctilious obligations of mourning—had begun to host at Shelford Hall. This unaccustomed invasion of county society was only slightly less daunting, in Callie's view, than the full round of gaiety in London during the season, but somehow she was a little less reticent than usual. When she found herself feeling intimidated amid a group of strangers, she thought of Trev feeding Hubert a tomato and grinning at her in the demolished kitchen of Dove House, and her lips would curl upward in a smile that seemed to make some guest smile back at her, and they would exchange a word or two, which was more pleasant than she would have expected in the circumstances.

She had never been obliged to suffer such a bustle of social doings at her home before. After harvest time, autumn and winter at Shelford had always been quiet. Though the Heythrop country was near enough for convenience, her father had held mixed opinions regarding foxhunting. He was by no means averse to the destruction of foxes, but he had the inborn objection of a true farmer to seeing his fences and

cattle overrun by cavalcades of youngbloods on their
bang-up high-bred hunters. So there had never been
any proper hunting parties held at Shelford, only a
few of her father's close friends who stabled their extra
mounts there when the stalls were full at Badminton,
and stayed over a day or two from time to time when
they came to retrieve their second string.

Now, though, with the end of cub hunting and
the true season about to begin, Lady Shelford seemed
to have enticed half the nobility to what she fondly
referred to as her family's ancestral seat. Callie tried not
to feel offended by this description of Shelford Hall.
It was true of course that the property now belonged
to Cousin Jasper, and thus to his wife, and eventually
to their eldest son, though an heir had not yet been
produced. Indeed, the Taillefaires did not seem prolific
of sons in their recent generations. Callie's own father
had outlived three wives without procuring a boy for
his trouble—and trouble it had been, from what Callie
recalled. Once he had even said to her, with some
anguish, that he would have been glad to leave her the
whole if he might, for she was as fine a successor as
any man could hope for, and then he could have done
without these plaguey women upsetting everything
with their vapors.

Callie had smiled at that but never allowed
herself to lose sight of the fact that she would be
leaving Shelford Hall. If there had been more fondness between them, she might have remained as a
companion to Lady Shelford, one of those maiden
aunts who made conversation over the needlework
and doted on the children, but no one had ever
contemplated that notion for more than an instant. In

truth, if Callie must dote on someone else's offspring, she preferred her sister's, or even Major Sturgeon's, for that matter. The changed atmosphere at Shelford was already painful enough.

This evening it was a formal dinner party large enough to fill the entire long table in the dining room. Callie partook of the extravagant meal with stiff care, dreading to make some faux pas that would draw Dolly's attention to her. She impressed her dinner partner—some viscount or other—only with her silence. Amid the murmur of conversation, the candles and glitter of silver and diamonds, she indulged herself in imagining a dining *salle* in Paris, with the conversation all in French, and herself the enchanting new bride of a duke—nameless, of course, but resembling Trev in every particular. Somewhere in her fantasy all the guests mysteriously vanished and he drew her up a gilded staircase to a bed that rather resembled the entire city of Byzantium, kissing her hands and then—

"Lady Callista?" Her dinner partner was standing, waiting to pull out her chair. Perforce, she took his arm and joined the guests in the drawing room.

Hermey had taken a place near the door with Sir Thomas, enjoying her time in the sun, accepting felicitations from some of the new arrivals who had been invited for the music after dinner. Callie had found her own brief betrothals and the attendant ceremonies to be excruciating, but clearly Hermey loved it. She readily offered her cheeks to be kissed and her gloved hands to be pressed. Her eyes sparkled when she looked toward the staid figure of Sir Thomas. It was pleasing to see. Her sister's evident happiness put Callie in such an expansive humor that she even exchanged a few words about the weather with the viscount.

He answered courteously as he seated her on the small sofa in the corner, screened as close behind one of the Corinthian columns as she could manage. His attention then being engaged by a fellow hunting-man regarding the condition of the coverts in the Cotswolds, and how it would affect the Beaufort pack, he forgot all about her. Callie accepted a cup of lemonade from a footman and sat looking at her toes, still drifting in her mind with Trev amid gilded towers and silken bedsheets, waiting for the first moment she could excuse herself to go out and feed the orphan calf.

"But where is your handsome French beau, *le duc très bon*?" a female voice murmured coyly. "Monceaux, was it? He didn't linger the other day. I had so hoped to have an introduction to him."

Callie's head came up in startlement. But no one was speaking to her—it was a lady on the other side of the column talking to Lady Shelford. Callie could just see the spangled train of Dolly's gown lying across the fringe of the India carpet.

"Oh, he sent his regrets tonight," Dolly said, with a low laugh. "*How* he regrets! His tiresome mother is ill."

"A dutiful son," the other voice said. And then, softer: "But that is so charming, *n'est-ce pas*? No doubt an attentive lover too."

"He's French, is he not?" Lady Shelford murmured.

"Let us pray his dear mother recovers sufficiently that he can leave her side," her friend said suggestively, "while I'm yet here at Shelford to offer him my sympathy."

"Indeed. But I fear I must claim precedence there, Fanny darling, as your hostess."

"No, it's too ungenerous of you!" The other woman had a smirk in her voice. "Didn't we always share everything at school?"

They giggled quietly and moved away, leaving Callie staring at the foot of the column. She was shocked, not least to find that Dolly must have sent him a card for the dinner. She sat fixed to the sofa, hardly knowing where to look. Trev grinning at her over the horns of a misplaced bull and the très bon duc de Monceaux were two entirely different persons, she realized. She came to that insight with great suddenness, on the heels of recalling that she was wearing a plain stuff gown that Hermey had cheerfully declared to be fit for a milkmaid, and her hair was unadorned except for a single ribbon in a shade of puce that Lady Shelford detested. Callie had not, when she dressed for dinner, taken any note of these opinions, because she intended to go out the barn later, but abruptly they took on a dangerous significance.

She was a spinster dowd. That was no fresh news, but she had rather a habit of forgetting it just recently, having been beguiled by the suggestion that her cheeks more closely resembled strawberries than a pudding, and the matter of certain gentlemen attempting to recover certain bulls on her behalf. But the knowledge was not something that she could afford to disregard, even under the allure of her daydreams. She and Trev were great friends, but he was indeed French. Flirtation and lovemaking were in his blood. He would say such things as he said to Callie to any lady. And now Dolly and her friend spoke of him in that horrid insinuating way, as if it were quite natural to suppose that they could share his attentions if they pleased.

Callie stood up abruptly, making her way toward the door before the violinist had even started to play. The room felt close and hot. Such a wave of resentment and despair had possessed her that she nearly grew ill. She had to go out into the chilly air to escape from this press of elegant strangers. She hurried down the stairs to the little vestibule on the ground floor where her cloak and muck boots awaited her. No one paid her any mind, though doubtless in the morning Lady Shelford would have some acid comment on her ungraciously early departure. Callie would say she had felt unwell. It was no more than the truth.

Major Sturgeon made his second and third calls without successfully cornering Callie alone. As the days passed, she observed with mild interest the colors of the bruise on his jaw fade from black and blue to green and purple. With each call he brought the latest news from Colonel Davenport regarding the search for Hubert, recounting the lack of success in grave tones. Poor Cousin Jasper was closely interested in this topic, asking anxious questions and proposing several absurdly optimistic theories about where the bull might have got off to—none of which would have comforted Callie in the least if she hadn't already known Hubert was safe.

Hermey also lent her chaperonage to the major's visits, sitting primly beside Callie and attempting to dislodge Cousin Jasper so that Callie could be left alone with her suitor. Their cousin seemed oblivious to all hints, however, chatting with the major in that slow, fretful way of his that always made Callie feel sorry for him. Major Sturgeon was relentlessly courteous, but by his third call, she could see that he was losing patience.

"Will you take a turn in the shrubbery with me, Lady Callista?" he demanded. It was phrased as an invitation, but clearly he was a man accustomed to giving orders.

She was to leave for Hereford at first light. Knowing that he could not continue to pursue her after today, she submitted to the inevitable. She had spent long hours staring into the dark canopy of her bed, considering her future. Of course she wasn't a beauty. Anyone could see that. She was far past the age of matrimony. She had no wit or even sensible conversation in company. She did possess a distinguished rank and pedigree, but there had always seemed to be more than an adequate supply of earls' daughters to fill the demand at Almack's, and she had been dismissed by the patronesses as a hopeless quiz after her first season anyway. Her jiltings had confirmed their judgment: Callie was a social outcast. The only thing that she possessed to attract a husband was her money.

She knew all that in her head, but since Trev had returned, he had confused her in her heart. His sentiments appeared to vary from the romantic to the unfeeling; he said he was going away, and yet he stayed. He mentioned in an offhand way that he might love her, but neglected to expand upon the topic to any particular purpose. She'd found no sense in it, but what she had overheard from Lady Shelford and her guest had brought Callie back to cold reality.

Trev might be her dear friend, but truthfully, what could a man like the duc de Monceaux possibly want with her? He had regained his own fortune. He was titled. He was rich. In spite of a penchant for devilry, he was perfectly fitted to the elevated continental society for which he had been bred. She had seen enough of the bon ton to know that. Callie at the head of a great French noble house? It was a preposterous idea. She was unsuitable in every way. She wasn't French, she wasn't Catholic, she wasn't young or gay or beautiful. She knew no better than to wear poppy orange with pink.

She imagined herself sitting against the wall in a Parisian salon the way she had sat in Almack's, conspicuously gauche, while the fashionable gossips whispered behind their fans and wondered what could have induced him to marry this unfortunate English thing. They would conjecture how she had trapped him and invent unpleasant stories about her. She knew well enough the sort of things people could say, having been jilted three times. Some no doubt would feel sorry for her and murmur that he had married her out of pity, a thought that made her feel wretched.

She allowed Major Sturgeon to escort her to the shrubbery. Hermey positively grabbed Cousin Jasper by the arm, detaining him from following. Callie sat on a stone bench and folded her hands, examining the polish on the major's boots as he took all the blame upon himself for the breaking of their previous betrothal—as well he might, she thought dryly— proclaimed that he was a reformed man, swore to devote the remainder of his life to her welfare, and declared himself to be prostrate at her feet. He did not, thankfully, claim to be in love with her. He seemed to have at least a smidgen of shame left to him.

She listened to his proposal in silence and then said that she must have a fortnight to think about it.

Twelve

CALLIE LOVED AGRICULTURAL FAIRS. HER SITTING
chamber at the Green Dragon, the same one she and
her papa had always used, directly overlooked the
wide street where all the stock would gather. They had
spent many hours standing in this same window and
trying to guess what sort of calves were hidden inside
Mr. Downie's tarpaulin enclosure, or commenting
on the suitability of some crossbred yearling ox for
plowing. The earl would lean out the window and
salute his friends, calling down to invite them inside
to share a breakfast.

There was no standing off or holding oneself up
stiffly above the others. Humble Farmer Lewis would
bring a jug of his best perry made from the celebrated
black pears of Worcester, touch his forelock respectfully, and be welcomed to sit down to the table with
the earl and everyone else. Callie always kept a place
on the little sofa near the window, taking effervescent
sips of pear cider and listening to the talk of sheep
and orchards. She enjoyed the familiar whiff of soap-
scrubbed skin and tobacco, the earnest mixture of best
Sunday clothes and work-toughened hands. There

was always a sense of gay excitement, especially on the first day as the animals arrived, much hearty laughter and dreams of silver cups and prizes. Everyone felt as if anything could happen.

She stood by the sitting room window now, the room silent and empty behind her. It was very hard not to cry. She saw Mr. Downie go by in the street below, but she felt too shy to wave or call out, and there was no need, for she couldn't host a breakfast as her father had—it would seem a very strange thing for a spinster lady to invite a group of gentlemen and farmers to her rooms.

She had felt conspicuous enough arriving alone at the Green Dragon with only Lilly in her company, but the innkeeper knew her well and made her comfortable, kindly sending Farmer Lewis's offering of a jug up to her room. She wrote the good farmer a note of thanks, with a mention of how her father had always especially enjoyed to drink the product of his orchards, and wished him the best of luck with his entries this year. She sent it down with the boot boy. Then she did weep, just a little.

Her own stock was not to arrive until this evening, moving at a careful, steady pace along the back lanes the fourteen miles from Shelford. She herself had embarked much earlier than usual. The brief note Trev had left for her in the medicine chest had not been very informative, instructing her only to arrive at the Green Dragon as early as she could, and send Lilly out to the shops directly.

A great deal of shouting erupted below her as some crated pigs and geese had to be moved in order to accommodate the passing of a large closed van drawn by a pair of oxen. Callie recognized one of the Agricultural Society officers, Mr. Price, trying to settle a dispute over how wide the lane for traffic must be kept. He made a valiant effort, but after the van had lumbered through, the space narrowed rapidly behind it again.

She watched the vehicle creak to a halt across the street, just past her window, waved into place by two very large and daunting men in powdered wigs and matching green coats that stretched taut over their broad shoulders. Even before the doors were opened, they set about erecting the pen and tarpaulins to hide their entry. Callie bit her lip, her heart beating faster. She had never seen any cattle brought in a van before, though crates of the smaller stock often arrived on drays. But while the patient oxen stood waiting, the body of the van shifted and rocked ponderously on its axles in a manner no sheep or pigs would ever cause.

The crisp tarpaulins spread out in the morning sun, displaying a richly painted coat of arms with the name *Malempré* beneath. A gentleman came to the door of the ancient half-timbered tavern opposite to observe the proceedings. She could not quite see his face, but he was dressed in a very smart cape and tall-crowned beaver hat. The way he lounged with elegant nonchalance against the doorway was all too familiar to Callie.

The pair of uniformed handlers paused as he spoke to them. A crowd was gathering, but more men in green coats seemed to appear from nowhere, waving and pushing the onlookers back. A boy who tried to peek under the tarp was summarily lifted by his collar and deposited in a watering trough, much to the amusement of his elders. Such curiosity about what lay behind the tarps was always discouraged by the jealously competitive herdsmen, and often not so gently.

From her vantage point above, Callie could see the doors opened, but she caught only a limited sight of horns and dark shoulders as the ramp thundered hollowly under the hooves of something obviously huge. It was Hubert, without a doubt. She stood holding her breath to see how he would accept the pen and tarps. But whoever handled him seemed to have him in control, no doubt aided by a number of Bath buns. The hanging tarps shook and shivered, waves passing over the coat of arms. Then they settled, showing only the pokes of elbows and occasional tug to keep the corners firmly closed.

Behind her, at a scratch on the door, Lilly entered with a bandbox on her arm. "You're desired to go to the dressmaker's shop in High Town, my lady," she said with a slight curtsy, her eyes dancing. "And here is a new bonnet for you to wear after you go there."

Lilly was clearly privy to a good deal more of the scheme than Callie yet knew, but the maid pressed her lips together and became provokingly mute about anything she had not been instructed to impart. Trev's charm had taken full effect on "Miss Lilly." Callie had already discovered that there was little hope of prying more out of her than she was willing to say.

Drawing a deep breath to fortify herself, Callie allowed the maid to help her with her cloak. Trev's plan was in full motion, and like someone caught in a rising flood, she would be swimming as fast as she could to keep her head above water now.

The dress was a deep gentian blue, with a high-waisted satin ribbon over a corset that cupped and prominently lifted Callie's breasts. From the puffy flounces at her shoulders, the neckline swept so low, she hardly dared look down. This expanse of her skin was covered, in a hypothetical sort of way, by a wisp of gauzy white scarf that seemed to want to work its way free with every move. Callie feared that this was no more than a false hope for modesty.

"*Magnifique!*" the dressmaker kept muttering to herself as she pinned and tucked and then placed the hat on Callie's head. She drew the sweeping front of the brim down over Callie's eyes and fluffed out the glittery blue veil that covered her face and the mass of red hair that was displayed behind. When Callie looked in the mirror through the veil, she saw a figure of mysterious fashion, slender and formidably stylish, perfectly dressed from the tight blue sleeves to the raking plume of the pale ostrich feather in her hat. "Magnifique!" The modiste congratulated herself again. "*Vous l'aimez, madame?*"

Callie could hardly breathe in the tight corset. She swallowed and gave a slight nod. Indeed, it was impossible to say she didn't like the dress—since she didn't even recognize the lady she saw in the mirror, she could only agree that it was a splendid costume. The modiste laid a soft cream-colored cashmere shawl over her shoulders, and Callie pulled it round herself, trying to hold it over her exposed breasts. But the dressmaker would have none of that.

"*Non, non, madame,*" she said in French, fussing with the shawl. "You will allow the drape, eh? There.

Perfect. If you will be so good…?" She gave a curtsy and opened her hand toward the door.

Callie had been informed by Lilly that she was now a Belgian lady of some wealth, who spoke both French and English, but she was to prefer French. Since Callie's French was only as polished as her ancient weekly lessons with Madame de Monceaux—and Trev's long-ago tutorials of quite another sort—she said nothing at all but did a great deal of nodding and murmuring wordlessly.

She emerged from the fitting room, looking about for Lilly. But the maid had vanished from the shop. Instead, against the light from the window, a tall figure turned toward her. Trev held his hat and a polished walking stick together in one gloved hand, looking extremely handsome and utterly continental. He smiled as he took her hand to his lips, raising his brows in a glance of pure masculine appreciation.

Callie felt the color rush up into her cheeks. She lowered her face quickly, but he lifted her chin on his fingers. "Magnifique, I must agree," he said softly. He also used French, which only reminded her more strongly of those long-ago days of ardent secrets between them. "Hold your head up, *ma chérie.* You're beautiful."

She raised her chin. She wasn't, of course, but she supposed that behind a dark veil she could play the part. As he stood close to her, he bent his head and let his lips drift over hers, with the gauze between them, while the dressmaker made little clucks of approving delight. Callie's heart felt as if it were beating too fast for her to breathe.

He took her arm and nodded to the modiste as he escorted Callie from the shop. Once on the street, she said, "Am I meant to be your... your—" She could not quite put into words the scandalous role it seemed she was to play.

"You are my wife, and I am so much in love with you that I can't keep my eyes away," he said, still insisting on French. "Do you object?"

She really felt quite unable to reply. She managed to shake her head and give a small shrug.

"We're come over from a small corner of Belgium near Luxembourg. You need not say much, as you have little English. Are you comfortable in the French?"

"I will do my best." Her spoken French was only fair, she felt, but she could understand it quite well after years of listening to Madame de Monceaux and her late daughter.

"Good," he said, as they strolled leisurely along. "I think it's safest. I wouldn't suppose too many of your stockmen and farmers would understand us."

"No," Callie agreed. "But of course the gentry will. And I'm afraid Colonel Davenport will know you by your face."

"I'll take care to avoid Colonel Davenport," he assured her. He paused to allow a carriage to go by, the sleek team of matched bays swinging in under the sign of Gerard's Hotel. "I've taken rooms here in the High Town. You'll be with me most of the day while the show is on, but from time to time we'll see that you make an appearance as yourself with your cattle. And at night, of course, you'll go back to the Green Dragon with Lilly."

This plan sounded both extremely alarming and enormously attractive at the same time. She was not at all looking forward to impersonating a Belgian lady, but the thought of three entire days in Trev's company, cast in the role of his adored wife, was... impossibly wonderful, to put a point on it.

"We are newly wed," he said, as he touched her waist, guiding her up the marble steps of Gerard's. "That will excuse a good deal."

Callie glanced through her veil at the footman who held the door, trying to swallow her agitation. Gerard's was one of the most exclusive hotels in the city, but Callie had never stayed there. She and her father had preferred the shabbier comfort of the Green Dragon, where they were close to the fair and sales.

Seeing the world through the gauze made it all the more like a dream. She was with Trev. They were going to his rooms. They would be alone together there, while everyone outside thought they were newlyweds. She lifted her skirts and climbed the stairs, preceding him into the chamber. The door closed behind them.

Callie stood looking at the gilded curves of the French chairs and reclining sofas, the draperies held back by golden tassels. It might have been any smart drawing room in Mayfair, with a silver tea tray and paper-thin slices of cake laid out on china and crisp linen. Lady Shelford would have felt quite at home at Gerard's, but Callie felt anxious, as if at any moment she might be called upon to make conversation at some tonnish party.

Trev tossed his hat and stick aside. He put his hands on her shoulders, turned her around, and pulled the veil free. She blinked and tried to smile, to show that she was primed for this adventure. He looked down at her a moment, his head tilted quizzically. Then he drew her close and kissed her.

All her uneasiness vanished in an instant, lost in the wonder of his touch. She let her head yield back under the searching kiss, the taste of him. She knew this—he had taught her. She lifted her arms in answer, clinging to him in spite of herself, or because of herself, because she wanted to feel him close to her so badly, and time was so short.

"Callie," he breathed against her skin. He held her cheeks between his palms. "Callie." He kissed her again. "I do look forward to this."

She gathered her wits enough to pull back a little. "You don't—I mean—we needn't pretend here, you know."

He laughed under his breath. "And decline the opportunity?" He held his hands at her waist and rocked her. "I have you in my evil clutches now, my lady. You may consider yourself lured to your doom."

It was only too true that he had her in his power. She seemed helpless to say or think a sensible thing. A part of her was looking on, warning her of peril in her father's troubled voice, but the most of her was simply full of joy at being here, at touching him, at being free to look up and return his smile without fear that anyone might notice.

It was only three days. It was a lark. Whatever Trev was—wild and a rogue and a teller of lies and tales—he had never abandoned her or allowed her to be hurt on one of their adventures. He'd always played the mother hen, constantly making certain she was safe and warning her of jeopardy, insisting that she remain in the background, so that it was all rather like a game in which she participated from within a cradle of his protection.

They were friends. There was nothing more to it, of course. Merely very dear friends.

But she had three days to live in the one daydream she had never dared to indulge.

She felt the corners of her lips turn upward. She lifted her face and forgot herself, put aside the thought that she was a wallflower and a spinster lady of advancing years, forgot she wasn't beautiful, forgot anything but that she was standing in Trev's arms and he was holding her tight and close as he bent to taste her lips again. He slid his hands up the curve of her waist, taking her face between his palms. With slow deliberation, he kissed the corner of her mouth, and then her chin, and her nose, and her temple. Then he stood back and looked down at her.

Callie met his eyes. They both smiled at once, as if it were a conspiracy between them.

She pressed her palms together and held them over her mouth in excitement. She giggled. "Oh my!" she said in a muffled voice.

Trev's smile turned into a grin. His dark lashes lowered. "Do you know," he said, "when you smile at me that way, I'd like to..." He broke off his sentence and cleared his throat. "Well. Slay dragons, or something along that line."

"Mere dragons?" she inquired. "I was hoping it would be giant squids."

"Take care, wicked Callie, or I shall stop hedging and tell you what I'd like to do in fact."

"Is it something very wicked?" she asked expectantly.

"Very," he murmured, pulling her close at the waist. "You know I have a particular talent for that."

She moved her hips in a daring way and had the pleasure of seeing him close his eyes and draw in his breath. It felt a bold thing to do, but not entirely unfamiliar to her. And the look on his face was reward enough; he had that dreamy, hot expression, his lips parting in a slight smile. Callie put her arms around his neck, above the high collar of his coat. "Will you show me?" she whispered.

He gave a low groan. "Ah, a little, perhaps." His fingers toyed with the single button that held the upswept folds of the dress at her back. "Maybe just a little."

That was a familiar thing too. He had said it before—just a kiss, just a touch, he always said—like a promise between them that they could never keep. Each time it had gone a bit further, a little more dangerous, until that moment in her father's carriage that halted everything for good.

Callie held her breath as he worked the button. One layer at a time, her dress loosened. His fingers slid down into the open seam. Her father wasn't here now. There was no one to interfere, nothing to hold back the cascade of sensation as the gauze slipped and the dress fell from her shoulder. She tilted her head aside as he kissed the curve of her throat and pulled her hips up against him.

With a light direction, he urged her toward a chaise longue and drew her down with him. He didn't look at her; he kissed her shoulder while he unfastened the dress and pulled at all the pins that the modiste had so lovingly inserted to set her hat.

The headpiece swept to the floor, along with the gauzy veil and shawl. He pressed her back down on the sofa, both of them breathing quickly. Callie held on to his lapels. As she laid her head back, she moved her hands inside his coat, feeling the solid shape of his chest under a satin waistcoat.

He made a fervent sound and sat back a little, yanking his waistcoat open and his shirt free, so that she could spread her palms against his bare skin. He closed his eyes as she stroked her hands up and down. His chest rose and fell under her touch. He swore roughly under his breath. When she ran her fingers along the edge of his trousers, slipping them between the fabric and his skin, he opened his eyes, putting his hand over hers, stilling her.

Callie gave him a naughty look. She knew—she remembered what he liked, what he had taught her, though she had hidden it away in the darkest corners of her recollections until now. It was something she had only allowed herself to remember in the deepest black of night, alone in her bed, dreaming.

He growled and leaned over her, brushing her chemise down off her shoulder, pulling it down until she felt her breasts exposed, pressed upward as they were by the corset. He bent his head, kissing and licking at the edge of the stiff garment until he teased her nipple free.

Callie gasped and clutched at him as the sensation shot through her. His tongue on her was hot and sweet, tugging gently, then harder as she arched up to him. She heard small sounds of delight working in her own throat, impossible to smother.

She lost herself in it, this stolen moment. It was bliss. Everything around her was him: his weight on her and his hair brushing her chin, his skin warm beneath her hands. All modesty deserted her, discarded as freely as her hat had been tossed to the floor. She spread her legs and pressed her body up to his. The air seemed to leave her lungs. Waves of sensation made her breasts seem to swell and rise to the delicious pull.

When he broke away, she could hardly gather her wits and recall who and where she was. He turned from her, sitting up and leaning back against the wall, staring at the tea table. He released a deep exhalation and closed his eyes. "I think—we had best stop there," he said.

"Oh," she said, vastly disappointed. "Gooseberries."

He laughed, turning to lean down to her again, his face close to hers. "I want you far too much," he said. "Miss Gooseberry."

Her eyes widened. "You do?"

"Oh no, I'm just about to have an apoplexy, that's all."

"An apoplexy!" She stuck out the tip of her tongue at him. "I suppose we don't want that."

"No indeed. Where would Hubert be if I fell dead on the floor?"

"I expect I should have to call in Major Sturgeon," she said airily.

He nipped her shoulder hard enough to make her yelp. Then he nuzzled her throat. "That pompous flatfish? What would you want with him?"

Callie giggled. "If you must know, he said he would do anything for me," she informed him in an arch voice.

Trev drew back a little. "He did, did he? And just when did he make this satisfying offer?"

"He has called *several* times," she said. "He was *most* obliging."

She expected that Trev would laugh, but his face changed subtly, grew cooler. "Several times!" he said. "I suppose one can guess what his object is." He pushed away from her, leaning on one elbow, his back propped against the wall. "Has he proposed to you yet?"

Callie began to be sorry she had mentioned Major Sturgeon, even to tease. It was hardly the moment to bring up the most persistent admirer of her fortune. She bit her lip.

"Has he?" Trev sat up. He began to tuck in his shirt and rebutton his waistcoat.

When Callie didn't reply, he stood, leaving her amid the disarray of her skirts and chemise. She pulled the fabric over herself and sat up also.

"Of course he has," Trev said. His mouth formed a hard line. "Did you fob him off?"

Callie held the dress to her breast. "I suppose I should have," she said faintly.

"You didn't?" His voice held a slight crack. "You're engaged to him?"

"No," Callie said. "Of course not."

He blew out a harsh breath. Callie watched him uncertainly. A notion occurred to her, one that she wished for so much that she didn't even dare entertain it for more than an instant. He took a few paces across the room. She thought he might speak. He stopped before the window and stood with his hand gripped on the drape, staring out.

"So you refused him?" he asked without turning.

She would have liked to say that she had. It seemed worse than a disgrace now, it seemed a betrayal to be here with Trev, to want him beyond anything else, and yet be entertaining a proposal from another man. But it was not as if Trev had asked for her hand. Indeed, he said he was going away back to France. And he had said nothing to suggest that he desired to wed her and take her home to his estates. She might indulge in a great number of fantastical daydreams, but that was one fantasy that she ruthlessly denied to herself.

She straightened and lifted her chin, pushing back a lock of her hair that had fallen loose. "I told him that I would consider it."

He gave a brief, cold nod, as if he had expected it.

"I don't think I'll be happy living with Hermey." She felt compelled to explain. "And so…" Her voice trailed off. "Well, I said to him I would think it over."

He tilted his head back and gave a short laugh. "Sturgeon!" he said bitterly. He turned to her. "I don't trust him, Callie. It's your money he wants."

"Yes," she said stiffly. "Of course."

He frowned at her, his jaw working.

She kept her chin lifted. "It would be foolish to expect at this juncture that I would marry out of affection or anything of that nature. If I married at all."

He stood looking at her, and then he shook his head. He put his hands up and ran them through his hair, as if he were quarreling with some recalcitrant and impossible child. He laughed again, a little wildly. "Accept him, then!" he exclaimed. "Why not? What's love to do with it, after all?"

She rose to her feet, gathering the white shawl from the floor. "I only told him I would think about it. But Hermey's fiancé doesn't want me. And I can't remain at Shelford. I won't. Trev, I don't know what I'm to do! If you—if I thought for a moment, if I thought that you—" She stopped, unable to complete the sentence, angry that she had said so much. She turned her back, clutching the dress and shawl against herself.

A heavy silence filled the chamber. Callie could hear her own breathing, rough with gathering tears. She stared at the mahogany leg of a chair, waiting for what she knew would not come, feeling her heart break with foolish hopes, fruitless wishes. The words that he didn't say hung between them.

"Of course I have no right to question you," he said in a low voice. "I beg your pardon."

She could think of no reply. She squeezed her eyes shut as she heard him come behind her. He put his hands on her bare shoulders, a light, warm touch that was like a sweet ache all down through her body.

"I want you to be happy," he whispered. "I don't want him to hurt you again."

She shook her head wordlessly. All she could think was that he would go away, and not take her, and it hardly mattered what she did then. He put his face down in the curve of her neck.

"I know," he said softly, as if she had spoken her misery aloud. "I know." He sighed, his breath a warmth against her skin. "We have a few days."

"Three," she said in a small voice.

He ran his hands down her arms and back up again, then held her against him, his lips at her throat. "Callie, I do love you. You know that."

She shook her head again, very quickly. "Don't," she implored. "Do not suppose you have to say that. I know you're my friend, my very best friend, and—that is quite enough."

"Friend," he said with a slight, derisive laugh. "Your friend." With a fierce move he clasped her hard and kissed her, burying his face in her shoulder. "Give me these three days, Callie."

She made a whimper of assent, nodding.

"It'll be our finest adventure," he whispered. "I promise you." He lifted his head and drew a deep breath against her hair. Then he slipped the chemise up over her shoulders and pulled the dress into place. With a few authoritative tugs, he buttoned the fabric over the tight corset while Callie held in her breath and smoothed down the front.

For a moment he stood behind her, resting his cheek on her head and holding her gently. Then he reached down and retrieved her hat.

"Now we must set you to rights and embark upon our first mission," he said briskly. "Procuring a steady source of Bath buns."

Thirteen

HAVING TAKEN DOWN AN ORDER, IN SPITE OF THE heavy accent of his customer, for twelve dozen Bath buns to be delivered daily to the exhibition pen of Monsieur Malempré, an elated baker escorted Monsieur and Madame into the street. He took leave of them with a surfeit of bowing and repeated pledges that his buns would most assuredly contain a generous measure of white currants. Having bespoke the buns, at a price so outrageous that it would have embarrassed His Majesty's pastry chef, Trev took Callie's arm and turned her toward the High Town.

He kept his hat brim low and gave the veiled lady on his arm the benefit of his full attention and gallantry. He was not overly concerned that Hubert would be recognized in the city of Hereford, but he was not so sanguine about himself. Here in the marches of the West Country, close by to Bristol—that first-rate source of burly butchers' boys anxious to enter the prize ring—the very soil seemed to produce prime pugilists. Trev had always limited his own scouting to the south and east, deliberately avoiding Hereford and Shelford and Callie, but he would be a fool to count himself perfectly safe here. He was too well-known among the Fancy.

Jock and Barton had been busy chasing up old acquaintance for the past several days, calling in all favors on Trev's behalf. And he had a wealth of credit to call upon, he found, for the thing he'd done for Jem Fowler's wife and baby boy. The hefty green-coated footman who now walked behind the Malemprés had only recently been pummeling a challenger in some set-to in a Bristol training yard. Across the way lounged a pair of regular brutes in the science, who owed their success and early opportunities largely to Trev's patronage. The men assigned to handle Hubert were experienced both in cattle yards and prizefights. There was a marvelous influx of boxing men to Hereford at the moment.

For his own part, Trev had discarded his Belcher necktie and adopted a sword cane and several other sartorial details to camouflage himself as a continental beau rather than a sporting buck. Walking beside Callie now, he regretted having chosen the name Malempré for their masquerade—he'd been in a hurry, arranging for the van and commanding the painting of the canvas to swathe Hubert's pen, and the first name he'd summoned to mind was a town in Belgium where he'd spent a few weeks of his imprisonment just after Napoleon's first abdication.

It had been an easy enough situation there. On his gentleman's honor to attempt no escape, he'd had the freedom of the pretty village and even waltzed at the *assemblée*. The sole inconvenience had been the wife of the local chevalier, who had conceived a most ardent fondness for Lieutenant LeBlanc on the basis of a single trifling kiss, which no amount of diplomacy—or indeed, discourtesy—had seemed to cool. She had been so relentless in her pursuit that he'd become the butt of the captive officers' mess until he was moved to Brussels to await a prisoner exchange that had never materialized—the defeated French apparently having no pressing need for one more LeBlanc littering their countryside.

He'd forgot about her until this morning, and that her name was also Malempré—a silly oversight that annoyed him. It seemed almost an insult to Callie. But it was too late to change now. He carried in his inner pocket several copies of a broadside imprinted with the handsome image of a dark bull and the breathless details of the Malempré Challenge:

The CERTIFIED Measurements of the Celebrated BELGIAN BULL of Malempré! Freshly Arrived in England, to Tour the Entire Country! The PRIZE offered to Any BULL of Any Breed that can be Proven GREATER in All Dimensions! 500 GUINEAS and a Silver Salver with the NAME of the Winner ENGRAVED beneath its Likeness!

He had made sure that Colonel Davenport would be absent for the formal announcement by the simple expedient of putting a man to spy on him and discovering his schedule. The good colonel was engaged this morning to determine which farm laborer had the honor of Supporting the Largest Number of Legitimate Offspring without Recourse to the Parish, for a prize of two pounds, and thereafter to judge turnips. Presumably he would be fully occupied in the counting of children and adjudicating of root vegetables, and unable to attend the public proclamation that Trev had arranged to give under the auspices of the president of the Agricultural Society. The colonel would not remain long in the dark, however, as Trev had caused a copy of the Challenge to be delivered to him by hand, courtesy of Monsieur Malempré, along with a bottle of excellent French wine to rub salt in the wound.

Trev had at first felt a twinge of guilt over leading Davenport a dance, but then he'd thought of how the fellow had taken Callie's bull and refused to sell it back for an honest price. When he remembered her tearstained cheeks hidden under the bonnet, his brief qualm vanished, replaced by a chilly desire to carve a liberal piece out of anyone who made her unhappy. Knowing that he himself was not entirely blameless in that regard did nothing to diminish his ire, but rather made him more inclined to exact revenge on whatever culprit he could reach.

"Something is amiss, Monsieur?" Callie asked in a worried tone, gamely keeping to French as she looked up sideways at him through the netting.

Trev realized that he was scowling, and softened his expression. "I beg your pardon," he replied, smiling down at her. "I was meditating on the shocking cost of pastries in this town."

"I understand you," she said with feeling. "Mrs. Farr would take to her smelling salts if she knew."

"We must pray that my bank will stand against the strain. But we have an hour or two before we issue our announcement—what would you like to do? Take in the shops?"

"I would rather look at the animals," she said. She spoke very pretty French, he thought, when she would venture to do so. It made him want to kiss her, to brush his mouth against her lips while she formed the words. "Would it be possible?"

"Certainly. Whatever would please you the best, ma chérie." He flourished his cane and pointed as they turned the corner to the wide street that was filling rapidly with all manner of livestock for the show. Under the shadow of the cathedral spire, the scent of a barnyard permeated the air. "Where shall we begin? Let us critique the pigs!"

"Do you make a study of pigs, Monsieur?" she asked, with a muffled note of amusement.

"Of course. I've observed them frequently on my breakfast plate." They had neared the first of the pens, where a stockman was lovingly bathing the ears of an enormously fat spotted sow. Five piglets squealed and gurgled about her panting bulk. "Note the marvelous coil of the tail." He gestured with his cane. "Absolute perfection!"

"And those ears," Callie said, nodding sagely. "She appears to have two!"

"Four legs," Trev added, cataloging all her points.

"Are you certain she has legs?" Callie asked dubiously. "I don't see any."

"They are hidden under her porcine vastness," he informed her. He tilted his head speculatively as they reached the pen. "Unless she has wheels. Perhaps she rolls from place to place?"

The handler glanced up, startled to hear a language not his own. Seeing a fashionable lady and gentleman observing him, he straightened up and pulled his forelock, red-faced.

"An animal *par excellence,*" Trev said in thickly accented English as he indicated the pig with an

approving nod. He reached inside his coat and drew
forth one of the printed broadsides. "Myself, I have
a bull."

The stockman took the bill and perused it with a
serious air. He seemed to read it, though Trev had
made sure there were numerals in addition to words,
for the edification of the illiterate. A working man
might not have book learning, but the number of
guineas was something that anyone would comprehend. "Looks to be a dead gun, sir," the stockman
said politely.

Trev was well aware of the local vernacular, but he
affected surprise. "Dead? No, he is alive, very much,
I assure you!"

"Aw, no sir, I mean to say, he looks a dead good
'un, sir. Them's his length and breadth, in'net?"

"And five hundred gold, you see there," Trev
pointed out, "to say there is none to match him."

The stockman grinned, showing spaces in his teeth.
He shook his head. "Naw, sir, I fear you'll be losing
it. Him's a good big 'un you got there, but we've the
biggest old bull ever you seen, right here, comin' up
today from Shelford."

"Indeed!" Trev said. "But I must see this animal.
Who belongs to him?"

"Colonel Davenport has him now, but 'tis his late
lordship's bull. The Earl of Shelford, sir. They call
him Hubert."

"Ah yes." Trev nodded wisely. "Of this bull I have
had a great description. With red and black—how do
you say this—the spots—ah, mottles, eh? Hubert." He
gave it the French pronunciation, "Oo-bear". "I long
to see him!"

"You'll see him, sir. Can't miss him, can you? He's the size of a house."

Trev turned to Callie and said in rapid French, "Good. Better to raise the challenge first, before they all learn he's gone missing." He patted her arm and reverted to English again. "And what do you think of this lovely pig, Madame?"

"A peeg of the first merit," she said obligingly, with such an earnest copy of his overwrought enunciation that Trev found it difficult to keep a straight countenance.

"Indeed," he agreed. "Great good luck to you with this peeg, *mon ami.*"

The stockman thanked Trev with a gruff acknowledgment. They left him turning to his curious neighbor with the broadside stretched out in his hand. From there, Trev was quite certain, the word would spread. He had planted news of a bout often enough to know how quickly intelligence could travel.

"But deplorably fat," Callie murmured as they walked away. "I cannot approve of it. She will overheat."

Trev nodded gravely. "I thought I smelled bacon burning."

She gave a gurgle of laughter under her veil but then added in a troubled tone, "It's not really a funning matter, though. It's become all the rage amongst the cottagers to show a poor pig so fat that it cannot even get up without help. I fear they suffer for it. I mean to write a letter to the society. I place full blame upon the judges for encouraging it."

He smiled. Only his Callie would champion the cause of leaner pigs for the greater good of pigdom. "I daresay they will be eager to know your view of the matter." He escorted her round a table where a woman was laying out molds of cheese in an artistic fashion.

"Of course they won't," she said wryly. "They will say that they are only pigs, and I am only a female—but pigs are most intelligent and feeling, I assure you. I taught one to play a wooden flute once."

"A flute!"

She nodded. "I secured it between a pair of fire-dogs, and he soon learned that he could procure a bit of molasses if he made a note upon it. I stopped the holes for him, and he would play 'Baa Baa Black Sheep.'"

"*Mon dieu.*" He shook his head. "And I was not there to see it." He slid his fingers between hers, so that their hands were clasped where they rested on his arm. She tilted her head aslant, glancing up at him, but he could not detect her expression through the veil. He wasn't sure if she knew just how difficult it had been for him to break off from their lovemaking. He was in a state of exquisite torment even to walk beside her, with her shoulder brushing his at every step. It was he who had conceived this grand plan of a manufactured marriage, but he found now that what had seemed as if it would be a diverting amusement was in fact a bittersweet ordeal.

If they had been married in truth, he would not have been strolling through a street full of straw and bawling calves, that was a certainty. He would have had her on the sofa—no, not the sofa, in the bed, stretched out on the sheets in very daylight, a long and slow and leisurely discovery of her white skin and golden red curls.

"I shall write to the officers of the Agricultural Society, in any event," she continued. "I would even—" She paused. "Well, they would never invite me to speak at the monthly meeting, so I needn't fear that, but I *would*."

He really very badly wanted to pull her up against him right there in the midst of the street and kiss her ruthlessly. "You are a heroine," he said, lifting her fingers briefly to his lips. "A heroine of overstout pigs everywhere!"

"I doubt even the pigs would thank me," she admitted with a rueful chuckle. "I'm sure they like their liberal dinners."

"Then you are my heroine," he said warmly.

Her fingertips moved slightly under his as she peeked up at him. He found that their slow stroll had stopped somehow; he was distantly aware of geese honking from inside their crates to his left, and a woman carrying a red hen on his right, but he stood looking down at Callie like a callow boy gazing helplessly at the adored object of his affections, unable to see more than a hazy shadow of her face but knowing just what her shy sparkling smile was beneath the veil.

He was not a man who thought much of the future. He'd had enough of the expectations and demands of his grandfather's extravagant fantasies as a boy. In the early days of his boxing promotions, he'd had dreams of backing Jem Fowler to the Championship of England, until that ended in the bout that killed Jem and left his wife and baby on Trev's hands. It was a lesson. There were no more friends of his heart in the ring.

He maintained no ambitions for himself beyond arranging the next prize bout or making good on the betting books he held. His very detachment was his strength. With no particular desires or emotions to burden his judgment of the outcome, he was very good at what he did. It did not ruin him to pay out on a losing stake, because he never made odds that would break him.

It made no odds for him to think of the future now, but he couldn't seem to help himself. It wasn't a real future; it was this moment of smiling down at her, extended somehow into tomorrow, and the next day and the next, and he would never have to say that he must go, or put her hand away from his, or hide what he felt, or lie. He was profoundly weary of lies. He wished to be himself—if he could have settled on any notion of who he might be.

Both of them seemed to realize at the same instant that they were stopping the way. Callie gave a slight "oh!" and Trev stepped aside, escorting her up onto the pavement to avoid a goat cart that desired to pass. As he raised his eyes from the curb and looked ahead down the crowded street, he saw the certain end of any wishful reveries.

"Sturgeon!" he uttered, forgetting himself far enough to lapse into English. "God curse the man."

Callie went stiff beside him. She gripped his arm and craned her neck to see past the crowd.

"Don't look," he said, quickly turning her away and reverting to French. "He's down beside the Green Dragon. The devil seize him, what's he doing here?" They were walking now away from the danger, Trev restricting himself with an effort to a more casual pace. He had thought Sturgeon had departed for London yesterday, when Colonel Davenport came up to Hereford. That had been the word from Jock. He paused for a moment, catching the eye of the "footman" who had been dogging them at a respectful distance.

The burly boxer came forward, bending his bewigged head to listen as Trev murmured to him. Charles gave a brief nod as he took his instructions and stood back again, folding his hands behind him.

"It seems I'm forced to be suddenly unwell, chérie," Trev said to Callie, pulling the sheaf of broadsides from his coat. "I'm afraid you'll have to make the announcement. Noon, at the prize platform."

"Me!" She gasped. "Oh no, I—"

"You must, love," he said. "I'm sorry. I can't let myself be recognized, or we'll all be in the soup. You won't have to speak to the crowd. Just hand one of these to the secretary and ask him to read it aloud on my behalf. Tell them I've been taken ill with a headache but will be better presently. You needn't say much—remember that you don't speak English well. Charles here will fetch the salver and the coins to display just before you take to the stage."

"But—"

"No, attend to me." He touched her shoulder, cutting her off. "Go back to the dressmakers' afterward to change. Lilly will be looking for you. Make some sort of appearance as yourself this afternoon—see to your animals, walk out with Lilly. I'm going back to Dove House for the night, to Maman, but I'll send word to you early tomorrow." He pressed the papers into her unwilling hand. Without lingering to answer her stammer of objections, he tipped his hat and kissed her fingers, and left her alone with Charles in the street.

Callie stood on the wooden platform with several of the officers of the society, feeling as if everyone in the crowd could see right through her veil. She hoped that Trev had made certain that her hair didn't show where the net was gathered at her nape. There were familiar faces in the audience—Farmer Lewis and Mr. Downie and any number of men who knew her perfectly well, waiting with looks of interest and speculation as the secretary of the Agricultural Society stepped to the fore. The colonel was not there—Trev had assured her he wouldn't be, but she was distressed to find that Major Sturgeon seemed to have some unaccountable interest in an event which should have held no importance to him whatsoever. She had told him during one of his visits that she would be attending the show, and he had nodded with polite but hardly urgent attention. She could not conceive of why he had come to Hereford at all, far less why he should linger about the platform as the early cattle classes were announced. She very much feared that he suspected something.

She did not dare to look directly toward him, but it seemed as if he were watching her while Mr. Price droned out the list of classes and the prizes that would be awarded for each. When he'd finished with the list of events, the club secretary turned and bowed deeply to Callie, and then took up Trev's broadside and read it through his glasses in a loud, official voice.

A murmur went through the crowd as the challenge was described. Charles lifted the heavy silver tray above his head. The trophy glinted in the sun as he turned left and right to show it off. Men in the audience elbowed one another, exchanging looks. There were a number of cattle breeders who had brought bulls to the show, but Callie was sure that not one of them approached Hubert's size. Still, with a such a grand prize, there was an eager push forward to sign animals onto the list of hopeful contestants for measure.

Mr. Price turned to her, beaming. It was a fine boost to the show, to have such an unusual and valuable challenge, he informed her with enthusiasm. Nothing could be better to generate excitement and bring attention. All the society officials were eager to attend to her, inquiring after her husband's health with some anxiety. Callie tried to assure them with a good many nods and a few broken English phrases that he was only feeling the effects of their recent journey.

Her stifled utterances were smothered entirely by the realization that Major Sturgeon had made his way onto the platform. As she stood frozen in dismay, he spoke to the president. That gentleman turned to her with a smile.

"Madame," he said gaily, "here's someone who tells me that he's visited your beautiful country and wishes an introduction. May I have the honor?"

Callie stared through her veil, not finding any way to avoid it without throwing herself bodily from the platform into the crowd. She gave a slight nod, turning her face downward so that the brim of her hat obscured her face even further.

"I give you Major Sturgeon, Madame," the president said. "Major, this is our honored guest, Madame Malempré, who adds such a mark of nobility to our humble agricultural affair!"

Callie allowed the major to take her hand, giving a faint curtsy as he bent over it.

"I am enchanted!" he said. He leaned close to her and said in a confiding voice, "But I have been to Malempré myself, Madame, and found it to be a charming place."

For an instant she felt as if she would simply dissolve, sinking to the floor in a puddle of terror. He had been to Malempré. She had no idea where Malempré was, except that it was presumably somewhere in Belgium. Never having been to Belgium, she could not even summon a speculation as to what sort of place it might be, if it was large or small, flat or mountainous, busy or rural. It might be dotted with pagodas and Chinamen for all she knew. Far worse, she didn't know if a visitor to Malempré would be likely to have met a Madame and Monsieur Malempré there.

"I do not... well speak," she said hesitantly, keeping her face lowered and her voice pitched low to disguise it.

He retained her hand in spite of her attempt to withdraw it. "Ah, I must beg your pardon," he replied in fluent French, lifting her fingers to his lips. "My command of your delightful language is poor, but let us converse in it."

His command of French appeared to be all too excellent. The veil seemed to become suffocating. "I must sit down!" she said faintly, drawing her hand away. She turned to the steps, but she could not avoid him. He caught her elbow and supported her as she went down the wooden steps.

"Come this way," he said, his grip firm as he directed her toward the door of the nearest inn. "Stand aside!" he barked in English. "Let the lady pass!"

The crowd parted at his sharp command. Callie

found herself helpless, propelled by his supporting arm about her waist in spite of attempts to draw back. She dreaded to enter the inn with him, where there would doubtless be a great fuss made over a lady feeling faint. They might even encourage her to remove her veil.

She allowed him to escort her as far as the walkway and then set her feet. "Monsieur, do not trouble yourself." She disengaged herself firmly. "If you please!" She put a little acid into her voice and made a point of removing his hand from her arm.

He stiffened for an instant and then bowed his head. "I beg you will consider me your humble servant, Madame! Are you feeling better?"

Callie took a deep breath. Seeing no other recourse open to her, she plunged with a whole heart into a masquerade of a haughty lady, bridling up and giving him a sideways glance of disdain. "I am well," she said coolly. "I do not believe I know you, Monsieur."

He stood quite still for a moment, looking at her with such intensity that she was sure he was trying to see through the veil. She turned her face away abruptly, fearing he would suddenly shout out her real name to the street.

"Of course," he said in an oddly light tone, doffing his plumed hat in the face of this direct cut. "But how could I be so foolish as to suppose you would remember me by name? I was among the liaison officers after the abdication. You were so kind as to open your home to us and give a luncheon al fresco, to celebrate the liberation of your country."

"Ah," Callie said, silently cursing Trev and his choice of towns and names. She put up her chin. "Yes, the picnic. You were there? I have a poor head for faces, Monsieur. A strange chance, to encounter you here, is it not? But you must pardon me, I will attend my husband now."

To her despair, he turned with her, persisting in walking alongside. "And where do you stay in Hereford, Madame? I would be pleased to return your hospitality, if you and your husband would do me the honor of joining me for dinner."

"I must regret," she said. "Monsieur Malempré is resting."

"I am devastated." He sounded truly sorry. "I would wish to make some return of your kindness. I have never forgot that sunny day in your gardens."

"Have you not, Monsieur?" Callie walked quickly, but he kept pace.

"Madame." He put his hand on her elbow as she turned the corner. He seemed to have no qualms about touching her. "Never," he said intensely. "My God, how could I?"

She cast a look aside at him, startled by the fierce note in his voice. He stopped, holding her, and then let her go as if he realized what he was doing. Callie took advantage of that to turn away in the direction of the dressmaker's shop. She thought that surely he would not follow her that far. But he came with her, keeping up easily with his longer stride. She began to feel hunted, frightened that he had recognized her and was playing some sly game. For the whole distance of the street he walked alongside her, saying nothing.

As they approached the shop, she debated with herself furiously. He appeared determined to keep company with her in spite of any rudeness she could summon. She had intended to go into the shop to change and emerge as herself, but she was afraid now that he would even try to accompany her in, or linger outside. She did not dare to go in as Madame Malempré and come out as Lady Callista Taillefaire.

She slowed her steps as she neared the door. She saw Lilly lingering across the street. Trev's footman trailed at a respectful distance. Lilly stared a moment toward them with an uncertain look, then turned quickly away, giving a coy smile to a pair of large young fellows lounging in a tailor's door.

Callie paused. The dressmaker's shop was impossible. He could see inside it. She nodded shortly and said, "I will leave you here, Monsieur. I must go to our hotel."

"Sofie!" he said under his breath. "Don't do this to me, I beg you!"

She stared at him through the veil. An astonishing suspicion came to her. He could not mean—surely he did not mean—it was shocking enough that there seemed to be a real Madame Malempré who he had met, but he appeared to believe that he had far more than a passing acquaintance with her.

He took her hand. "Don't tell me you have truly forgotten me," he murmured. "The garden. The summerhouse. I know you might not recall my name, but—" He broke off, looking down. "It was not so much to you as to me, perhaps."

As the full import of his words sank in, Callie began to feel an upwelling of outrage. He not only knew this Madame Malempré, but it was becoming quite clear that he'd had some romantic encounter with her in a summerhouse. And it appeared that he would be quite willing to renew the acquaintance, in spite of the fact that he had been diligently courting Callie for the past week.

As the realization sank in, a new recklessness possessed her, the sort of feeling that she had not experienced in a very long time. Not since her last adventure with Trev, in fact, in which she had been obliged to steal a melon from a canvas bag and replace it with a large hedgehog. Instead of marching away, she allowed the major to take her gloved fingers to his lips.

He smiled over her hand. "You have not forgot," he whispered. "Tell me it is so."

From the corner of her eye, Callie could see that Charles had drawn closer. His bulk towered over the major's height. At a word, she thought, she could have Major Sturgeon deposited in a watering trough. The picture of it made her give a low laugh as she let him kiss her hand. "Forget?" she asked noncommittally. "What do you mean, Monsieur?"

He turned away from Charles, drawing her arm through his, leaning very close to her ear. "Is it your husband?" he murmured. "I didn't think he was a jealous man."

Callie's heart beat faster. She found it difficult to believe that he did not recognize her from so close. But if he did, he was playing a very deep game. She should repulse him immediately, she was sure, but the desire to take some small revenge was growing.

"You must have a better knowledge of him than I, if you suppose that," she said.

"But it's not very handsome of him to leave you alone at a dirty cattle fair, Madame."

Callie instantly wanted to protest that the Hereford

show maintained exceptionally high standards of cleanliness, but she suppressed her annoyance. "He has the headache," she said, allowing her fingers to play over his arm the way she had once seen Dolly do as she flirted discreetly with a gentleman houseguest. "Refresh my poor memory, Monsieur, if you please. I met you at the Waterloo picnic?"

His hand tightened on her a little. "I see that I made scant impression on you. I'm humbled. But a lady of your loveliness must have many admirers."

"You flatter me," she said, putting a sultry note into her voice. She was pleased to encourage him to suppose himself forgettable. "But there aren't so many. I'm very sorry—I cannot understand how I have not recalled you. The summerhouse...?" She let her words trail off suggestively.

"Perhaps you recall more than you wish to confess," he said. There was a hint of bitterness in his words.

"La, if only you would give me some hint. Some detail that might prod my memory."

"Are you angry with me, Sofie?" he asked huskily. Apparently it didn't suit him to believe any woman might not remember an encounter with him. "You know I could make you no promises, nor return again."

"Oh?" she asked with a dawning interest. "Why not?"

"You do remember!" he exclaimed instantly. "But then you know why, my love. How could I promise to come back, when I was to wed the moment I returned to England?"

"I see," Callie said. She stopped. She could feel her cheeks growing hot under the veil. "You were engaged to an English lady?"

He shrugged, walking on with her. "Yes. I told you then, Sofie. I didn't hide it. I thought you understood."

"So of course, you were in love."

He gave a brusque snort. "Nothing of the sort. In fact I didn't care for her—she's a chilly woman, with a dull wit and no beauty. What little time I had with you was precious, when I knew what I must go back to."

Callie blinked. She bit her lip. With a sense of turning a knife in her own breast, she said, "How sad for you, Monsieur. A man like you, to marry a plain woman."

"Not a pleasant prospect, I admit. But fate intervened, and I didn't marry her after all," he said.

"Fate?" she inquired with an effort. "Did you discover some prettier heiress?"

He took her hand, kissing it. "Of course not. Do you think me a fortune hunter? She died before the wedding."

Callie hid her gasp in a choked laugh. "What a fortunate escape for you, then! And still you didn't return to me?"

"I could not, my love. I was posted to the West Indies."

She stood frozen in sick amazement at his gall. After breaking off with her, he had wed Miss Ladd and gone to Norwich to have three children; he had not been posted to the West Indies. For a moment she could think of nothing to say. They had been strolling slowly, and the door of the Gerard lay only a few steps ahead. It seemed to her to be a portal of escape now, a place she could run away and hide. A furious part of her wanted to tear off her veil and reveal herself, but she could not be so rash in spite of the ugly lump in her throat. She had to be rid of him.

"It's a very affecting story, Monsieur," she said, assuming a cold hauteur. "I thank you for telling me, but still I don't recall anything of our meeting. I think perhaps you have confused me with another lady. Now I must leave you. Adieu."

She detached her arm forcibly from his clasp, in spite of his quick objection, and glanced back toward Charles. The footman came forward with a determined look on his face. Callie felt a wave of relief as the big servant imposed himself between her and Major Sturgeon. Charles escorted her up the steps. She dared to glance back once and was alarmed to see that the major followed them right into the hotel. She hurried her pace, going directly to the staircase. Only when she reached the upper floor did she pause, catching her breath. He hadn't the effrontery to pursue her that far, at least.

She looked at Charles. "*Merci,*" she said in grateful French. "I did not know how to escape him."

"Ma'am, I don't speak that Froggie talk, I'm sorry." The footman bobbed his head apologetically.

"Oh." It was a relief to slip back into her own language. She'd thought he must be one of Trev's French retinue. "I'll be pleased to thank you in English, in that case! I'm very glad to be rid of him."

"Was that officer swell taking liberties, then, ma'am? I weren't certain. I'd 'a made a dice box of his swallow, if ma'am just give me the office."

His thick slang was almost as foreign to her as the French, but she understood his meaning. "Yes, I'm sure you would have, but I didn't wish to make a scene." She paused, not sure if she should speak openly of Trev's plans. "Do you know my maid, Lilly?"

"Aye, ma'am." He nodded toward the street. "The little chick-a-biddy what's giving Monsieur's bruisers the chaffin' gammon up the tailor shop."

She was entirely mystified by this description of Lilly's activities but decided not to inquire into it too deeply. "Go down and tell her to wait for me at the dressmaker's," she said, "but she mustn't let the major see her. I'll stay here until he goes away, and then I'll be obliged to you if you'll take me to join her."

"Now you just leave that officer nob to old Charlie, ma'am. We'll give him some proper pepper, me and Monsieur's lads. He'll bolt off right handy, or we'll dislodge some of his ivories for 'im."

"Oh no. No, you must not start a fight—is that what you mean?"

He shrugged. "Won't be much of a fight, ma'am," he said with some regret. "Not unless he's got a screw loose."

"I don't want any sort of fight at all," she said hastily.

"We'll just carry him out, then," Charles offered.

"No no, nothing of that sort. We mustn't draw undue attention."

The footman submitted to this, though he seemed disappointed. "S'pec so, ma'am. It might blow the gaff, aye."

Callie realized that under his powdered wig and formal coat, the muscular Charles was quite a "bruiser" himself. Trev seemed in the habit of hiring very large menservants, for which she was rather grateful at the moment.

"I think it's best to wait quietly until he leaves," she said. "I'm sure he won't linger." She only wanted be out of this disguise, to retreat into the safety of her own rooms to lick her wounds, but the chambers at the Gerard were at least a refuge for the moment. She was glad now that Trev was gone for the night, so that she wouldn't have to tell him of her encounter with the philandering major. Not, at least, until she had composed herself. "Send word up to me when you're certain that he's gone away entirely. Make sure of it first. I don't dare to let him see me again."

Fourteen

A FIRE BURNED GENTLY, WARMING THE ELEGANT PARLOR. The tea tray still stood waiting on the table set for two. If not for Major Sturgeon, she might have been sitting here cheerfully with Trev, celebrating the successful announcement of the Malempré Challenge. Instead she was feeling as if she had been soundly slapped. She took off the veil and sat down heavily.

She had not desired to marry the major, but with no other happy prospect before her, she had allowed herself to consider it as a practical possibility. A marriage of convenience merely, but at least she would have her own home. He was so eager to marry her fortune, she was sure that she could negotiate anything she pleased in terms of her livestock. She was not averse to a household with children in it. She had a talent with them, as she had a talent with animals.

Infidelity—she had assumed that she could tolerate that. It wasn't as if she hadn't known what sort of man he was already. If she had taken a moment to think it through, she wouldn't have been surprised to find him entangled with another woman again even as he courted her.

But knowing precisely what he thought of her, hearing it said so bluntly—she felt as if a miserable thick stone were lodged in her throat. He gave her pretty compliments to her face, while in fact he thought she was cold and plain and dull. And she was. It was the truth of it that made what he'd said so painful. She did not really care what Major Sturgeon thought of her, but he wasn't the only gentleman she knew who could tell a lie with convincing skill.

She sprang up, gripping her hands together as she paced to the fireplace and back again. A horrid notion began to possess her. It was mortifying to think of how much she must have revealed of herself to Trev. He meant to give her three days of happiness, in the best way that he could. Husband and wife, deep in love, a little pretense of what she longed to have.

How Lady Shelford and her friend would laugh at that! Dowdy Callie, wed to a man who might have a love affair with any woman he chose. And she would have to sit with her eyes fixed on the toes of her shoes and listen to the whispers about it. She would rather live in a ditch and eat worms.

With Major Sturgeon's cold words to steady her mind and prevent any flights of fancy, she tried to think back on the things Trev had said to her, the contradictions and awkward moments. He did care about her, she had no doubt of that. He didn't wish for her to be unhappy. He'd tried to buy Hubert back for her, he'd created this outlandish scheme to make an adventure for her, he worried that Major Sturgeon would hurt her. He said... he said that he loved her.

She should put no great stock in that, of course. Trev could not endure to see unhappiness around him.

Nearly every adventure she had shared with him had been a rescue of some hapless creature from captivity, or a clandestine attempt to emulate Robin Hood on behalf of a downtrodden victim. If truth be told, she had known him to go to absurd lengths in his efforts to heal the smallest hurt or suffering in those he cared for. And if he could not do it, he would disappear.

She felt a deep chill inside, a prickle at the nape of her neck. She squeezed her eyes shut, remembering how she had almost—almost—blurted her dream out loud to him. He had understood her perfectly, of course, but he had not betrayed it. It was like a play, and they each had their parts. She could be Madame Malempré and enjoy this moment that he offered, understanding that it was only as enduring as a single waltz, but better at least than sitting out every dance.

Callie's throat felt closed and swollen, but she did not weep. She felt no anger now when she thought of Major Sturgeon, only a vague distaste, and a sharp hole in her heart that was impossible to fathom. With mechanical moves she made tea for herself, pouring water into the polished kettle and placing it on an ornate hob beside the fire. She sat down, toying with one of the delicate slices of cake.

They were friends. She should not, could not, must not, think of more.

It calmed her to reach this conclusion. She had been struggling in a welter of confused feelings ever since his return, unable to make sense of his intentions. As it all came clear to her now, the heavy feeling in her chest receded. It was not as if she had ever really believed that she would marry Trev. She couldn't even imagine it, in truth: living in France among

strangers, dealing with aristocratic guests and the evil
Buzot and great vats of wine. It was as improbable as
her fantasies of Trev as a pirate and herself the captive
governess who stole his heart by learning to wield a
cutlass like a Cossack.

She smiled a little at her own absurdity. The kettle
began to boil, a soft rumble in the quiet room. Callie
made her tea and sat sipping it, trying to take a sensible
view of her future. It was high time that she left
behind these silly daydreams, before she became odd
and ended up locked in some attic, collecting bits of
string and candle wax and muttering.

She must exert herself to make the best of things
as they were. She was dull and plain; a definite
pronouncement had been made on the subject, and it
was stupid to argue the point any further, no matter
what Hermey and her father and the village goats
might claim. They loved her—at least Hermey and
her father did; she couldn't say about the goats—and
people who loved one saw a different person, a person
bathed in the flattering light of affection. Look at how
Hermey seemed so taken with Sir Thomas, who was
certainly as dull as Callie, and perhaps even duller.

No, to live out her life as a spinster sister, politely
unwanted, was impossible. She would marry Major
Sturgeon in spite of his faithlessness. There was no
other tolerable prospect. She knew the truth about
him, and while she didn't enjoy knowing, there could
be no further wound in it. Her eyes were open. It was
a common thing among the ton, she believed, for a
married couple to live quite-unrelated lives.

Before Trev went away, she would make sure
that he knew she had accepted the officer's very

flattering proposal. He wouldn't depart thinking she was unhappy with her choice. She had never lied to him before, but she would.

A gentle knock made her put down her cup. The boot boy's muffled voice spoke the name of Madame briefly as he slipped a folded paper underneath the door. She stood and peered down at the handwriting.

Major Sturgeon had not yet given up and gone away, it seemed. The preposterous man—he had sent up a letter, which Callie put into the fire without breaking the seal. She had a pretty exact idea of what it would say. He must be desperate indeed, to be so rash as to send a missive to the very chamber where Monsieur Malempré himself was supposed to be resting with the headache! No doubt the thought that he might find himself engaged at any moment to the tedious Lady Callista made him wish to cement a more agreeable alliance at once.

For an instant she wished Trev were there to share the bleak comedy of it all. She laughed in spite of herself, thinking of what he would say about Sturgeon lurking at the hotel door and writing fraught pleas to Callie under the illusion that she was his long-lost paramour.

Just what the world needs: more bloody fools.

In the wee hours of the morning, a sleepy groom threw a blanket over Trev's horse and led it away, its breath frosting in the lantern light. After a warm autumn afternoon, the wind had arisen and the temperatures dropped suddenly to a bone-cracking cold. By the time Trev reached Hereford, well after midnight, his muffler was frozen and his hands were stiff inside his gloves.

Fortunately he'd left word that he would return late. The boots unlocked the door promptly, greeted him in a cordial, low voice, relieved him of his great coat, and led him upstairs with a shielded candle. The service at the Gerard was excellent.

Trev sat down by the fire, pleased to see that it was still well tended. He allowed the boy to pull off his boots, gave him a generous coin, and then sent him away, murmuring that he could do for himself tonight. By the red glow of the coals he stripped, feeling prickly sensation come into his toes as they warmed after a long ride in the icy night. He sat drowsing in his shirttails, his bare feet stretched out beside the fire.

He'd lingered late with his maman, for she'd been in a lively humor, full of questions and gentle gibes, laughing over the portly "peeg," and demanding a full description of what the couturier had done for Lady Callista's wardrobe. She'd scowled at the intrusion of Major Sturgeon, as engaged in the difficulties as if she'd been in the midst of the Hereford scheme herself. He could see that she expected him to announce at any moment that Callie had agreed to marry him. He did not disabuse her of this notion. To be perfectly candid, he might even have encouraged it a little, because it pleased him to see her look so knowing and contented, smiling like a cat over a bowl of fresh cream.

What difference did it make? He'd not yet brought himself to mention anything about putting her affairs in order. His maman didn't have any affairs that he knew of anyway—there were those spiritual matters that the Reverend Hartman had been so eager to address, of course, but he could leave that to her priest. She didn't appear as if she were going to fail within a short time. She seemed to him to be improving each night that he visited her, with more energy and strength, but the doctor had warned him to take no comfort from that.

He sighed heavily, standing up. His nightclothes were in the bedchamber, but he'd sent the candle away with the boots, so he pulled his shirt over his head and left his clothes by the fire in the parlor. He padded to the closed door. The bedroom was pitch-black, the air frigid. He moved quickly across the cold floor, feeling his way by the faint light of the fire through the door. The bed curtains were already closed, a good sign that the maid would have put a hot brick between the sheets. He climbed hurriedly into the warm cavern of the bed.

He froze in the motion of pulling the bedclothes over himself. A flash of alarm went through him as someone turned over—someone waiting in the bed—he reached instinctively for his pistol, found himself naked, and then just as suddenly relaxed, lying back on the pillow with a low, surprised laugh.

"Callie?" he whispered, feeling toward her in the dark. Her warm, sweet hay scent filled the close confines of the bed; her hair was spread loose over the counterpane. He touched her shoulder—shocked to find it bare—and she responded with a sleeper's sigh, a delicate sound that spoke to his body like a wild flute in a dark, beckoning forest.

He was instantly aflame for her. He had kept it brutally at bay until now, using every mental trick he'd ever learned from his grandfather and the considerably more crude methods he'd discovered on his own. He'd always prided himself on his self-control concerning women. In the circles he frequented, it had served him well on more than one occasion. At seven and twenty, he had no bastards or vengeful mistresses to trouble him. He conducted his love affairs the same way he conducted his business, with cold caution and ruthless disinterest.

But it had cost him. Until this moment he had not known how much. He carried always a slow simmer of lust—that was as much a part of his life as breathing. The loneliness he dealt with. He thought he did. He could just see a coppery glint, an outline of her hair riding down in a lovely curve to the shape of her hips, and suddenly it was as if every time he had denied himself was compounded and concentrated, years of turning away, of sleeping alone, all coalesced into this one warm girl in his bed.

He held himself still, staring into the dark toward her, trying to bring sense and distance to the hot physical flood that engulfed him. If this was an offer, it was an unexpected one. She should have been at the Green Dragon for the night—he was sure he'd explained that clearly to her. Callie had always been careful to attend to every detail of her role in their adventures—she was too nervous of making a mistake to do otherwise.

He didn't think she'd misunderstood him. And Lilly wasn't here to provide propriety. But then, Lilly belonged to Lady Callista, not to Madame Malempré. And he'd said he wouldn't be back until morning. He was having difficulty thinking rationally with the feel of her hair drifting over his bare arm, the soft shape of her body pressing down the feather bed. He ached with a longing that was lust and something beyond lust, almost a sickness of desire. He tried to reason it, to tell himself that whatever the circumstance or error, he'd best get up and leave the bed, but his mind wasn't making much headway against his body.

He turned abruptly onto his back and lay staring upward, listening to her soft breath. He should sleep in the sitting room. He could close the door and ring for coffee—roust the poor boots off his cot again and annoy the kitchen staff. Or just dress and go downstairs to the parlor.

He ran his hand over his face and then thrust it through the curtains, testing the freezing air outside. He drew back quickly. The bed was thoroughly warmed where she lay, an invitation drawing him near. He moved a little closer to her, pulling the counterpane over her bare arm where her skin had cooled in the open air. She stirred but did not waken. He tucked it around her, trying to be protective, or something like it. He didn't want her to be cold.

He laughed silently at his own excuses, turning fully toward her and putting his arm across her shoulders. She felt indescribably soft, moving a little, settling into him. There was a thin slip of silk between them, some low-cut confection that pressed tight across her breasts. He could feel them, their tips taut against the inside of his arm.

He was going to die. He really thought it possible. He knew a number of ways to make love safely, to please a woman without undue risk, but he wanted to fumble now like a untaught boy, so hot he could not think past the fact that he could feel her nipples. His ears were roaring. Memories of erotic kisses they had shared engulfed him, instants of passion that he had carried in his memory for years, the images he used to take his own pleasure.

He held himself very still and ran his fingertip around one small nub, feeling it rise in response. Her leg stretched out, sliding along his as she sighed in her sleep. She had wanted more this afternoon; he told himself he would satisfy her now. Gratify her and please her and go no further.

He bent his forehead against the nape of her neck, his mouth and jaw locked in an ironic smile. Self-controlled lover that he was, he was trembling, his full member pressed against her just below her buttocks. He'd never been in a bed with Callie. He doubted he was able to move without losing mastery of himself.

She stirred, rolling over toward him. He pulled back, feeling her awaken, expecting her to jerk away and cry out in surprise. But she only stiffened a little, holding herself still. His hand was resting on her shoulder.

"Trev," she mumbled drowsily.

"Wicked Callie," he whispered.

She came into his embrace suddenly and fully, making a thankful little sound, as if she'd been having a nightmare and awoken to find safety. He drew her tight against him in spite of his arousal, touched to his heart by the simple way she reached for him.

"I couldn't leave," she said, her face buried in his throat. "I didn't know what to do."

"It's all right," he said against her temple.

"Major Sturgeon followed me. He's taken a room here."

"Meddlesome devil." He might have been alarmed by this news at some other time, but he had scant interest in Sturgeon just now.

She held him close, but he could feel a change come into her, a dawning awareness of the state of his body, of their entanglement together. He felt her swallow.

"But I thought—you weren't to come back tonight," she whispered.

"Mmmm," he said, nuzzling her face. "Do you want me to go away?"

She let out an unsteady breath, a half-surprised, half-scared flutter of sound. It made him want to roll her onto her back and take her fiercely, all caution tossed away to the cold night outside.

For a long moment she was silent. He could feel her heart beating, the light touch of her hair falling across his skin.

"I should go," he said reluctantly, when she didn't speak.

Her arms tightened. "No," she said in a small voice. "Stay."

His breath left his chest. He almost wished that she had banished him. He wasn't in command of himself. "You want to kill me," he muttered, only half in jest.

She shook her head, a movement in the dark against his throat. "I want... everything," she whispered, the words a mere breath of air on his skin. "I don't want to stop this time."

Trev lay very still, closing his eyes as a wave of white-hot urgency possessed him. He turned onto his back, his arm flung wide, a low laugh in his chest. "It would be heaven, wouldn't it?"

"Do you think so?" she whispered, and he could see her face in his mind, her soft, shy eyes looking up at him like a wild deer watching from the wood.

He laughed aloud. "My God, Callie, have a little mercy. We'd better not start it. A man can only go so far and contain himself."

"Oh," she said.

It was not that she sounded disappointed or miffed or offended, the way any number of women of his past had sounded when he had tactfully refused their very agreeable offers. She didn't weep or withdraw. There was only that single small syllable she spoke, but he heard all the damage, the hurt they must have given her, those bastards who had left her standing at the altar or alone in the line of chairs against the wall, all their excuses and lies, those blind, blind, stupid bastards who never saw what was right before their eyes.

Here he lay, burning, and she thought he didn't want her. He could hear it in her voice, feel it in the faint slackening of her fingers on his arm.

He sat up on his elbow. "It's not a good idea," he said, trying to explain. "There are risks. We're not wed." He felt helpless. "What if I... what if you... what if we..." His voice trailed off. A green boy would have explained it better, but now he was drowning in visions of Callie carrying his child. He took a deep breath. "Do you understand me?"

"Yes, of course," she said quickly. "I understand."

"Oh Christ." He fell back on the pillow. "*Ma vie,* you don't understand." He swore. "There's so much you don't understand."

"Yes I do. Truly. It's all right." She had taken her hand away. "I know what you mean."

"Marry me," he said suddenly. "Callie."

She drew back. "Marry?"

He would reckon it all out somehow. He'd tell her everything. And she'd take him anyway, and they would go to France or America or Italy. He'd buy her all the prize bulls she wanted, and they'd make love in haystacks all over the world. He realized from her shocked reaction that he'd been deplorably blunt. "Of course I meant—Lady Callista, will you do me the honor—"

"No!" she exclaimed, the bed rocking as she sat up. "You're very obliging, sir," she said in distress, "but please, you must not."

He sat up also. "Callie, I'm in earnest. If you would consider…" Consider marriage to a convicted criminal. Consider fleeing the country and never coming back. Consider tying herself for life to a fraud. She thought he had vast estates, a place in society, titles that were more than pretty words and air. He trailed off, staring uneasily into the darkness toward her.

"I'm sorry," she said quietly. "We wouldn't suit. But I do thank you, Trev." Her voice was sincere, a little shaky. "Truly. It's very kind of you to offer."

He ran his hand through his hair. It seemed like a blow, one of the lethal sort that didn't hurt at first, only sent a strange shock through the body, a few moments of numbness before the pain would come roaring in. All he could think was that he hadn't even told her the worst yet, and already she said no.

"Well," he said at last.

She leaned down, searching for his lips. Her hair fell over his chest as she kissed him with a shy tenderness, a questioning, as if she weren't sure of his response. Still floating in the numbed delay before reality, he put his hands up and cupped her face. Ferociously he kissed her, angrily, pulling her down on top of him. He thrust his fingers into the mass of her hair and carried her over onto her back in one swift move. Cold air washed his bared shoulders.

He held himself over her, his mouth hovering just above hers. "You want it all?" he breathed. He felt wild now, unreasonable. "You want me?"

She made a faint nod in the darkness. He wanted her with a need that had the blood hammering in his veins. He felt her lips part. Her body was delicate and soft beneath him, freed of all the petticoats and corsets and limits.

He slid his hand down the shape of her, kissing her deeply at the same time, feeling her back arch toward him as he drew up the silk. She was so beautiful; he could imagine what she would look like in the light, with her hair loose, with her nether curls of pretty golden rose—he knew that much of her, glimpses of bright curls against white skin. He remembered it, he ran his fingers through it, drawing a willing whimper from her lips.

She pulled at him, opening her legs as he touched her, and he lost all strength of mind. He ought to give her time, to play and coax, but he was desperate now. The anger had disintegrated; he had to be inside her, part of her. He kissed her throat, breathing the scent of her deeply into his chest. He would have tried to be gentle, but she pushed herself up against him as if she couldn't wait—the sensation of her beneath him, spreading for him, went to his brain like a firestorm, burning away everything in his mind but her body as he mounted her.

"Trev," she gasped. He felt her flinch, but he thrust hard and deep, reveling with a primitive pleasure in being the first. He would have been, so long ago—he should have been. She was his, and all the endless days and nights of exile fell away as she held him tight to her, gripping him so hard that her fingernails dug into his skin.

He turned his head down and kissed her temple, holding himself still inside her. He wanted to move so badly that he was shaking, but he waited in exquisite torment. *"Je t'adore,"* he whispered. *"Je t'aime.* Do you want me?"

Her tension softened. Her hands opened across his back. "Oh yes," she breathed.

He pressed into her. She whimpered, but it was a sweet, passionate sound, frantic, her body closing and squeezing around him.

"Do you want me?" He drew back slowly, torturing himself.

"Yes." She arched up, taking him deep as he pressed again. A moan escaped her.

Trev arched his head back, his eyes closed. "You want me?"

"Yes. Yes." She was panting now, clutching him, pulling him into her. He was going to explode; only the kittenish sounds she made held him back, those woman sounds, Callie sounds, rising to ecstasy as he thrust into her. He knew them, but he had never heard them this way, from inside her, coming on waves of hot, pure pleasure. He lifted himself on his palms with no thought beyond how it felt, how deep he could go. Her body fit his, rising and yielding, meeting him until it seemed he had no air in his lungs.

He threw his head back as the climax came over him, a powerful shudder, a hoarse breath as she cried out beneath him, both of them suspended together for an infinite instant of bliss.

Callie lay with him, cradled close, feeling his heated bare skin on hers, the mingled scents of what they had done. She felt numb with the impact of it, joyful and frightened and confused all at once. Her body still throbbed with the sensation of taking him into her, pain and delight mingled. He said nothing afterward, only holding her tight, his head buried against the nape of her neck. She could feel his deep breathing as he recovered himself. Her own heart was beating in her ears.

She had asked for him to do it. And now it was done. She bit her lip in the darkness. Shyness overcame her. She tried to shift away from him, but he made a low sound in his throat and caught her back. His arm came round her, stronger than she had realized, pulling her against his chest. He kissed her shoulder. He was all heat and maleness; she loved the feel of him, a great warm carnal shape enfolding her.

It was bewildering. To think of herself lying in bed with a man was too incredible. She could try to imagine herself as sultry Madame Malempré, but that fantasy had been besmirched by her encounter with Major Sturgeon. Her mind flitted through all her daydreams, pirates and naval officers and handsome alpine shepherds, finding nothing to light upon.

It was real. It was not a daydream, or even an adventure. It truly was herself, and him, in a bed, united as lovers, as husband and wife would be. She felt him fall asleep against her, his arm slipping slowly downward as his body relaxed. She would have stayed this way forever if she could, in this particular reality, this moment, this pose. It was almost better than all the passion that had come before, to lie beside him in perfect trust.

She closed her eyes. She twined her fingers with his and kissed them lightly. He made a sound in his chest, pulling her close again, but did not fully wake.

Fifteen

CALLIE SAT UP IN BED AND PEEKED OUT FROM THE closed curtains. Her nose was cold. The chill in the room surprised her. Buried under the counterpane and protected by the curtains, she had not realized how the temperature had fallen.

Her first thought was for her animals. They had arrived in Hereford last evening, before this cold snap, but she had been trapped at the Gerard and only received word of them through a complicated exchange of messages that traveled through several envoys, from Callie to Charles to Lilly to her herdsman to Lilly to Charles and back again to Callie. By the time she received her reply, it was so mangled by Lilly's ignorance of livestock jargon and garbled by Charles's imposition of cant that all she could make out was that she did possess cattle, they were somewhere in Hereford, and the whole countryside was in an uproar searching for Hubert.

She did not forget Trev or what had happened. But the thought of it in the morning light was like a tender bruise that she was not quite ready to touch. The instant she awoke, she had been aware that she was alone in the bed, surrounded by the lingering warmth where he had been.

A deep blue robe lay across the counterpane, along with her cashmere shawl. Callie had undressed with the help of the chambermaid and slept in her shift, but she had not laid out anything for the morning. She touched the robe, knowing that Trev had left it there for her. When she pulled it around her shoulders, she breathed the scent of him.

The fire had been lit in the grate, but it had yet done little to warm the bedchamber. A soft chink of china came from the parlor, and the sound of a servant withdrawing. Callie pulled the robe and shawl around her and slid out of the bed. With her toes curling on the cold floor, she went to the doorway and looked in.

Trev stood by the table, shaved and fully dressed, pouring a cup from the coffeepot. He glanced up as he saw her. Callie immediately dropped her eyes, her face growing fiery.

"Good morning." His greeting was a little too loud in the quiet room.

"Good morning." She stood in the door, uncertain. When she stole a look toward him, he turned his face down to the cup before their eyes met.

He picked up a newspaper lying on the table, folded it, and tossed it aside. "Come in, it's warmer here."

Callie moved a little way into the room. He walked behind her and closed the bedroom door. She was very aware of her bare feet and her loose hair and the tumbled bedclothes behind her. If he had any similar sensation, he did not show it. They evaded one another politely, like strangers.

"Tea or coffee?" he asked briskly. "They've brought us some breakfast, if you like."

"I really should see to my cattle," she said. "It's turned cold."

"Yes, of course." He paused. "I suppose you have no slippers. I'm sorry. I didn't think of that." He poured tea for her. "I hadn't expected you to be here overnight."

Callie sat down on a chaise and curled her feet tightly under her. "I didn't expect you to come back," she countered, on a slight note of defense.

"No," he said. "I realize that." He brought her the cup. She could make nothing of his neutral tone, but as she took it, he stepped back with a small bow, as formal as if he were a butler. She began to feel more awkward yet. There were volumes of unspoken words between them.

"Did you tell me that Sturgeon had taken rooms here?" he asked.

Callie nodded. "He followed me. That is—he followed Madame Malempré. He seems to be acquainted with her."

"Acquainted with her!" Trev stopped in the motion of lifting his cup. "The deuce you say."

Callie raised her face. "He says he met her in Belgium, at a picnic after Waterloo. He seems to"—she cleared her throat—"to know her rather intimately."

He swore under his breath. "That's impossible. He must be feigning it. He suspects something. Damn, he followed you here?" He paced a step and turned. "It's as well you didn't go out again."

"He isn't pretending," Callie said. "I think he does know Madame Malempré. I think he knows her very well."

Trev looked at her sharply. "You do?"

Callie nodded. She lowered her eyes and took a sip of her tea.

"What did he say to you?" There was a taut edge in his voice.

"Not to me," she said. "He thought he was speaking to her."

"Indeed," Trev said suspiciously. "And just what did he say?"

Callie thought a moment. She wasn't sure she wished for Trev to know everything he had said. "He seems to have had an encounter with her, in a garden summerhouse."

He snorted. "An encounter in—" He stopped short. He stared, as if at some distant place, and then turned his back to her, looking out the window.

"Who is she, this Madame Malempré? Do you know her too?" Callie asked.

"*Mordieu,* it's just the name of a town I passed through once!" He made an impatient gesture, as if tossing something away from him. "I remembered it when I ordered the tarpaulins, that's all."

She gazed at his back. "It was quite an unfortunate choice, then." She gave a little shrug. "He would like to renew his acquaintance with her."

"Oh, he would, would he?" He turned back swiftly his jaw hardening. "He didn't touch you? You should have called Charles—" He stopped again. He frowned and then gave Callie an amazed look. "And he's been courting *you,* hasn't he?" It had taken a few moments longer for him to notice the incongruity of the situation than it had for her. He seemed shocked, as if he could not quite comprehend what he had just realized. "Callie!"

She lifted her eyebrows, trying to look arch. "Yes, it's rather a blunder on his part. That's why I think he isn't pretending."

"That whoreson *bastard*!" he exclaimed, striding across the room. He followed it up with several words in French that she had never heard in any lessons. He was not as amused by it all as she had expected. "By God, I'll kill him."

He had reached as far as the door by the time Callie had untangled herself from the robe and shawl. He seemed to have come to his senses, or at least paused to consider what method by which to eradicate the major, for he stopped and turned around. Callie was on her feet by then.

"Let me be certain I understand you," he said. "Sturgeon has asked you to marry him?"

"Yes," she said.

"And you are presently considering his proposal?" His voice was steely. He stood very still, looking at her.

Callie couldn't hold his eyes. Suddenly she could not seem to think of anything but his arms around her, his body over hers. She found it difficult to breathe. She could not at that instant recall why she had said, in the middle of the night, that they would not suit. It seemed mad, as mad as those moments themselves, and equally dreamlike now. He had asked her to marry him, and she had remembered just in time that for some reason she must say no. And afterward...

She hugged herself, standing in her bare feet, covered in mortification. "Trev," she said, turning with an agitated move. "We must—could we—discuss something?"

"What happened between us last night?" he asked bluntly.

She took a deep breath, daring to lift her eyes. "Yes, I… suppose… that."

"It was, of course, iniquitous of me to take advantage of you." He gave a short bow and spoke as if he were reciting something that he had memorized. "Let me repeat, my lady, that I beg of you to become my wife, if you would see fit to accept me."

From the sound of it, the last thing he hoped was that she should do so. Callie looked down and fiddled with the fringe of the cashmere shawl. All her reasons for refusing him came back to her in a rush.

"I know you feel that you must offer now," she said with difficulty. "But I don't think we would suit."

"Yes," he said. "You mentioned that, I believe."

"I'm rather… awkward and not very clever in company, you know. I fear that I wouldn't be a fitting wife for you."

She glanced up at him, half hoping to be contradicted, but he seemed to find the hem of her gown to be of more interest than her face. He remained silent, his jaw set.

"I'm not a lady of fashion," she added, trying to make a clean breast of the whole. "I'm seven and twenty. And I'm English, of course. And not a Catholic."

He made a slight deprecating shrug. But still he said nothing, altering his attention to some painting on the wall, frowning at it as if it offended him.

"I suppose that might be overcome," she said, trying to reply sensibly to his silence. "But—you may have noticed—I'm rather dull and plain. I can't see myself living amid the *haut ton*. I was really quite a failure at it before, you know. I'd have to be like Madame Malempré and wear a veil all the time, so that no one would see me," she added, in a stupid attempt at humor.

His expression grew darker as she spoke. "Nonsense," he snapped. "Don't talk that way."

Callie wet her lips and gave him one more chance. "But you must wish to find someone who would be more worthy of Monceaux."

He gave a short laugh and turned away, his hands shoved into his pockets. "Do not concern yourself on that head, ma'am."

So. She lifted her chin, growing more sure, and at the same time more disheartened. He had been eager in the night, and passionate, but what was that vulgar phrase she had overheard once among the stable lads? *All cats look alike in the dark.* She had fairly well thrown herself at him, even if she hadn't meant for him to find her in his bed, playing a trick like that impudent housemaid who had tried to entice the parson on a dare. If he had even a slight wish to marry her, he would certainly show more delight at the idea. Even her jilts had managed to summon a greater show of gratification at the prospect than Trev appeared to feel.

She had a gloomy vision of becoming betrothed to him now, in this moment of crisis, and then in a month or two receiving one of those polite, reserved letters in which he expressed his deep regret at breaking off their engagement because he found he was unable to make her a praiseworthy husband. Her jilts would be a nice round number: a wretched prospect.

Or worse, far worse, a thousand times worse—for him to wed her because he felt he must, and then to be sitting some evening in some drawing room, listening to the whispers, to overhear that he was seeing Lady So-and-So, or Madame Vis-à-Vis, or whatever reigning beauty it might be, and how mortifying for his dreary little mouse of a wife, poor thing!

"Well!" she said quickly, turning and walking to the table, where she started to pick up the teapot and then put it down when the exasperating lid *would* rattle under her trembling hands. "It is most kind of you, but I find that I cannot accept. I hope… I hope that we may remain friends."

He inclined his head coolly. "Of course. We will certainly remain friends."

She knew in that moment that she had been right to refuse him. He didn't wish to marry her. A tiny remaining hope that he might dispute her decision died a final death. She poured tea in spite of the fact that she spilled several drops into the saucer.

"I suppose," he remarked, still in that dispassionate voice, "since you find you cannot accept me, we must pray that no natural consequences will result from my mistake."

Callie felt herself grow cold, her blood seeming to recede from her head to her feet. It was a "mistake" now. She sat down abruptly, feeling light-headed. "No," she whispered. "I don't think that likely."

The chamber was so quiet that she could hear a horse's hooves ring distantly against the cobbles in the stable yard.

"At my age, you know," she added, to fill the silence, fumbling among the cups and spoons. "I'm not a girl any longer. It's very unlikely. Would you be so good as to ring for the chambermaid? And arrange some way that I may go out as myself? I must see how my cattle go on in this weather."

He gave her a long, smoldering look. Then he bowed and left the room.

It took all of Callie's courage to show herself in Broad Street. She was certain anyone could see that she had been walking abroad there the day before, dressed in a gentian blue hat and veil and speaking French. But when she appeared as herself, there were only welcoming grins and brusque farmers' greetings, the familiar faces of her drover and his boys—no one accosted her with accusations or stopped in the street and pointed with scandalized horror at the woman who had slept in Monsieur Malempré's bed last night.

In fact she found herself quickly drawn into her own life, regaled with all the small incidents of moving the livestock to town, leaning down to check the knees of a calf that had stumbled and to see that sufficient ointment had been applied. With her warmest cloak and hood wrapped close about her, she accepted a cup of hot cider from Farmer Lewis. Lilly distributed mincemeat pies from a basket—the traditional hospitality at the Shelford pens. Callie could almost have forgot that there was anything amiss about this cattle show, but that her father wasn't there and all the talk was of Hubert and the Malempré bull, and she could still feel the physical consequence of what she and Trev had done in faint tingles and strange sensations that made her blink and blush. But her cheeks were already as pink as they could be from the cold, and no one seemed to notice anything different about her at all.

"I don't believe it," she said, dutifully giving her opinion of the challenge to Mr. Downie when he stopped to chat. She spoke softly, because she wasn't very good at prevarication, and somehow it seemed as if keeping her voice low might make her sound more believable. "I can't credit that this Belgian animal would be larger than Hubert."

"Certainly not," Mr. Downie said indignantly. Then he cleared his throat. "Have you seen the published measurements, my lady?"

"No, I haven't," she lied, pulling her hood closer in the frigid air. The scent of smoke from street fires mingled with the odors of the show. "I understand that they are said to be certified?"

"It's what the paper claims," he admitted, his breath frosting in the cold. "Has there been no progress in locating the Shelford bull?"

She shook her head. Everyone spoke of Hubert as belonging to Shelford, though it was common knowledge that Colonel Davenport now owned him. Mr. Downie harrumphed. "It's a bad business, my lady," he said. "A sorry day when your father passed away, God rest him. This wouldn't have happened if the earl had been alive."

Callie could agree with that in all honesty. She listened to the rumors as more agricultural people gathered at the Shelford pens, pausing to greet her kindly and regale themselves on mince pies and steaming cider. The most common gossip suggested that Hubert had been taken swiftly from the vicinity and either moved by some old abandoned drovers' road to the north, or already baited and slaughtered, never to be seen again. She hated both notions and had to keep reminding herself that he was lying in a well-kept pen not fifteen yards away. The edge of a thick bed of straw overflowed from under the Malempré tarps, and she could see a big hoof tip and the smooth black lock of his tail just under the canvas. A baker's sack, presumably full of Bath buns, sat on the Malempré herdsman's enameled green show box.

Colonel Davenport himself arrived, his cheeks flushed with cold and bluster. He accosted Callie immediately, demanding to know if she had heard of this havey-cavey Belgian business. He was of the dark opinion that Hubert had been made off with, probably by this Malempré fellow himself. The whole thing had the strong smell of criminal activity. He did not mean to frighten her, but he was a magistrate. He had long experience of rogues and rascals, and they were not all of the lowest classes. He very much doubted that Monsieur Malempré was what he represented himself to be. Colonel Davenport didn't suppose for one moment that Malempré was an honest gentleman, and it was unconscionable for the Agricultural Society to give him any countenance when he had stolen Hubert.

"No, I believe it was your fence," Callie said quietly, finally lifting her face at this. "I saw the break myself. You don't keep secure fences, I'm sorry to have to say, Colonel Davenport. No one stole Hubert—he simply pushed through your fence and got out."

A silence greeted her pronouncement. Every herdsman and farmer who had been standing about eating mince pies and listening to the colonel—and there were many—looked at Callie in something like awe. She had never said so much in public before.

As the representative of the late Earl of Shelford, who remained in everyone's mind the proper owner of the bull, her opinion of the matter carried considerable weight. When her drover chimed in, muttering that he'd seen the break too, and there weren't no way such a rupture in the wood had been made by the hand of man, the weight of judgment began to go against Colonel Davenport's theory. He was a little put out, defending his fence and trying to argue with her, but Callie found that she had more friends than she knew: Mr. Downie and Farmer Lewis, her drover and her herdsman and the cottager with the fat pig, several other cowmen and farmers, and the wife of the Shelford butcher—even Mr. Price stopped as he was passing and took up Callie's point with vigor. A great discussion erupted over the usual sounds of clucking and lowing, filling Broad Street with the echo of voices in loud dispute. Callie could imagine Trev's wicked enjoyment as he observed the scene from whatever place he had chosen to conceal himself. He had told her that he would be watching.

Monsieur Malempré's reputation gained considerably in respect when some bystander said he'd spoke to the banker, and the five hundred guineas were deposited under seal, good as gold, and if no bull met the challenge, they were to be donated to the society itself to be used for improvement of the local breeds. The big fellow who imparted this stunning information was a stranger to Callie, but his size and diction—there was a strong flavor of Charles's rough style to his speech—made her suspect he was no random passerby.

Mr. Price turned round at this, expressing astonishment and gratification at the news. He demanded to know why the officials of the society had not been apprised of this aspect of the challenge.

"Dunno nothin' more of it." The stranger shrugged. "I'm just a stockyard man myself, from up Bristol. Guess he don't want some swindle," he suggested innocently, pulling a straw out of his mouth. "Like them society fellows might shuffle off the biggest bull here roundabouts if they knew they'd get them guineas themselves. Dunno what them aggi-culture coves might do, eh?"

"The *society* hide him? By God, we'd never—"

Colonel Davenport cut him off. "Mr. Price! How long has the society been aware of the Malempré Challenge?" he demanded.

"Why, we just found it out yesterday!" Mr. Price cried. "And precisely what are you implying, Colonel, by asking me such a question?"

The colonel seemed to realize he had crossed the line to insult, and held himself up stiffly. "I merely inquired," he said. He gave a small bow. "I beg your pardon, sir. I meant no offense."

The secretary of the society relaxed a little but kept his brows raised. "No offense taken. I comprehend your upset, Colonel. It's an unfortunate situation for you, no doubt, to have misplaced the Shelford animal at this juncture."

Colonel Davenport drew in a sharp breath as if he might give an angry retort, but then he seemed to crumple under the weight of the secretary's words.

"I cannot comprehend it," he said in despair. "How that bull could have disappeared so suddenly, under my very nose! Gone without a trace! A week before the show—and now this... this... *Belgian*! Five hundred guineas, I say! What would you think?"

"Dark doings," Mr. Price agreed. "We've had seven animals measured since yesterday, but none approaches the dimensions of this imported animal." He glanced toward Callie. "My lady, I beg your pardon, did your father ever have Hubert's measure taken?"

"He was measured last year at the Bromyard show," she said promptly. "After he took the premium for Best Bull under Four Years," she added, to remind them of Hubert's value. "But he's grown since. I daresay he's larger now."

Colonel Davenport gave a faint moan. "Egad, what an animal," he said miserably. "And I've lost him!"

"You've no leads at all?" Mr. Price inquired.

"I'm having all the yards searched from here to London," the colonel said. "I've sent letters to the shorthorn breeders and the society secretaries in ten counties, in case someone attempts to sell him or show him. I've even alerted Bow Street, should he be taken to the Home Counties. Gave 'em a description of that shady fellow who tried to buy him of me. And that French rascal who attacked poor Sturgeon—*he's* still abroad! I dare swear he's mixed up in it too."

"Perhaps he pulled down your fence," Callie murmured.

"It was a perfectly sufficient fence!" the colonel declared, glaring at her.

"We always keep our largest stock behind stone walls," she said modestly.

"There's a frost break in my stone," he grumbled. "That's why I had to put him in the wood paddock."

Farmer Lewis cleared his throat meaningfully and took a bite of mince pie. Several of the herdsmen chuckled. Callie felt her point about the condition of the colonel's fences had been made. A new bystander, muffled up to his eyes against the cold, winked at her.

She glanced quickly away, blushing at this importunity from a stranger. Then she looked back at him, suddenly suspicious. He tossed the ragged woolen scarf over his shoulder and shoved his hands in his pockets, a nondescript working man in a shabby drover's jacket and fingerless mitts. He met her look with a directness that no common herdsman would ever dare. Callie felt her cheeks flame, growing hot even in the chill.

"Good morning, my lady!" Major Sturgeon's voice came from just behind her, loud and cheerful. Caught gazing at the muffled drover, she startled and turned, her hood falling back from her hair. He bowed and gave her a warm smile. He wore his uniform again, with braids of gold on the collar points of his heavy cloak. "How cold it is!" he remarked, clapping his hands together. "Did your animals fare well on the journey? They've all arrived safe and sound, I pray."

Callie gave him a nod and a slight curtsy. She was still flustered from discovering that Trev was nearby; she wasn't prepared to deal civilly with Major Sturgeon at the same time. "They've arrived in good order," she managed to reply, hoping that he wouldn't recognize her voice. "But... I didn't expect to see you here at a cattle show, Major." She almost said, "a dirty cattle show," but stopped herself in time.

"I hope to enter into your interests with enthusiasm," he replied, doffing his plumed hat. If he heard any similarity between her voice and Madame Malempré's, he gave no indication of it. "Morning, Davenport!" He nodded to the colonel. "I missed sharing that glass with you last night, but I was a little indisposed. We'll make it up this evening, eh? I'll join you at the Black Lion—I find the Gerard doesn't suit me."

Callie gave him a sidelong glance, recalling that the proprietor of the Gerard had approached Monsieur Malempré as they were leaving the hotel, murmuring that the unfortunate matter had been taken care of and Madame would not be troubled further. She wondered if Trev had had the major turfed out of his room, or if the officer had merely grown tired of waiting for Madame to appear. Whichever it was, it did not appear to have dampened Major Sturgeon's opinion of himself. He seemed to be in an expansive mood, perfectly certain that Callie must be pleased to see him. But of course, he didn't know that she was Madame Malempré herself, or that in the time since he had made his proposal, she had made love to another man.

She ought to be ashamed, Callie supposed, but there was too much irony in it all. Clearly he would have done the same if Madame Malempré had given him the chance, and she didn't doubt that Miss Ladd had been his lover too while he was betrothed to Callie. So they were even now. She had sunk to his level. It was not a particularly consoling thought.

The little crowd of herdsmen and farmers had begun to drift away now that the mince pies had run out, though the muffled drover lingered, leaning against a wagon with his arms crossed. Callie avoided looking toward him. She sent Lilly back into the Green Dragon for more pies. Colonel Davenport excused himself, clapping his friend on the shoulder and advising him to take good care of Lady Callista, as if somehow the major had already taken possession of her, and left them standing alone together.

"May I bring you a hot cider, my lady?" Major Sturgeon turned to Callie again. When she demurred, he looked about him at the rows and pens of her cattle neatly lined up along her assigned portion of the street. Callie had not bothered with tarps to conceal the Shelford stock, as there were no surprises there. She could pride herself at least that it was Shelford's usual excellent showing, except for the lack of Hubert. "This is an exciting moment, to see you here among your entries," he said expansively. "What do you feed to bring your calves up to this great size? I'm not an expert on livestock, but I fancy myself a quick study, if you'll honor me with a tour of the various points of interest."

His attention might have been manufactured, but he made a good show of it. And she had an aim—she meant to convince Trev that she was content with him as a potential husband. More than ever now, after last night. After this morning. After hearing Trev's stony silence as she listed her obvious shortcomings as a wife. She could feel the shabby drover in his muffler watching her.

"Yes, if you like," she said, taking a deep breath of icy air to fortify herself. She allowed the major to take her arm and tuck it under his.

He patted her fingers. "Are you warm enough, my lady?" He bent his head near hers, the way he had when he'd thought she was Madame Malempré, and took it upon himself to tweak her hood back into place. "I've missed your company in Shelford," he murmured.

As she had only been gone one day from Shelford, it hardly required any wit to realize this was nonsense, but she forced herself to smile. "Have you, sir? But it's only been a few hours since I saw you last."

"Long enough that I couldn't help myself—I found after I started out yesterday that I was on the road to Hereford, when I'd certainly meant to go up to London for a fortnight. But I had the greatest urge to see this agricultural fair of yours."

Callie wished he'd fought off the urge. If he hadn't come, if he hadn't thought she was his long-lost paramour, she might still have had her three days of adventure with Trev. Now it was all a shambles. She had lost her best friend with one splendid, delirious mistake. Trev had parted with her at the dressmaker's without giving her any instructions to return. And indeed—how could she go back to the Gerard as Madame Malempré now?

She kept smiling, but there was a stinging blur in her eyes. She blinked, hoping that it would only seem to be the cold, and looked up at Major Sturgeon. "I haven't had much time to consider your offer," she said softly.

"Of course not!" He affected a great dismay. "I beg you not to suppose that I mean to worry you on that head. Tell me, what premium class do you most hope to win?"

She answered at random, finding that she wished to move away from her own stock and the man who still loitered there, rubbing his hands in the fingerless mitts over her herdsman's fire. She turned her back on him, directing the major toward the pavement, stopping to speak vaguely of a fine draft pony that stood harnessed to a farm cart in the next row, its mane braided, its hoof feathers lovingly brushed out to perfect unstained white. Major Sturgeon made gallant attempts to compliment her expertise. He had to make do with that, she supposed, since he couldn't compliment her looks or charm.

Sixteen

TREV HAD THOUGHT HE COULD TAKE IT. HE'D THOUGHT he could endure the idea that she would marry another man. For near a decade he'd assumed she already had, reckoned she was a happy wife with all her children about her, an image which had been sufficient to keep him on the other side of the Channel, if not the other side of the world, for a good part of the last ten years. He'd wandered back to England finally, having failed to recover Monceaux and botched pretty much everything else he'd set his hand to before he discovered in himself a particular talent for arranging boxing spectacles of both fixed and fair varieties. By then she had faded to a soft-edged memory, blunted in the golden autumn mist of his past, the mere image of a copper-haired, kissable waif in an outmoded gown. He'd hardly been eating his heart out for her. In truth, he'd remembered her father with stronger feeling.

The knowledge that she was even tolerating Sturgeon's company, allowing him to call on her—at first Trev had not taken it in seriousness, supposing she'd merely been unable to summon sufficient daring to refuse to admit the man. He'd been perfectly ready to undertake a visit to Sturgeon on her behalf if she required assistance in the matter, and finish up what he'd started by giving the major a matching pair of black eyes to go with his swollen jaw.

To discover that she was entertaining an actual proposal had set Trev well off his stride. Perhaps a little more than that. Perhaps he had finally admitted the truth to himself—that he was utterly distracted and still crazy in love with her mischievous smile and that way she had of looking up at him sidelong while she discussed the various merits of an overweight peeg. He was worse off than even his mother suspected, and she suspected a good deal.

He was, in fact, dying by inches. He stood near the fire, glowering at an innocent cow and rhythmically opening and closing his fists while Sturgeon made up to her in the open street. She knew Trev was there too. After she'd turned him down, with all that bosh about how unworthy she was of Monceaux; turned him down, and he couldn't argue with her, couldn't tell her what he felt or prove it was the other way round—*C'est à chier*, his exalted *grand-père* had always said of him, *not worth a shit,* and God knew it was true at that moment.

He watched sullenly as Sturgeon pulled her hood round her face in a mawkish little gesture of caring. The fellow was a damned hum. How she could allow him to touch her, knowing what she did, that he'd dangle after some Belgian slut at the very moment he was supposed to be courting her—Trev set his jaw and narrowed his eyes. He slapped his hands against his arms, more out of frustrated violence than cold.

It seemed like a nightmare that he stood here wrapped up to his eyebrows to hide himself, doing nothing while his lover walked away with another man. He ought to have cut off all her silly objections and dragged her down to the cathedral, found a priest, or a bishop, or whoever did these things quietly and fast—he'd convert to the Church of England while he was at it and let his grandfather turn over in his grave. He didn't think, if he'd insisted, that she would have refused him very long. He rather thought she'd been hoping for it.

But then he'd have to tell her the truth.

C'est à chier, he thought, *eh, grand-père?* Thrusting his cold hands in his coat, he strode away from the fire. Callie and her beau were strolling along the opposite pavement, pausing now and then to observe some exhibitor's cheese or pies. Trev shadowed them, jerking his chin to one of his boys. The big boxer stood up and fell in with him casually, passing the signal on. In a moment, there were a dozen of them, spread across the street and among the exhibits, ready for trouble.

Trev was in the mood for it. He wished it were all done with, over now, this juvenile adventure, so he could get on with the vast sum of nothing that was his life stretching before him. *Italy,* he thought, but no, that wasn't far enough. He needed an ocean between them if she was going to marry Sturgeon. Boston, perhaps, where he could get himself a tomahawk and live with the rest of the savages, busting up tea crates for entertainment.

Across the way, the happy couple stopped at the pen with the obese pig. Trev halted. He felt his reason slipping. Sturgeon made some remark and pointed at the animal, and Callie laughed and shook her head.

Something cracked, some final thin sliver of sanity. Absurdly, all he could think was that it was *his* pig, his and Callie's, and Sturgeon had made her laugh. He stood still for a moment, suffused with rage. She looked up then and saw him. Across the width of the street full of geese and chicken crates, he stared at her, breathing through the woolen scarf concealing his face.

She gazed back as if she were transfixed. Trev narrowed his eyes, expressing his opinion of this betrayal. She lost all her color, leaving only two bright spots burning on her cheeks in the cold. Her hand went out and found Sturgeon's arm for support.

Trev realized then that he must be a figure of more than ordinary menace in his mask. He turned abruptly away, prowling along the street. She liked adventure. He would give it to her. The fair had begun to attract more people now, as the shadows of early morning retreated and the sun took off the worst of the frost. He moved near the tarps that concealed Hubert's pen.

"Untie the bull," he muttered. "Get him on his feet."

Charles poked his head from inside the canvas. "Aye, sir." He pulled back and vanished.

Trev moved away as the tarps began to sway and tremble. He gave a low instruction to one of his boys.

"Eh?" Bristol's finest hope for the next Champion of the Noble Art rolled a startled eye toward him.

"Do it," Trev said. "And man the fires—keep 'em clear when it starts."

"Oh, there's the dandy," his cohort said with understated violence. "Mind we don't burn down the town."

"Aye, mind it," Trev said, giving him a clap on the shoulder to send him off.

While the word spread, he loitered by a stack of crated turkey hens, listening to their soft gobbles. After a moment he reached down surreptitiously and flipped the wooden latches open, holding the doors closed with his knee. He kept his eyes down the street on Callie and Sturgeon as they sampled bread and honey at a vendor's stall. Sturgeon sampled it, at any rate. Callie just stood holding hers, looking nervous, the way she always looked just before he gave her the office to act on whatever outrageous part he had assigned her in their schemes.

A tight smile curled his mouth. Only that one look between them, and she knew. And in spite of the desperate expression, she would perform her role to perfection, even if she didn't yet know what it was. She always managed to carry it off, as clever and cool as a schoolmistress once the sport commenced.

Ah God, he would miss her. No good-byes, no farewells, which was better. Last night was his good-bye. *Remember me,* he thought.

Off by the sheep, one of his boys leaned over the pen as if to observe a ram more closely. Then he stood back, his hand nonchalantly resting on the gate, and made the high sign with a swipe of his arm across his forehead. Trev looked from one end of the wide street to the other. They all waited on him, an odd sprinkling of Samsons and Goliaths amid the fairgoers, rubbing their chins or whistling and gazing artlessly up at the sky.

He nodded and stepped away from the turkey coops, turning his back as the doors swung open. With a sharp kick of his heel, he cried havoc and let slip the hens of war.

It all started with the turkeys, a sudden burst of black wings and wattles as the birds exploded from a falling stack of crates. Four big hens tumbled and recovered themselves amid a flutter of feathers and splintering wood. As their owner shouted in alarm, they began to run, sleek ebony missiles darting hither and thither between the legs of goats and through fences and under the skirt of a cottager's wife.

Callie had just begun to calm herself a little, thinking she must have misunderstood the intent of that malevolent stare from Trev, that it was merely the particular effect of his dark gypsy eyes that made it seem as if he intended to commit some sinister mayhem at any moment. But she went stiff at the sound of shouting from just at the place he had been standing. God in heaven, what mad thing did he think was he doing?

All about, every animal came alert for danger. One frightened beast startled the next, and suddenly the pens seemed no more than flimsy toothpicks. The cart pony reared as a turkey dashed under its belly, its silken hoof feathers flying while pumpkins smashed onto the pavement. They bounced and rolled beneath the feet of an uneasy yearling calf. It bucked and bolted away from the attack of these alien objects, lead rope trailing. Suddenly there were geese waddling free, flapping their wings to flee from sheep crowding through an open gate and flooding onto the pavement. The air filled with bleats and quacks, disorder mushrooming into chaos.

Callie picked up her skirts and ran. A big drover waved his arms and shouted, spooking the loose calf and sheep away from a street fire. The frantic calf sheared off; Callie grabbed hold of its lead just before it leaped through a shop window. The rope burned across her gloved fingers as she threw herself backward to turn the animal. When the calf hit the end of the lead, the momentum hurled her to her knees. Her head struck hard on the wooden window sash. For an instant she was stunned, the pain ringing down through her whole body like a bright, terrible bell. Tears sprang in her eyes. But she held herself upright with her arm against the sill, her head spinning, refusing to let go of the lead.

Someone helped her up. She didn't stop to see who it was. She took a loop of the calf's rope and pulled it along with her, plunging for the Malempré pens. Amid the chaos they passed the corpulent pig—the only animal sitting calmly, contemplating the open gate of its pen without even trying to rise. Callie grabbed a loose piglet with one hand just before it tottered out, tossed it back, and slammed the barrier shut. She picked herself up from another half stumble and plowed through the confusion, reaching the Malempré pen in time to see the canvas rock and sway as if the earth quaked.

She panted and lunged forward, almost going down on her knees again when she stepped off the curb. A strong hand caught at her elbow, saving her. The tarps lifted and flailed. With a squealing bellow, Hubert burst forth, tossing a sheet of canvas and a green-coated herdsman aside with one powerful sweep of his head. The herdsman went down on his rear and Hubert broke into a thunderous trot, flinging his nose from side to side, his eyes rolling white as he emerged into the street.

Callie stood still, her mouth open, as he put his head down and hooked a bag of potatoes, pitching them on his horns right through a trestle table full of jam and preserves. The board collapsed, sending jelly flying through the air. Farmwives screamed and scattered.

"Hubert!" Callie cried, as the bull swung his great head and threw a barrel aside. It rolled along the street, barely missing Colonel Davenport as he ran pell-mell toward them. He leaped out of its path, losing his hat, but came on, closing with Callie on the rampaging beast. From somewhere Trev's footman Charles had appeared, running at her side. Everyone else scattered away, wise in the ways of enraged bulls.

"Hold!" Callie screamed at Charles, flinging out her arm before he could run past her. "Colonel! Stop! Don't go near him!"

The men froze in midstride. Hubert bellowed, the strange squealing sound echoing over the turmoil in the street. He turned toward her, searching, his breath frosting in the air like great puffs from a steam engine. Callie's knees were failing under her. Her head spun with pain. Someone pulled the calf's lead from her hand, but she never took her eyes from the bull.

"Hubert!" she called, tasting blood in her mouth. "Come now, Hubert…" She put that little note in her voice, the sweet note that promised treats and an ear scratch, but the bull was confused and angry, uncertain of where he was. He lowered his head and pawed the street.

"Come along," she crooned. A red hen trotted past her, zigzagging toward the bull and away. Hubert made a charge at it, almost taking out its tail feathers before it squawked and flew out of range. "Come along," Callie warbled desperately. "Walk on, Hubert. There's a good boy."

He swung his head, eyeing a kid goat that pranced too close. Callie held her breath, dreading for him to strike out with his horns. But the little animal stood with its legs spread, staring up at the snorting giant above it as if Hubert were the eighth wonder of the world. Hubert lowered his horns and pawed once, staring back balefully.

Everything had gone quiet around them. Even the loose animals seemed to pause. The kid gave one tiny, uncertain bleat. The bull snuffled. They touched noses.

As if some question had been answered between them, Hubert heaved a great sigh and gave the little fellow a lick that near bowled it over.

"Good boy," Callie said. She began to walk toward him slowly. Her knees were knocking. The kid darted away as she approached, but Hubert merely swayed his head toward her and blinked in a dreamy way. She caught the lead dangling from his nose ring.

A crowd had gathered in a wide, wary circle around them. The Malempré pen lay in ruins.

"It's Hubert," she managed to say in a small voice, remembering her part. The darkness at the edge of her vision seemed to close in on her. Her breath failed. "This isn't... a Belgian bull. It's... Hubert."

Everything seemed to slide away from her at once. The last thing she remembered, before the spinning world closed in, was Trev's muffled face above her, his arms catching her up just before she hit the ground.

She was already awake before they conveyed her into the Green Dragon. She knew it was Trev who carried her; she heard him snarl a fierce command at the others to stand back, but she couldn't seem to gather her wits to speak or even lift her head. And then he was gone somehow, and she was lying on a sofa surrounded by a great number of anxious onlookers, bewildered as to how she had got there.

"Hubert?" she mumbled, trying to sit up.

"He's penned all right now, my lady, good and tight." She recognized her drover's familiar voice. "Don't you worry."

She could trust Shelford's own drover, who had handled Hubert since he was a baby calf. She subsided for the moment, closing her eyes, allowing someone to take her hand and squeeze it reassuringly. The top of her head hurt abominably. She wanted Trev, wanted him to be holding her close while she ripped his character to shreds, beginning with his unforgivable foolishness and continuing through his criminal negligence and winding up with his unpardonable stupidity, and then starting on it all over again, louder.

"Was anyone hurt?" she mumbled.

"Only a few scratches." She thought it was Mr. Price who spoke. "But for you, my lady. You took a sharp rap, eh? The doctor's on his way."

A vial of hartshorn appeared under her nose. She wasn't fond of smelling salts, but just at this moment, a deep whiff went straight to her brain and cleared some of the mist. "The animals?" she asked, blinking her eyes open.

"We're making a head count," he said. "No injuries or losses reported yet. We may be fortunate, thank the good Lord. Only there was a good deal of damage to property. But don't you try to talk, ma'am. We've sent word to Shelford."

"Oh no," she said, with a drifting vision of Lady Shelford's reaction to this news. "Where's—" She broke off, realizing that she shouldn't ask openly for Trev. She looked about her and saw him standing at the foot of the sofa, his scarf slipped down off his nose and only covering his mouth. His expression was white and set, almost frightening. She wanted to tell him that he should take care, but her brain was a little confused, and she thought it better to say nothing rather than risk a mistake.

She wondered vaguely, since Trev was standing there, who it was holding her hand. Peculiar lights seemed to go off in flashes when she turned her head, but she discovered Major Sturgeon kneeling at her side, rubbing his palm over the back of her hand.

"Oh," she said and sat up, pulling free.

Everyone chided and clucked at her, but she closed her eyes and took a deep breath of the salts to make the world stop whirling and straighten itself again.

"I'm quite all right," she said, when the horizon had settled. "May I have some tea?"

"Bring her some tea," the major ordered, just as if a bustle had not already broken out to accomplish this task. People hurried back and forth and said things, and it was all rather confusing. She kept her hands folded tightly in her lap, except for once she dared to look aside at Trev and brush her fingers up her cheek to try to tell him that his disguise was slipping.

He didn't seem to comprehend her, or if he did, he didn't appear to care. He met her eyes with that look again, such a look, his eyes a deep black glitter, so that she didn't know if he was nearer to tears or to cold-blooded murder. It seemed it could be either.

Callie herself felt inclined to murder, if only her head had not felt as if a blacksmith were using it as an anvil and pounding horseshoes into shape on top. She accepted the teacup, sitting up straight as it rattled in her hand. "Where is this Monsieur Malempré?" she demanded, as loudly as she could manage. Her voice was shaky, but strong enough to draw the attention of everyone around her.

From the corner of her eye—if she turned, she feared that her wobbly stomach would betray her—she saw that Trev finally took her hint and pulled his collar and scarf up about his face. Fortune and the general disarray of things favored them; no one even looked at him twice as a clamor went up regarding the where-abouts of the mysterious Belgian gentleman.

"Shabbed off, I'll wager," a deep voice rumbled. Callie recognized the drover who'd prevented the panicked calf from running into the fire. "His jig's up, ain't it?"

"Look for him at the Gerard." Major Sturgeon stood up beside her, scowling. "He was there last night."

"Major," she said plaintively, reaching for his hand. "Will you find him for me?"

"Certainly, my lady." He bent down and kissed her fingers. "Davenport, can you send someone? I don't want to leave her side."

"No, please—" She pulled her hand away. "I wish to go to my room. But… Colonel, you were right after all, he did steal Hubert." She looked again at Major Sturgeon, putting on her best imitation of a lost puppy. "But you have such resolution, Major—will you hunt for him yourself? I hope you won't let him get away."

It seemed to have a good effect. "Of course. Of course not." Reluctantly he let go of her and then caught her elbow again as she pushed herself to her feet. "Let me help you—no, that's the wrong way, my dear."

She turned, ignoring him, tottering a step toward the foot of the sofa. She managed to trip on her skirts and fall against Trev's chest. "Oh," she muttered. "I beg your pardon. Where is… where is my maid?"

His arm came round her, holding her up as she allowed her knees to crumple. "Have a care, Miss," he muttered through his scarf. Then, without further ceremony, he bent down and picked her up bodily. "Where's 'er lady's slavey?" His voice was a rough growl, a fair imitation of a local drawl muffled within the scarf. The sound of it rumbled against her cheek. "You, inn'it? Lead us on up, then, and sharp about it. Shove over, let me through."

The knot of spectators parted. He swung her round, mounting the stairs as Lilly hurried ahead. Callie closed her eyes, clinging to his neck. She was aware of the sound of many people on the stairs, of talk of the doctor's arrival, and then of passing under the door to her rooms. Trev carried her through to the bedroom. As he laid her down, she held on to him and hissed into his ear, "Don't you dare leave!"

He grunted and stepped away. Lilly bustled about, ejecting several interested persons who had followed them upstairs. She allowed the doctor in, so Callie sat up quickly, pretending to a considerably stronger state of revival than she felt. She submitted to an examination of the bump on her head, trying not to wince every time the doctor touched it, promised that she would rest quietly and not go out for several days, and positively refused the administration of laudanum. The doctor shook his head and went away complaining that a young lady ought to have a guardian with her when she traveled, someone who could keep her from bumping her head and make her mind her elders.

Callie waited until the door clicked closed behind him. She had been well aware that all the time she was being examined, Trev and Lilly had been standing in a corner of the bedroom, speaking in low tones to one another, so that the doctor took them both for her servants.

"Lilly," she said. "Pray close the bedroom door. Stand outside and make certain that no one comes in."

Lilly cast a glance at Trev and bit her lip. "But Sir wants me to—"

"Do as I ask, if you please," Callie interrupted. Her head hurt. She put her hand to her temple. "I don't care what 'sir' would like at the moment."

The maidservant bit her lip and curtsied. She turned away to the door. Trev moved a step, and Callie lifted her head.

"Do *not* leave!" she ordered him.

He stopped. Lilly closed the bedroom door behind her, leaving them alone. Callie sat on the bed, looking at him. He'd pulled down the scarf to show his face, but still the sinister gypsy effect was powerful.

"I can't stay long," he said.

"Really!" Callie favored him with a dry look. "And how do you plan to accomplish an exit, when half the county is loitering below looking for you?"

He returned a sardonic smile. "By the window."

"Oh, of course." She blinked, touching her hand gingerly to the bump on her head. The doctor's probing had only made it worse. She realized that her hair was falling down.

"Are you all right?" he asked. There was a peculiar tautness about his mouth.

"I am excessively put out with you!" she said, taking this as an invitation to vent her spleen. "*You* started that rout, didn't you? And you had those men helping to let the animals loose! Whatever possessed you to do such a thing? Any number of them might have been hurt or lost. And think of the prize pies!" She paused, her lip trembling. "Someone could have been *killed*! It was abominable of you."

"I'd not thought of the prize pies, I'll admit."

"Well, you should have. And the preserves and cheeses. I'm sure poor Mrs. Franklin is weeping her heart out right now, after Hubert threw a barrel through her pear tarts. She is a new bride, you know."

"No. I didn't know."

"And you haven't the least regret, have you?" Her resentment grew. "It's all quite a game to you, isn't it? You stroll into some unsuspecting town and cause a riot, and then you can't stay long." She stood up, holding on to the bedpost when the room had a tendency to rotate about her. "You just go away and leave the rest of us to put everything to rights."

"Yes," he said.

The fact that he stood there without defending himself only fed her wrath. "Why did you do it? You didn't warn me. You didn't stop and think. Surely there was some other way to reveal Hubert, something a little less—spectacular! I thought we were to do it on the last day of the fair."

"We were," he said shortly.

"Then *why*?" she demanded.

His lip curled. "I was angry."

"Angry?" She blinked. "At what?"

"You showed him the pig." There was a note of self-mockery in his voice.

"The pig?" She had no notion what he meant.

"And laughed at what he said. Of course I had to put a stop to that at once."

"The pig? Do you mean that fat sow?"

He gave a slight shrug of assent, like a schoolboy called up on the carpet.

"You started all that—you put us all in danger—because I laughed about a *pig*? Are you mad?" she exclaimed.

"It was our pig, do you see?" His voice rose to match hers. "God damn it. I haven't asked for much. Give me a goddamned pig at least."

She shook her head, bewildered. "It's not my pig."

He threw back his head and gave a brief, hard laugh. "No. Right. I'm sorry you were hurt. Scared the daylights out of me. It's true, it could have been far more serious, I didn't realize until it got out of hand." He sounded mortified. "I'm sorry. My damnable temper."

"I only laughed because Major Sturgeon was so stupid. He asked me if she was a Berkshire hog, when anyone could see that she's an Old Spot."

He took a stride toward her. Callie leaned back against the bedpost with her hands behind her. In his rough jacket and heavy stockman's boots, he seemed much larger than he ought, his dark, satyric features fit for a highwayman. For an instant she thought he might shake her, but instead he took her cheeks between his hands.

She felt the rough wool of the mitts, and his fingertips resting on her cheeks. He bent his face to hers. "Callie—know something, believe something. I must go, but believe that I love you. Marry that fellow if you must; I know you have your reasons. I know I've let you down at every turn. I'm not the man who could give you the sort of life you deserve. But wherever I go, *mon trésor,* it doesn't matter where—I'll think of you. You're in my heart. Believe me. You're the only true and honest thing in my life."

She stood with her face turned up to his, biting her lower lip.

"And you're beautiful," he said. "Believe that too. Not like some damned society diamond, no. You're beautiful like the leaves in autumn, like a spring colt kicking its heels, you're beautiful the way your animals are beautiful, even that fool pig. Do you believe me?"

She didn't answer. He pushed back a lock of her hair and kissed her gently, so sweetly that she was near to weeping.

"I want to make love to you in a field," he whispered. "In the green grass or in the fresh hay. I want you beyond reason."

"I don't believe you," she said woodenly. "Tell me the truth."

His breath touched her skin. "I am."

Slowly she shook her head.

"The truth about me, you mean," he said, lifting his head and looking down at her under his dark lashes.

"Tell me in truth why you're leaving. If you want me to believe—whatever else you say."

He stood back, his hands sliding to her shoulders. "I suppose I owe you that much, don't I?" He looked aside and suddenly let go of her, pushing away. In a voice that went to icy derision, he said, "The truth is I've been convicted of forgery and sentenced to hang."

Callie blinked. Then she pushed back her falling hair from her face. "Oh come now. I'm sure I might have swallowed the rest, even about the pig, but I'm not a complete flat, you know!"

He had been standing before her with a hard, sullen expression; at that, his lip quirked upward. "Yes, you are," he informed her. "You're a pea-goose. It's one of the most charming things about you."

She gave a little huff. "Perhaps so, but I'm sure I'm not going to believe that you're laboring under a sentence of death."

He tilted his head. "Why not?"

"Well… *because*," she said, not quite certain of the look in his eyes. "For forgery, you say? I can perfectly suppose that you gave Major Sturgeon a black eye, and so the constable is after you, but I can't imagine that you did any such thing as commit a forgery. Why would you do so? You're already excessively wealthy. And besides, I don't think anyone would be hung for it. It's not a case of murder or something on that order. It's just a piece of paper."

He leaned back against the chest of drawers, a wry smile touching the corner of his mouth. "Very sensible, I admit. I wish the bench might have taken your point of view."

"And here you are, quite alive," she pointed out with some satisfaction in discovering another large hole in his claim.

"Just so," he said. "I was given a conditional pardon the day before they finished building the gallows. I must leave the country and never return."

Callie had been about to poke further punctures in his ridiculous tale, but she paused at that. "Never return?"

"It is a hanging offense, Callie," he said gently. "It's a crime against commerce, and that's near-worse than murder in the eyes of the magistrates."

"I... don't see how that can be so," she said. But she remembered suddenly that all the newspapers and even the ladies' magazines had been full of some great trial not long ago; she hadn't paid any mind to the details herself, but Dolly had followed the course of the events avidly and read them aloud at breakfast every morning at interminable length. Callie thought it had involved a lady with a very young child, and a gentleman of the sporting crowd, and a great number of sordid insinuations and accusations. And yes—it had been a trial for forgery—she remembered that now, and the lady's life had been in peril if she were found guilty, but it had turned out to be the gentleman instead.

She wet her lips. "Trev—" she said uncertainly. She looked up at him with a sinking feeling at the pit of her stomach.

His faint smile vanished, and his jaw hardened. He gave a bitter laugh. "Please. Go on refusing to believe me. It's not something a man cares to admit, I assure you."

The words seemed to go past her, then spin in strange echoes round her head. "A hanging offense," she repeated slowly, hearing it as if from a great distance. She stared at him, every limb in her body going to water. If she had not been holding on to the bedpost, she would have slid to the floor.

"It was not a pleasant experience," he said. "And so you see, I must depart." He gave a slight mechanical bow, a move full of suppressed violence.

"What happens if they discover you here?" she asked, hardly able to command her voice.

"They hang me," he said simply.

"Oh good God," she breathed. Her legs were failing her. "Oh dear God."

He stepped forward, supporting her. "Don't faint— Callie, my sweet life—oh no, please don't weep. Come here now. They haven't caught me yet."

She realized that tears had sprung to her eyes, but they were not of sorrow. She gave a sob of pure terror, clinging tightly to him as he pulled her into his arms. "You must go!" She gasped into his shoulder. "Why are you still here?"

He held her close, kissing her temple. "You can't guess?"

"Your mother!" She pulled back sharply. "Does your mother know?"

His mouth flattened. "No. God grant she never will."

"Of course not." Callie turned from him, hugging herself. "No, she mustn't know." She turned back. "But you must flee directly—they're all hunting you now as Malempré." Her head was a painful whirlwind. "Oh lord, the duchesse—what shall I say to her? I can't go back to Shelford and—"

"Hush, *mon ange.*" He caught her again, more gently. "I've thought of all these things."

"You have?"

He nuzzled her temple, his breath soft on her skin. "Most of them."

"Where will you go? To Monceaux?"

He pulled her close. "It doesn't matter, if you aren't there."

Callie turned her face up. He gazed down at her for a moment and then kissed her roughly.

"Don't forget me," he whispered. He put her away from him. Callie held out her hands numbly. He caught them up and kissed them, and then without another word, he left her—not by the window, by the door, but she hurried to the window and stood there, looking out through the wavy glass with her heart beating hard until he appeared in the street below.

He crossed swiftly to the far side, his face muffled up again, only another drover among the working people cleaning up smashed preserves and setting pens and crates and tables to rights. At the corner he turned, looking back up at her. She put her palm to the glass.

He nodded once and vanished from her view.

Seventeen

MAJOR STURGEON STRODE VIGOROUSLY TOWARD THE Black Lion in the long shadows of evening, his collar turned up against the cold. Clearly he meant to keep his appointment with Colonel Davenport this time. As the cathedral bells rang out, echoing deeply across the roofs and down in the back lanes and alleys, the streets emptied, deserted by the fair crowds for the warmth of taverns and inns.

Trev straightened from the wall where he'd been loitering, hunched down in his ragged jacket, and stepped into the major's path, shouldering him hard. The officer grunted and recoiled, exclaiming at a damned stupid oaf, but before he could get far with this rebuke, Trev grabbed him by his gilded braids and shoved him into the alley.

Sturgeon caught on instantly—he turned, trying to reach his sword and shout, but Trev kneed him hard, doubling him over before he could draw steel. Trev had his own knife at the ready, and he let Sturgeon feel it, but the man was no fading flower even with a knife at his ribs. He seized Trev's wrist and shoved the weapon away, throwing a short, hard punch at his face. Trev ducked, to take the hit on the top of his skull—a cheap boxer's trick that hurt like the devil but could break the officer's hand if Trev got lucky. He didn't stop to discover if it worked: he clubbed Sturgeon in the side of the head with an elbow, jammed his forearm against the officer's throat, and wrenched his knife hand free. With Sturgeon blocked up against the wall, Trev shook his head to loosen the scarf from his face.

"*You!*" The officer showed his teeth in a sneer, resisting Trev's grip until both their hands trembled with the strain.

"Aye, it's me," Trev said cordially, moving the knife downward. "Now shut up and listen, or I'll cut off your pretty baubles and have done with it."

Their huffs of frosted breath mingled in the fading light. Sturgeon made a wordless growl, his teeth bared, but Trev's arm across his windpipe and the knife at his groin appeared to be sufficient persuasion. He stood still.

"I've got some good advice for you, Sturgeon." Trev spoke through his teeth. "If the lady chooses to take you, you'll treat her right, do you follow me?"

For an instant, the officer just stared at him, breathing hoarsely against the pressure at his throat. Then a half degree of tension left his body, though he held himself stiff against the wall, well away from Trev's knife point. "Shelford's girl, do you mean?" He lifted his lip in derision. "Is that all? Damn, I thought you a common footpad."

"I could be," Trev said in a silken tone. "I could strip you and leave you bleeding in the street, and I may yet. But you'll give up your bobtails and keep your trousers closed, starting now. You won't shame her or hurt her; you'll treat her like a queen, do you comprehend me?" He pressed the knife closer.

Sturgeon tried to back up with a little scrabble against the brick. "Good Christ," he snarled. "What is it you have in for me? I caved to your bloody blackmail the first time, I broke it off with her— damned if I crawl for the likes of you again. I'll kill you first."

"Blackmail?" Trev held him hard, his eyes narrowed. "Somebody got the advantage of you, Sturgeon?"

"You know what I mean. What's your game? What do you want from me?" Sturgeon made a grunt as he tried to break free. "Take your blade away, fight me like a man." He gasped through Trev's constriction on his throat.

"This is how I fight." As Sturgeon's hand moved, reaching, searching for the knife, Trev kneed him again. The officer wheezed, well caught between his windmill and his waterpipe.

"Like a bloodsucking thief." Sturgeon's teeth were white in the shadows. "Blackmailer!"

"I never blackmailed you, you maggot," Trev hissed. "I don't know what you're talking about."

"Lie like the two-faced French devil you are!" Sturgeon gasped for air. "I know you did it. You were there."

"Where? I was where?"

The officer held stiff, glaring at Trev over his arm, his lips compressed. "You were there. Who else but Hixson could have known?"

"Are you talking about Salamanca?" Trev asked in wonder. "Good God, is that it?"

Sturgeon didn't answer, but his look was answer enough.

Trev held him. "That courier's orders? Someone blackmailed you with it?"

"Oh, the innocence," Sturgeon sneered. "All these years I never realized it must be you, you turncoat worm, until I saw you with her! It's too bad I didn't have you shot the day Hixson brought you in."

There was truth enough to the word "turncoat" that Trev had to swallow back an urge to beat the man to a bloody pulp. His breath came harsh, but he kept his voice dead even. "Tell me all of it. You were blackmailed into jilting her? Did they ask for money too?"

"They?" Sturgeon gave him a look of scorn. "You! No money, and you know it. But Shelford wrung me to the last penny for sheering off, if it gives you any satisfaction."

"Oh, it does," Trev said. "Believe me."

"And you didn't manage to get your claws on her fortune after all." His lip curled. "What happened, did the old earl have you whipped away at the tail end of a cart?"

Trev held himself back from strangling the man on the wave of rage that suffused him. Instead he blew air through his teeth and gave a bitter laugh. Suddenly he let go, all at once, and stepped back, well out of range of the heavy blow that Sturgeon threw. He blocked the next punch, still laughing, an angry sound that echoed in the alleyway until Sturgeon stood back, huffing for air, looking at Trev as if he were mad.

"I didn't blackmail you, Sturgeon," he said. "I was a prisoner until after Waterloo, you jackass, how'd you suppose I'd know anything about you, or give a damn? I didn't even know your name at Salamanca. Hell and the devil, I was grateful to you for taking that tent out of artillery range. You were welcome to ignore all the orders you liked, by my lights, as long as you didn't get me shot."

"Shut up about it." The officer looked as if he'd like to enter into a further brawl, but Trev could see him thinking in spite of himself, calculating history and distance.

"I didn't return to England till '17," Trev said, to aid him with his mathematics. He held himself ready, watching Sturgeon put his hand on his sword. "I'd say if someone blackmailed you, it's Geordie Hixson must be your man, though I'd not have thought it in his style."

"Hixson was already dead a two-month before I got the note."

"Geordie's dead?" Trev scowled. "How?"

"A damned kettle of turtle soup," Sturgeon said. "Cook left it in a copper pot overnight, so they said. Or it was poisoned on purpose, belike. Convenient for you that he's not alive to say his piece."

"Oh, isn't it? You think I murdered him and then blackmailed you out of marrying her? All the while I was incarcerated at Wellington's behest. The bastard kept me right through the Paris treaty, and you're welcome to question the Foreign Office on that if you like." Trev began to chuckle again on a wilder note. "Or save yourself the trouble and ask Madame Malempré where I was." He gave the officer a swift bow, backing away to make sure he was out of range as he did. "Were you before me with her, or after, Sturgeon? Quite a willing little piece, that one."

The officer stood upright, stiffening. His face went white. "I will kill you," he said low.

"I'm sorry to enlighten you as to her liberal character." Trev pulled his pistol from his pocket. "But you won't be entertaining yourself with that sort of thing anyway," he informed the officer. "You think me capable of blackmail—I assure you that I am. If my friends tell me you're embarrassing my lady with any escapades of a romantic nature, or distressing her in any way, you'll find yourself drummed before a court-martial, and I'll be very pleased to tell them what I saw that day."

"The word of a French coward against mine!" Sturgeon spat in the street.

"I'd advise you not to take the risk," Trev said softly. "The exposure alone—the rumors, the questions. Think about it, while you turn about and walk out to the street."

The officer glared at him. For a long moment, they faced one another across the dark, garbage-strewn distance between them. Then Sturgeon pulled his cloak about him and turned, striding swiftly toward the open street.

Everyone supposed it was the blow to her head that made Callie stare vaguely out of windows and lose the tail of her sentences. Hermey watched her with a worried little frown and asked if she was in pain at least once an hour. To pacify her sister's concern, Callie submitted to daily attention from Shelford's mumbling old doctor and then locked herself in her bedchamber to provide Hermey with the happy impression that she was resting quietly. It was a convenient excuse to avoid Major Sturgeon's frequent calls to leave flowers and inquire after her condition. And to avoid making a visit to Dove House.

She spent the time pacing and leafing through every copy of an outdated paper or magazine that she had been able to discover at Shelford Hall. She was down to the fish wrappings, but she'd found nothing that hinted at the trial that had so fascinated Dolly. In spite of all the concentration she could muster, Callie couldn't recall precisely when it had taken place. Some time ago: after last Christmas she was certain, but had it been in the spring or the early summer? *The Lady's Magazine* of March was mute on the topic. The latest copy, October, had been whisked away by Hermey and was nowhere to be found amid the gowns and hats and peculiar assortment of possible costumes for the upcoming masquerade ball that lay cast about her room. All the volumes in between were making their way along the village circuit, passed from house to house in a strictly defined order of precedence before being returned to Shelford Hall, where they would be bound and shelved in neat gilded leather bindings at the end of each year.

She'd found nothing more informative than a folded month-old page of the *Gazetteer and New Daily Advertiser*, which had slid under a cushion in the library and been missed by the charwoman. The page contained an odd and passionate letter to the editor from a Mrs. Fowler, who accused her enemies of besmirching her name in the attempt to "murder the good reputation of an innocent creature and impose upon the public." Mrs. Fowler insisted that her whole heart belonged to one man, and one alone, and though he was no longer at her side, those who knew her best would never doubt this.

It was a strange letter, fervently written but repellent to Callie's mind; a washing of one's linen in a public newspaper that hardly seemed appropriate to any situation. The name Fowler seemed distantly familiar, but it was common enough and there was no reference in the letter to any trial. The remainder of the page was taken up with a description of a concert by an Italian violinist, a discussion of the new Navigation Act, and three advertisements for linen drapers. Callie had smoothed the paper, folded it again, and placed it in her pocket diary. It disturbed her in some way that she couldn't quite fathom, but she found it impossible to discard.

She was carrying the diary when at last she had herself driven to Dove House a week after her return from the disastrous fair at Hereford. She dreaded to call, but when she heard that Lilly had sent to Mrs. Adam for the ingredients for a chest plaster, Callie felt she must look in on the duchesse. Constable Hubble was sitting opposite the garden gate, perched on a crate with the remains of a substantial luncheon about him. He put aside his mug and a half-eaten pie and stood hastily as the trap drew up, straightening his coat with a stern look.

When he recognized Callie, he eased his severe expression and pulled off his hat. "Afternoon, my lady." He offered a rough hand to help her down.

"We ain't caught 'im yet, ma'am, but I've set a net, as you can see. We'll snap him up if he comes near, mark my words."

"A net?" She paused, glancing up from the generously packed food basket at his feet.

"Aye, ma'am. I'm here m'self, in the flesh, as you might say, and I got my boys posted both ends up the village, that I do, my lady. He won't get past us!"

Callie relaxed slightly. She had thought for a moment that he meant a real net, one capable of actually trapping someone. Once she understood that it consisted of the constable and his two lads barricading the single road through Shelford—well provisioned by Cook, too, it appeared—her immediate alarm receded. Trev was out of the country by now in any case, so there was little fear that Constable Hubble would be required to desert his picnic basket in the line of duty.

"Thank you," she said. "That relieves my mind. I hope you enjoyed your dinner?"

"Aye, my lady, that I did. Her's a mighty cook, that woman come to work for the poor duchesse. Her can make a kidney pudding to rival my old Fanny's, rest her soul, and I wouldn't say that about nobody else."

It was high praise indeed, this comparison to Constable Hubble's beloved late wife. Callie nodded. "I'm pleased to hear it. But do you say the duchesse is poorly?"

He gave a solemn nod. "Cook tells me the lady ain't got no appetite—that's why her brings us out so much broken victuals." He twisted his hat and ducked his head. "We wouldn't gobble so much otherwise, my lady, but Cook don't want it to go waste, y'see."

"I understand." Callie was glad at least to know that Trev must have arranged for ample provisions to the house. She could see that someone had been working in the garden, clearing away the chaos that Hubert had left and trimming the plants down to winter crowns. There was a pot of Michaelmas daisies on the stoop, with purple petals and cheerful yellow eyes.

She took a deep breath, gathered her skirt, and walked up to the door. Lilly answered the bell promptly.

"Oh, my lady!" The maid stepped aside as Callie entered, closing the door. "I'm so thankful you've come—Madame asks so many questions and looks at me so odd, and I don't know what to say! My lord told me that I mustn't worry her, and I've tried, my lady— I've tried, but—" Suddenly her eyes filled and she dropped a belated curtsy. "I beg your pardon, but—" She put her apron over her face and burst into tears.

Callie felt all the guilty weight of her neglect in delaying to call. She put her arm about the girl and guided a sobbing Lilly toward the kitchen. Cook turned about from her chopping, took one look at them, and lifted the teakettle from the hob. Lilly wiped her eyes and plopped down in a chair.

"She asked me when the duke was to call again!" the maid exclaimed in tragic tones. "And I knew I was meant to say that he would be here soon, b-but I c-couldn't seem to say it a-right. And she looks at me *so*! And now her cough is worse, and her fever is high—Nurse says she's in a bad way, even with the mustard plasters."

"Nurse." Cook snorted, sitting down and reaching over with her great arm to fill the teapot amid clouds of steam. "Don't put much stock on what her says,

I don't. That grim sort, them likes to make out like as all's going to wrack and ruin. Gives 'em position, they suppose."

Lilly sniffed. "Do you think?"

"Ma'am's been eatin'. Not in great swallows, her ain't, but I seen that tray don't come back quite so full as it goes up."

In spite of a desire to hurry to Madame's bedside at this news, Callie delayed to share a cup of tea. It was always best to learn what the servants had to say of a situation. Lady Shelford would never countenance a chat in the kitchen with the staff, but Callie had no such qualms. "So there's been no word from the duke this past week?" she asked, careful to keep her voice level and unconcerned.

"No, my lady," Lilly said. She glanced toward Cook and then averted her eyes, heaping lumps of sugar into her tea.

Callie noted the heavy inroads on the sugarloaf, which had been reduced from a neatly peaked cone to a shapeless lump wrapped in blue paper. "You have enough to buy what provisions you need?" she asked.

"Oh aye," Cook said comfortably. "We got us an open account at the greengrocer and the butcher too, and I told the duke I've no need to have recourse to the cookshop. Whatever Ma'am needs, I can make right here, I told him. There was a little trouble when that Easley woman tried to buy a ham off the butcher, claiming her was working here at Dove House, but I took care of that. And I'll send *that* one on her way if she comes round about here again, no matter if Ma'am wants to waste her time on such rubbish and don't know her own good." Cook nodded and thumped her knuckles on the table, making the teacups rattle.

"Mrs. Easley has come here?" Callie asked in surprise.

"Twice!" Cook said indignantly. "Come asking to see Ma'am, and got herself in too!" She glared at Lilly.

"Madame said she wanted to see her!" Lilly protested. "It's not my place to say she can't see anyone she likes, is it?"

Callie shook her head. "Of course not. I'm sure the duchesse wanted to make certain that poor Mrs. Easley was—that her situation had not deteriorated after she was turned off."

"'Poor Mrs. Easley,'" Cook mocked with a snort. "Her's top-heavy from the gin, that's all o' her situation a body needs to know."

Callie could not argue this point. She nodded. "Well, I don't want her to worry the duchesse—if she comes again, you may turn her away."

"But Madame said in particular that she was to be allowed to call," Lilly said plaintively.

Callie frowned. "I see. If that's the case, I suppose we must allow it. I'm sure the duchesse feels some gratitude toward Mrs. Easley, in spite of her faults. She was the cook here for a good while, after all, before—" She cleared her throat. "Before Madame's circumstances were recently improved," she finished.

"Too soft-hearted by half," Cook grumbled.

"I perfectly comprehend you, Cook. And do make sure to count the silver whenever she leaves." Callie stood. "I'll go up now. You may bring us some tea and whatever you think Madame might be persuaded to partake."

Cook nodded and heaved herself to her feet, turning briskly in spite of her bulk. Lilly dried her eyes and shook out her apron. She began to collect clean cups from the cupboard. Callie paused at the door and watched for a moment. A wave of gratitude came over her for these two humble and good-hearted people. While she had been cravenly putting off a call on the duchesse, for fear of what questions she might face, they had been taking care of their mistress with staunch loyalty. "Thank you," she said. "Madame is very fortunate to have you both."

Lilly blushed and curtsied. Cook grunted an assent. "Her's not a bit o' trouble," she said. "Now that mad Frenchie son o' hers—" She shook her head and took a deep breath, preparing for what Callie could see would be a lengthy exposition on the topic of the duke.

"I must go up," she said hastily and closed the door before Cook could get a start on her next sentence.

It didn't take long for Callie to understand why Lilly had been reduced to tears. The duchesse was neither gloomy nor distressed; she sat up and smiled and conversed in her elegant, accented English, but she seemed spun fragile and slight as a thread of glass, as fleeting as a web that glistened in morning dew. She asked no questions about her son, but her bright, feverish glance followed Callie with an intensity that seemed to look right through her, as if in search of answers.

They spoke of the cattle fair and Callie's knock on the head. Madame inquired as to Hubert's health and nodded in satisfaction when she learned that the bull was residing temporarily in his home pasture at Shelford Hall again while Colonel Davenport repaired his stone walls to Callie's strict specifications. That lesson, at least, had been learned.

Callie wondered if Trev had found a way to see his mother before he left, but she was simply too craven to ask. Instead, to fill the time with safer topics, she asked if she might read to the duchesse, and picked up a periodical from a stack on the bedside table.

"Please, if you will," Madame said faintly, smiling and closing her eyes. "Such a world beyond—our village. And such people it is. I am never at a loss to be amused."

Callie nodded. She brushed her thumb through a copy of *The Lady's Spectator*, one of the more daring of the new journals that Dolly had brought to Shelford. Although it was much sought after in some quarters, several of the ladies of the village would not even allow it within their doors. Doubtless that was why Madame—languishing at the low end of village precedence—had a copy only a few months old at her bedside. It was a summer number, full of town gossip and moralizing in equal measure, warning ladies against the unwholesome activities of the bon ton while describing them in rich and titillating detail. Callie was suddenly glad that her appearance as Madame Malempré had occurred in such a backwater as Hereford, or she suspected that she would have found the entire escapade described in detail in the upcoming Christmas volume. The editors of *The Lady's Spectator* appeared to know a great deal about all manner of personal and public activities.

She searched for something she could read aloud without blushing, and finally found an article on a financial scandal, in which the perpetrator had, according to the affronted editors, "sold out his own holdings in good time while keeping the true state of affairs from the public." When the stock company in question failed, this malefactor had fled to Naples, where he was now residing comfortably on the sixty thousand pounds he had previously settled on his wife, much to the fury and financial embarrassment of his creditors.

The article editorialized at length on the shameful tendency of the justices to allow these villains of both sexes to impose upon society without fear of retribution. Callie added emphasis to her reading voice as the author summed up with high flourishes of moral contempt. Then she paused. She frowned as she finished the article's last sentence, which compared this disgraceful situation to that of Mrs. Fowler's escape from a just penalty for her crime of forgery.

"Oh," the duchesse said, opening her eyes suddenly. She lifted one slender hand. "Pray do not read me of this tiresome Mrs. Fowler. I have no interest in that... sordid affair."

Callie found to her chagrin that she did. Prurient and low though it might be, she had a burning desire to discover more of the woman who protested her innocence in the public papers. And now, finding that Mrs. Fowler was apparently accused of forgery—Callie hardly seemed able to hold the journal steady. She riffled through the pages quickly, following the indication pointing to *Further Articles Relating to the Trials of Mrs. Fowler and Monsieur LeBlanc, Page 24.* Fortunately the designated page included a story about a well-known actress driving herself alone in Hyde Park, an uneventful progress, which was nevertheless endowed by the editors with broad hints of sinister meaning. Callie read it aloud, trying to examine the articles about Mrs. Fowler from the corner of her eye.

They detailed the lady's history with the salacious enjoyment of a first-rate village gossip. The pretty daughter of a Yorkshire gentleman with both money and connections, Mrs. Fowler might have made a respectable match, but instead she had obliged *The Lady's Spectator* by running away with an impoverished poet at sixteen. After his early demise in a sponging house, she straight away wed a famous prizefighter— Mr. Jem "The Rooster" Fowler—and became the reigning toast of the Corinthian set, only to witness his death in the ring under suspicious circumstances. But it was the description of her companion Monsieur LeBlanc that made Callie stumble as she tried to read. He figured prominently in the latter part of the story, first as the friend, then as the lover, then as the secret spouse of Mrs. Fowler.

He was French, but according to *The Lady's Spectator,* no one who knew him personally could hold that against him. The journal seemed to take a tolerant, even an admiring view of his activities. Monsieur LeBlanc was a member of the demimonde and the boxing fancy, a bookmaker and organizer of bouts, a close friend of Gentleman Jackson and the Rooster, and a man of impeccable character and noble manners. The journal saved its disdain for the hapless widow, Mrs. Fowler, who had been detected in the attempt to pass a forged note of hand in payment for her large debt at a dressmaker.

Upon exposure, this unfortunate lady had at first seemed bewildered by the idea that anything could be amiss. Learning that the crime was subject to capital punishment, however, she had instantly insisted that her friend Monsieur LeBlanc had given her the note, which she had merely delivered in all innocence. At her trial, she had caused a sensation by revealing that he acted as trustee of the considerable public sum that had been collected to support her and her child after her husband's untimely death in the boxing ring. Upon examination, she tearfully suggested that Monsieur had gambled away her money and been reduced to forgery to hide it from her.

Several affecting drawings of Mrs. Fowler accompanied the description of her trial. She was shown in her prison cell, in the dock, and praying outside the courtroom with her young son, each time in a different gown. But however plausible and touching it might be, *The Lady's Spectator* did not swallow her story for an instant. There was no indication, upon the court's summoning of the account books, that Monsieur LeBlanc had mismanaged Mrs. Fowler's trust. Indeed, it appeared that when she had exhausted the stipend with her spending, he had given her a generous amount of money from his own funds as well.

It was this last fact that riveted Callie's attention and caught that of the eager public too, it seemed. The discovery that he had been supporting Mrs. Fowler for some years prior to the scandal put a new light on their relationship. Witnesses spoke of how often he was in her company, how tenderly he treated her. While it had never been brought up at the trial itself, *The Lady's Spectator* confidently stated that they had married on the day after the Rooster's death and kept it secret so as not to offend the mood of public mourning for the famous boxer. Thus he made no defense at his own trial, taking the part of tragic honor and allowing himself to be convicted so that his lover might be declared innocent.

Callie looked up, realizing that she had long since ceased to read aloud. She stared blankly at the bedpost. Her heart was beating wildly, but she sat very still.

It was Trev, of course. She knew that with a certainty that went to her bones. He had not come home from France. He had been in England all along. All his huge menservants—they were prizefighters. He had been convicted of forgery, and it was precisely the sort of gallant thing he would do, sacrifice himself for a woman.

For his wife.

The duchesse said nothing. When Callie looked up at her, their eyes met for a long moment. Madame bit her lip and turned her face away with an unhappy look. It came upon Callie suddenly that she knew— that the guilt and sadness in Madame's face were because she knew.

"Oh my," Callie said. She was numb, but she struggled to speak. "Oh."

The duchesse reached toward her. "My dear, if I may—"

"I'm sorry, I... I must go." She couldn't hold the magazine for another moment; she let it fall to the floor as she stood and hurried to the door. "I really must go!" she exclaimed. She closed the door behind her, ran down the stairs, and flew out the door, leaving Lilly standing with some unanswered query on her lips.

Eighteen

"I FEEL A DEEP LOVE AND ABIDING RESPECT FOR YOU, my dear," Major Sturgeon said. "You have made me the happiest man alive."

"Congratulations," Callie remarked wryly, holding her bucket with both hands as she lugged it to the stove. "How pleased I am for you."

He glanced up at her from his position on the requisite bended knee. He had worn his full dress uniform, all burnished and plumed, as he made his call in reply to her note that she had made up her mind in the matter. The Shelford yard and cattle stalls were quite clean, but he had paused and looked carefully at the ground before he lowered himself to put his question to her.

"Oh dear," she added, seeing his expression as she set the bucket down. "That's someone else's line, isn't it? I've done this so often that I become confused."

He had the grace to made a gesture of rueful admission. "You haven't been treated as you ought, dearest, and I am the first to blame for that."

She gave him a faintly acid smile. "Only the first."

He stood up, looking down for a moment and brushing at his knees. Then he took a step toward her and caught both of her hands in his. "I hope I can make you as happy as you have made me."

She raised her lashes. "You might lift this bucket up onto the stove, in that case," she said.

"Certainly!" He let go of her and reached down, hefting the bucket of mash and molasses onto the hot surface with a grunt. He stood back, brushing his palms together. "I beg your pardon, I ought to have done so instantly, but I was… distracted."

"By your deep love and abiding respect." Callie took up the wooden paddle and began to stir the mix. "I understand completely." She peered down into the dark syrup. "I have one stipulation that I must mention."

"Of course. Tell me anything that would please you."

"I hope you won't object to a marriage of convenience."

"Convenience?" He drew her away from the stove, taking her hand again lightly. "I'm not certain that I understand you."

Heat rose in her cheeks. She held the paddle out over the pail to prevent molasses from dripping to the floor. "I mean that I prefer not to interfere in your conduct. You may feel free to indulge—"

"My dear!" He interrupted her, catching the paddle from her and dropping it into the mash. "We needn't speak of this sort of thing. I mean to make up fully for my past fault, of that I assure you. Tell me—where would you like to live? Somewhere that you may raise your cattle, I'm certain, and I've had my eye on the broads country round about Norwich. Have you seen it? What do you think of the forage there?"

Callie pulled her fingers free. She looked down at her muck boots and then up again. "I believe you understand me perfectly well. I do not wish to be touched."

Surprise flitted across his features, followed by a lightly concealed impatience. "Delicacy of feeling is perfectly understandable in a virtuous maiden such as yourself, of course. I hope that I can assuage your fears. I'm not an insensitive man."

"It isn't delicacy of feeling," Callie said frankly. "It is you, sir. I do not wish to be touched by you. You may consider it a personal aversion, if you like. I well understand that you wish to marry me for my money. You must understand that I have purely practical motives to accept you. You may, of course, feel free to withdraw your suit if that offends you."

He stared at her. "My lady—" He seemed unable to summon a reply. Callie had the notion that he actually noticed her for the first time and was not pleased with what he perceived. She turned to the pail and began to stir vigorously before the syrup could congeal.

"You feel a personal aversion to me?" he asked, as if the very thought bewildered him.

The notion that any female could hold him in aversion appeared to be a supremely difficult concept for him to grasp. She let go of the spoon and turned. "I beg your pardon," she said with a slight curtsy. "I am known to have poor taste."

He stood observing her with a frown. "I'm sorry to hear that you feel this way."

She offered a consoling glance and went back to her task. "I'm sure I'm in the minority."

Major Sturgeon stroked his plumed hat. Callie waited for him to say that the engagement was off.

She wondered if she had been engaged long enough for it to count as a fourth jilt. Going for a record, Trev would have said. But she did not want to think of Trev. She was done with Trev. She walked Trev to the end of a plank at sword point and poked him in the back and watched him step off into shark-infested waters with a huff of satisfaction. Before he even hit the water, she was stirring hard as she boiled him in a vat of molasses and made him march, covered in goose feathers, down the center of Broad Street in Hereford, while farmwives jeered and threw pear tarts at his back.

She stiffened a little as the major took a step toward her. He noticed it. He paused in midstride and held himself up. Callie stopped stirring her mash pail. For an instant they were like two tin soldiers facing one another.

"My lady," he said. A degree of the rigid affront left him. He lifted his hat and dropped it with a helpless move. "I'll admit that I hardly know what to say. Are we to be strangers to one another, then? Do you wish to live separately? I had hoped that my children—" He stopped.

Callie supposed that he was hesitant to admit quite so openly that he needed a mother for his family. Her cheeks were flaming with bright red spots, she was sure. She wiped her hands on her apron and glanced over the stall partitions to be sure no one was nearby. "It isn't that. I look forward to becoming acquainted with your children. I don't—I suppose I don't wish to live separately." She took a breath, feeling as if she were smothered in molasses herself. "This is a difficult topic to discuss. I would prefer not to live as man and wife. Of course I understand that you will have— other interests—and I wish you to understand that is perfectly acceptable to me."

He stood looking at her, a slight frown creasing his brow. He shook his head slightly. "A mistress, I comprehend you mean. Pardon my bluntness. No, my lady, I had not contemplated such a thing."

"Oh come," she said, adding another scoop of barley and giving the mash a hard stir. "Pray do not lie to me."

A silence stretched between them. He averted his eyes and shrugged. "Perhaps at one time I did." He looked at her askance, his lowered glance traveling from her hem to her throat. "I cannot, at the moment, comprehend why."

"Perhaps you will remember later," Callie said dryly. She would hardly be an object of admiration in her canvas apron and mucking boots. "It doesn't matter. That is my stipulation, along with my choice of property for our home and a settlement in which I have ample allowance to pursue my cattle husbandry."

He examined the plume on his hat, running his fingers over the feathers. Then he shrugged. "I will agree to that, my dear, if it's truly what you wish."

Callie found herself even more flustered. She'd rather hoped that he would find her requirements too onerous, but of course except for his pride, there was little to burden him in her requests. Her mouth was dry as she nodded. "Very well."

He reached as if to take her hand to kiss it, then stopped himself, looking conscious. He substituted with a brisk military bow. Callie gave him a shallow curtsy in return.

It was settled, then; she would truly marry this man and go away from Shelford Hall with him.

"Ah yes!" he exclaimed with a forced brightness. "But in the excitement of our coming to an understanding, I'd forgot that I've news for you. You'll be pleased to hear that my efforts to apprehend that so-called Belgian scoundrel for you have borne fruit."

She lifted her eyes quickly. "Indeed?"

"Yes, I had word from some men I hired out of Bow Street. He was spotted boarding a ship, but when the port police learned that there was warrant for him, they sent an officer out to take him off before it left harbor."

"Oh?" To hide her reaction, Callie turned to the bucket of mash on the stove. She took up a cloth and clasped both hands about the wooden handle of the pail, gripping it tightly.

He reached to help her lift it from the stove. "They're low fellows, those thief-takers, but they know the criminal mind. Careful! Allow me, my dear. They tracked him from Hereford to the Bristol docks. He's jailed and awaiting the assizes by now. Take care!" He leaped back as the bucket tilted and clattered to the floor, spilling a flood of hot molasses and barley grain.

Trev should have been on a packet ship for Boston instead of under his mother's bed. His trunk—and Jock along with it—were aboard. But Trev had gone ashore with the last mail, telling himself he ought to leave a final note for his maman and that he'd somehow find the words to write it on the Bristol quay. He hadn't, of course. Six beakers of blue ruin in a dockside gin house had not loosened his pen, but they had succeeded in making him miss the last call for the ship tender.

Jock was doubtless a little put out. Trev sincerely hoped that Boston had excellent tailors.

He'd woken up with a thundering headache and no purse. By the time his head was clear, he'd been halfway to London on borrowed blunt, with the intent to track down whoever it was who had blackmailed Sturgeon. It was a bothersome itch in the back of his mind—though not as bothersome as the dust ball that was tickling his nose at the moment. He stifled a sneeze.

"Why is this window wide open to the cold night air?" Nurse demanded. Her sturdy shoes clumped across the floor, making the boards vibrate under Trev's cheek. He'd just made it under the bed before the door opened. "The plain truth is, that young maid is a good-for-nothing! I'd supposed Madame would be asleep," she added severely. "And the candle still lit!" There was an ominous pause. "I daresay you didn't think to ring for me to snuff it?"

"You may put it out now," his maman said faintly. "No—ah no, pray—there is no need for you to… occupy the dressing room tonight."

Nurse's feet clumped indignantly. "My duty to you, Madame."

"But… you wish me to sleep," the duchesse said in a plaintive tone. "Do you not?"

"Certainly, Madame."

"Then I think… " His maman trailed off. "I do not say that the snore would… wake the dead. But perhaps I think it might."

Trev pressed his fist to his mouth and nose, subduing a sneeze and a laugh. It was said with such a pretty, tremulous naïveté that the nurse didn't even feel the sting. She huffed and clumped about, grumbling, but after slamming shut the window, placing all the utensils of her black art to her satisfaction, and snuffing the lamp, she made a decisive effort to tiptoe on the way to the door, threatening to rattle the medicine bottles off the shelf.

After the door closed behind her, a silence descended on the room. Trev waited. The sound of Nurse's shoes receded, replaced by the creaks of the floorboards overhead as she took possession of the attic.

"Mon trésor," his mother murmured. "The toast is clear."

Trev worked himself from beneath the bed frame, wincing as he bumped his head. "The 'coast,' Maman. The *coast* is clear." He fumbled to light the bed candle that Nurse had just extinguished.

"That is a great relief to me." She gave a faint smile. "Toast I never could comprehend to be clear. Particularly as the English... put butter on it. Are you hungry?"

He observed her intently, suspicious that his first impression had been correct—that her eyes had filled with tears when she first reached out her hand to him. "I'll eat later. Constable Hubble is presently engaged on some murky business with Cook in the kitchen, which I prefer not to know too much about."

"You have been... traveling?" She seemed unconcerned that he had entered through the window. It seemed to be his typical means of ingress and egress to any respectable establishment these days.

"Yes." He did not elaborate but sat down on the bed and put his finger under her chin. "What is this?" He examined her face from side to side. "You've been gay and raking while I wasn't here to restrain you, I see. Too many parties, Maman. You're run off your feet."

She smiled. Then she gripped his hand and pressed it against her cheek, kissing his palm fiercely. Her eyes glittered as she took a single sobbing breath.

When she released him, he brushed his fingertips tenderly over her pale hair and down her chin. She greeted him with tears. Tears, and he had never seen his maman weep before except when his brother had died. She had lost four more children, but if she shed tears, she had done it in someplace beyond where anyone could see or hear.

"I won't leave again," he murmured.

"But the constable…" she said.

"Aye, and the Bow Street Runners too," he said, dropping his hand with a sigh. "I'll be put to some lengths to dodge them, I fear, but I won't leave you again, Maman."

He hadn't expected to have the Runners on his track. After a narrow escape from a brickyard where he'd been meeting with a clerk from the Bank of England, they'd made London too warm for him in the circles where he was asking questions. So even while he was developing a deep suspicion that there was something amiss with Callie's fortune, he'd been forced to abandon the inquiry and leave for a little holiday in the country.

He should have avoided Shelford, of course. He'd meant only to make a brief pause there to face his final farewells. Getting inside Dove House had not proved to be difficult, but staying only a moment with his maman proved impossible.

"Who are these... Runners?" she asked, frowning a little.

"Fellows from London. Thief-takers by trade." He saw her glance up at him quickly and gave her an easy shrug. "It's about the bull, I suppose. Lady Callista's magistrate friend is a determined prosecutor, but they'll never discover me under your bed, eh?"

She looked at him in that way she had, sidelong beneath her lashes—the one that reminded him where he had inherited his unsteady nature. Not from his upright patrician grandfather, certainly. "Oh yes," she said with a little dismissive gesture of her hand. "I have had news of Lady... Callista. She engages herself again... to marry. It is a very stupid thing."

Trev grew still. He said nothing, only let it wash over him and past, a wave of emotion and anger and all the things he had no right to feel. So, she had done it. He'd advised her to. He gave his mother a tight smile. "Congratulations to her. Sturgeon, I suppose?"

"That military man... who left her at the altar before." She made a sound of vexation. "It is because... you went away. I cannot approve!"

"It isn't your place to approve, Maman, after all." He took firm hold of his composure, building a wall between himself and the space Callie occupied in his heart. "It's not a bad match for her. She wants to have a home of her own and a place for her cattle. He should be able to give her that much, at least."

The duchesse sniffed, wrinkling her nose. "He doesn't love her."

"What's that to say? It's a marriage, not a love affair. He'll respect her as his wife, that I can promise you."

"Bah, how is that so, that you can promise it?"

Trev shrugged. "I had a little talk with him on the subject. In a back alley."

She lifted her slender eyebrows.

"You know I won't let him hurt her, Maman."

His mother gave a vexed sigh. She put her handkerchief to her face as it become a cough. He watched her, concerned and guilty to see how weakly she moved.

"You should sleep now, before Nurse hears you and comes back to discover you dancing jigs against her advice," he said.

"One thing… would make me dance," she whispered hoarsely.

"Maman—"

"You make me… cross," she said, speaking with effort. "Go and sleep… on the floor. And if these Runners should come into my… house, you must pull the… blanket over your head!"

The news that Lady Callista Taillefaire was engaged to be married to Major Sturgeon had created a sense of wonder and awe among the inhabitants of Shelford that equaled the appearance of a comet or some other profound astronomical event. Certainly it had occurred with less warning. But the gentlefolk of Shelford overcame their astonishment in their eager kindness and sent such a number of small gifts, congratulatory cards, and perfumed letters that the pile threatened to overwhelm the porter's table in the hall, and this in spite of the fact that no formal announcement had yet been made.

Callie knew where to lay the blame. Obviously the major had mentioned it to someone—probably Colonel Davenport, in strict confidentiality—and from there the word raced with that mysterious speed and force that only a secret in a small country village could obtain. By the next day after her interview with the major, it was known to Mrs. Adam, Mr. Rankin, Miss Cummins, and Miss Poole. By the second, Reverend Hartman, Mrs. Farr, and Polly Parrot were acquainted with the facts of the matter. By the third day, it was old news to the goats. Callie was only left to wonder if she ought to make a formal announcement to Hubert. She supposed he must know, through the goats, but she wouldn't want to hurt his feelings by being the last to mention it to him.

"Pssst!"

She paused, uncertain if she had heard the whisper, which seemed to emanate from somewhere behind the bales of silk and shawls and cloaks piled high in what passed for the fashion showroom of Miss Poole's mantua-shop. There was no one else in the back room; nothing but fabrics and a faint sour-sweet scent that Callie could not quite place. She had wandered there on the excuse that she was looking over the fabrics, but in truth to escape the frequent congratulations from Miss Poole, which seemed to be unremitting. Callie herself felt rather numb and lacked an appetite, but she could not quite tell if it was from being engaged or expecting momentarily to hear that Monsieur Malempré had been sent to his trial in Bristol.

The hissing sound came again. Callie frowned and looked about the dim corners. Her sister and Dolly drank tea in the front room, poring over the fashion book while Dolly made acidic comments on the poor selection in a country town. It was only an emergency that had brought them to the length of consulting Miss Poole. Having got wind that Callie had used up her sister's rejected coquelicot wool for a costume to be worn at the masquerade ball two days hence, Dolly had positively shrieked with disgust. The impossibility of allowing this cloth to be viewed in public by the guests at Shelford Hall, particularly on Callie, had precipitated a sudden crisis. It was to be a royal blue, or she could appear in her petticoat, Dolly declared. Callie would have preferred to simply remain in her room, but Hermey protested that this would make her appear as if she wished to hog all the attention, when everyone knew that Callie was engaged now too. They would appear together—in suitably harmonious colors—or Hermey would break off her betrothal and enter a convent, or become a milkmaid, or something on that order, but worse. So Callie was at Miss Poole's, to be judged against the silks.

"My lady!" A plump white hand appeared from behind the mantled shape of a dress form. It held a note, the folded paper waving in the faint light. Callie peered around the form. Mrs. Easley crouched down behind it against the back door, holding her bottle in her lap. Callie recognized the sweet scent of gin now.

The woman pushed herself to her feet and leaned against the door frame. "The madame," she said, pushing a loose lock of hair from her forehead.

At that, Callie snapped the note from her hand. She opened it hurriedly. It said only, *My good dear Lady Callista—I beg of you to come to me at once.* The handwriting was shaky, and the duchesse's signature trailed off at the end to a fine thread.

Callie did not hesitate. She edged behind the dress form and followed Mrs. Easley out the back door of the shop.

"An' so you're to be married, m'lady!" Mrs. Easley mumbled as she made weaving but gallant attempts to keep up with Callie's stride. A fine sprinkle and lowering clouds threatened rain, but as yet it was only a misting. "Dare s'y you'll be wantin' a cook for the new establishmuum?"

Callie ignored this, drawing her shawl up over her head against the light dust of raindrops. Her heart was too far in her throat to compose any sort of reply that would not come back to trouble her in the future, so she merely kept walking and hoped Mrs. Easley would fall behind. That hope took on substance when the former cook halted abruptly, barely keeping her balance, as they came upon Dove Lane and saw a man in the distance ahead of them. Callie would have hurried ahead, but Mrs. Easley grabbed her elbow.

"Hssst! M'lady! That's a one of 'em!" Her slurred voice took on sharp urgency, and her fingers dug into Callie's arm. "Stop!"

Callie had little choice, as Mrs. Easley seemed bent on dragging her bodily back. "One of who?" she asked, trying to disengage herself from the drunken cook's grip.

"'Em runner fellows, up from London. Thief-takers, m'lady!"

Callie looked back. She could see the man loitering far up the lane, moving from side to side in a strange manner, as if he were inspecting something in the dirt. She gave an exasperated sigh. A genuine thief-taker was a rare article in Shelford. The occasional disappearance of a farm implement, which was usually discovered next spring where it had been left under a rick during the last haying season, was what passed for a wave of criminal activity in Shelford. In fact Callie could not remember ever hearing of one of the profes-sional policemen in the vicinity before. But doubtless if they were looking about for thieves, Mrs. Easley had her reasons to avoid them. "You may go back, then," she said. "The duchesse needs me."

Mrs. Easley seemed readily willing to take this advice, but she retained her hold, muttering, "Have a care, m'lady! Don't 'er go near 'em!"

"I'll say nothing of your activities, I can promise you," Callie assured her. She pulled away and took a determined stride toward Dove House. Mrs. Easley tried to cling, uttering some further slurred objection, but Callie shook her off and turned down the lane. She doubted any thief-taker would dare to accost a lady. She was walking quite quickly by the time she reached him, and didn't hesitate or give him notice. She merely hastened past, aware that he stopped and stared at her as she turned in at the gate of Dove House.

The garden gate swung closed behind her with a bang. She didn't pause to ring, but to her surprise the cottage door was locked. She rattled at the latch, then rang the bell with a clamor. After a few interminable moments, Lilly's muffled voice came through the door, demanding in a rather quavering tone who was calling.

"Lady Callista!" Callie responded impatiently. Her fear of the duchesse's condition was rising with every obstacle that delayed her. "Do let me in!"

The door cracked. Lily peeked out, grabbed her arm, and pulled Callie inside, slamming the door and turning the key in the lock. "Upstairs, my lady!" she said urgently. "Oh, hurry!"

Callie ran up the stairs, almost colliding with the nurse at the top. "I'm sending Lilly for the doctor, my lady," Nurse exclaimed. "She won't let me in the door, Madame won't!"

Callie looked at Nurse in dismay. She could hear the duchesse coughing violently. "Won't let you in?"

"Locked me out!" Nurse said. "I fear the worst, my lady." She looked grim. "She's gone out of her head."

"Go for the doctor yourself," Callie ordered. "And send Lilly to the Antlers to fetch Mr. Rankin. He'll be able to unlock the door. I'll see if I can coax Madame to let me in. Hurry."

As the nurse pounded down the stairs, Callie faced the duchesse's closed door. The coughing beyond had ceased, which frightened her even more. She put her hand on the latch and pushed, expecting it to resist her.

It gave way easily. She opened the door. A strong hand grabbed her arm. For the second time in a few moments, she was yanked inside as a door shut behind her with a sharp thump.

She caught herself and turned, looking from the duchesse, who was sitting up in bed, to Trevelyan, who was engaged in locking the door. She had expected to find the duchesse alone and dreaded to discover her in the midst of fatal spasms. Instead she was looking quite animated and gesturing at the door with her handkerchief. For an instant Callie was unable to perfectly comprehend the scene.

She glared at Trev.

"*You!*" Her whole body seemed to lose any sense of up or down; her hands went slack and then began to tremble. "What are you—" She blinked back a peculiar stinging in her eyes and nose. It was difficult to find any air for a moment, and then all her feeling came rushing back upon her at once. "*You!*"

He gave her a look, a little shamefaced, a wry half smile, and a shrug, so much like him that she put her hands to her mouth, closed her eyes, and took a deep breath into her lungs. When she opened them again, he was still standing there. He was not a figment of her strained nerves or imagination.

"What are *you* doing here?" she cried. "And that man... that man outside..." She paused as the ramifications all came clear to her. "Oh my God—he's a *thief-taker!*"

Nineteen

"MY DEAR—WE MUST BEG FOR YOUR AID—IF YOU WILL assist us one more time. I am so sorry to trouble you again! But there is a thief-taker, yes. I fear so."

The duchesse gave a little wry smile, and Callie saw where her son had inherited that particular expression of self-deprecating appeal. But Callie hadn't gone through coaxing Hubert out of a kitchen, masquerading as a Belgian lady, suffering an animal rout at the cattle fair, and then discovering that Trev was married to some person who forged bank notes, without learning anything. She resisted forcefully the danger of succumbing to any Gallic charm.

"I'm very sorry," she said, holding herself stiff. "I had thought you were unwell, ma'am, and so I came as quickly as I received your note. I'm happy to see that you aren't in danger. Regarding thief-takers, I don't see what I can do in such matters. If you'll excuse me, I'll go and prevent Nurse from fetching the doctor."

She turned toward the door, half expecting that Trev would endeavor to stop her. He didn't. The duchesse said nothing. Callie reached for the latch with silence in the room behind her. She paused with her hand on the knob.

His mother made a very small cough, a faint, muffled sound, as if she tried to stifle it.

Callie dropped her hand. She turned about. "Oh, very well!" she exclaimed. "What is it?"

"It's nothing," Trev said. He stood across the room from her, making no attempt to move closer. "I didn't know that my mother had contacted you—I asked her not to do so." He gave the duchesse a brief glance. "I'll inquire into how you managed that under my very nose, Maman, but later. Please, Lady Callista, if you'll just contrive to forget that you've seen me here, you needn't concern yourself further in the situation."

"Excellent." She threw up her hands. "The last I was told, you were arrested on the Bristol quay and put to trial, and now I'm to forget I've seen you here while a thief-taker out of Bow Street lurks in the garden."

"Hired by your new fiancé, as I understand," he replied acidly. "I could wish you'd suggested to him that he call off the hounds. I've had his pursuers on my heels since I left Hereford."

For herself, she could have wished that he had mentioned he was married. But she was determined to say nothing of that. She had spent a number of nights weeping into her pillow over the disclosure, but she would die rather than allow him to know it. It was quite certain to her now that she had made the veriest fool of herself. She could not remember with any clarity their brief discussion of marriage in Hereford, though she had spent long hours trying to recall what precisely he had said about it. All she could seem to draw from her memory, with considerable blushing, were the parts that had little to do with conversation. He had not wished to marry her in the morning, however—that much she remembered perfectly.

"I beg your pardon," she said. "If you mean Major Sturgeon, the topic of you has not arisen between us in conversation."

She felt that she adhered to the spirit of the truth, if not the letter. After the incident of spilling hot bran mash all over his boots, which he had taken very well, considering, the topic had not arisen again. She lifted her chin a little. Let Trev suppose she had forgot him the moment he had disappeared by vanishing into an alley.

"It makes no matter. My apologies for disturbing you." Trev leaned a shoulder against the wall. "Please go on about your day, my lady." He seemed to find some spot on the fading wallpaper to be of deep interest, observing it with his lashes lowered.

"But you will have to go away, Trevelyan," his mother said. "I cannot... abide the strain of... worry that these thief men will discover you here."

"I'm not going away again, Maman," he said strongly, glancing at her.

"But they will come here, and come again... as they did this... morning... until I am driven... mad."

"I'll simply have to hide when they come."

"Hide where? You cannot... be under my bed... all the day while Nurse comes and goes." She clutched nervously at the bedclothes. "Already I am thinking all night, how will I make sure she does not... see you in the dressing room? It is exhausting."

"I'll think of something," Trev said.

"And now the doctor is on... his way. He must pass that thief person who... lurks outside."

"I'll think of something." Trev swung away from the wall. He gave Callie a brief, polite smile. "Let me offer my best wishes to you and Major Sturgeon on your engagement, my lady. I'm sorry that I can't make a formal call, but you'll comprehend that circumstances prevent me."

The duchesse began to cough. "Do not… pretend—" She wheezed and caught her breath. "As if… it is a drawing room! You must… have a hiding—"

"I'll think of something, Maman," he said in an edged voice. Callie looked at the duchesse, who could not seem to draw air enough into her lungs, but only put her hand to her face and covered her eyes, her body trembling with the effort.

"Well, something must be done," Callie snapped. "Your mother will fret herself to death!"

"And what precisely do you suggest, my lady?" He threw her an angry look. "Dress myself as a footman and serve you and the major your tea?"

"Or secret yourself in my bedchamber, perhaps," she retorted. "I'm certain no one would ever look for you there."

The duchesse recovered her breath. She sat up. "Perfect!" She gasped and subsided in another cough. "It's… perfect. I knew you would… aid us—"

"Maman, for God's sake—"

A distant sound of the bell made them all turn and look with apprehension toward the locked door.

"That will be Mr. Rankin," Callie said. "I'll go down and tell him he's not required."

It was indeed Mr. Rankin, but to Callie's dismay and annoyance, he hadn't arrived alone. Lilly met her on the stairs, hurrying up with her apron lifted. "They're coming into the garden, my lady!" She looked harassed. "Oh, but he's brought that awful major with him!" She stopped on the stairs, giving a little gasp, and then dropped her eyes. "Oh, I forgot—my lady. Begging your pardon, but I meant—why has *he* come? Madame duchesse won't want to see *him*!"

Callie didn't want to see him either. She recalled belatedly that he was putting up at the Antlers now; he must have heard the summons for Mr. Rankin. She closed her eyes for a moment to gather some composure. "I'll speak to them," she said. "Send them into the parlor."

Just then the constable emerged from the depths of the kitchen, holding a large bun between his teeth and shouldering on his coat. He looked as if he'd just got out of bed; his hair and neck cloth oddly disordered for the middle of the day. When he saw Callie, he stopped and quickly dropped the bun from his teeth, stuffing it into his pocket. "Good morning, my lady!" He bobbed his head. "We've not caught that scoundrel yet, but we're on the job here, my lads and I, as you can see!"

Callie paused on her way to the sitting room. "Constable Hubble. Have you spoken to this new thief-taker?"

He looked puzzled. "An' who would that be, my lady? Only fellow paid to take thieves round and about Shelford is myself. And my boys, if I want to share a bit with 'em."

"He's from London, I understand."

The constable's jaw dropped. "London!"

Callie nodded, beckoning him into the parlor. "Yes. From the city. Come in, Constable. Perhaps you can discover more about him, and what he knows of the duke's location. You may wish to work together."

"I have my doubts about that, my lady." The constable followed her, dusting flour from his sleeve. "He's after the duke too, is he?" He snorted. "I did hear they thought they'd caught him, up to Bristol, and he slipped out of their hands. He's a sly fox, ain't he? Got to respect that in a criminal. So they think he's come here to his mama's, and s'pose I wouldn't know of it, do they? We'll see about that."

She sat down in a chair and folded her hands as Lilly ushered the gentlemen into the house. The maid brought them to the door of the parlor, gave a curtsy, and said in a resentful tone, "Major Sturgeon, my lady." She glanced at the innkeeper and added with more pleasantry, "And Mr. Rankin."

Mr. Rankin, stood back, holding his hat in his hands, to let Major Sturgeon come ahead of him. Before the major could speak, Callie said quickly, "Mr. Rankin—it was very good of you to come. I'm afraid I've brought you out of your way to no use. It was all a misunderstanding, and I've seen the duchesse. She is as well as might be expected."

"Well, I'm glad to know that, my lady." The innkeeper stood on the threshold with Lilly lingering behind him. "I was sorry to hear the poor madame went out of her mind."

"Her feelings are in considerable distress," Callie said. "I understand that this thief-taker out of London has been troubling her." She glanced at Major

Sturgeon. "I should like you to ask him to remain at some distance from this house, Major. As a favor to me. In fact, I really see no need at this time for him to continue in pursuit of the Belgian gentleman. All's well that ends well, is it not?"

"Belgian?" the constable asked. "I was told he was French, my lady."

"It's all the same, I'm sure," Callie said quickly. The stories had multiplied to such an extent that she hardly knew who was pursuing Trev under what guise anymore. His misdeeds appeared to be uncountable— another reason to maintain a severe detachment between him and her heart.

"Aye, my lady." Constable Hubble nodded. "Belgian, French, they're none of 'em English." He ducked his head toward Major Sturgeon. "And you won't take it ill, sir, I hope, if I just humbly say that being the representative of the king's law in Shelford, I didn't give my permit to some London fellow to come pokin' about here for thieves."

Major Sturgeon had said nothing before; at that, his mouth tightened. "I spoke to the Bow Street man just before we came in, my lady. And I've reason to believe the criminal in question—be he Belgian or French or a Hindoostani—is hidden in this house at this very moment."

Lilly gave an audible gasp, peeking round Mr. Rankin with wide eyes. Callie would have liked to gasp herself, or at least shriek and tear her hair out, but she managed to stifle it. "If that's the case," she lied blithely, "I haven't noticed him, though I've been with the duchesse quite some time. And Lilly, *you* may go up and see to Madame until Nurse returns with the doctor." She gave the maid a pointed look. "You're not required here."

Lilly ducked her head and curtsied. "Yes, my lady." She vanished up the stairs.

"He's hiding, of course," Major Sturgeon said. "Most likely in the attic, or perhaps in the kitchen, if there's a cellar attached. It's only been out of respect for the lady's illness that we've not moved to take him yet." He inclined his head toward Callie. "I know she's a particular friend of yours, my lady, and as such I don't wish to cause her any undue distress. But her son is wanted for breaking the law in several instances. So we're waiting for him to come out."

"He ain't in the kitchen," the constable said bluntly. "That I know. And he ain't in this house at all, come to that. Do you think I wouldn't have taken him up myself if he had been? I s'pose your fancy thief-takers from up London think they can discover what we country fellows can't."

"It seems unlikely, I must agree, Constable," Callie said. "Would he return to where it must be known he's a wanted man?"

"He's in here," the major said with certainty. He looked at her. "Do you doubt me, ma'am?"

"Well, I—" For one fatal moment, in the face of his hard blue stare, she allowed herself to glance away. When she looked back again immediately, a strange expression came into his face. He tilted his head, as if to observe her more closely.

Callie fidgeted with the fingers on her gloves. He made her feel as if she had a fly on her nose, he looked at her so intently. "It's not a matter of doubting you, sir," she said, forcing some backbone into her tone. "I've requested that you call off your pursuit. If it doesn't please you to do so at my request, then I suppose there's no more to be said." She stood up. "I must be going now; my sister and Lady Shelford will be missing me at Miss Poole's."

"Allow me to drive you, my lady," he said swiftly. "I was just on my way to call at the Hall; my landau stops outside."

"No, no, there's no need. They brought the Shelford carriage." She was flustered at the way he looked at her so. "Please don't trouble yourself."

"Then do me the honor of riding with me," he insisted. "It's coming on to rain; I can take you home directly. We'll send a message to let them know."

Lilly appeared at the door, making a light cough. Callie turned to her, thankful for the diversion. "Yes, what is it?"

"Madame says that if the men must search the house, then they ought to do it this very minute," the maid said with a curtsy. "She wishes to have it over directly."

Lilly stood with her eyes lowered. Callie had no trouble reaching the obvious conclusion that Trev had concealed himself or got away somehow. She turned to Major Sturgeon. "Well, then." She lifted her eyebrows. "Here is your opportunity, sir."

He bowed his head slightly, but still he observed her in the oddest manner, as if he would make note of her every smallest move. He had been suspicious of Trev in the house; now he seemed suspicious of her too. But he said only, "If you prefer that we not disturb the duchesse, then I won't have anyone come into the house, now or in the future. Let us simply drive on to Shelford Hall, shall we? I'm at your service." He bowed.

Callie judged that it was best to remove him from the place, even if Trev had hidden himself. She gave a curt nod. "Then let us go. Lilly, you'll give my compliments to Madame, and please tell her that she needn't fear any further intrusion."

Outside, her judgment of the preferred course of action took a sudden turn. As she passed through the door ahead of the major, she glanced up at the landau, which had both of its canopies raised to make it a closed carriage in the inclement weather. The driver sat up on his perch with his back to them, hunched down against the mist, a shapeless hat pulled over his eyes.

She almost stopped in her tracks. Then she forced herself not to pause or stare at the driver, who had an all-too-familiar cut of black hair just barely showing under the hat. She made a great demonstration of being unable to lift her shawl over her hat to cover it, which required such aid from the major as kept his attention occupied until they reached the carriage door. He held it open for her and Callie stepped up inside.

As Major Sturgeon swung in beside her, he called out a command to drive on. The vehicle jerked into motion. He sat back on the seat and turned to her.

"You're in love with him, aren't you?" he said.

She sat bolt upright. "I beg your pardon."

"I understand you now." He gave a slight laugh. "You're carrying a torch for that French scoundrel. That's why you don't want me to touch you and asked me to call off the Runners."

In spite of the fact that it was nothing but the whole ghastly truth, Callie exclaimed, "Are you mad?" She sat away from him. "The poor duchesse is my friend. I don't want her to be tortured while she's ill."

"Certainly," he agreed. "I understand that."

He said nothing more but merely looked ahead at the black leather of the landau's canopy, a slight frown on his strong, handsome features. Callie was beyond any words. She kept expecting him to call off the engagement, but he did not. She stared out the window at the gray sky and slowly passing fields.

As the carriage turned in at the gates of the Hall, the major said, "You're better off with me, you know." His voice was not unkind. "I won't tell you what sort of man he is—I think you're well aware, or you would have run away with him already. But that's an ill way to win you, is it not? Disparaging my rival for your heart." He lifted her hand and kissed it lightly. "I'll strive to make my own place in your affections."

"I'm sure—there's no necessity—I do not require—"

He released her before she could pull away. "Do you say I must not make the attempt?" He gave a wry smile. "Will you be that cruel to me, my dear heart?"

Callie looked at him in astonishment. "Please, I would prefer that we—"

"That we go our own ways. Yes, I comprehend you. Completely. I only ask that, as you have been so generous as to say I may take any woman I choose, you allow me to choose you."

The carriage rolled to a halt beside the stairs. A Shelford footman stepped briskly forward, opening the door. He would have helped her out, but Major Sturgeon jumped down first and held up his hand. Callie had no choice but to take it or remain confined in the coach, which seemed like a promising course of action when she thought about it. She could just take up residence there and simplify her life. As she descended the steps, she took one sideways glance at the driver again, to make sure she hadn't been deceiving herself.

She hadn't. Trev sat holding the lines of a team of placid job horses, staring out ahead of him. The Antlers' postboy stood in front of the team, holding their heads, a vastly innocent expression on his face.

Major Sturgeon took her arm and guided her up the stairs.

The most dangerous moment for Trev wasn't getting out of Dove House, or exchanging places with the Antlers' grinning driver, or climbing into Callie's unlocked window in broad daylight. It was offering a bribe to the gruff old charwoman who first discovered him in her bedchamber.

In the old days, the Shelford servants had not been susceptible to bribes. The butler kept his staff firmly in line but looked kindly enough on Trev that recourse to sweeteners hadn't been useful or necessary. It was a risk now to assume that things were different under the management of Lady Shelford. The moment he heard the doorknob turn, he laid a stack of gold sovereigns in the middle of the floor where it would be instantly noted and stood to the side, trying to look as harmless as possible.

The charwoman saw the coins first. She froze, holding her broom and ash bucket. Trev cleared his throat and said in a soft, easy voice, "They're yours, if you're a friend to Lady Callista."

She startled and looked up. The instant in which she saw him rated well up in the category of the longest in his life, along with sitting in the dock waiting for the judge to read his fate.

No expression flitted across her face, no recognizable thought process. She leaned on the broom. It trembled a little in her blue-veined hand.

"I mean her no harm," Trev said. "I love her."

She took a slow step into the room. With a bang of her bucket, she closed the door so that they were alone. "Sir's the Frenchie gentleman," she said, jutting her chin toward him. It was not quite a question. "Outta Dove House."

Trev nodded. "Aye, my mother is the duchesse."

The old woman lifted her broom, indicating the canopied bed. "M'lady's been weepin' of a night, sir. Even though her got bespoke to marry that officer, eh?"

That was a shaft directly to his heart, but he had no reply for it. He looked down at his boots and up again.

"Well, sir," she said after a moment, in her rough, old voice. "I reckon I ought to call up the hall boy and say there's a housebreaker, eh?" She peered at the coins on the floor. Then she bent over and gathered them up, dropping them into her apron pocket. "If I find m'lady's been weepin' in her pillow in the morning, I will, sir," she said and went about sweeping the ashes from the hearth.

Twenty

BY THE TIME CALLIE MANAGED TO EXTRICATE HERSELF from Major Sturgeon's suddenly ardent turn of mind, and Lady Shelford's strong rebuke over vanishing from Miss Poole's shop without warning, and Hermey's delighted description of the discovery of the perfect butter-spotted sarcenet for spring at a bargain price, she wanted nothing more than to sit alone in her room with a cup of tea and stare stupidly out the window.

Her excuse of a headache was no exaggeration—she was long over the effects of the bump on her skull, but the events of the morning had brought on a splitting pain in her temples. She sat down beside the window and requested the maid to close the door gently behind her after leaving the tray. Outside, the rain had come on to pour. Callie sipped her tea, staring with grim satisfaction at the cascades of water beating against the windowpanes. On the assumption that Trev was not going to be arrested, tried, and hung—not in the next half hour, at any rate—she hoped he drowned.

She indulged in a small reverie in which she piloted a rowboat, saving puppies and kittens and the occasional lamb from a raging flood, ferrying them to warm safety while Trev and Major Sturgeon clung to trees, forced to await her aid, which she was in no hurry to provide. She finally got round to them, fighting wind and torrents in her oilskins, as she was stirring sugar into her second cup. Her headache receded as she treated herself to this fantasy. She disposed of Major Sturgeon in some vague but laudable manner and then found herself wrapped in a blanket with Trev, with water dripping from his hair onto his bared shoulders as he held her in his arms and kissed her fiercely…

She took a slow breath, dreaming. A sensation grew on her: a feeling of his presence, now that she brought the mute awareness to the forefront of her mind. A scent below perception, a still sound of life and breath—the things that the animals knew, and she knew too when she gave them the proper attention.

She looked up and saw the note placed on her pillow.

Abruptly she put the cup aside and strode to the bed. *Don't be alarmed,* the paper said, in familiar black strokes made from her own inkpot. It wasn't signed. It hardly needed to be. She dropped to her knees and looked under the bed. The space was empty. Callie glanced toward her wardrobe, but that was far too full of the hopeful contributions Hermey had made to her growing trousseau. She looked toward the door to her dressing room.

Irrational pleasure and rational consternation warred for a moment. Rationality won out and was all the more enraged by the moment of foolish weakness. She stood up and snapped, "Show yourself this instant."

There was no reply. Callie glared at the door. She refused to go over and peer into it as if she were looking for a mouse that had escaped round the corner.

"If you don't come out, I shall scream," she threatened, her voice taut.

After a long moment, Trev appeared in the doorway. He didn't move into the room, but put his hand against the frame and looked at her under a sullen lowering of his lashes. "You wouldn't scream," he murmured. "I've never heard you scream in all your life."

He was, of course, perfectly correct, but that gained him no prizes in her estimation. "I beg you will explain to me, sir, precisely what you're doing in my bedchamber."

"Raiding your jewelry casket, of course. I already have a Runner after me and a price on my head, why not actually commit a crime?"

"Oh, have you a price on your head too?" Her eyebrows arched. "I hadn't heard that much."

"Courtesy of Colonel Davenport. There are broadsides pasted up in town. Seven guineas for my capture."

"Seven guineas! How unfortunate that I missed them. I might have turned you in and spared myself this visitation in my room."

He appeared a little taken aback at that. "I'm sorry—I know it's awkward, but my mother's taken it into her head that I must leave Dove House."

"I see," Callie said coldly. "And therefore naturally you felt my bedroom was your obvious destination."

"It's ridiculous, of course. I won't leave her again, though, and I need a safe place. Hide in plain sight, you know. I didn't suppose you would..." He stopped, looking as if he couldn't quite discover the tail to his own sentence.

"You didn't suppose I would object? Why should I? A gentleman in my bedroom—how handy. Perhaps you'll discover the cause of this chimney smoking when the wind is in the south. Or you might investigate the way the floorboard creaks under the wardrobe. Do you plan to stay indefinitely? I must inform you that I'm engaged to be married, and must leave you to your own devices if you're to be ensconced here after Boxing Day."

"I know you're engaged," he said, his voice going harsh and icy. "How could I not? You're the talk of the town."

Callie grew stiff. She turned away. "That is unkind."

She felt him come to her and stand close behind her. "I'm sorry." He touched her hair and slid his fingers down to her throat gently. "I'm sorry, Callie. For everything."

"Quite," she said, trembling. But she did not move away as she should have. "Do you never simply ring the bell and hand in a card?"

He put his arms round her and turned her toward him. "Are you all right?" He drew a breath against her hair and then passed the backs of his fingers over her cheek. "God forgive me, I've done nothing but worry about you after what happened."

She clenched her hands together, pushing away. "If you mean, was there any unfortunate result, no," she said, turning her back to him. "I can confirm that. So you need not concern yourself about it further."

She wanted desperately to turn back and cry out her anger and bewilderment, that he was married, that he had let her fall in love with him all over again and never told her. But then she would have betrayed herself wholly. Between him and Major Sturgeon, what silly vestige of pride she had left had been lacerated enough. The one thing she would never admit was that she hadn't known all along. While she stood frozen, aching with the loss of his touch, she heard him move away.

"It was simply a… a fling out, is that what they call it now?" she said to the opposite wall. The steadiness of her own voice surprised her. "I suppose I'm not the sort of person one would expect to fling, but really, one must have one's moment before marriage, don't you think? As the horses have a kick before they're put in harness."

The dull, rushing sound of the rain drummed on the windows. She forced herself to unclench her fingers and turn toward him. He stood looking out at the downpour. His profile was silhouetted against the window so that she couldn't see his expression in the dusky light. As she looked at the straight, brooding lines of his face, she bit her lip. She could not expel him into the rain, at the mercy of Runners and broadsides. But she had no intention of allowing him to see her true heart.

He looked at her sidelong. "Will it be a harness?" he asked, lifting one eyebrow. "Marriage to him?"

"Certainly not," she said instantly. "That was merely a figure of speech. Now that I've come to know him better, I believe that we shall be excessively happy together. He's developed the greatest admiration for me. He—" She searched quickly for some evidence of the major's affection. "He brings me any number of posies and is forever kissing my hand."

"I see," Trev said. She glared at him suspiciously, in case he should be inclined to laugh, but he maintained a perfectly sober countenance. "Very gallant of him."

"Yes, and he said it would be cruel of me if I wouldn't allow him to make an attempt to win my heart," she added, to seal her case. "Just now, in fact, in the carriage, he said so."

"Oh?" He turned to face her, his features darkened by the light behind. "Then it isn't won already?"

"Very near," she lied stoutly. "I believe I can come to love him."

He made a small, taut motion, something between a nod and a jerk of his chin.

"I'm sure that once we've begun our own family," she added, expanding on her theme, "we'll be exceptionally devoted."

"Doubtless," he said in a clipped voice. "I'm charmed by this vision of connubial bliss. I assure you that I'll do all in my power to stay out of sight, so that you may continue to enjoy his attentions to the full."

"I suppose you've bribed the servants?" she asked dryly.

"Of course."

Callie expelled a deep breath. "You may remain for the night." She pointed and then crossed her arms. "In the dressing room."

He walked away to the door of the adjacent closet. "Certainly. Just toss me a biscuit now and again, like the rest of the dogs."

Trev closed the door behind him with something just short of a bang. He stood in the small dressing room, contemplating his many options. He could sleep on the bare floor, as he'd done the night before in his mother's room, or prop himself against the wall next to the chest of drawers, padded by a pillow of clean rags that were neatly folded in one corner—their use was uncertain, but he thought it likely she was more concerned to polish some heifer to a high sheen than to have her footwear buffed. For entertainment, he saw that he could avail himself of any number of books, starting with *CATTLE: Being a Treatise on their BREEDS, MANAGEMENT, AND DISEASES, Comprising a FULL HISTORY OF THE VARIOUS RACES; Their Origin, Breeding and Merits; Their Capacity for Beef and Milk; The Nature and Treatment of Their Diseases; THE WHOLE FORMING A COMPLETE GUIDE for the FARMER, THE AMATEUR, and VETERINARY SURGEON*, with 100 illustrations. If that didn't put him to sleep, he could turn to *THE COMPLETE GRAZIER, or Farmer's and Cattle Breeder's and Dealer's Assistant,* and get an overview of neat cattle, sheep, horses, and swine, the present state of the wool trade, and an appendix on *Prize Cattle, Farm Accounts, and Other Subjects Connected with Agriculture*, all courtesy of A Lincolnshire Grazier, assisted by Several Eminent Agriculturalists.

He sat down on a stool and looked at her stockings instead. They were of the practical sort, plain white, knitted with warmth and not style in mind. But they hung over a wooden rack, along with her petticoats, and showed the shape and outline of a feminine leg very well. He gazed at them, indulging himself in some highly provocative thoughts, until his imagination was stimulated beyond the point of comfort.

It wouldn't be easy remaining here. At first, when his mother had seized on the idea, he'd mocked it, but on finding that he had to make a quick escape he'd snatched at the first opportunity that presented itself—a pair of postboys from the Antlers who were more than willing to indulge in a lark for a few coins. That had taken him as far as Shelford Hall. Once here, the scheme had shown some advantages.

He was, for the moment, as safe in Callie's rooms as anywhere else. With a little care, he could come and go by the branches of the ancient yew to Dove House. He wanted to look into his suspicions regarding her fortune, and a glance at any account books he could manage to find might be illuminating. That would require some prowling about the house and offices in the wee hours, and perhaps a lock picking or two—not a harmless prospect, but it would give him something to do besides sit here and bleat to himself about the torture of sleeping a few feet away from her.

It would keep other thoughts at bay too. Thoughts about how he'd deserted her after he'd made love to her and about killing Sturgeon for any excuse he could come up with. The sort of thoughts that had kept him drinking in a gin house until he'd missed his ship sailing. He surprised himself. Usually he was more successful at such things as leaving his past and all its strings behind him.

The same old argument began to play in his mind. What was best for her against what he wanted, which was to be with her, even if it was just hiding out in her dressing room while she was engaged to another man.

When he got to the part about smuggling her aboard a ship with him while they left the country for France, where he would show her conclusively that he'd lied about everything from the evil Buzot to the coach and six and the restored château—at that point, when he was wishing heartily for another bottle of gin, his unpleasant reflections were interrupted by a soft rap on the closet door and Callie's hissed warning to him to stay concealed.

He grew still, listening to the sounds of a girlish voice begging entry to Callie's bedroom. Trev laid his ear to the door. After the thumps and creaks of entry—she did have an inconveniently creaky floor, he noted with exasperation—he heard Lady Hermione say, "Are you feeling better? Can you let Anne make her measures? Because she'll be sewing half the night as it is, you know, to have a costume ready for you by tomorrow."

"Oh dear," Callie said, her voice muffled, "I'd forgot about the masquerade. Really, I—"

"Don't say you won't appear!" her sister said pleadingly. "Please. It will be great fun, you'll see. And Sir Thomas has had the greatest news! Lord Sidmouth himself is to come! Right here to Shelford Hall to attend the masquerade."

"Lord Sidmouth?" Callie asked in a blank voice. "Why is he to come?"

"Callie." Hermione took on the tone of a patient but prodded teacher. "He's the Lord *Secretary* of the *Home* Office," she explained, as if speaking to a dull but beloved child. "And it's the greatest honor, because he's frightfully busy with convicts and laws and the king and all that, so he almost *never* leaves

London. I daresay he'll bring a hundred undersecretaries with him. Sir Thomas is in alt!"

"Oh," Callie said. Then she seemed to catch on to the matter. "Oh, these are his colleagues from the Home Office?"

"Yes, so you see what an honor it is. He says that it almost certainly means he'll be advanced in the next election."

"That's excellent news," Callie said. "A hundred undersecretaries."

Lady Hermione giggled. She dropped her voice confidingly, though it still came through clear enough as she moved closer to the dressing room. "Major Sturgeon is going to come as a sultan; he told me so. And here, I've just the thing to make you into a veiled sultana from a harem! See this blue and green gauze? Even Dolly agreed it would be perfect. Will wonders never cease?"

Trev moved back quickly, seeing the dressing room knob turn. He was just contemplating how fast he could open the window and leap out when Callie said in a hurried voice, "Yes, of course, that's lovely! Is Anne in your room? Let's go there and measure. It's half dusk with this weather, and the light is so much better on your side."

"You'll wear it, then?" Lady Hermione let go of the door knob with a gay laugh. "Come, it won't take a moment, and then you may go back to dreaming of how you'll arrange the cattle sheds on your new home farm. I vow, I can't think for wonder at it all. Sir Thomas has said I may fit up his town house just as I please. We'll have our own homes, and I can bring the children to visit you in the country, and…" Her naïvely happy voice faded as the outer door closed behind them.

Callie didn't speak to him or acknowledge his presence when she returned from her sister's bedchamber. Trev stayed discreetly out of sight in the dressing room, brushing up on animal husbandry in the unlikely event he should ever have reason to deliver a calf or cure the gripes, and wondering how he had allowed his life to sink to this point. He did not care for the idea of costumes of veiled harem girls and Callie playing sultana to Sturgeon's sultan. For one thing, it made him imagine her wrapped in sparkling blue gauze that grew more and more transparent the more he thought about it, until he was strongly in the mood to visit a harem himself. For another, he was going to strangle Sturgeon with his own turban.

And now Sidmouth of all people would be in the house, along with some army of undersecretaries, any one of whom might have seen Trev at his trial. Not that he wouldn't mind having a few pointed words with the Lord Secretary. He'd understood the deal to be that he'd receive a full pardon in return for putting up no defense—but when the royal pardon came down from the king's council, signed by Sidmouth, it was conditional and made an explicit point that he'd leave the country or hang. Trev had never met the Home Secretary, but he wondered if the fellow had something in for him. A bad bet, perhaps, or a fixed match that he blamed on Trev or the Rooster. Or perhaps he simply believed Trev was guilty.

It would have been gratifying to have the answer to this burning question, but confronting Sidmouth with a complaint about his pardon didn't seem the wisest course. He'd lived for a fortnight in Newgate under a sentence of death before any sort of pardon at all had come down; an experience he did not care to repeat. As a condemned felon, one got rapidly off the scaffold at the first opportunity and didn't look a gift horse in the mouth.

He sat glumly in the dimming room, propped against the wall. He couldn't even pace, because the damned floor creaked. He heard her take supper on a tray in her room and noted that she didn't invite him to join her. She was turned against him, looking forward to starting a family with Sturgeon, which was precisely what Trev had wanted, of course. He was perfectly delighted.

Boston was too close. It would have to be Shanghai.

They spent the evening hours in mutually ignoring one another while the incessant rain rumbled in the gutters. As it neared full dark, he finally opened the dressing room door, stood for a moment without precisely looking at her, and announced to the air in general that he was going to take supper with his mother. She bade him a chilly good evening from her seat by the fire, in a tone that suggested that he need not hurry back. Trev stalked to the window. He opened the inner shutters. Even in the dark, he could see that the rain was beating against the glass in sheets. If he raised it, the window seat—not to mention himself—would be deluged.

He closed the shutters again and turned round.

She appeared to be wholly occupied by the tatting

that was spread across her lap, moving a shuttle briskly in and out of some knotted lace with deep concentration. The firelight brought a rosy bloom to her cheek, a warm copper glint to her hair. She wore it in a stylish upswept bun today, instead of her usual neat braids, but her thick curls seemed inclined to revolt against the more fashionable style and drape gently down to the nape of her neck. He watched her for a moment.

"Shouldn't you thread some yarn in that needle?" he asked dryly. "I'd think it would make the work go more efficiently."

She threw the shuttle down in her lap and glared up at him. Trev tried not to smile, as she appeared to be in no mood to be amused at herself.

"I thought you were going to make a call on your mother," she said stiffly.

"You'll observe that the weather is somewhat inclement."

She gave a great sigh, as if he had arranged for the downpour merely to inconvenience her. Trev walked over and helped himself to a decanter of wine from her tray, pouring it into the untouched glass. He sat down in the other chair. "Can we not be civil at least? If we're no longer friends."

She bit her lip, turning her face toward the fire. For an instant there was a faint quiver at the corner of her mouth, which made him long to go down on his knees and gather her still hands and press them to his face. He took a sip of wine instead.

"I'm still your friend, Callie," he said. "And I always will be."

She nodded, looking down. "Of course."

"This masquerade is opportune," he said conversationally. "I want to investigate the Shelford account books. Are they locked away?"

"You want to see the Shelford accounts? Whatever for?"

He debated whether to tell her of his suspicions. He didn't want to frighten her. But since he had every intention of seeing that any money that had been embezzled from her fortune was replaced, even if he had to fund it himself, he thought it safe to be open. "I had a talk with Sturgeon before I went away. I'm concerned that something's not right with your trust."

"My trust?" She looked baffled. "I don't understand. You spoke to the major about my money?"

He gave a brief nod. "Indirectly. There's something odd, Callie. Not about Sturgeon; I don't mean that. But I discovered that he was blackmailed out of your first engagement."

She gazed at him. "What on earth do you mean?"

"I mean that he didn't want to break it off. He was forced to do so."

The shuttle slid from her fingers to the floor. "Blackmail? Oh come, that's nonsense."

"It's true. It's nothing to do with you, or your marriage now, you needn't concern yourself with that. It has to do with his honor as an officer. He made a decision during the war—saved men's lives, in fact—but he disobeyed direct orders. It isn't something he wants to come out in public."

"Oh?" she said in a dubious voice.

"I don't fault him for what he did, myself." He retrieved the shuttle for her, careful that their hands did not touch. "He had his reasons. But he's an officer, and if it were known, he'd be like enough to lose his commission and face a court-martial. So he broke off the engagement to prevent it coming out."

She shook her head slowly. "Are you certain? Blackmail, of all things!" Then she pursed her lips. "No. I don't believe it. I think he simply didn't care to marry me and preferred another." Then she glanced at him and raised her chin. "At that time. He assures me that he feels quite differently now."

Trev gave her a small smile. It didn't surprise him that Sturgeon was coming to love Callie in spite of himself. And well enough, if it would make him a better husband to her. Trev would be in Shanghai, making arrangements to become an opium addict.

"You aren't saying this just to butter up my feelings, are you?" she asked suspiciously. "I don't mind that he broke it off before. You needn't make up silly stories about it just to make me feel better."

He scowled. "It's not a made-up story. And it's hardly silly if you've been embezzled of your fortune."

She gave a little gasp. "Nonsense! What are you talking about?"

"You'll have your money back, I'll make certain of that," he said. "But he was *blackmailed*, Callie. Why would someone try to prevent him from marrying you? And then the rest of them cried off too, on the thinnest of reasons. It's devilish strange, and I've been doing some looking into the matter."

"In between your escapes from the Bow Street Runners, I suppose?" she asked haughtily.

He held his temper. "Who would be most likely to have access to the accounts and the trust? Who's your trustee?"

"My cousin, of course," she said. "Are you saying poor Jasper blackmailed Major Sturgeon and stole all my money, and then made the rest of them cry off too? And this while my father would have been alive—I don't suppose you're accusing *him* of embezzling me?"

"Of course not." Trev was becoming annoyed at her resistance. "But stranger things have happened, you know, than the heir apparent wishing to help himself a bit early. How many years has your cousin had access to the Shelford accounts? I want to see the books."

"I believe you've run mad. You don't suppose he altered the accounts! Cousin Jasper couldn't add a sum correctly if it were two plus two."

"Couldn't he? I'd like to be certain of that."

"It's quite impossible. I manage the accounts. At least I supervise him at it, because he's hopeless at the task."

"Perhaps that's all a show. It was damned odd of him to gamble Hubert away—he may have come short in his reckoning and required money to cover himself. Or perhaps it could be the countess behind him? God knows she's as cold as any thief in Newgate."

Callie made a face. "I'll confess that I'm not fond of Dolly, but I don't suppose she's a criminal." She reached down to her basket and pulled out a ball of white yarn. "Perhaps you may have been too much with that class of person and become excessively suspicious."

Trev flung himself out of the chair, almost knocking over his wine. Callie looked up, wide-eyed, which made him realize the violence of his action. He took command of himself. "Perhaps I have," he said coolly. "And it's taught me that anyone is capable of deceit, from the pink of the ton to a dustman."

She gave him a long, clear look, then turned her face down to her work, taking a turn of yarn around the shuttle. "Undoubtedly," she said.

They both watched the shuttle move in and out of her tatting. Trev stood feeling much as he had in the dock: judged, tried, and condemned. "You may doubt me, if you please," he said finally. "But someone blackmailed Sturgeon, and they did it for a reason."

"Very well," she said. She stood up and set her work aside, crossing the room to her dressing table. "Here is a key to the desk in my cousin's study. It's on the ground floor, in the south wing. Please be certain to tell Major Sturgeon if you discover that all my money is gone, so that he may jilt me in good time before the wedding." She held out the key, making a stiff little curtsy. "And of course you'll want to be prepared to escape through the window when you're discovered breaking into the earl's desk. I'd recommend the one to the far right, nearest the fireplace, as the others have a tendency to stick in humid weather."

Trev caught the key from her hand and closed it in his fist. "He won't jilt you. I won't allow that to happen."

"Of course he will," she said calmly, "if it's true that I have no fortune. And perhaps it's for the best. I'm sure my hand would grow quite sore from all the kissing, and the posies merely wilt."

Trev gripped the key. "Damn it," he said, taking a stride to her. He put his arm about her waist and held her up close against him and kissed her passionately, countering the moment of resistance in her, asking and demanding at once, until she made a helpless sound and her arms slid round his neck and a thousand nights of being without her ended in this hard embrace, clinging to one another as if they were drowning together.

She leaned against him, her fingers opening through his hair, pulling him down to her. The sound of the rain seemed to grow to a roar in his ears as her lips opened under his. Trev lost all reason. He drew her down, dragging them both to their knees in a deep, long kiss. He retained just enough sense to know that he must not lay her down on the carpet and take her there. They were in her bedroom, in Shelford Hall—as the world spun around him in sweet, hot lust and he outlined the shape of her body with his hands, he saved one mite of sanity and confined himself to kissing her mouth and her chin and her ear and throat and anything he could reach without pulling her gown entirely open—only down off her shoulder, only that much, or more, until the little modest ribbons and catches gave way and he tasted the ivory white skin just above her breasts.

She was making those feminine sounds that drove him to wildness, lifting herself to him, her body pressed against him in an invitation to much more. Trev squeezed his eyes shut. With an effort that was physical pain, he let go of her. He sat back to gain some control, and then stood up and walked across the room.

He threw open the shutters. He would have liked to open the window and douse his head under the roaring cascade off the roof, but all he did was lean his arm and forehead against the glass, breathing deeply of the chill air.

When finally he regained some composure and turned, she was standing, holding the gown up to her shoulder and trying to refasten it. Her hair had come down, cascading in a wave of tangled copper to one side, giving her a tousled and bewildered look. She glanced up at him, her face all warmed and softened by his kisses.

"Now I feel remarkably foolish," she said resentfully. She turned her face aside. The firelight outlined the curve of her bared throat, and he thought perhaps he would die just looking at her.

"Well, you appear remarkably desirable," he said. "Which is awkward, under the circumstances."

Her lashes swept downward as her chin came up. "I must beg your pardon for inconveniencing you," she retorted. "I didn't wish to… to succumb… to that sort of thing."

"I fear you only make it worse by looking at me that way."

"What way?" She looked down at herself and up, tugging nervously to straighten her skirts.

"As if you'd like to slap me and be kissed at the same time." He strolled over, made as if he would pass by her, and then at the last moment caught her waist and leaned his face into her throat. He brushed a light kiss over her skin. "Where can I find a mask?"

"A mask?" she repeated helplessly.

"I think it best if I don't remain here where we might… succumb, as you put it." He nuzzled her ear. "Unless you'd prefer it?"

He felt her breasts rise and fall with unsteady breath. "Oh, that is brilliant," she said in a voice that would have been sarcastic if it hadn't ended on a slightly cracked and upward note. "So you intend to prowl about the house in a mask instead?"

"Take your choice, *mon amour*."

"I'm not your love."

"You are," he murmured into her hair. "You always will be."

She swallowed. "I'm your friend merely."

"Is it so?" He drew her against him, opening his lips against her temple. "Callie. A mere friend?"

A tremor went through her, but she was soft in his arms. "Don't," she said. "Oh don't."

He shouldn't, he knew. But her body pleaded in spite of her words. She wanted him—he could feel her desire vibrate under every touch. She'd be in Sturgeon's arms; the vision froze his heart, crushed what little remained of his tattered honor. His embrace tightened as if he could hold on to her by strength alone. When she yielded and turned and lifted her face, Trev was lost to it.

He took her to the bed in a swift move, pressing her backward until he tumbled her atop the counterpane. He leaned over her, braced on his hands, looking down at her face. "I want to see your stockings," he growled. "The plain white ones."

Her lips parted, as if to make a refusal, and then she blinked. Her puzzled look only made her more adorable to him.

"Yes, I was driven demented in your closet." He bent down to kiss her. "I'm passionately in love with your hosiery."

She twisted her ankles together. He could see that she tried to frown. Then she clutched his shoulder, tilting her head back as he ran his fingers along her leg and under her garter. She made a breathless sound and drew up her knee when he explored further, following the smooth muscle of her thigh upward. Her petticoat fell back, revealing the curve of her leg, the pale, pure white stocking and simple garter lit by firelight down to shadowed rosy curls, half-glimpsed and half-imagined. For a moment she looked up at him like an innocent, all fresh and maidenly with her shimmering red hair framing her face.

Then her lips curled and puckered. She began to giggle. "I'm keeping a gentleman in my closet," she said and laughed aloud.

He gazed at her as the sounds of mirth bubbled up. Her body quivered. She pressed her hand to her mouth, trying to suppress it, but the corners of her eyelids tilted up with hilarity.

Trev bent down and put his lips beside her ear, feeling her laughter all the way through him. "My little cabbage," he murmured, sliding his fingers into the warmth of her, "you really aren't supposed to find it amusing when I do this to you."

She whimpered, arching to him. "Oh don't," she moaned. "It's not amusing."

He watched her with pleasure. There was nothing and no one in his life like Callie when she giggled. "You don't want me to go about in a mask instead," he said innocently, stroking his thumb over the place that made her shudder.

"No," she said breathlessly. "Oh!"

"You could pack me off to your closet, to a cruel sentence of nothing to do but moon over your drawers," he offered.

She laughed and gasped, holding tight to him. "Trev! We shouldn't."

"Of course not," he said, bending to kiss her offered breast. "If you'll just release this delicate grip on my arm—"

She showed no inclination to do so. When he moved atop her, her embrace welcomed him. She smelled of warm skin and female desire, but it was her laughter that impelled him. She was laughing as he kissed her, a sweet shaking deep inside. He pushed into it, into her, a union that carried both of them beyond any doubt or words to pure and simple joy.

Twenty-One

CALLIE HAD SLEPT LATE. VERY LATE. NORMALLY SHE was up by dawn to bring Hubert his loaves of bread. His sad, complaining bellow could be heard faintly even now through the closed shutters. She was still trying to sort through her hair to find the displaced pins and make some sense of this à la mode fashion of Hermey's design when Anne scratched at the door.

Callie blushed and kept her eyes strictly on the mirror at the dressing table as the maid entered. She knew already that Trev had vacated her chambers while she slept, but she seemed to breathe his scent on her and everywhere in the room. If Anne noticed, she made no mention of it, but came quickly to Callie and began to tuck up the trailing weight of her hair. "The countess wants you downstairs directly, my lady," she said. "There's a caller for you, and my lady says you're to be at home to her."

Callie sighed. "It must be one of her friends, to congratulate me. Are they talking? I'm sure she won't miss me until after I feed Hubert."

"You're wanted to hurry, my lady." Anne placed a pin and stood back from an attempt to secure Callie's hair that was only partially successful. "There. I'll send the hall boy with some bread to the poor hungry beast. But you must hurry down." She met Callie's gaze in the mirror with an expression that they both understood. If Callie delayed, the countess would make her life miserable in consequence.

"Very well." Callie rose. "Thank you, Anne, that will do, then."

"You looks very pretty, my lady, if I may say. The curls about your face become you."

"I only hope it won't fall down." Callie cast one last glance in the mirror and was surprised and discomfited to see that she did look rather well, but in a tousled and pink sort of way, very much as if she had just risen from bed after making love to a gentleman. Which of course was quite the fashion according to Hermey, but it was rather unnerving, considering the recent circumstances.

An impassive footman opened the door of the drawing room, which was even more alarming, since normally John would have returned a nod and smile to her greeting. Instead he stared straight above her head, which meant Lady Shelford was in high force this morning. But as Callie passed, he turned just slightly, lowering his lashes and lifting an eyebrow, and gave her what could only be described as a wink.

She hardly knew what to make of that. Just as she took in the fact that Major Sturgeon was also present, in addition to Lord and Lady Shelford and several persons who were strangers to her, she recalled that Trev had bribed the servants. The thought, and the footman's wink, combined to make her lose all hope of maintaining any composure as Major Sturgeon rose to take her hand and lead her into the room. She was so flustered that she hardly knew what she was saying in reply to the introductions.

"But I'm enchanted to meet you!" A very pretty lady stood up from her seat beside the countess. She was small and fairylike, with a twinkling smile and a confiding air, quite as if she truly had been longing to meet Callie. "The duchesse has told me everything about you!" She turned to Lady Shelford as she caught Callie's hand. "It's most kind of you to receive me, ma'am, out of the very blue this way. But the duchesse insisted that I call on Lady Callista and give her my wishes to be happy."

"Mrs. James Fowler," Lady Shelford said belatedly. Her demeanor was not quite as coolly restrained as usual, and she glanced from the young woman to Callie in an odd, energized manner.

It was that peculiar look more than her words that struck Callie first. She was in the midst of some disjointed attempt at a courteous rejoinder when the realization dawned upon her. She stopped speaking, and before she could recover herself, the other woman smiled at her apologetically.

"Yes, I am *that* Mrs. Fowler," she said, managing to look abashed and charming at once. "I'm very notorious, I'm afraid."

Callie was simply speechless. She apprehended that her hand was limp as Mrs. Fowler grasped it warmly; she understood that she had to speak, to appear normal and at ease. But it was utterly out of her power. "Mrs. Fowler," she repeated stupidly.

She managed to return a slight pressure to the friendly handshake. Next to this delightful and delicate creature, she felt like Hubert standing beside a fawn. She was amazed that Lady Shelford had admitted such an infamous caller, but then Dolly had been fascinated and obsessed by reports of the crime and trial. She had even considering leasing a window overlooking the scaffold, but Lord Shelford had proved too squeamish to allow it and protested that she would be exposed to vulgar crowds. It was uncommon for the countess to submit to her husband's will, but the suggestion of vulgarity had impressed her, and she had reluctantly given up the plan. To have the scandalous Mrs. Fowler drop into her lap, or at least into her drawing room, must seem a windfall of no small proportions.

Callie summoned a shred of self-control, fearing that her shock would appear to be disapproval. "I'm pleased to meet you," she managed to say. "You are a friend of Madame de Monceaux?"

"An acquaintance merely," Mrs. Fowler said vaguely. "But I was on my way north to reunite with my little boy, and I couldn't but pause to look in on her, she is so amiable, is she not?" She gave Callie's hand a pat and looked directly into her eyes. "She particularly said that I must leave a card on you, Lady Callista." She paused. "Of course I didn't hope to find you at home, but what an honor it is!"

"Thank you. Pray be seated," Callie said weakly. This was Trev's wife, this exquisite small creature with the pixie eyes. And that pressure on her hand— Mrs. Fowler had been sent by the duchesse—she was here not to congratulate Callie but to find her husband, of course.

As Mrs. Fowler returned to her chair, a gaunt and balding gentleman stepped forward, the wispy remains of his hair floating behind his ears. He placed one hand at his back and offered the other to her. "Sidmouth. Your servant, my lady," he said, briefly bending over her fingers. "Accept my wishes for health and great happiness in your union."

A large dose of smelling salts would have been more useful to her. "Thank you," she whispered. She sat down abruptly in the chair that the major provided and clasped her hands.

Dolly turned to Mrs. Fowler and began to inquire about the conditions of women in the Fleet Prison, apparently oblivious to any crudeness in her enthusiasm to satisfy her curiosity and gather some morbid tidbits to spread. Mrs. Fowler replied gracefully and without any sign of resentment, describing her treatment as perfectly humane. She even glanced at the Home Secretary with a confidential smile, as if they were both connoisseurs of prisons, which Callie supposed they were. Lord Sidmouth, however, returned the familiarity with a cool and impassive glance.

A servant handed Callie a cup of tea. She sipped, finding herself so far beyond frantic that she was almost calm, sitting with her fiancé on one hand, the Home Secretary on the other, and directly opposite—but she could not even quite compose the thought in her mind. Mrs. Fowler kept glancing at her, even while replying so tolerantly to Lady Shelford's questions. With every look, Callie felt more naked, as if her hair had fallen down and her clothes vanished and she were lying tumbled in the bed with Trev the way they had been all night together, with his outraged wife standing over them in righteous fury.

Mrs. Fowler did not appear furious, however. She couldn't know the truth, of course—though Callie had rather the idea that a wife could somehow deduce these things by intuition or mesmeric currents or something on that order. It was the most disconcerting thing of all, to suddenly think of herself as the other woman, particularly in regard to this petite elfin beauty. Callie could perfectly comprehend that a gentleman would sacrifice his life and honor for a woman like Mrs. Fowler. She was a princess from a fairy tale, lovely and sweet and charming, with lips like a rosebud and petal-soft skin. Dolly seemed fascinated, and Callie could hardly blame her. It was absurd to think of this delicate creature sitting in a prison cell, and even more ridiculous to suppose that she could be hung for a crime.

But for the Home Secretary, who appeared to find her uninteresting, all the gentlemen in the room seemed quite taken with Mrs. Fowler. Only Major Sturgeon made any particular effort to keep himself from smiling foolishly at her. Callie saw him catch himself once and look deliberately away, glancing toward Callie to see if she had noticed. She took a gulp of her tea and lowered her lashes. She hardly blamed him. If Major Sturgeon had not been strongly attracted to Mrs. Fowler, Callie would have feared he was coming on with some sort of condition.

But while all the masculine attention was fixated on the fairy princess, her attention seemed to be fastened on Callie. After a polite period of bearing with Lady Shelford's avid interest, the infamous caller found some means to excuse herself and come to sit beside Callie, evicting the major from his seat with a pretty pleasantry.

"Now," she said, sitting down with a bright look, "we must have our private whisper together, as all the ladies do with the bride-to-be, you know!"

Callie didn't know anything of the sort, but she nodded dutifully. "The picture gallery at Shelford is thought to be of interest. Perhaps you would like to view it?"

"You're kindness itself, Lady Callista. The duchesse assured me it was so. Of course I should be honored if you'll show me the paintings."

They rose together. Dolly and the earl both wanted to accompany them in order to acquaint Mrs. Fowler with the illustrious history of the artworks, but she put them off, insisting that they must not desert their distinguished guests for such a nobody as herself. Lord Sidmouth, who seemed a perceptive gentleman, said that he would be glad to view the gallery but only after another cup of tea. So Callie and the nobody were allowed to depart without a full escort.

The long, gloomy promenade at Shelford, with paintings on one wall and a line of tall, narrow windows on the other, offered an excellent location for a tête-à-tête. The weather still waxed inclement, and hisses of rain added to the usual echoes, creating a suitably murky background for any private exchange. Mrs. Fowler nodded and walked slowly along, pretending an interest in the historical account that Callie pretended to give her, but when they reached a safe distance from the drawing room door, the petite lady paused and turned.

"The duchesse told me that you're hiding her son here," she said hurriedly, interrupting Callie's monotone on the comparisons between the Gainsborough portrait of her great-grandmother and the Reynolds of the same subject.

Callie bit her lip. She glanced along the gallery to make sure they were still alone. She gave a quick nod.

"Where is he? I must see him," Mrs. Fowler said.

Callie could not bring herself to say that he was staying in her bedroom. But the woman had every right to see her husband, of course.

When she hesitated, Mrs. Fowler said anxiously, "Can you arrange it?"

"Yes." Seeing her fretfulness, Callie felt a sharp wave of guilt. She debated and discarded a number of possible meeting places in her mind. Even the carriage house wouldn't be safe, as all the vehicles were being readied to fetch guests for the masquerade. "Oh!" An impulsive thought came to her. "Mrs. Fowler, can you come by a costume of some sort? A mask?"

The other woman looked at her and then smiled mischievously. "Can you get me a ticket?"

An instant after she made it, Callie was already regretting the suggestion. Anyone must recognize Mrs. Fowler, it seemed to her, even masked. And it meant that Trev would have to be abroad at the masquerade too—a thought that appalled her. "I'm not certain. Where are you staying? If I can, I'll have it sent."

"Thank you!" Mrs. Fowler clasped Callie's hand between hers. "I haven't a room bespoken, I fear. Is there an inn?"

"The Antlers," Callie said. "In the village."

"Oh, I do thank you!" Then she fumbled in her reticule and pulled out a note folded over so many times and covered with so much wax that it was only a lump. "Give him this." She pressed it into Callie's palm. "You are a heroine to do this for us! *Thank* you!"

By the time Callie reached her bedroom, she had found a target for the roil of emotion in her breast. And he was so amiable as to be waiting for her, stepping out from behind her door to take her about the waist and bestow an ardent kiss on the nape of her neck. As Trev turned her in his arms she trembled with fury, which he seemed to misinterpret as romantic passion, so that he was taken entirely by surprise when she planted a shove in the center of his chest that set him reeling backward.

"Do... not... touch me," she said through her teeth. As he caught himself on the bedpost, she lifted one eyebrow in scorn. She waited, breathing deeply, until he pushed away from the bed and stood upright. "A Mrs. Fowler wishes to see you."

He'd glanced down to straighten his coat sleeve. At her words, his body stilled. He looked up at her. "I beg your pardon?"

She held out the folded note. "Here."

He ignored it. "Mrs. Fowler?"

With a supreme effort, Callie held herself back from a vulgar display of her feelings, such as screaming aloud or stabbing him with a hairpin. Instead, she said with a dangerous coolness, "I believe you are acquainted with her?"

Trev stood looking at her. "Are you making a jest?"

Callie had a moment's pause. He made no attempt to soothe her or offer any excuse or explanation for himself. He appeared to have no desire to hurry to Mrs. Fowler's side or even to read her note. He didn't do anything but give Callie a look of slightly affronted disbelief.

"I am not," she said, maintaining her rigid spine. "I wouldn't jest about such a thing. She wishes to see you." Once again she held out the note.

He regarded it with all the fondness one might feel for an overripe kipper. They stood facing one another, a few feet apart, as if a bottomless chasm had opened in the floor between them.

"She sent this. She wishes to see you," she repeated, feeling he must not properly comprehend the case.

"Well, I do not wish to see her," he replied sweetly. "Good God, what can she want, the little—" He stopped himself. "You didn't tell her I was here, did you?"

The tone of this callous rejoinder, while not entirely unwelcome to her feelings, somewhat shocked Callie. She'd been feeling miserably ashamed, awakened from a brief dream in his arms to reality again—a reality now graced by the woman he loved so deeply that he had been willing to sacrifice his very life for her. But he didn't appear to understand the situation at all.

"Of course I told her," she said. "I've arranged for her to come here masked tonight, so that you can safely meet."

He shook his head slowly. "Callie. Do you despise me that much?"

She lowered her hand, curling her fingers over the note. "But… she's come to find you."

"What a gratifying thought. Doubtless she may offer me some further opportunity to hang on her behalf. Thank you, I believe I'll avoid the prospect—and the adorable Mrs. Fowler—altogether."

Callie turned away, walking across to her dressing table. She dropped the note in an empty pin holder and sat down in bewilderment. "I thought you would wish to see her."

"What possible reason could I have to want to see her?" he demanded. "I've had done with the woman, you may be sure."

She picked up a discarded scarf and began to fold it mechanically. "I suppose... I can understand that you've come to regret your... sacrifice... on her behalf."

He gave a low laugh. "Oh my God." He leaned his head back and closed his eyes. "Regret!"

"I thought—" She paused. "Then you don't love her anymore?"

"Been reading the newspapers, have you?" His voice was full of scorn.

"I did read of it, yes," she said uncomfortably. She tied a knot in the scarf.

"I see." He gave her a civil bow. "I collect that you subscribe to the school of scandal rags that casts me as a hero for shielding my wife, rather than a scoundrel who forged a note of hand for her to pass to her creditors." He made a casual, contemptuous flick of his fingers. "I'm not sure which is more flattering, being thought a criminal or a screaming fool."

"Nothing of the sort!" she exclaimed. "I never thought you a criminal. I hope I know you better than that. And however much a miscarriage of justice it might be, surely no one would suggest a gentleman was a fool to risk his own life to protect his wife."

"Doubtless it would be exceedingly chivalrous, if she *were* my wife."

"If she—" Callie started to speak, then broke off and blinked at him. "She isn't?"

"You have to ask me that?" he inquired bitterly. "I would have thought... you, of everyone—" He blew out a harsh breath. "But what difference does it make?" He shrugged. "No, she isn't. I've never married. Much to my mother's disgust." He gave a slight laugh and leaned against the bedpost, watching her from under lowered lashes. "I've been in love with you, you know, since I was sixteen years old."

He said it in such a composed way, that for a moment she didn't quite take his meaning. She blinked down at the contorted scarf in her hands, frowning. She forgot, sometimes, how fine and carelessly handsome he was, but it came upon her now with strong force. She forgot because he was her friend; he was simply Trev, who made her laugh. She had adventured with him and had trusted him, slept in his arms.

"But why do I trouble myself to tell you?" he continued, as if he were speaking to someone else. "You never believe me, and it's not as if I can do anything to the point about it. I might as well be in love with your hosiery, for all the future there is in it."

"I don't—" She struggled with words. "I don't know that I don't believe you, precisely. You're very dear to me, and I'm sure I'm dear to you too. We're excellent friends."

"Of course." He nodded. "Friends. And now I'll just go and find a suitable cliff from which to cast myself."

"Oh come," she said with a wan smile.

"My God." He pushed away from the bedpost. "Friends! And do you fall into bed with any man who's 'dear' to you? How am I to take that?"

"Of course I don't." She stood up, letting the knotted scarf slip away. "I can't seem to help myself. With you. About that. It's extremely vexing."

"You're quite right on that count," he said sullenly. "I'm damned vexed. I'd like to vex you right here on the floor, in fact. And the idea of Sturgeon vexing you is enough to dispose me to murder. Is that clear? Do you comprehend me?" He took a reckless stride toward her and caught her chin between his fingers. "I'm not your *friend*, my lady. I'm your lover."

She was startled into immobility, except to blink rapidly as he looked down into her eyes from so close. He bent and kissed her, a featherlight touch that belied the strength in his hand, a kiss that deepened and invaded her until she was quivering in every limb.

He broke it off, still holding her face. "Has he kissed you like that?"

Wordlessly, she shook her head.

"Have any of them kissed you like that?" he demanded. "Have you had any other?"

She drew a deep breath and thrust out her lower lip. "Have you?"

He held her, looking down with a grim hauteur. "That's not an answer. But would you care if I had?"

It ought to have been uncomfortable to be held in such a forceful manner, but for some reason Callie was merely breathless. "I suppose I——" She faltered. She found the truth excruciatingly difficult to admit. "I'm sure a gentleman such as yourself has a number of... of opportunities, and it would be unnatural, doubtless, if you had not responded."

He let go of her and swung away impatiently. "Oh, I've had other opportunities, true enough."

As Callie had not herself had any prospects of that nature, she felt at a considerable disadvantage. "Well, then. Perhaps I might care. A little. That is human nature, is it not?" She confessed that much with some effort. "But I would not allow it to disturb me unduly."

He put his arm along the mantel and stared into the cold fireplace. "You're quite worldly about it, I see," he said with a tight smile. "And here I've been saving myself like some boy virgin."

She gave him a doubtful look. "I beg your pardon?"

He leaned on his fist. "To answer your question— yes, I've had other opportunities," he said brusquely. "Yes, I've taken some up. But something always stopped me in the breach. I don't know if you can understand that. I don't know that I understood it myself until lately. But I seem to be yours, Callie. Body and soul." He didn't sound as if it made him happy. "I will be till I die."

She stood silent, turning the words over in her mind as if they were a strange device that she could not find the key to understand. With a shy move, she looked away and caught a glimpse of both of them in the mirror on her dressing table. Herself, with red hair and a high-colored complexion—if not quite dread-fully plain, then certainly with no particular beauty— and him, watching her in the glass, dark-eyed and masculine, exceptionally handsome by any measure.

The flush on her cheeks deepened. She felt strange to herself, mortified and confused. "I don't see how that can be true," she whispered.

"No," he said. His mouth was grim. "No, you can't, because all you can see is what's in that mirror. So! *Eh bien!* Sell yourself to Sturgeon. I'll be removing to France in any event," he added, "where I'll find myself some vintner who'll overcome his republican scruples so that his daughter can call herself a duchesse. And everything will be *très convenable,* n'est-ce pas?"

"You're mine?" she asked in a faint voice, still bemused by his words.

"I'll do my best to overcome the sentiment, so do not concern yourself about it." He thrust his hands in his pockets. "Ah, and here is your key." He withdrew the key and tossed it onto her dressing table. "I found nothing amiss with the books. They conform to the bank ledgers perfectly, so no hope that the good major can be dissuaded from his engagement to marry your fortune."

She picked up the key and turned it over in her palm, looking down at it. "Did you wish to dissuade him?"

"No such thing," he said in a curt voice. "I merely wanted to satisfy myself as to who had blackmailed him. But it remains a mystery, and I daresay it always will now. Since Mrs. Fowler has managed to locate me, and you've all these assistant secretaries running haphazardly about the house, I don't think I'll tarry here much longer."

"I don't understand you. If you weren't married—if you never loved her—then why—" She clenched her fist on the key. "*Why* did you do such a thing for her?"

"Because I *am* a screaming fool, that's why!" he snapped. "It wasn't out of love for *her*, you may be sure. I did it for a friend."

"A friend!" she cried indignantly. "What sort of friend would ask such a thing of you?"

"Hush. Do you want to bring the secretaries down upon on us?"

Callie plopped down in a chair, looking up at him. "What I want is to know how you came to be convicted of a crime on behalf of this Mrs. Fowler. I'm coming to dislike her extremely now, and perhaps I may turn her over to one of these secretaries myself."

He shrugged. "A benevolent thought, but it would do no good. There's no evidence against her that hasn't already been dismissed by the court. You'd have to bring her to confess to Sidmouth himself, and there's slim chance of that. She may complain of her notoriety, but she likes having her neck spared well enough."

"But why did you do it? You didn't raise a finger to defend yourself!"

"It was ill-judged, I'll admit. Though it might have been worse."

"So it might!" she agreed angrily. "I should like to know what so-called friend caused you to put yourself in such peril! And then I should like to see him tossed head over heels on Hubert's horns." She paused. "Or her," she added conscientiously.

"Him," Trev said. "But you'd have liked him, Callie. And I know he would have very much liked you. We had a quip between us—" He stopped himself, looking conscious. "Well, that's no matter. Perhaps a female wouldn't appreciate the humor."

"Perhaps," she said. Some of her rigidity left her, but she felt dissatisfied that she wasn't to be let in on whatever humor this might be. "I collect he is no longer living?"

"No," Trev said shortly. "He's dead."

"I'm sorry." Callie lowered her eyes. To be candid, she found herself jealous of any friend who commanded such loyalty from him. "I'm sure you miss him," she said, attempting to enter into his feelings. "Was he a Frenchman?"

He gave a laugh. "The Rooster? No, not hardly! Though I met him in France."

"Oh," she said. "Oh, of course. The pugilist." Callie supposed she shouldn't be taken aback; the papers had mentioned his association with Mrs. Fowler's late husband, but she had never imagined that Trev would have a close rapport with one of the great, hulking men who pounded one another to bloody, raw flesh in their illegal bouts.

He seemed to read her thoughts, for he clasped his hands behind his back and bowed. "I haven't led a very respectable life since I left Shelford, my lady."

She bent her head. "No, I suppose you haven't."

"I expect if you've read the papers, you know that I've got no property in France, either," he added gruffly. "It's all a great fabrication that I made up to please my mother."

She had deduced that, in fact, and spent a number of her nights composing scornful remarks to her pillow on his general perfidy and falsehood. But she only said, "I see."

"I made an attempt to recover it," he said, "and all I received for my trouble was to find myself in the clutches of a moneylender the likes of whom I'd knife in the back if I met him today. But I was young and witless, and I wanted to have Monceaux; I wanted to go to my grandfather and tell him I had it back. Sadly for these fine ambitions, what I got was beaten sense-less in a back alley of Paris."

Callie listened with her eyes lowered. In mockery he called her worldly wise, but she had stayed in Shelford, dreaming of adventures, reading his letters

full of humor and invented tales, while he had gone
out and been beaten up in an alley.

"But to shorten this unedifying story," he
continued, "I fell in with some English deserters after
the war. Big fellows. We were all starving to death."
He gave a humorless laugh. "I had the lucky notion
of making an exhibition of English boxing in Paris.
None of us knew a thing about fighting, so we fixed
it. It was a sensation. I'd call for a volunteer to take on
these English *goddamns*—you'll pardon another lesson
in my language, Mademoiselle, but I'm afraid that's
what we French call your countrymen under certain
circumstances—and we'd have some hulking local
géant ready to come up and fight. There'd be a lot
of sound and fury before we made sure he won, and
split the takings with him." He crossed his arms and
leaned back against the mantel. "But Jem got tired of
it. He began to fight in earnest. And he was good."
His voice softened, and he shook his head a little.
"He was amazing. But we couldn't make any profit
in France by thrashing Frenchmen. So we changed his
name, came back to England, and made a bid for the
championship."

"Instead of coming home to your family," she said
tartly, "as you might have done in place of starving on
the streets of Paris or becoming a... a—"

"An operator of the Fancy," he supplied. "I
arranged bouts and held the stakes. I didn't want to
come back. My grandfather was still alive." He paused.
"Among other reasons."

That cause she did comprehend. The old duc had
used mockery and scorn like a rapier on his grandson;
Trev had always ignored it or turned it away with a

shrug, but Callie knew. Their wildest adventures were driven by his grandfather's sneering voice. Trev would give his alley-cat yowl under her window in the middle of the night, and all the rules were at naught then. There would be a hint of violence in his laughter that only some journey to the edge of disaster could quell. To stand before his grandfather and admit that he had tried to regain Monceaux and failed—no. She understood that much.

"But this is a boring topic," he said with a shrug. "We did well enough for ourselves. Jem fell in love with the adorable Emma, and they had a son, and everyone loved them all, and when the Rooster lay there dying on the grass, he asked me to take care of Emma and the boy." His tone was light and careless, but his expression was rather hard. "Perhaps they didn't print that part in the newspapers."

"No," she said quietly, "they didn't print that."

"God knows I tried to do it," he said, drawing a deep breath. "She'd listen to Jem. She's a remarkably silly woman, but she doted on him. Once he was gone—we couldn't deal at all, she and I. There was a nice sum of money that was meant for her and the boy. I had charge of it, but I could see she'd run through it before he was out of short coats. And she did. So I made her an allowance myself—aye, you may lift your eyebrows, but I'd built up a pretty fortune, and a good deal of it was from making book on the Rooster's fights, so I reckoned it was only what I owed him. But she got herself on tick with some jeweler, and he frightened her, and she was too stupid or stubborn to come to me." He blew a scoffing breath. "As if we'd let a bill broker carry her off without breaking his legs for him first."

She sat looking at him, sorting out this new Trevelyan in her mind: this rather fierce gentleman of fisticuffs and a friendship that outlasted death. In truth, it suited him better than presiding gravely over a grand châteaus, something that she had always had a difficult time envisioning even with his letters from France full of details and embellishments.

But there was a certain force, a hint of real brutality about him now. In all her fantasies of pirates and swords, amid the skewering and cannon fire—clean and bloodless in imagination—Trev had been at the center. It had always been a part of him, that violence: hidden and checked, but understood. The world had brought it out in him, she thought. No, he'd never allow anyone under his protection to be carried off or threatened—not when Callie had been tagging along with him on adventures, and not now.

"I marvel at her lack of sense," she said thoughtfully. "Certainly you would break his legs."

He gave her a sardonic smile. "Well, I wouldn't do it personally, of course."

"I did wonder why all your menservants were so large."

He made a slight bow.

"I ought to be shocked," she said.

He tilted his head to the side. "Aren't you, *ma mie?*"

Callie's forehead creased as she considered the question. She stood up and took a turn across the carpet. "I am exceedingly cross with you, certainly."

"So I had noticed," he murmured.

"Trevelyan," she said with determination. She stopped and faced him, taking a deep breath into her lungs in preparation to speak her mind.

"Call me 'Seigneur,'" he suggested to her mildly. "If you wish to reduce me to a quivering dish of jelly in the most efficient manner."

She ignored this. "I was led to believe you were *married* to that woman." She gathered her skirt, strode across the room again, and then looked back at him. "Married!"

"I'm sure I never said so."

This was so reasonable that it merely fed her displeasure. "You also never said you weren't!"

"At what point did the topic enter into our conversation?" he inquired.

"And that is another thing!" she expostulated. "Previous to this, sir, your conversation has been singularly uninformative regarding anything of any consequence whatsoever."

"I beg your pardon, Madame," he said, thrusting himself away from the mantel. "In that case I'll endeavor to confine myself to subjects of more worth and significance than my admiration for you."

She was cast into confusion by that, but recovered and began to pace the carpet again. "Indeed, it's been an excellent diversion, all this making up to me. I collect it was your intention to keep me wholly in the dark about everything!"

"Well of course," he said. "I always tell women I'm in love with them in order to produce mystification and bafflement. What other reason could I possibly have?"

"I can comprehend that you didn't wish to reveal these things to your mother, about making money off of boxing matches, and not truly owning Monceaux, and nearly being hung—but you might have told *me* and saved us a good deal of trial and tribulation."

"I didn't want you to know," he said curtly.

"What's more," she added, "you talk a great deal of how you admire and… and… whatever it is that you say—"

"That I love you?" he interrupted.

"Well, that. Yes, you seem to say that." She became flustered. "You have said that, several times. And that you would like to murder Major Sturgeon, and that sort of thing, which of course is quite nonsensical, and perhaps it is all nonsense." Callie stopped her pacing. She looked over at him where he stood beside the fireplace. The hard expression had returned to his face.

"I think it is all nonsense, because it is only words," she ventured. She wet her lips and then blurted out: "Like your letters, and everything you've said before. Words, with nothing behind them."

She glanced toward him under her lashes. White lines had appeared at the corners of his mouth. For a long moment they stood in silence, but her heart was beating so hard that it seemed to fill her ears. She had never seen him look so forbidding.

"Because if…" she said, summoning all her nerve, "if you aren't already married, then…" She broke off, realizing with horror that she was as near as was practical to demanding that he propose to her instead. Her courage failed her, overcome by a miserable wave of shyness. "Of course I understand now," she continued hurriedly, trying to appear as if she had meant nothing of the sort, "your circumstances are—with what you've told me, it's quite plain—you have abundant reason for not seeking matrimony with any respectable lady."

"Any respectable lady such as yourself?" he asked in a smothered voice.

"Myself!" she said with a dismissive flurry of her hands. Three gentlemen had assured Callie that they loved her, and then reexamined their characters and belatedly determined that they were not worthy of taking so bold a step as to actually escort her to the altar. He was going to say he wasn't worthy to marry her. She could feel it coming. "Oh no. I wasn't speaking of myself, of course. You wouldn't be offering for me!" She gave an unconvincing laugh. "I'm betrothed, am I not? I didn't mean that at all. I merely meant—some chance respectable lady."

He examined the coals in the fireplace. Callie examined the hem of her skirt.

"In fact," he said slowly, "you are correct. It was all nonsense. Merely words, with nothing behind them."

· Since she had entered into the room, Callie's emotions had spun from fury and shame to astonishment—and then a feeling that she could hardly put a name to, something rather like a fragile joy, but half-disbelieved, too tentative and tender to fully show itself. At these words, it snapped back into hiding like a frightened turtle.

"To be frank," he went on grimly, "I never wanted to see you again. I assumed you were married and long moved away from here. If I'd known you were in Shelford, I'd never have come back at all."

"Would you not?" she asked lightly, assuming a defensive shell of hauteur against the shock of this attack. "Perhaps, after all, that would have been best."

"Certainly it would." He plucked her scarf from the floor and tossed it on her dressing table. "In point of fact, I don't care to be your lover." His voice gained strength. "I didn't want to tell you anything at all about what my life has been. Not a goddamned thing! Here you are in this quaint little village, a respectable lady with your fortune and your cattle, where you're safe and comfortable, where a goat up a tree is the about the greatest threat to anybody's peace of mind. If there's one thing that's certain, it's that I don't belong in this pretty scene—as your father made perfectly clear years ago. When I saw you in that ballroom, I should have turned on my heel and walked out. And that, as you suggest, would have saved us all a great deal of trial and tribulation."

"Of course!" She was forced to agree immediately, and indeed to raise the stakes. "I'm sure that would have been the best for all of us!" she exclaimed in an unsteady voice. "Except for your mother, and if you did her a great deal of good at first, I believe with these Runners and constables besetting her, you may be the death of her yet!"

The instant she spoke, she wished the words back. She lifted her hand quickly, but he was already turning away.

"I'll remedy that at once," he snapped. "I bid you adieu, my lady. Accept my felicitations on your marriage." He threw open the shutters and the sash. It had come on to rain heavily again, and a gust of cold air blew her scarf from the table.

"Wait!" she said hastily. "Of course, I didn't mean—please wait. Oh, please wait!"

He paused with his hand on the sash, the wind blowing past him, tousling his hair. "What is it? Quickly, before I'm seen here in broad daylight."

A tumble of words fought to reach her tongue, but all she could manage to utter was, "Where are you going?"

"Where I've always been going." He swung his legs fully over the windowsill and ducked out. "To the devil."

Twenty-Two

THE DOWNPOUR HELD ONE ADVANTAGE, WHICH WAS
that the Bow Street Runner apparently didn't care
to stand outside in it and watch Dove House. Trev
actually entered by the front door, a rare treat in
his life lately. He had to shake off his coat, strip to
his shirtsleeves in the entryway, and towel his hair
dry with a cloth brought by Lilly, before he could
step into the dining room. His mother seemed to
have gained enough strength to sit up and have her
breakfast there.

She glanced up at him from a newspaper spread out
on the table. "Lilly, bring the fresh coffee. And then
you must—" She caught her breath on a light cough.
"You must do a guard at the kitchen door."

"Yes, ma'am." Lilly curtsied and gave Trev a pert
glance, ogling him in his shirtsleeves as she left the
room.

He pulled out a chair. "You frighten me, *ma mère*.
I hope this doesn't mean Cook is entertaining the
constable again."

"No, this time it is the Runner," she said, taking a
sip from her cup.

"Excellent," he said. "A redoubtable woman."

"But why are you here, *mon enfant*?" She coughed again, covering her lips with a lacy handkerchief.

"Where is Nurse?" he countered. "Should you be cavorting out of bed in this frivolous manner?"

"I have made Nurse an errand, to walk very far in the rain."

"Making a nuisance of herself, is she?"

"She is a good woman, but she troubles… me very much, that I must be bled, which I do not wish."

"Never mind her, then. But you look well, Maman. You look well." He gazed down at one of the heavy old knives of sterling, running his finger over the ornate coronet engraved above the flowing initial *M*. "Je t'aime, ma mère," he said to the tablecloth. "I must leave England."

He heard her give another small cough, but he didn't look up. Lilly scratched at the door. Trev gave a gruff assent, and the maid entered. She poured his coffee, set the pot down, and retreated.

"*Voyons,* it is just as good that you go, then, eh?" his mother said, when Lilly had closed the door behind her. There was a hint of anger in her thin voice. "What need do we… have with you here?"

He took a deep drink of coffee, not caring that it burned him. "C'est à chier, non?" he said, closing his eyes briefly.

"Oh my son!" She reached across and caught his hand. "I am sorry! It was a sting of the moment only. Forgive me! Forgive me."

He pressed her fingers. "You've nothing to forgive. Not you." He let her go, still not meeting her eyes. He rolled the sterling knife over, watching the dull light gleam on ancient silver. "But let us for once be frank with one another. How much do you know, Maman?"

She drew a shuddering breath. He looked at her sidelong.

"Very much, I think," she admitted, "that I deduce, but do not know."

He waited, spinning the knife with his fingertip.

"Monceaux is gone, is it not?" she asked quietly.

The sadness in her voice was like a mortal wound to him. "It is a pig farm," he said, his lip curling a little. "Except for the vineyards. They've been honored by Jacobins and royalists alike. A mistress of the duc de Berri now enjoys possession, I believe."

A steady tap of rain beat on the old glass panes. He watched the watery flow of green and brown and gray outside. His mother did not speak.

"I could not bring myself to tell you," he said. He leaned on his elbows and rubbed his hands over his face. "I could not."

She said, "I have only one regret for it. That you never saw it as it was. What belonged to you."

"It never belonged to me. It was yours, and my father's and grandfather's. I wanted it for you. For you and Hélène and Aimée. I wanted you to dance again at Monceaux, those dances that you used to teach us." He shook his head. "It was never mine. It's why Grand-père hated me, because my heart was born between. I was happy here; I loved to come home from school and be with you in this shabby old house. And Callie—my God—" He laughed. "What would he have done to me if he'd known? I don't know where I belong, Maman. But I wanted—ah, I wanted to come back and hand you a golden key, and make it all right again."

"And so you could not come back at all, which makes me hate Monceaux now."

He shrugged. "I should have come. At least after—" He broke off.

"After you fought for Bonaparte?" she asked wisely. "No, not then. Your grand-père would have killed you for certain if he had discovered it. Or you would have made a duel, which would be very shocking—here in such a *petit* place as... Shelford."

He frowned at her. "You know of that? How?"

She hid her face behind her handkerchief for a moment to cough and then lowered it elegantly. "Your English friend. The officer. Hixson? He came to call on me, to assure me that you were safe."

"Geordie Hixson?" Trev was astonished. "That was damned handsome of him."

"Yes, he said that he was making... calls on the families of his men while he was on leave. He said that you were captured but allowed to go about freely on your honor as a gentleman." She caught her breath. "It was a great comfort to me. But I did not mention it—to your grand-père—of course."

Trev was left without words for a moment. Then he only said: "You see? We were in school together. That's what makes me love the English."

"They are a most stout people," she agreed. "Very kind friends. But you have been a good friend also, I think? To the Chicken?"

He regarded her with unwilling amusement. "The Rooster." He took the coffeepot from her shaky hand

and poured for her. "So I find, after all my toil and trouble, that I have no secrets from you at all?" he asked ironically.

She gave him an apologetic glance. "The ladies of Shelford are so liberal as to bring the monthlies to me—they are a little out-of-date, but I find them—*très piquant*. I cannot always be—reading my prayer book, you know."

"The ladies of Shelford appear to be preoccupied beyond reason with the scandal papers."

"Of course," she said, lifting her cup by its double handles and looking at him over the rim. "Particularly when young Frenchmen of a certain description appear prominently in the pages."

He ran his hand through his damp hair. "You understand my situation, then."

"In truth, mon trésor, I am not certain that I do." She set down her cup. "You tell me you must leave the country? I thought you safe to remain concealed at Shelford Hall?"

"Safe?" he echoed sarcastically. "Shelford Hall is presently host to the Home Secretary himself, along with some uncounted number of his minions." At her questioning expression, he added, "He's minister in charge over such fellows as Cook's been taken to entertaining in her kitchen lately. Constables and Bow Street Runners and the like."

She did not appear to be alarmed. "But I do not think his bunions expect you to be there. As they might expect to discover you here, for instance, though I am happy for you to call briefly."

"'Minions,' Maman. But that's not the worst."

She gazed at him with wide eyes. "What is worst?"

His mouth flattened. "Mrs. Fowler," he said. "The devil only knows how she's found me. But she presented herself at the Hall and managed to get herself a word with Lady Callista."

His mother straightened a spoon and fork on the well-worn linen cloth. "Mon dieu," she said mildly.

"Mon dieu, indeed." He shoved away from the table, causing the cups to rattle as he stood. "Callie taxed me with having wed the woman, thanks to what she read in some scandal rag. She even had a plan for us to meet at the masquerade tonight."

"Oh, the poor child. Breaking her heart."

"Hah. She near pushed me out the window," he informed her. "'The poor child.'"

His mother sat up a little. "She was angry with you?"

"Yes."

"But you explained to her, of course? That you are not such a fool as to be in love as the magazines say? With a woman such as that. I brought you up to know better."

"I explained to her," he said shortly.

She put a spoon in her empty cup and stirred as if there were coffee there. "And now you must go away, you tell me?" Her voice broke upward. She dropped the spoon and took up her handkerchief to her mouth.

"Yes."

"What did you say to her?" The question was more like an exclamation. She balled the handkerchief in her fingers.

"I told her the truth."

"Oh, you must have made a great spoil of it all! She did not accept it?"

"She accepted it well enough, Maman," he said, as gently as he could. "And still I must go away."

His mother stood up, leaning on the table. She was trembling, but she managed to say, "What have you done to her?"

"It's what I will not do to her."

"And what is that? You do not offer a... a carte blanche... not to such a lady. You would ask her to wed you."

"Ma mère, I'm afraid to ask. I'm afraid she would say yes."

She stared at him. "But of course yes. And why not?"

"Because she would go with me!" He paced across the small room. "You know that she would; she is a little heroine: she is all heart. She's never refused me any mad thing I asked, never once. And I want her—my God, I want her with me. But I will not. I will not ask her to live as I do. I was wrong to linger here, wrong to speak to her at all." He closed his eyes. "What I've said, what I've done—knowing that I had no right!" He shook his head helplessly. "You don't know this life, Maman, and neither does she. It would be exile for her, from everything she holds dear."

"And so?" his mother demanded. "Do you think I do not know exile?"

He stopped and looked around at her.

"Trevelyan," she said, more quietly. "I will tell you something, mon ange. It is you who condemn her to exile."

He gazed at her. Then he looked away blindly.

She lowered herself to the chair again. "What will the life be with this officer who cares only for her money?"

"She says they're growing to love one another."

His mother gave him a look of scorn. "You will let another man take her from you?" she asked provocatively.

"I'm not fit for her," he said, scowling at the fading gilt on a pier mirror that was older than he was.

"*Chut!* Your grand-père will strike us with lightning bolts! The duc de Monceaux, twenty generations in Bourgogne, and to say you are not *worthy* of some English girl."

He gave a reluctant laugh at her exact imitation of his grandfather's frosty tone. "How many times have I heard that? Twenty generations in Bourgogne."

"At the measured pace you are proceeding, *mon fils*, I will not live to see twenty one, not any place at all."

He gave her a speaking look. "I'm not quite past that point, ma'am," he said dryly. "But if you mean to talk in this shockingly forward manner to a gentleman of my advanced years, while sitting up in your morning negligee, then you'll find yourself swept off your feet and carried directly to your sickbed."

"Bien," she said with a sigh. "You may carry me, so that Nurse will not scold, but do not disturb the Runner with a great noise on the stairs."

"I doubt a full cannonade would disturb him," Trev said and gave his hand to help his mother from her chair. "But what's this, Mademoiselle?" As she stood up, he noticed a pair of billowy yellow trousers that had been lying folded over the chair back. "Have you been cheating on me?"

"Never!" she declared, placing her arms lightly about his neck as he lifted her. "It is most mysterious.

Nurse found them hung over a rafter in the attic, and we have no notion how they arrived. I meant to have Lilly put them in the rag bag."

"The rag bag! I'll have you know those cossacks cost thirty guineas."

Her fingers tightened as he mounted the stairs. "Assure me that they can't be yours, my son."

"Hmmm," he murmured. "I may have to discover if they fit me now."

"*S'il te plaît!*" she begged. "Spare my frail health."

Callie tried to make a daydream for herself. It was what she always did when she could not quite bear what was real. She was, as most of those who knew her had informed her with some exasperation at one time or another, quite capable of becoming so lost in her thoughts that she did not hear any words spoken to her. But this time she could find no way to lose herself in any reverie—or delusion, as they all seemed.

So she heard her sister clearly when Hermey came to her door, but she didn't rise from her place on the window seat in answer to the knock.

"At least the sky has cleared," Hermey was saying to Anne as she came in without waiting for a reply. "The mud will be horrid, but—" She stopped on the threshold, a vision in pink in her costume of Venus rising from the waves, a necklace of seashells about her throat and a foam of sparkling net and lace at her hem. "My dear sister," she said with gay reproof, "it's nearly half past six—haven't you begun to dress?"

Callie bit her lip and shook her head. "Not yet."

"Callie!" Hermey came forward. "What is it? Do you feel quite well?"

"Oh yes." She summoned a smile. "I'm all right."

Hermey reached for the bell pull. "We'll have something to eat. *The Lady's Spectator* strongly advises that one should always eat before a ball and take a short nap. Come and sit down, I've brought some plumes to try in your hair."

In numb obedience Callie sat before the mirror and turned her head from side to side as Hermey held up the feathers. She ate the slices of buttered bread and drank some wine without protest. She allowed Anne and her sister to dress her in the costume that the maid had created by cutting up two of Hermey's overgowns, then swath her with spangles and the blue and green gauze. Below a shortened hem, her ankles were covered by a pair of puffy silken pantaloons drawn up with ribbons, and Hermey had tied tiny bells to her slippers.

It was only when her sister, reaching for some pins, instead accidentally swept a folded note out of a dish on her dressing table, that Callie awakened from her deadened state and made a sudden move. "That's nothing," she said quickly. "I'll take it." She held out her hand for the oddly shaped paper.

Hermey had been about to toss the note aside, but she paused then, a teasing expression on her lips. "What is it? Are you keeping secrets?"

"*No,*" Callie said, with too much emphasis.

Hermey giggled. "Well, it's a night for secrets, is it not? A masquerade." She held the note just out of Callie's reach. "Is it from the major?"

"No, it is not," she retorted, realizing that she had made a grave tactical error by drawing any attention to the paper at all. She turned back to the mirror. "This plume is drooping," she said, pulling it out of the turban Anne had wrapped about her hair. "I look like Mrs. Farr's cockatoo after a disorderly night on the town."

Hermey made as if to unfold the note, and Callie grabbed for it. She managed to seize it from her sister's hand, but then there was no escape. She felt herself blushing fiercely as Hermey and Anne both stared at her.

"I heard a whisper about something," Hermey said with a smirk.

Callie felt her heart go to her feet. She glanced at Anne, saw the maid bite her lower lip, and suddenly knew that the servants had been talking. Her mouth went dry. She gripped the note in her hand and turned away.

"Callie?" The bantering tone left her sister's voice, replaced by wonder, as if before she had only been teasing but now she saw more than she had expected in Callie's reaction.

"I'd like to take my nap now," Callie said.

"You can't lie down now that you're dressed," Hermey pointed out, "or you *will* look like a demented parrot. You should have rested earlier. What have you been doing in here all afternoon?" she demanded.

"Merely watching the rain and reading a little." Callie plucked all the feathers from her headdress. "I'll come to your room in a little while, and you can put them in again. I only want to doze for a few minutes first, to refresh myself."

Hermey looked at her and then at Anne. The maid cast down her eyes and stood with the dumb and blind expression that Lady Shelford encouraged in her servants. "All right," she said, favoring Callie with another speculative glance. "You may read your love letter in peace. I'll send for you at quarter to eight. That should give us time."

Callie waited until they had both gone out. She waited for some little time longer, just to be sure Hermey would not find some excuse to come back. Then she opened her fist and looked down at the note in it.

She had meant to tear it up. Almost, as she fingered the thick seal of wax, she did so. She hadn't sent any ticket for the masquerade to the Antlers, of course. If Mrs. Fowler wished to find him, she would have to chase after him herself. On a broomstick.

The thickly folded note lay in her palm. He'd said so many things to her, one lie upon the other, that it could hardly matter what more the infamous Mrs. Fowler might have to add to the whole sordid story now. Callie had a masquerade to attend, and never had the notion of hiding behind a mask seemed more appealing. She would have preferred to spend the evening in a cowshed, but there was small of chance of her being allowed to do that. She made a gesture, tossing the note toward the grate, but her fingers closed on it before it left her palm.

Instead, she broke the seal. Almost without her conscious approval, she found her fingers pressing the paper half open, as if she wished to worry at a wound and could not help herself. The writing was thin and florid—a thought crossed her mind that it was nothing like Trev's concise, elegant strokes; a piece of evidence that one might have supposed a jury would have noticed, but perhaps they were twelve good men and blind instead of true.

She tilted her head. At first glance she was unable to make out the opening line, but then she realized that the letters spelled out *"M. Tib L.B.,"* rather than what she had thought at first: a very contorted rendering of *Trevelyan.*

Monsieur Thibaut LeBlanc, of course. Callie had disliked the name immensely from the first time she had seen it printed on the pages of *The Lady's Spectator.* Morbid curiosity prompted her to spread the sheet full open, some dark desire to disgust herself as thoroughly as possible. The first sentence provided a promising start to this endeavor.

> *You will surely Suppose me to be the Most Madcap of the Female race, and I know you Think me so, but dear M. L.B., I dare to Plead for your Aid.*

Callie made a face. She held the note with the tips of her fingers, as if it might stain her skin, and read down the page.

> *Once before out of the Loyalty and Friendship which you bore So Nobly for my Late and Dearest Husband, you put Yourself at Great and indeed Mortal Peril for that which you Did Not Do. I depend on You then, that You will Not let that Sacrifice be in Vain, not on My Behalf, but in the Sacred Memory of Mr. Jem Fowler and to Protect his Innocent Child. I am in a Desperate way to*

Remove from England. I will tell you the Truth,
that you may understand the Extreme Gravity of
my Present Situation—I uttered a Second note,
and it has now been Discovered. I will not attempt
to justify my actions to you of all People. I was
Imprudent, that I will Acknowledge. Jem would
Forgive me, and I Beg that you will also and Help
Me and my Blessed Child to Depart from England
and reach Safety. E.F.

"Imprudent!" Callie whispered, opening her eyes wide. She stared at the swirling signature. She blinked and read the missive again. It still said the same things that it had said before. "Dear God."

It was a confession. It was not meant it to be so, of course. Trev had said she was a silly woman—she struck Callie as something very near to a raving imbecile to have written this and handed it to a stranger.

Callie sat slowly, her knees buckling under her. She frowned down at the letter in her hands for a very long time. Once she started up from her chair, thinking to ring the bell and send to Dove House, and then sank down again without touching the pull. When she finally did send for a footman, it was to dispatch two messages—one, by word of mouth—to the Antlers, and the other, by a quickly written card, to Hermey's fiancé, Sir Thomas.

Finally Anne's discreet scratch came at the door, summoning her to have her feathers inserted. Callie folded the note carefully and slipped it into her bodice under the layers of gauze.

It had been Hermey's dashing idea to hold a masquerade, one taken up by Dolly with considerable enthusiasm. Callie had been too preoccupied with the circumstances of secretly entertaining a gentleman in her bedroom to pay much mind to the preparations, so that even though Hermey had regaled her with reports of the progress, she was astonished when she saw the transformation. The ballroom at Shelford Hall, which had not seen any large parties in Callie's lifetime, was fitted up as an enormous tent, canopied and draped with swags that alternated green and white with pink and lilac and yellow—all festooned with multicolored fringes and tassels. Under the radiance of the great crystal chandelier, with the music and the mixing of masked and costumed guests, the effect was dizzying.

As it was a masquerade, a dinner and reception would be quite silly, Hermey had declared, for how ridiculous would they appear standing in their masks and greeting guests they weren't supposed to recognize when they had just sat next to them at table? Dolly, in an unusually obliging temper, had agreed to substitute an unmasking at the midnight supper.

Callie entered arm in arm with her sister, but soon lost Venus to the music of a country dance. She seated herself on the row of chairs against the wall, but she was not left alone for long: an Egyptian Mamluk—Major Sturgeon in his regimentals and a turban—found her almost immediately. This was no great feat of detection. Among the several sultanas present, Callie was the only one with red hair and one plume that was determined to keep drooping down over her nose in spite of Hermey pausing to straighten it several times.

The major was in an amorous mood. He bent over her fingers, looking quite imposing in his black mask and clean-shaven jaw. "An exotic!" he murmured. "Will you dance with me, lovely odalisque?"

She accepted, reckoning it best to humor him now, as she would be otherwise occupied in a short time. Besides, she found that wearing a mask went a great way toward making one feel less shy in public. There was something to be said for the protocol of ostriches. She entered the dance for once without being too nervous to enjoy it.

He returned her a little breathless after two sets, with her plume askew and the gauze drifting loose from several places that she could see through the mask and several more that she suspected from the attention that her Mamluk seemed to give her bodice. She put her hand up to check the safety of the note, and his eyes behind the black silk followed her motion. He grinned and bent to her ear.

"My God, my lady—do you wish to slay me?"

She did wish to be rid of him, but not quite that permanently. "I must go straighten my… my plume," she said. "If you will excuse me."

"You look charmingly just as you are," he said, giving her elbow a squeeze.

"Thank you," Callie said. She caught a glimpse of Sir Thomas taking Hermey toward the stairs. "But there, my sister is going down too. I must speak to her. If you will bring me a lemonade when I return, I would be much obliged." Without waiting for a reply, she deserted her fiancé as rapidly as the crowd would allow.

She hurried down the stairs and found Sir Thomas lingering outside the room set aside for the ladies to repair their toilettes. Instead of joining Hermey, she went to Sir Thomas and put her arm through his, walking with determination down the spine passage to the servants' stairs. He allowed her to lead him, though she could see that he was rather ruffled.

"In here." Callie took him through a door into the dark recesses of the boiler room.

"My lady," he said in a whisper, "this is quite irregular. What is it?"

"Can you bring Lord Sidmouth to me?" she asked, pushing the plume back over her head. "It's a matter of the utmost importance. A terrible miscarriage of justice has been done, and I believe he should be informed."

"So your note said, or I shouldn't be standing here in a coal cellar! I'm sure I'm pleased to do whatever I may for Lady Hermione's sister, but what can you mean? What miscarriage?"

"Regarding Monsieur LeBlanc and that forgery," she said urgently. "I have a confession from Mrs. Fowler."

Even in the dark, she felt him stiffen. "The deuce you say. Pardon me—but… a confession? How is this? She was here today, Lady Hermione told me. She made you a confession of guilt?"

"Yes! Well, no. Not precisely. She wrote it down."

"Wrote it down!" he exclaimed.

Her eyes were adjusting to the darkness and the dim red gleam of the boiler. "I have it here. And she's coming back to Shelford Hall tonight. Can you ask Lord Sidmouth to meet me?"

He was silent. Callie watched him. She would have to try to accost the secretary herself if he would not aid her, but she was sure the minister would give one of his own assistants a more serious ear.

"She's passed a forged note again," Callie added ruthlessly. "And doubtless will continue, if she isn't stopped." It was unfeeling, perhaps—even wicked—to reveal Mrs. Fowler and put her in danger of the noose, but she had served Trev the same turn without apparent remorse. Callie had thought long on the issue. She hardly knew if Trev would thank her—he might think it rendered what he had done pointless, and there was this child somewhere in the north, his friend's son—but in the end Trev was gone and Callie was adamant. It was for the duchesse, if nothing else.

"You have evidence of that?" Sir Thomas asked sharply.

"Yes, she wrote of it. And the second note has been discovered. She's attempting to find a way to leave the country; that's why she's here."

That was enough. He made a sound of assent. "I'll speak to the secretary."

"Do so directly," she urged. "And bring him here at quarter past eleven."

Callie's message to Mrs. Fowler had warned her that on no account must she come to the porter at the front facade, but to enter by the laundry court. She would have no trouble locating this, for Callie had instructed the same footman to return to the Antlers with a sedan chair and escort her to the Hall at the appointed time. Under a full moon and racing clouds, a pair of hefty retainers trotted up to the rear of Shelford Hall bearing the chair. A figure swathed in a dark domino emerged and stepped daintily to the washroom door.

Callie met her, still masked, feeling much as if she ought to have thirty pieces of silver jangling in her pockets when Mrs. Fowler thanked her with such a pretty profusion. But then she thought of the note and stiffened her resolve. The one forgery—that might have been excused as a naïve mistake—but when she uttered the second counterfeit note, she had known full well how heavy the consequences were. And then she came to Trev again as her savior from her own folly!

Callie had provided a blank card and writing materials on the big ironing table in the dry laundry. "I couldn't find an extra ticket," she said, drawing a closed lantern near. "But this is out of the card stock from Lady Shelford's desk." She set the lantern on the table and shone light on the paper. "Here is ink. Write it as: 'The Pleasure of your company is requested at a Masked Ball'—and you must make a capital of *P* and *M*—yes, just so." Callie had noted the peculiar and unique manner in which Mrs. Fowler inscribed these letters. The original invitations had been engraved, and Callie had been ready to explain that these had run out and the latter ones written by hand, but in the event Mrs. Fowler didn't question writing her own ticket. She did it so readily that Callie thought perhaps she had some experience of the practice.

"Where am I to meet him?" Mrs. Fowler asked, looking up from the table. She had procured a half mask on a stick; she picked it up with the card and turned to Callie.

"He's waiting for you," she said. "He says that you must be ready to fly on the instant."

"Oh, I am ready!" she exclaimed. "I can go tonight if I must."

"What of your son?" Callie asked, the point on which she was most uneasy with this snare.

"Oh, he's well enough where he is; I've left him with Mr. Fowler's parents. They dote on him, I assure you!" She gave a nervous giggle. "I think he would much rather his mama escape with her life than take the time to fetch him, don't you?"

"It must be terrifying." Callie watched Mrs. Fowler through her mask. "Monsieur told me a little of how he felt, fearing for what might be done to him."

"Indeed—I thought from what you said he must have told you—and I'm quite in mortal danger, you know!"

"You must be very courageous, though."

"Oh, I'm the veriest coward, I do assure you, my lady."

"But to forge a note of hand, not once but twice, and then pass them both. You must be as daring as any highwayman, I think."

She lifted the mask to her eyes and gave a pert twitch of her head. "I suppose it was rather daring of me," she said. "I shouldn't speak to you of it, though." Her eyes danced with mischief. "You might witness against me!"

"We need not call my lady to witness, I believe," said a man's voice. Lord Sidmouth stepped from the shadows behind the tall laundry mangle. The courtyard door swung shut and revealed Sir Thomas standing behind it.

Mrs. Fowler gave a shriek. The outer door was blocked, but she threw herself past Callie, making a rush across the laundry room for the corridor. In the dim light, Lord Sidmouth tried to catch her, but after an instant's struggle, he was left with only her black cloak in his hand. She escaped to the passage. Hermey's fiancé started to run after her, but the secretary stopped him with a raised hand.

"Sir Thomas," Lord Sidmouth said calmly, "we don't wish to cause a scene at her ladyship's excellent fete. Let her go."

"Let her go, sir?" Sir Thomas frowned.

"Let her go." He picked up the card Mrs. Foster had written, and then asked Callie for the note in which she had confessed. For a time that seemed to stretch to infinity, he stood reading and comparing the two by the lamplight.

Finally he looked up at Sir Thomas. "You may rejoin your betrothed. I'm certain that she's wondering what's become of you." Lord Sidmouth tucked the two papers inside his coat and turned to Callie. "My lady—would you do me the honor of allowing me to escort you?"

Callie's heart sank. She saw her hope of clearing Trev's name vanish before her eyes in his easy dismissal of the whole incident. But he held out his arm, and she could think of nothing to do but accept it. "Thank you," she said in a small voice.

They followed Sir Thomas out into the dimly lit corridor. As his figure disappeared up the stairs, Lord Sidmouth murmured, "I should like to speak to you in privacy, my dear. I'm sure all is at sixes and sevens, but is there some respectable place that we may be quiet?"

Callie was quite familiar with the servants' range. "The housekeeper's parlor," she said, swallowing her nerves. "She can look in, but she won't disturb us."

"Excellent. And perhaps she'll see that we have a cup of strong tea—I've had a surfeit of punch for the night."

This plan was carried out easily enough, Callie being a favorite belowstairs. In the plain, cozy sitting room, Lord Sidmouth dropped a lump of sugar in his tea and sat back in the housekeeper's overstuffed chair. Callie perched on a straight-backed stool, feeling much like a frightened maid called up to account.

"My lady," he said, "I must admire your cleverness. The episode produced an abundance of evidence that can be used in a court of law. But I was brought into it rather suddenly and find myself a little at sea. If you will be so good as to explain to me, why did she come to you in search of LeBlanc?"

Callie bit her lip. She still retained her mask, for which she was grateful as she felt the blood rise hotly in her face. But it was time and enough to speak some truth, she thought. "He isn't Monsieur LeBlanc. He is the duc de Monceaux. His mother has resided here in the village for many years after they escaped from France."

"I see." The secretary accepted that with a thoughtful nod. "He is a friend of your family, then."

Callie cleared her throat. "Yes," she said, not quite adhering to her intention to speak the whole truth. "That is, his mother is very dear to me. He came here to say farewell to her before he left England. He's gone now."

A faint smile flickered over his thin lips. "Doubtless." He regarded her for a few moments. "I must tell you, Lady Callista, that whatever his name may be, I was under a great deal of political pressure after his conviction. The king most sincerely wished to pardon him."

She said nothing to that, not knowing what reply to make.

"I can't blame you if you don't follow these matters, of course. It was a most unpleasant case: a young

LESSONS IN FRENCH 421

woman of such… attractive manners. The public does not hold with hanging the young and lovely, and who can blame them? The newspapers became involved. Sides were taken. We'd have had riots. Yet a great crime had been committed, and the law must be satisfied. Particularly in a case of forgery. The faith of the nation rests on a signature, my dear. Our banks would fail if we could not trust the notes that are passed."

She nodded, feeling a little sick.

"Yes, I can see that you don't like what you hear. But a full pardon was not possible. He did not defend himself. The lady did. With vigor."

She frowned behind her mask. "But the evidence…"

"Such evidence as there was spared his life. The jury convicted him, and the judge condemned him to death, in accordance with the law. He received a conditional pardon. He was not transported by force or sent to the hulks. I felt at the time that a reasonable compromise had been reached between the demands of the law and humanity."

"At the time?" she asked, her voice trembling.

"Outright pardon is an infrequent grace, my lady, by necessity. The awful power of the law is tempered by the king's mercy, but you will understand that it must not be casually extended."

She blinked behind the mask. "But the king himself, you said—"

Lord Sidmouth's lips flattened. "His Majesty in his compassion would pardon the entire roll of felons in Newgate," he said. "Your king, ma'am, has a very soft heart. And certain gentlemen of the sporting crowd had his ear in this case. It falls to me and his council to examine the petitions with a little more severity. When all the circumstances and the effect on the public mind were taken into consideration, we did not feel that this petition merited full pardon."

She bent her head, gripping her hands together and trying not to show her emotion. This seemed so unjust and capricious that she could not even speak— that he allowed Mrs. Fowler to escape in order not to disturb a mere ball, but would make an example to the country of Trev when they must have known he was not guilty.

"However," Lord Sidmouth continued evenly. "There are those rare cases in which the evidence of innocence is overwhelming." He looked up at her. "Reconsideration must be made. As you seem to take a friendly interest in his… ah… his mother… you may inform her that on the basis of what I have witnessed tonight, and these notes in evidence, the petition will be reopened. He will receive a full and unconditional pardon."

Callie sprang up from her seat. "Sir!" she exclaimed. "Oh, sir."

"Full and unconditional. She has my word on it."

Twenty-Three

SUCH WAS HER EUPHORIA THAT CALLIE WAS ALL THE way up the stairs and hurrying into the crowd of guests before she brought to mind that she had no one to tell the news. She paused, pushing the dangling plume from its favored position covering the right eyehole of her mask. All day she had felt benumbed, until she had discovered Mrs. Fowler's note, and then her determination to act on it had kept all other feelings at bay. But now the full impact of his absence came over her. It was nearly midnight; she couldn't even go to the duchesse. She experienced such a rapid descent in her emotion that she nearly stood there in the midst of the masqueraders and burst into tears.

"My lady." A gentleman spoke low, very near her ear.

Callie turned. Her mask and the plume obscured her vision, but that voice sent a shock of recognition down her spine.

"I've come for you," he said. He laid his hand on her arm.

She turned and saw him: masked, dressed in loose shirtsleeves, his collar open and a bloodred sash about his waist. He carried a sword in a glittering sheath, a real one—she recognized the elegant weapon that hung above the mantelpiece at Dove House. With his black hair and dark skin and a pair of yellow breeches thrust down inside his tall boots in the billowing Cossack style, he looked a corsair indeed.

She could have blurted out her news. It was her first thought, but hard on that came the memory of his leaving and what he had said to her. She stiffened, resisting his touch.

Guests nearby gave them curious glances, as well they might, for of all the costumes, his was the most simple and yet the most dramatic. Scandalous, without a waistcoat or cover for his shirt, with the muscle in his shoulders obvious and his collar points dangling carelessly down so that his throat and chest were half-revealed. Dolly, in a small coterie of her friends, was staring openly.

"I'm shocked to see you here," she said, with more dignity than she could have summoned without a mask to hide her face.

He did not reply. He looked down at her, his mouth grim below the black mask tied across his eyes. The first notes of a waltz drifted above the crowd of guests. He caught her about the waist and swept her into the dance.

"I thought you were going elsewhere," she said, blowing the plume from her face as they turned.

Still he did not speak. Resentment began to rise in her, that he would come back again. Again! How many times was she to be teased and mocked? If he said again that he loved her, and that he must go away, she would scream. Perversely, she suddenly wanted to keep her hard-gained victory on his behalf to herself.

"To the devil, in fact," she added, lifting her chin.

"Oh yes," he murmured. "And this time I'm taking you with me."

Callie glanced up at him, tripping a little. He held her up in balance, turning them both to the music. Through the mask, his eyes glinted. She was already flushed from the dance, but these words caused her to lose her breath for an instant.

Her agitation increased as she noticed Major Sturgeon coming toward them across the floor. Her fingers tightened on Trev's shoulder. He glanced over her head and then gave a smile that was most piratical under the mask.

"Oh dear," she whispered. "Don't make a scene."

The smile vanished. He gazed down at her steadily. "Is that what you want? No scenes?"

As they swung and whirled to the music, his arms held her firmly but lightly, like a question. Another turn, and Callie saw the major again. He had stopped to let another couple dance past. She was having trouble finding her breath. Dolly and Hermey and Sir Thomas were standing along the edge of the floor, all looking toward her. Lord Sidmouth also watched, tall and grave, without a mask to hide his stern features and flyaway hair. With each circle, she realized that the audience to her waltz was growing, speculative glances and whispers behind fans. Callie felt herself shrinking. She was what she had dreaded to be all her life: the center of attention.

The music began to sweep to a close. Major Sturgeon reached them just as the orchestra ceased to play and a gong started to toll midnight. It was the signal for everyone to unmask, but instead, when the bell fell silent there was a frozen stillness; everyone paused and turned to look at Callie and her partner.

"Unhand my betrothed," the major said, his voice low but carrying in the weird quietness of the ballroom.

Trev ignored him. Instead he stood looking down at Callie. She was aware of her costume all disordered, her mask askew from the dance and her feathers fallen down. She must appear a ridiculous figure. But Trev tilted his head a little, an inquiry. "Make your choice, my lady," he murmured.

Her fingers rested on his open palm. The answer was hers to make: he would let her go in a moment.

Callie took a deep breath, in hopes of preventing herself from swooning on the spot. She turned to Major Sturgeon. He wasn't even looking at her; he was glaring through his mask at Trev, reaching for the weapon at his side. He appeared to have forgot that it was a scimitar of pasteboard.

"I beg your pardon," she said. Her voice seemed to catch, but she cleared her throat and pushed her mask up above her face as he glanced at her. "I beg your pardon, Major," she said, so much more strongly that her voice made an echo in the hushed room.

He turned to her, making a slight bow of acknowledgment. "My lady. I must ask you to allow me the honor of escorting you to the refreshments."

"Thank you," she said, "but I wish—"

"Pray consider what you say, ma'am," he said in a warning tone.

"Major—"

"Do you not see where we are?"

"Major, I—"

His face was turning red. "Do not speak!" he hissed under his breath, so viciously that she drew back a little.

Trev's hand closed over hers. He stood beside her, regarding Callie with a faint quirk at the corner of his mouth. Then through the eyehole of his mask, he positively winked at her.

She gathered herself, giving one look around her at all the staring faces.

"Major Sturgeon," she said in a level, carrying voice, "I'm sorry to say that after all we should not suit. My affections are previously engaged."

In the silence that met her words, she bit her lip and brushed the feather back out of her eyes. Major Sturgeon stared at her, his mouth a hard, set line.

Trev pulled his mask down from his face. A ripple of sound went about the ballroom, faint murmurs of surprise and wonder.

With a slight, ugly laugh, the major said, "As you will, then, madam. I wish you joy of your bargain." He gave a short bow and turned his back on them, striding away with the crowd parting before him.

Someone began to clap enthusiastically. It was Hermey. Her fiancé joined her. Another took it up. Callie blinked around her, realizing with bewilderment that everyone was applauding. Trev grinned and took her hand, bending deeply to kiss it. Then he pulled her close to him, as if to kiss her cheek, but instead he whispered fiercely in her ear, "We must go. No farewells, I'm sorry."

She let him lead her—if not quite drag her—past Hermey and Dolly and the other clapping guests, who seemed to be taking it all as part of the entertainment. Even Dolly was applauding with a rather wild enthusiasm. She gave a frenzied wave toward the conductor, and the orchestra started up again, so that Callie and Trev made a grand exit to the rising strains of an Austrian galop.

He still had her by the hand when they reached the archway to the stable range. There he stopped and pulled her into his arms and kissed her until Callie was in danger of losing not only her feathers but her wits.

"We'll have to steal a horse, I fear," he said, letting go. "You've cast in your lot with me now; I hope you won't shy away from a felony here and there."

Callie lifted her foot to worry at a piece of gravel that had found its way into her slipper as they'd run pell-mell across the drive. "Steal a horse? Why?" She hopped on one leg, holding onto him for balance.

"We're in a great hurry, ma mie. You'll have to become accustomed to it, at least until we're out of England. Sit down." He pushed her onto the mounting block and reached down to pull her slipper free, shaking it out. But he paused in his great hurry long enough to slide his hand up her ankle. He lifted her stockinged foot and kissed the arch of it. "I adore your petticoats and bells, my love, but this is the last time you show them in public."

Callie retrieved her shoe from him. "Let's steal my horse," she suggested.

He gave a nod, rising. "A good notion," he said approvingly. "Strictly speaking, it won't be a crime, eh?"

She followed him into the shadow of the stable yard. "Where are we going?" she asked curiously.

"We're for Liverpool and the Boston packet," he answered, keeping his voice low. "I'm sorry you had no time to say your good-byes, but you can write from there."

"Very true," she agreed. "Hubert will want to know where I've gone."

He pulled her close to him again, holding her tightly. "I'm sorry. We'll find someplace for your cattle—some land. There's a great deal of land in America."

"So I understand," she said in an equitable voice. "Let me have the groom harness my mare to the gig. I'll drive out and pick you up at the archway.

He gave her a squeeze. "Intrepid girl."

"Certainly," she said. "I collect we're eloping?"

"We are," he said. "Unless you'd prefer it to be a forcible seizure. I don't know when we'll find a proper parson."

"Kidnapped from a masquerade!" she said with relish. "After I jilted my betrothed in front of a great crowd of people. On behalf of the editors of *The Lady's Spectator*, I thank you."

He laughed and straightened her feather. "Bring out our escape vehicle, you notorious female"—he kissed her on both of her eyelids—"before the Home Secretary remembers where he saw me last."

A few minutes later, still feeling satisfactorily rosy from the slight delay due to the need for further kisses in spite of the Home Secretary hot on their heels, she trotted her mare out of the stable yard, leaving a startled groom behind her. Trev swung up from the darkness and settled onto the seat beside her. He leaned over and kissed her again. He would have taken the reins, but Callie retained them, feeling that he might not drive quite straight while afflicted with this continued compulsion to kiss her. She flicked the whip and asked her horse to break into a brisk canter, sending up a spray of gravel as they flew down the drive.

While Trev lounged back on the seat, his arm about her shoulders in a most warming manner, she allowed the mare to maintain this great pace as far as the gate lodge. There she reined in, for the trees shadowed the road and the moonlight was not as bright. The horse came to a halt before the closed gates. The lodge keeper stared up. "My lady, is it you? But—begging your pardon—where are you driving out at this hour?"

Callie looked over at Trev. "America, did you say?"

He leaned across her. "Or Shanghai, if you prefer it," he countered.

"You needn't leave the gates unlocked in that case," she informed the bemused gatekeeper as the gig rolled through. Outside, she turned the mare toward Shelford village.

"We'd best take the north road from here," Trev said. Their mingled breath frosted in the pale dark. "No need to go this direction."

"This is a short cut," Callie told him.

"Is it? Good. Damn, I'm a fool—I ought at least to have lifted a cloak for you on our way out. I don't think it would be wise to stop in Bromyard, except to leave your mare. But if you can endure it as far as Leominster, we'll take a chamber there. That's fourteen miles or so."

"I'm not in the least cold," she said truthfully. Not while he was holding her close in this gratifying manner.

"You're a heroine," he said, kissing her neck. "Je t'adore."

She accepted this compliment calmly. "But pray, will you enlighten me... when last we spoke, you wished you had never seen me again."

"I was out of my mind," he explained. "I entirely blame your stockings."

She cast him a sideways glance.

He withdrew his arm and put his hand across her wrists, causing the mare to come to a walk. "Callie," he said, turning her face to him. His voice dropped harshly. "Do you understand—you won't even have your own money? Your father made certain of that long ago."

She felt much colder when he sat away from her. "Did he?"

"Aye, he was pleased to inform me that your trust was made ironclad to protect you from fortune-hunting scoundrels." In the moonlight she could see a derisive smile curl his lips. "Taking myself as the pattern and type."

"He didn't yet know Major Sturgeon, I suppose."

"And we'll be living abroad," he said doggedly. "I can't bring you back to see your sister or Shelford or England. And I don't keep respectable company. I've money enough, but—"

"Are you trying to make me jilt you too?" she demanded.

"No, damn it all, but you ought to."

"Yes," she mused, "I should return to the masquerade and announce that I've changed my mind and prefer after all not to be forcibly seized. Doubtless that would make heads spin even on the editors of *The Lady's Spectator*."

"I daresay they'd thank you for the increase in their circulation numbers, at any rate."

She clucked the mare to a trot. "I feel they've been given adequate stimulation. As for me, I should like to break it off with you, of course, after having discovered these dismaying facts, but it was such great fun to jilt Major Sturgeon that I daren't encourage that sort of fickle behavior in myself."

He fell silent. The mare splashed through a puddle, and Callie allowed her to slow again on the muddy track. "This is Dove Lane," he said, as if he had just noticed it.

"Yes, and I hope it will dry a little by morning," she said. "Lord Sidmouth intends to pay a call on your mother tomorrow, if he isn't kept up too late at the masquerade."

Trev sat bolt upright. "Sidmouth?"

"The Home Secretary, you know."

"He intends to call...? Good God, has that Runner been to see him? Why the devil is Sidmouth to call here?" Then he stopped and said in an appalled voice: "Did Emma Fowler tell him I was here?"

"No, nothing of that sort," Callie said soothingly. "I mentioned to him that your mother has been feeling ill and very low about you, and he thought that perhaps a visit from him might raise her spirits."

"Are you mad?" They had halted at the garden gate in front of Dove House. Moonlight shone dimly on the whitewashed fence and the silvery rose canes. "Callie, don't stop here," he hissed. "She's asleep. She knows I can't come back. For the love of God, let us go and be done with it. "

"I have something to say to her."

He closed his eyes and took a breath. "I won't prevent you," he muttered in a constricted voice, "but we'd best be damned quick about it, if Sidmouth's in the way of things."

She had been enjoying to the full her opportunity to serve him back some of his own sauce, but seeing his anguish, Callie relented. "Perhaps I should tell you too," she said. "Before we go all the way to America."

"Well?" he asked gruffly. "What is it? You prefer somewhere closer. Italy? I warn you that it won't make much difference, except that perhaps you might be able to make a visit on your own now and again."

"I really don't think we need leave England at all, unless you very much wish to do so."

He shook his head. "I knew you didn't truly understand what it would mean to go with me."

"I know you suppose I'm a flat—"

"A pea-goose, damn it," he corrected. "Flat is a vulgar canting word."

She cocked an eye at him. "Perhaps you should teach me some cant, as we're not planning to keep respectable company," she suggested.

"No," he said in smothered outrage.

"A pea-goose, then," she said mildly, "but as I was saying—since Lord Sidmouth comes tomorrow to tell your mother that you're going to receive a full and unconditional pardon, and I understand that the climate in Shanghai is not entirely salubrious, I was thinking perhaps we could take a look at property in the neighborhood of Hereford instead."

He took her hands. "Ma chérie," he said gently, "you must know it's not possible—*what* did you say?"

"I said that Lord Sidmouth is going to give you a full and unconditional pardon."

He let go of her. There was a long and charged silence, with only the sound of the mare's soft snorting breath and the creak of a wheel on the gig.

"He gave his word on it," she added, feeling a little uneasy now that she had pushed her amusement to the limits of what any reasonable man might be expected to bear. "Because the evidence of your innocence is now overwhelming."

"Now overwhelming?" he repeated blankly. "When did he discover this?"

"Only an hour ago, perhaps."

"Don't jest with me. It's not a topic I find amusing. And don't suppose you can hoax me, either."

"It's not a hoax. I merely asked Mrs. Fowler several questions, and she wrote a sample of her handwriting on a card, and—well, perhaps she wasn't aware that Sir Thomas and the Home Secretary were witnessing what she said." She wriggled uncomfortably. "It might have been a bit dark in the corners of the dry laundry, and so she didn't see them. And you're right, Trev, I may be a pea-goose, but she's a… a veritable *saphead*. If you could have read the letter she wrote to you! That folded-up one you wouldn't touch, and I can't blame you for it. She's forged a second note of hand, and she wrote all about it to you, saying that you had taken the blame for her before and in hopes you would help her to escape England this time, and so you see, when the invitation ticket she wrote matched the handwriting in the note—and Lord Sidmouth heard what she said—" Her voice trailed off.

He was sitting beside her, his body very, very still.

"I hope you're not angry," she said. "She was allowed to flee."

"Who arranged this?" he asked in a strange voice.

"Well, I suppose—one could say—that I arranged it," she admitted rather nervously. He did not seem to be as glad as she had hoped he would be.

"When?"

"Just today. This evening."

"After I left you."

She nodded, though it was dark.

"A full pardon?" he asked again. "Unconditional?"

"Yes. Lord Sidmouth gave me his word."

"A full pardon?" he repeated and shook his head as if he found the very idea alarming.

"I think he has the power to arrange such matters."

"Oh, he does," Trev said harshly. "They sit at that table in council and decide life and death at their whim after every session. I don't doubt he has the power to arrange it. It's only that—" He stopped and scowled at her in the dim moonlight. "This puts a new complexion on matters."

She regarded him doubtfully. The night seemed to have grown colder. A faint shiver ran through her. She couldn't quite discern from the tone of his voice exactly what the new complexion on matters might be. He might wish to reconsider his position. He might even wish to reconsider marrying her at all. Now that he was a free man, he might want to find some other heiress, one who wouldn't have so readily agreed to accompany him to Shanghai. She bent her head, preparing herself to appear perfectly unconcerned if he should suddenly become unworthy to abduct her.

"For one thing," he said, "it means we don't have to drive fourteen miles to Leominster and arrive looking as if we took a wrong turn at the Barbary Coast."

"I rather like you as a pirate," she said shyly.

"I assure you, Mademoiselle, my feelings about you as a harem girl are beyond description," he informed her. "But I don't arrange a very good abduction, I'm afraid. In my haste to seize you and carry you off to the ends of the earth, I seem to have forgotten a few of the important articles. Such as baggage."

"It was a perfect abduction," she declared. "Pray do not carp about the details."

"No doubt the press will add such embellishments as are required to satisfy the public taste. And since I had already determined that my life is a vast wasteland without you, in spite of my best and repeated efforts to abscond like a worthless cad—"

"Usually through a window," she interposed.

"—and you appear to have agreed that you would accompany me to Shanghai if you must—"

"With the greatest happiness," she concurred.

"—I wonder if I might prevail upon you to forgo some of the minor particulars of this plan, such as driving all night to Leominster and sailing to Boston in the dead of winter, in favor of the simpler expedient of sleeping in a warm bed here at Dove House tonight?"

Callie tilted her head, considering. "Well, I'd been hoping for a Chinese adventure, but if you're so poor-spirited as to want to forgo storm and shipwreck…"

"Shabby of me, I must admit, but there's the added advantage that I'll be able to debauch you thoroughly before sunrise," he pointed out.

She gave a contented sigh. "I daresay your mother will be shocked."

"I daresay she'll be purring like a hat in a cream pitcher," he said. "And I must warn you that if you continue to giggle in that provocative manner, I shall be forced to accost you right here on a carriage seat, in my customary French scoundrel style. Drive on to the stable, my sweet life, before *The Lady's Spectator* catches us in the open."

Epilogue

"IT'S TIME."

Trev started up from a deep sleep. His stockinged feet hit the floor. For an instant he had no notion of where he was, only that this was important news and he had to react quickly. "I'm coming," he mumbled. "I'm here. Stay calm."

His fumbling hand found his shirt; he was pulling it on as he rose from the cot. He grabbed his boots in the dark and took a step toward the door, cracking his shin on the corner of an unexpected obstacle. "Stay calm," he muttered to himself, hopping on one foot. "Damn it."

"Hurry!" Callie's voice drifted to him. "Oh!" Her voice rose in pitch. "Oh my!"

Trev's heart was pounding. He drew a deep breath into his lungs. He remembered that he was in the cattle yard, not in his bedroom. Faint lamplight outlined the door of the tool room. He picked his way more carefully and leaned a shoulder against the doorjamb, dragging on one boot. Callie urged him again to come quickly, her voice echoing in the eaves.

"On my way!" he responded, rolling up his shirt-sleeves and attempting to sound as if he were wide awake. He could just see the clay-paved corridor as he hobbled past the granary on the way to the cattle stalls, carrying one boot. Down the long row, she was standing with her stockman and a farm boy at the edge of the lamp glow, her palms pressed together and her eyes alight.

"Look!" she said, pointing toward a lush bed of straw.

Trev blew out a breath of relief. He'd been deputized to provide added manpower in case it was required, a task which *The Complete Grazier* had not made to sound inviting, but from her joyful expression he could see that all was well. As he reached the open stall, a large cow heaved herself to her feet, revealing a wet and unprepossessing bundle of calf in the straw. Trev appeared to have slept through the grittier details of the procedure, for the tiny beast was already licked clean and attempting to get its hind legs under it in a wobbly effort to rise.

"It's a bull calf," Callie whispered, leaning toward him. "Our first!"

"Congratulations," Trev said low, winking at her.

She took his arm and watched as the calf struggled to get its legs in order, collapsed, and tried again. This time he made it, standing with his feet splayed, trembling but upright, his damp tail flapping from side to side.

"Oh, bravo! On the second try!" She cast a glowing look up at Trev. "I never tire of seeing this," she confided, resting against him in a gratifying manner that fully made up for his cracked shin and the fact that he still only had one boot on. "Look at his perfect mottling! He looks a great deal like Hubert, don't you think?"

"Exceedingly like," Trev agreed with a sage nod, privately considering that he had never seen anything that looked less like Hubert than this wobbly scrap of life that seemed to be all legs and eyes. As if to disagree with his assessment, the proud father favored them from somewhere in the distance with a prolonged, plaintive bellow.

"Is it that late? The sun must be coming up." Callie glanced over her shoulder. Hubert had removed with them to the new property at Hereford, a wedding gift from Colonel Davenport—which was damned decent of the man, Trev thought, considering that the bridegroom had punched him in the breadbox. She had accepted the gift with fervent gratitude and promised the colonel one of Hubert's offspring, but it was not to be this particular one, Trev surmised. She was leaning over and baby-talking to the calf, cooing and encouraging its first step like a new mother.

Trev might have been a bit jealous if it weren't for the fact that she made equally foolish babble over their own two-month-old son. Master Etienne Shelford d'Augustin had also been pronounced to be the perfect image of his father, so Trev could feel satisfied that he rated well up with Hubert on the paternal scale of things. Hubert, of course, got by with lying about in a pasture, having done his duty, eating and sleeping himself to another championship, while Trev was sitting up with Callie for late-night feedings, walking the halls with a crying infant, and applying himself to a new life of bonds and cent per cents and bank shares instead of sporting bets.

He had a family of his own. Etienne's program rather resembled Hubert's: eat and sleep, with the addition of periodic howling sessions. Trev had never realized that babies were so consistently raucous, but if that was the price of admission, he was more than willing to pay. He experienced some indescribable prickle of sensation across his skin every time he watched his wife and son together, sitting up late at night in the house he had bought for her, just the three of them together.

Assured that the new calf was up and nursing, Callie left her stockman with a lengthy set of instructions and then allowed Trev to escort her back to the house, kindly pointing out to him that he ought to put his boot on first. Faint light barely touched the horizon, outlining the heavy, strange shapes of ancient oaks. Trev carried a bucket of warm molasses mash, walking over the dewy grass beside her. They had been here only a six-month, but all the fences were in trim, and the hay fields ripening. Their house stood elegantly on level ground overlooking the River Wye: nothing so great and magnificent as Shelford Hall, but a pretty mansion, recently built, with six bedrooms, two drawing rooms, and a modern kitchen that had almost brought Cook to tears of delight.

Callie paused at the gate to felicitate Hubert on his accomplishment, covering him with compliments that would have made a debutante blush. Trev merely told him that he was a jolly good fellow and offered the mash. Hubert appeared to fully appreciate the gesture, tipping the bucket over with relish and consuming the treat off the grass with his great tongue.

Around them, birds had begun to twitter in the growing light. On the far side of the pasture, a fox trotted into the open, stopped and stared at them a moment, and then vanished into the hedgerow. Callie stood tiptoe on the fence, a little disheveled, her hair trailing loose and her collar turned up on one side.

The thought that he might have been in Shanghai at this moment, instead of where he was, brought such a fierce tenderness to Trev's chest that he blinked twice and then informed her brusquely that he would like a moment in private with her, as he had a mind to do some highly indecent things to her person. It was not precisely what he would have liked to say, but he had no words sufficient for that.

She turned with one of her sidelong, mischievous smiles and gave him her hand, hopping down from the fence and into his arms. Beyond that, it seemed, words were not presently required.

"It's a bull!" Callie informed the duchesse when she came down for breakfast.

"Voyons, did I not predict?" Madame said with satisfaction. She allowed Nurse to seat her at the table. "You owe me a guinea, Trevelyan, and do not wager against the brave Hubert again, if you are wise."

"Strip me of my fortune, will you?" Trev kissed his mother's hand and carried his newspaper back to the window. "Take care you don't become a hardened gambler on the strength of this success."

"But no, can I help myself to bring young men to ruin?" She lifted a hand as Callie moved toward the door. "*Ma fille,* pray allow Nurse to attend to Etienne and have a cup of tea with me to celebrate this great event. Then we will go and dote on him together, eh?

He has not yet been sufficiently spoiled by his grand-
maman today."

Callie assented to this agreeable plan and sat down
again. The duchesse had made a recovery that even
the London physician called miraculous, though Callie
privately thought it could be attributed largely to
having her son back with no cloud over his situation.
Trev claimed it was because he wouldn't allow any
lancets for bleeding in the house. The duchesse had
merely smiled at all their speculations and asked to
hold Etienne very often.

"Good God," Trev exclaimed suddenly, rattling
the newspaper. "Listen to this!" He folded the paper
back. "'The marriage of John L. Sturgeon and Emma
Fowler, née Braddock, took place in Florence, Italy, in
a private ceremony.'" He laughed and shook his head.
"I never thought I'd feel for Sturgeon, but Lord save
the poor devil. I wonder how she managed that?"

"She's very taking," Callie said. This news, while
surprising, somehow made her smile behind her
teacup. "I think he likes that."

Trev made a sound of disgust. "Taking, indeed. She'll
take his hide and tan it for a new pair of gloves."

"It pleases me to see that I have brought you up wisely,
Trevelyan," the duchesse murmured. "I never believed
that you would fall in love with such a one as that."

"Nary a chance," he said, smiling at Callie. "I was in a
hopeless case long before I ever met the lovely Fowler."

Callie blushed and peeked at him over her cup. "I
wonder what the magazines will make of this?"

"At least ten volumes, I'm sure. What I wonder,
my love, is who blackmailed that unlucky devil out
of marrying you? Not that I don't bless 'em every

day, but I've turned over every angle I can conceive, and still I can't reckon who it would benefit—" He stopped abruptly. An arrested expression came over his face. He looked toward his mother.

"And now I go to puddle my grandson, I think," the duchesse said lightly, laying her napkin aside and rising from her chair. "Will you come with me, *ma bonne fille*, and leave this boring son to his newspaper?"

"'Cuddle,' ma'am," Callie said, suppressing a smile. "Of course I will come."

"A moment, Maman," Trev said sternly, standing up. "Geordie Hixson called on you, did you tell me once? When was that?"

"Ah!" She made a careless gesture. "I'm much too old to recall such a detail. But a charming young man. I was so sorry to learn that he had passed away. I liked him very much. We were great friends in one afternoon."

"I can imagine," Trev said dryly. "No doubt he told you many stories of the war."

"Several," she agreed. She lifted her thin brows. "I fear he didn't like his commanding officer and unburdened himself to me on the topic."

"Did he!"

"Yes, and perhaps it was not well done of me, but when I mentioned to him that my young friend at the great house was engaged to marry this same officer, he was most dismayed."

Trev shook his head slowly. "No, it wasn't Geordie. Sturgeon said he was dead before he got the blackmail note."

"Of course it was not him!" she said, shocked. "He was far too honorable a young man to stoop to such a thing! In fact, it was upon a point of military honor that he took greatest exception to his officer's behavior, I believe."

Trev's mouth quirked. "I see. And how did you dispatch the other two, ma mère?"

Callie took a sharp breath. She looked back and forth between her husband and the duchesse. "Trev! You can't be accusing your mother of... of—"

"Of blackmailing them all into jilting you?" He grinned. "Indeed not. I'm not accusing her. I'm about to get down on my knees and express my burning gratitude to her."

"It was nothing, my son," she said demurely. "Mrs. Easley obliged me by cutting up the papers and pasting them and seeing the notes delivered."

"*Ma'am!*" Callie exclaimed.

"I hope you are not too angry with me, chérie. I know that it hurt you a little each time, and for that I am very, very sorry." She gave Callie a worried look. "You did not greatly wish to marry any of them, did you?"

"Well, no, I didn't, but—"

The duchesse lifted her chin. "None of those men could have loved you as you deserve," she declared, "or they would not have paid the slightest heed to a silly note."

Callie was much struck by this view of the matter. "I suppose you're right," she said wonderingly. "Though I never thought any of them loved me at all."

"*Fools*," the duchesse and her son said at one and the same time.

They sounded so much alike, the one word so full of haughty French disdain, that Callie laughed and put her hands over her mouth. She wrinkled her nose against the sting that came to her eyes. "Oh," she said, "I am so fortunate to have you both."

Trev took her chin between his fingers and bent to kiss her gently on the nose. "Not you. I'm the lucky one here, ma mie. You are my fortune."

The End

Author's Note

After I finished *Shadowheart*, long before it was on the shelves and there was any controversy among readers about it, I'd already decided that I wanted to do a much lighter book this time. So I've pulled a complete 180—if books have family ties, *Lessons in French* is a first cousin to *Midsummer Moon* and only a very, very distant relation of *Shadowheart*. I wanted to revisit some of the character styles that I've enjoyed in the past—what I think of as "hedgehog humor." I find writing "light" to be even more demanding than writing "dark," and so I owe a great deal to Charles Rutledge and Beth Kingston, my team in charge of Plot Twists and Witty Banter. They kept me laughing hysterically even while I was suffering through the usual trials and torments of finishing a manuscript. A deep curtsy and profuse thanks; I couldn't have done it without your help. This one stayed in the drawer awhile, and to be honest I forgot about it, but there comes a time for every story to see the light, and now is the time for this one. Thanks to Deb Werksman of Sourcebooks for reminding me!

About the Author

Laura Kinsale, a former geologist, is the *New York Times* bestselling author of *Flowers from the Storm*, *The Prince of Midnight*, and *Seize the Fire*. She and her husband divide their time between Santa Fe and Dallas.

Uncertain Magic

One

RODERICA DELAMORE CLUTCHED HARD AT THE BILLOWING silk folds of her father's pavilion as the horses came pounding down the turf. The blood-bay stallion was in the lead, a flash of living fire, pulling away from the challenger with each ground-eating stride as the crowd's rumble gathered to a piercing howl. The noise and emotion rose up around Roddy like a breaking wave, beating at her, drowning her, crushing the barriers that she'd built in her mind. Her cursed gift laid her open to everything, the sound, the sight, the combined aggression and excitement of ten thousand screaming spectators. The intensity of emotion threatened to overwhelm her, and she tore the silk with her twisting fingers as she sought madly for some way to block it out.

Her parents had been right—she should never have come. She should have stayed home on the quiet Yorkshire estate where her father raised his blooded running stock, safe in the country solitude. She was not ready for this; she'd had no concept of what it would be like to suffer the full force of her talent in the grip of a hysterical crowd. In desperation she narrowed her concentration to the animals, pushing away the tide of human feeling with terrific effort.

The trick worked. The impact of the crowd faded and changed, becoming a background roar of sound as Roddy let herself be sucked into the mind of the stallion in the lead, the bright bay, whose will and power filled her like a flood of molten fire. Her world became the world of the racehorse: the taste of copper and foam, the smell of sweat and crushed grass and hot wind; stretching, seeking, ears flicked back to the thunder of the challenger, eyes focused on the terrain ahead; reaching and reaching and reaching forward—

The sudden pain struck her as if it were her own. It shot down the stallion's left foreleg, and he broke stride for one fraction of a second, sending the jockey's live weight forward onto the horse's shoulders. The whip flashed, not hitting, but the brandishment was enough. The stallion sprang ahead. The pain increased. It grew, spreading across the animal's chest and striking into his neck and right leg. Still he ran, defying it, his stallion's mind set in aggression and pride—stay ahead, stay ahead, damn the pain—while Roddy pressed her fists to her mouth and bit down until her knuckles bled with vicarious agony.

In a back corner of her mind she was aware of fear, a human dread of the moment when the great beast would collapse and take down his jockey and the challenger behind in a savage tangle of flesh and hooves. She'd felt this kind of pain before, at home, when an exhausted gelding had collapsed of heart failure after a twenty-mile race between parish steeples. It was death, close and dreadful, and yet the stallion drove on, opening the lead. His stride lengthened, his black-tipped legs devouring turf like the rhythmic spokes of a giant wheel. As he neared the finish, the crowd noise rose to a crescendo. The pair flashed by Roddy. She was screaming, too, hardly aware of the tears that streamed down her cheeks for the animal's pain and courage, for the will that carried him past the finish a full length ahead of his rival, for the spirit that made him toss his head and fight the restraining hand of his jockey when every single step was anguish. She broke from her hiding place in the pavilion, in the rough stableboy's clothes and the cap she'd worn to conceal her bright blond curls, and pushed with unfeminine force through the mob that closed in on the victor.

She reached the stallion just as the silk-clad jockey swung off. A groom ran forward to take the puffing animal's bridle; his hand clashed with Roddy's as they both lunged. Roddy's fingers closed first and she tore the reins away.

"*Yo!*" he shouted amid the din, and made a move to yank them back.

Roddy screamed, "Don't move him!" forgetting entirely she was supposed to be a boy. "He'll die if you move him now!"

"Are ye crazed?" the groom cried. Roddy stumbled under his shove, then gritted her teeth and held her ground.

The stallion stood still beside her, awash in pain. He lowered his head, giving in to weakness for the first time, and at that motion the protests of the groom faded momentarily. But the man's pride was aroused now, his authority questioned. Roddy felt the stallion begin to tremble in delayed reaction. The groom made another grab for the reins. He captured them, pushing Roddy aside as he led the horse forward.

The stallion faltered, and went to his knees. All around, a dismayed cry flew up, and then a cheer as the horse clambered back to all fours. Roddy gave the groom a savage look. She felt the man's antagonism, sharp and quick as a stabbing knife within the wash of emotion from the crowd. She knew before he did it that he was going to drag the horse forward again. "Damn you! Don't—" she shouted, and found herself cut short by another voice that sliced across the noise.

"Leave it, Patrick. Let him stand."

Roddy stiffened, unused to being taken by surprise. She did not turn toward the newcomer—that was habit—but opened her special gift to his mind, expecting to pluck out a name and identity before she even saw his face.

Instead, she found only blankness.

That jolted her. She focused her gift more sharply. But the other remained a silence, a void, as disconcerting as the space where a newly lost tooth should have been.

A bubble of panic rose to her throat. For the first time in her life, Roddy felt herself reaching out instead of turning away, probing for emotion or thought instead of rejecting it. When finally she turned, it was as if she could not quite see the man beside her; only a vague figure, tall and elegant in a black coat and doeskin breeches. She spared a single glance up into his face.

His features came into focus with a sudden, wrenching clarity. He stood quite still amid the clamor, watching her intently, his eyes a startling blue

beneath thick black lashes—light against dark, like
the bright evening sky behind stark silhouettes. The
expression on his fiercely carved face was closed, set
in lines impossible to read. She blinked stupidly and
gaped, like a person set down in a foreign country,
unable to cope with an unknown tongue.

The silence spread to the watching throng, the real
silence, the one her ears heard instead of her mind.
Shouts and talk faded into hush. And in the crowd-
thoughts behind the silence she found a name.

Her eyes widened. She looked quickly toward the
stranger from under her lashes.

Saints preserve us.

Iveragh. The Devil Earl of Ireland.

She found herself in deeper water than she'd
wanted. A lot deeper. She should have guessed. Oh,
God, how had she not guessed? He *owned* the beast,
for the Lord's sake. Rumor had been rife that the
horse would go for a fortune to Lord Derby or the
Duke of Grafton if it won today.

Roddy stole another look. The man could have
been Satan himself, with his hell-black hair and
burning blue eyes. Every improbable tale of the Devil
Earl took on believability: if anyone could be a blackmailer and a thief and a pitiless corrupter of innocent
maids, this was surely the man.

People moved. The crowd shuffled and shifted, and
opened way again with that instinct they had for a fine
coat and a gentleman's air. She knew the newcomer
this time—Lord Derby himself, eager to lay his claim
to the horse.

He hailed Iveragh and pumped his hand, congratulations on the win. "We'll call this an agreement."

Derby pumped harder, looking sillier than he knew against Iveragh's trenchant silence. The excited lord babbled something about the next heat, and Roddy swung round in dismay. "Don't race him again! You musn't—"

"Gor—" The groom shoved her roughly. "Mind yer business, ye little bastard. The horse 'twere never better. Get on wi' ye."

Roddy thrust his hands away with hot indignation, remembering too late that she could hardly be taken for a lady of quality just now. She turned again to Iveragh—a look up to those uninterpretable blue eyes as steady as she could make it, which wasn't very. From somewhere she still had enough sense left to use her best country accents. "He ain't fit, m'lor'. He's sick. 'Twill kill him to run again. I've felt—" She stopped herself, knowing that these strangers would never believe in the talent that was taken for granted in her father's stable. "I've seen this before. 'Tis his heart, m'lor'."

"Sick, is it?" The groom moved a step. "Sick be damned, ye bleedin'—" Roddy felt his intention a moment before the action and stiffened—fool, fool, when she should have ducked—and the cracking blow took her across the face and sent her reeling into the solid wall of the earl's chest.

ALSO AVAILABLE

MIDSUMMER MOON

BY LAURA KINSALE

New York Times bestselling author

IF HE REALLY LOVED HER,
WOULDN'T HE HELP HER REALIZE HER DREAM?

When inventor Merlin Lambourne is endangered by Napoleon's advancing forces, Lord Ransom Falconer, in service of his government, comes to her rescue and falls under the spell of her beauty and absent-minded brilliance. But he is horrified by her dream of building a flying machine—and not only because he is determined to keep her safe.

THE
PRINCE
OF
MIDNIGHT

BY LAURA KINSALE
New York Times bestselling author

"Readers should be enchanted."
—*Publishers Weekly*

INTENT ON REVENGE, ALL SHE WANTS FROM
HIM IS TO LEARN HOW TO KILL

Lady Leigh Strachan has crossed all of France in search of S.T. Maitland, nobleman, highwayman, and legendary swordsman, once known as the Prince of Midnight. Now he's hiding out in a crumbing castle with a tame wolf as his only companion, trying to conceal his deafness and desperation. Leigh is terribly disappointed to find the man behind the legend doesn't meet her expectations. But when they're forced on a quest together, she discovers the dangerous and vital man behind the mask, and he finds a way to touch her ice cold heart.

"No one—repeat, no one—writes historical romance better." —Mary Jo Putney

Seize the Fire

BY LAURA KINSALE
New York Times bestselling author

"Magic and beauty flow from
Laura Kinsale's pen." —*Romantic Times*

AN UNLIKELY PRINCESS SHIPWRECKED
WITH A WAR HERO WHO'S GOT HELL TO PAY

Her Serene Highness Olympia of Oriens—plump, demure,
and idealistic—longs to return to her tiny, embattled land
and lead her people to justice and freedom. Famous hero
Captain Sheridan Drake, destitute and tormented by nightmares of the carnage he's seen, means only to rob and abandon her. What is Olympia to do with the tortured man
behind the hero's façade? And how will they cope when
their very survival depends on each other?

"One of the best writers in the history of the
romance genre." —*All About Romance*

The WILDEST HEART

BY ROSEMARY ROGERS

Two destinies intertwined under the blazing New Mexico sun

When passionate, headstrong Lady Rowena Dangerfield travels to the savage New Mexico frontier to lay claim to her inheritance, she finally meets a man as strong as she is: Lucas Cord, a dark, dangerously handsome, half-Apache outlaw. Fighting scandal, treachery, and murder, Luke is determined to have Rowena for his own, and as their all-consuming passion mounts, no one is going to stop him...

WHAT READERS SAY:

"It makes you cry, it makes you wish, and it makes you dream. It's what a romance novel is all about."

"The Wildest Heart *kept me captivated well beyond the last page..."*

PRAISE FOR ROSEMARY ROGERS:

"The queen of historical romance."

—New York Times Book Review

"Her novels are filled with adventure, excitement and, always, wildly tempestuous romance."
—Fort Worth Star-Telegram

A *Duke* to *Die For*

BY AMELIA GREY

THE RAKISH FIFTH DUKE OF BLAKEWELL'S UNEXPECTED AND shockingly lovely new ward has just arrived, claiming to carry a curse that has brought each of her previous guardians to an untimely end…

Praise for Amelia Grey's Regency romances:

A *Marquis* TO *Marry*

BY AMELIA GREY

"A captivating mix of discreet intrigue
and potent passion." —*Booklist*

"A gripping plot, great love scenes, and well-drawn
characters make this book impossible to put down."
—*The Romance Studio*

The Marquis of Raceworth is shocked to find a young and
beautiful Duchess on his doorstep—especially when she
accuses him of stealing her family's priceless pearls! Susannah,
Duchess of Brookfield, refuses to be intimidated by the
Marquis's commanding presence and chiseled good looks.
And when the pearls disappear, Race and Susannah will have
to work together—and discover they can't live apart...

Praise for *A Duke to Die For:*

"A lusciously spicy romp." —*Library Journal*

"Deliciously sensual... storyteller extraordinaire Amelia Grey
grabs you by the heart, draws you in, and does not let go."
—*Romance Junkies*

"Intriguing danger, sharp humor, and plenty of simmering
sexual chemistry." —*Booklist*

My UNFAIR Lady

by Kathryne Kennedy

A Wild West beauty takes Victorian London by storm

The impoverished Duke of Monchester despises the rich Americans who flock to London, seeking to buy their way into the ranks of the British peerage. Frontier-bred Summer Wine Lee has no interest in winning over London society—it's the New York bluebloods and her future mother-in-law she's determined to impress. She knows the cost of smoothing her rough-and-tumble frontier edges will be high. But she never imagined it might cost her heart...

"Kennedy is going places." —Romantic Times

"Kathryne Kennedy creates a unique, exquisite flavor that makes her romance a pure delight page after page, book after book." —Merrimon Book Reviews

"Kathryne Kennedy's computer must smolder from the power she creates in her stories! I simply cannot describe how awesome or how thrilling I found this novel to be." —Huntress Book Reviews

"Kennedy is one of the hottest new sensations in the romance genre." —Merrimon Reviews

Highland Rebel

BY JUDITH JAMES

"An unforgettable tale." —*The Romance Studio*

RAISED TO RULE HER CLAN, SHE'LL STOP AT NOTHING TO PROTECT HER OWN

Daughter of a Highland laird, Catherine Drummond rebels against ladylike expectations and rides fearlessly into battle against the English forces sent to quell the Scots' rebellion. When Catherine falls into the hands of vicious mercenaries, she is saved from a grim fate by an unlikely hero. Jamie Sinclair only wants to finish one last mission for his king and collect his reward. But in a world where princes cannot be trusted and faith fuels intolerance, hatred, and war, no good deed goes unpunished...

"Complex, compelling characters and a good, galloping plot... Upscale historical romance at its best!"
—*Historical Novel Review*

"The romance is tender, yet molten hot."
—*Wendy's Minding Spot*

"Wonderfully written. It's captivating and heart wrenching." —*Anna's Book Blog*

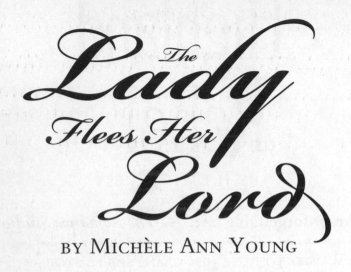

The Lady Flees Her Lord

BY MICHÈLE ANN YOUNG

DESPERATE FOR PEACE AND SAFETY...

Lucinda, Lady Denbigh, is running from a husband who physically and emotionally abused her. Posing as a widow, she seeks refuge in the quiet countryside, where she meets Lord Hugo Wanstead. Returning from the wars with a wound that won't heal, he finds his estate impoverished, his sleep torn by nightmares, and brandy the only solace. When he meets Lucinda, he thinks she just might give him something to live for...

Praise for Michèle Ann Young's *No Regrets*

"Dark heroes, courageous heroines, intrigue, heartbreak, and heaps of sexual tension. Do not miss this fabulous new author." —Molly O'Keefe, *Harlequin Superromance*

"Readers will never want to put her book down!" —Bronwyn Scott, author of *Pickpocket Countess*

No Regrets

by Michèle Ann Young

"A remarkable talent that taps your emotions
with each and every page." —Gerry Russel,
award winning author of *The Warrior Trainer*

A Most Unusual Heroine

Voluptuous and bespectacled, Caroline Torrington feels
dowdy and unattractive beside the slim beauties of her
day. Little does she know that Lord Lucas Foxhaven
thinks her curves are breathtaking, and can barely keep
his hands off her.

"The suspense and sexual tension accelerate
throughout." —*Romance Reviews Today*

June, 2011